ALICE CA

A DOOR CLC

MYSTERIES BY ALICE CAMPBELL

1. *Juggernaut* (1928)
2. *Water Weed* (1929)
3. *Spiderweb* (1930)
4. *The Click of the Gate* (1932)
5. *The Murder of Caroline Bundy* (1933)
6. *Desire to Kill* (1934)
7. *Keep Away from Water!* (1935)
8. *Death Framed in Silver* (1937)
9. *Flying Blind* (1938)
10. *A Door Closed Softly* (1939)
11. *They Hunted a Fox* (1940)
12. *No Murder of Mine* (1941)
13. *No Light Came On* (1942)
14. *Ringed with Fire* (1943)
15. *Travelling Butcher* (1944)
16. *The Cockroach Sings* (1946)
17. *Child's Play* (1947)
18. *The Bloodstained Toy* (1948)
19. *The Corpse Had Red Hair* (1950)

ALICE CAMPBELL

A DOOR CLOSED SOFTLY

With an introduction
by Curtis Evans

DEAN STREET PRESS

ALICE IN MURDERLAND

CRIME WRITER ALICE CAMPBELL, THE OTHER "AC"

IN 1927 Alice Dorothy Ormond Campbell—a thirty-nine-year-old native
of Atlanta, Georgia who for the last fifteen years had lived successively
in New York, Paris and London, never once returning to the so-called
Empire City of the South, published her first novel, an unstoppable
crime thriller called *Juggernaut*, selling the serialization rights to the
Chicago Tribune for $4000 ($60,000 today), a tremendous sum for a
brand new author. On its publication in January 1928, both the book and
its author caught the keen eye of Bessie S. Stafford, society page editor
of the *Atlanta Constitution*. Back when Alice Ormond, as she was then
known, lived in Atlanta, Miss Bessie breathlessly informed her readers,
she had been "an ethereal blonde-like type of beauty, extremely popular, and always thought she was in love with somebody. She took high
honors in school; and her gentleness of manner and breeding bespoke
an aristocratic lineage. She grew to a charming womanhood—"

Let us stop Miss Bessie right there, because there is rather more
to the story of Alice Campbell, the mystery genre's other "AC," who
published nineteen crime novels between 1928 and 1950. Allow me to
plunge boldly forward with the tale of Atlanta's great Golden Age crime
writer, who as an American expatriate in England, went on to achieve
fame and fortune as an atmospheric writer of murder and mystery and
become one of the early members of the Detection Club.

Alice Campbell's lineage was distinguished. Alice was born in Atlanta
on November 29, 1887, the youngest of the four surviving children of
prominent Atlantans James Ormond IV and Florence Root. Both of
Alice's grandfathers had been wealthy Atlanta merchants who settled in
the city in the years before the American Civil War. Alice's uncles, John
Wellborn Root and Walter Clark Root, were noted architects, while her
brothers, Sidney James and Walter Emanuel Ormond, were respectively
a drama critic and political writer for the *Atlanta Constitution* and an
attorney and justice of the peace. Both brothers died untimely deaths
before Alice had even turned thirty, as did her uncle John Wellborn
Root and her father.

Alice precociously published her first piece of fiction, a fairy story,
in the *Atlanta Constitution* in 1897, when she was nine years old. Four
years later, the ambitious child was said to be in the final stage of complet-

ing a two-volume novel. In 1907, by which time she was nineteen, Alice relocated to New York City, chaperoned by Florence.

In New York Alice became friends with writers Inez Haynes Irwin, a prominent feminist, and Jacques Futrelle, the creator of "The Thinking Machine" detective who was soon to go down with the ship on RMS *Titanic,* and scored her first published short story in *Ladies Home Journal* in 1911. Simultaneously she threw herself pell-mell into the causes of women's suffrage and equal pay for equal work. The same year she herself became engaged, but this was soon broken off and in February 1913 Alice sailed to Paris with her mother to further her cultural education.

Three months later in Paris, on May 22, 1913, twenty-five-year-old Alice married James Lawrence Campbell, a twenty-four-year-old theatrical agent of good looks and good family from Virginia. Jamie, as he was known, had arrived in Paris a couple of years earlier, after a failed stint in New York City as an actor. In Paris he served, more successfully, as an agent for prominent New York play brokers Arch and Edgar Selwyn.

After the wedding Alice Ormond Campbell, as she now was known, remained in Paris with her husband Jamie until hostilities between France and Germany loomed the next year. At this point the couple prudently relocated to England, along with their newborn son, James Lawrence Campbell, Jr., a future artist and critic. After the war the Campbells, living in London, bought an attractive house in St. John's Wood, London, where they established a literary and theatrical salon. There Alice oversaw the raising of the couple's two sons, Lawrence and Robert, and their daughter, named Chita Florence Ormond ("Ormond" for short), while Jamie spent much of his time abroad, brokering play productions in Paris, New York and other cities.

Like Alice, Jamie harbored dreams of personal literary accomplishment; and in 1927 he published a novel entitled *Face Value*, which for a brief time became that much-prized thing by publishers, a putatively "scandalous" novel that gets Talked About. The story of a gentle orphan boy named Serge, the son an emigre Russian prostitute, who grows up in a Parisian "disorderly house," as reviews often blushingly put it, *Face Value* divided critics, but ended up on American bestseller lists. The success of his first novel led to the author being invited out to Hollywood to work as a scriptwriter, and his name appears on credits to a trio of films in 1927-28, including *French Dressing*, a "gay" divorce comedy set among sexually scatterbrained Americans in Paris. One wonders whether in Hollywood Jamie ever came across future crime writer Cornell Wool-rich, who was scripting there too at the time.

Alice remained in England with the children, enjoying her own literary splash with her debut thriller *Juggernaut*, which concerned the murderous machinations of an inexorably ruthless French Riviera society doctor, opposed by a valiant young nurse. The novel racked up rave reviews and sales in the UK and US, in the latter country spurred on by its nationwide newspaper serialization, which promised readers

> . . . the open door to adventure! *Juggernaut* by Alice Camp-bell will sweep you out of the humdrum of everyday life into the gay, swift-moving Arabian-nights existence of the Riviera!

London's *Daily Mail* declared that the irresistible *Juggernaut* "should rank among the 'best sellers' of the year"; and, sure enough, *Juggernaut*'s English publisher, Hodder & Stoughton, boasted, several months after the novel's English publication in July 1928, that they already had run through six printings in an attempt to satisfy customer demand. In 1936 *Juggernaut* was adapted in England as a film vehicle for horror great Boris Karloff, making it the only Alice Campbell novel filmed to date. The film was remade in England under the title *The Temptress* in 1949.

Water Weed (1929) and *Spiderweb* (1930) (*Murder in Paris* in the US), the immediate successors, held up well to their predecessor's performance. Alice chose this moment to return for a fortnight to Atlanta, ostensibly to visit her sister, but doubtlessly in part to parade through her hometown as a conquering, albeit commercial, literary hero. And who was there to welcome Alice in the pages of the *Constitution* but Bessie S. Stafford, who pronounced Alice's hair still looked like spun gold while her eyes remarkably had turned an even deeper shade of blue. To Miss Bessie, Alice imparted enchanting tales of salon chats with such personages as George Bernard Shaw, Lady Asquith, H. G. Wells and (his lover) Rebecca West, the latter of whom a simpatico Alice met and conversed with frequently. Admitting that her political sympathies in England "inclined toward the conservatives," Alice yet urged "the absolute necessity of having two strong parties." English women, she had been pleased to see, evinced more informed interest in politics than their American sisters.

Alice, Miss Bessie declared, diligently devoted every afternoon to her writing, shutting her study door behind her "as a sign that she is not to be interrupted." This commitment to her craft enabled Alice to produce an additional sixteen crime novels between 1932 and 1950, beginning with *The Click of the Gate* and ending with *The Corpse Had Red Hair*.

Altogether nearly half of Alice's crime novels were standalones, in contravention of convention at this time, when series sleuths were so popular. In *The Click of the Gate* the author introduced one of her main recurring characters, intrepid Paris journalist Tommy Rostetter, who appears in three additional novels: *Desire to Kill* (1934), *Flying Blind* (1938) and *The Bloodstained Toy* (1948). In the two latter novels, Tommy appears with Alice's other major recurring character, dauntless Inspector Headcorn of Scotland Yard, who also pursues murderers and other malefactors in *Death Framed in Silver* (1937), *They Hunted a Fox* (1940), *No Murder of Mine* (1941) and *The Cockroach Sings* (1946) (*With Bated Breath* in the US).

Additional recurring characters in Alice's books are Geoffrey Macadam and Catherine West, who appear in *Spiderweb* and *No Light Came On* (1942), and Colin Ladbrooke, who appears in *Death Framed in Silver*, *A Door Closed Softly* (1939) and *They Hunted a Fox*. In the latter two books Colin with his romantic interest Alison Young and in the first and third book with Inspector Headcorn, who also appears, as mentioned, in *Flying Blind* and *The Bloodstained Toy* with Tommy Rosstetter, making Headcorn the connecting link in this universe of sleuths, although the inspector does not appear with Geoffrey Macadam and Catherine West. It is all a rather complicated state of criminal affairs; and this lack of a consistent and enduring central sleuth character in Alice's crime fiction may help explain why her work faded in the Fifties, after the author retired from writing.

Be that as it may, Alice Campbell is a figure of significance in the history of crime fiction. In a 1946 review of *The Cockroach Sings* in the London *Observer*, crime fiction critic Maurice Richardson asserted that "[s]he belongs to the atmospheric school, of which one of the outstanding exponents was the late Ethel Lina White," the author of *The Wheel Spins* (1936), famously filmed in 1938, under the title *The Lady Vanishes*, by director Alfred Hitchcock. This "atmospheric school," as Richardson termed it, had more students in the demonstrative United States than in the decorous United Kingdom, to be sure, the United States being the home of such hugely popular suspense writers as Mary Roberts Rinehart and Mignon Eberhart, to name but a couple of the most prominent examples.

Like the novels of the American Eber-Rinehart school and English authors Ethel Lina White and Marie Belloc Lowndes, the latter the author of the acknowledged landmark 1911 thriller *The Lodger*, Alice Campbell's books are not pure puzzle detective tales, but rather broader mysteries which put a premium on the storytelling imperatives of atmosphere and suspense. "She could not be unexciting if she tried," raved the *Times Literary Supplement* of Alice, stressing the author's remoteness from the so-called "Humdrum" school of detective fiction headed by British authors Freeman Wills Crofts, John Street and J. J. Connington. However, as Maurice Richardson, a great fan of Alice's crime writing, put it, "she generally binds her homework together with a reasonable plot," so the "Humdrum" fans out there need not be put off by what American detective novelist S. S. Van Dine, creator of Philo Vance, dogmatically dismissed as "literary dallying." In her novels Alice Campbell offered people bone-rattling good reads, which explains their popularity in the past and their revival today. Lines from a review of her 1941 crime novel *No Murder of Mine* by "H.V.A." in the *Hartford Courant* suggests the general nature of her work's appeal: "The excitement and mystery of this Class A shocker start on page 1 and continue right to the end of the book. You won't put it down, once you've begun it. And if you like romance mixed with your thrills, you'll find it here."

The protagonist of *No Murder of Mine* is Rowan Wilde, "an attractive young American girl studying in England." Frequently in her books Alice, like the great Anglo-American author Henry James, pits ingenuous but goodhearted Americans, male or female, up against dangerously sophisticated Europeans, drawing on autobiographical details from her and Jamie's own lives. Many of her crime novels, which often are lengthier than the norm for the period, recall, in terms of their length and content, the Victorian sensation novel, which seemingly had been in its dying throes when the author was a precocious child; yet, in their emphasis on morbid psychology and their sexual frankness, they also anticipate the modern crime novel. One can discern this tendency most dramatically, perhaps, in the engrossing *Water Weed*, concerning a sexual affair between a middle-aged Englishwoman and a young American man that has dreadful consequences, and *Desire to Kill*, about murder among a clique of decadent bohemians in Paris. In both of these mysteries the exploration of aberrant sexuality is striking. Indeed, in its depiction of sexual psychosis *Water Weed* bears rather more resemblance to, say, the crime novels of Patricia Highsmith than it does to the cozy mysteries of Patricia Wentworth. One might well term it Alice Campbell's *Deep Water*.

In this context it should be noted that in 1935 Alice Campbell authored a sexual problem play, *Two Share a Dwelling*, which the *New York*

Times described as a "grim, vivid, psychological treatment of dual personality." Although it ran for only twenty-two performances during October 8-26 at the West End's celebrated St. James' Theatre, the play had done well on its provincial tour and it received a standing ovation from the audience on opening night at the West End, primarily on account of the compelling performance of the half-Jewish German stage actress Grete Mosheim, who had fled Germany two years earlier and was making her English stage debut in the play's lead role of a schizophrenic, sexually compulsive woman. Mosheim was described as young and "blondely beautiful," bringing to mind the author herself.

Unfortunately priggish London critics were put off by the play's morbid sexual subject, which put Alice in an impossible position. One reviewer scathingly observed that "Miss Alice Campbell . . . has chosen to give her audience a study in pathology as a pleasant method of spending the evening. . . . one leaves the theatre rather wishing that playwrights would leave medical books on their shelves." Another sniffed that "it is to be hoped that the fashion of plumbing the depths of Freudian theory for dramatic fare will not spread. It is so much more easy to be interested in the doings of the sane." The play died a quick death in London and its author went back, for another fifteen years, to "plumbing the depths" in her crime fiction.

What impelled Alice Campbell, like her husband, to avidly explore human sexuality in her work? Doubtless their writing reflected the temper of modern times, but it also likely was driven by personal imperatives. The child of an unhappy marriage who at a young age had been deprived of a father figure, Alice appears to have wanted to use her crime fiction to explore the human devastation wrought by disordered lives. Sadly, evidence suggests that discord had entered the lives of Alice and Jamie by the 1930s, as they reached middle age and their children entered adulthood. In 1939, as the Second World War loomed, Alice was residing in rural southwestern England with her daughter Ormond at a cottage—the inspiration for her murder setting in *No Murder of Mine*, one guesses—near the bucolic town of Beaminster, Dorset, known for its medieval Anglican church and its charming reference in a poem by English dialect poet William Barnes:

> Sweet Be'mi'ster, that bist a-bound
> By green and woody hills all round,
> Wi'hedges, reachen up between
> A thousand vields o' zummer green.

Alice's elder son Lawrence was living, unemployed, in New York City at this time and he would enlist in the US Army when the country entered the war a couple of years later, serving as a master sergeant throughout the conflict. In December 1939, twenty-three-year-old Ormond, who seems to have herself preferred going by the name Chita, wed the prominent antiques dealer, interior decorator, home restorer and racehorse owner Ernest Thornton-Smith, who at the age of fifty-eight was fully thirty-five years older than she. Antiques would play a crucial role in Alice's 1944 wartime crime novel *Travelling Butcher*, which blogger Kate Jackson at *Cross Examining Crime* deemed "a thrilling read." The author's most comprehensive wartime novel, however, was the highly-praised *Ringed with Fire* (1943). Native Englishman S. Morgan-Powell, the dean of Canadian drama critics, in the *Montreal Star* pronounced *Ringed with Fire* one of the "best spy stories the war has produced," adding, in one of Alice's best notices:

"Ringed with Fire" begins with mystery and exudes mystery from every chapter. Its clues are most ingeniously developed, and keep the reader guessing in all directions. For once there is a mystery which will, I think, mislead the most adroit and experienced of amateur sleuths. Some time ago there used to be a practice of sealing up the final section of mystery stores with the object of stirring up curiosity and developing the detective instinct among readers. If you sealed up the last forty-two pages of "Ringed with Fire" and then offered a prize of $250 to the person who guessed the mystery correctly, I think that money would be as safe as if you put it in victory bonds.

A few years later, on the back of the dust jacket to the American edition of Alice's *The Cockroach Sings* (1946), which Random House, her new American publisher, less queasily titled *With Bated Breath*, readers learned a little about what the author had been up to during the late war and its recent aftermath: "I got used to oil lamps. . . . and also to riding nine miles in a crowded bus once a week to do the shopping—if there was anything to buy. We thought it rather a lark then, but as a matter of fact we are still suffering from all sorts of shortages and restrictions." Jamie Campbell, on the other hand, spent his war years in Santa Barbara, California. It is unclear whether he and Alice ever lived together again.

Alice remained domiciled for the rest of her life in Dorset, although she returned to London in 1946, when she was inducted into the Detection Club. A number of her novels from this period, all of which were published in England by the Collins Crime Club, more resemble, in tone and form, classic detective fiction, such as *They Hunted a Fox* (1940). This event may have been a moment of triumph for the author, but it was also something of a last hurrah. After 1946 she published only three more crime novels, including the entertaining Tommy Rostetter-Inspector Headcorn mashup *The Bloodstained Toy*, before retiring in 1950. She lived out the remaining five years of her life quietly at her home in the coastal city of Bridport, Dorset, expiring "suddenly" on November 27, 1955, two days before her sixty-eighth birthday. Her brief death notice in the *Daily Telegraph* refers to her only as the "very dear mother of Lawrence, Chita and Robert."

Jamie Campbell had died in 1954 aged sixty-five. Earlier in the year his play *The Praying Mantis*, billed as a "naughty comedy by James Lawrence Campbell," scored hits at the Q Theatre in London and at the Dolphin Theatre in Brighton. (A very young Joan Collins played the eponymous man-eating leading role at the latter venue.) In spite of this, Jamie near the end of the year checked into a hotel in Cannes and fatally imbibed poison. The American consulate sent the report on Jamie's death to Chita in Maida Vale, London, and to Jamie's brother Colonel George Campbell in Washington, D. C., though not to Alice. This was far from the Riviera romance that the publishers of *Juggernaut* had long ago promised. Perhaps the "humdrum of everyday life" had been too much with him.

Alice Campbell own work fell into obscurity after her death, with not one of her novels being reprinted in English for more than seven decades. Happily the ongoing revival of vintage English and American mystery fiction from the twentieth century is rectifying such cases of criminal neglect. It may well be true that it "is impossible not to be thrilled by Edgar Wallace," as the great thriller writer's publishers pronounced, but let us not forget that, as Maurice Richardson put it: "We can always do with Mrs. Alice Campbell." Mystery fans will now have nineteen of them from which to choose—a veritable embarrassment of felonious riches, all from the hand of the other AC.

Curtis Evans

CHAPTER ONE

MISTAKES WILL HAPPEN

THERE was a thickish mist over Hampstead. Oh, not a real fog—as Alison was careful to explain.

"Wait," she scoffed, "till you've had a whole year of London, as I have. You'll see."

David Beddoes grunted. After the hot murk of the Tube the clammy white haze went through him as no American cold had ever done. Taking longer strides and turning up his collar to protect his dress-shirt front from the damp, he let his cousin brag airily about the pea-soupers she had known.

"Last time," she informed him, her cheeks more than ever like an Indian peach as she manfully led the way to heights masked in mystery, "my taxi-driver got lost, and had to keep borrowing my matches to read the street-signs. He and I got so chummy I asked him in at the finish and filled him with hot rum. Of course first thing in the morning that landlady of mine had me on the mat!"

"Well, living in sin as you do, you know darned well what to expect! The look that female gave me tonight was an eye-opener. Cousin, forsooth, it said, I've heard that yarn too many times. . . . Say, where's this benighted house you're carting me to?"

"Oh, close! Hold on a minute. Isn't this marvellous?"

Before them lay the Heath, a soft blur, with faint skeletons of trees thrusting up out of amorphous blobs of shadow and remote lights, like stars, sifting through the pale gauze. David approved.

"Whistler stuff." He flicked away his cigarette in a shower of red sparks. "Very swell."

"Turner, you moron! That is, when it's day and you can get the long, sandy slides. Down here's a hollow. They hold fairs in it, with merry-go-rounds. Over there's Jack Straw's Castle—and The Spaniards. Pickwick, you know. Don't fall in the pond. Now, then, shake your feet!"

They skirted the Heath, bearing left.

"And just who," asked David, "is this good woman who's throwing the party?"

"I told you—Lady Wibbe. Cynthia—wrote *Caravans*. She's a good seller. We're bringing out her next three books over our side. I've been to her only once before—sherry-party, in September—but when she heard I had a cousin staying with me she said to bring you along. Now, which house is it?"

Alison halted before a dark, curving road abutting on the Heath. In this obscurity all houses looked much of a muchness, but her real thoughts were occupied with the someone who on the former occasion had driven her home from Lady Wibbe's. It had been her first meeting with him—oddly exciting, making the otherwise dull sherry-party stand out. Too bad he couldn't be here to-night. Still, there was to-morrow. . . .

"It had a big garden," she meditated aloud, "and a sort of turret. Would it be that one?" She pointed to the second house, like its wide-spaced neighbours well retired from the road. "I want my glasses for this. How are your eyes?"

"Well, there's your turret, anyhow."

They crossed, and got a better view of what was certainly a tower, empty-eyed and black against the blankness of mist. It looked a suitable home for bats, part and parcel of the hideous mid-Victorian architecture stamping the whole edifice, which was large and erupted all over in cramped balconies and pseudo-Gothic pinnacles.

"Sure you've got the right date?" David accused. Hand on the gate, Alison frowned. To be sure most houses were at their worst in a shrouding of cold mist, but this one, crouched amongst sooty laurels, seemed quite dismally decayed. Almost repellent in its gloom.

"Rot, you saw me look at the card. Curtains drawn, that's all. The English don't blazon their doings to the world the way we do."

She pushed the sagging gates inward and saw a vaguely-familiar drive curving to a columned portico also recognisable. This old-fashioned bell-pull, though! Still it produced a competent jangle, and before the dead stillness inside had grown too oppressive the door opened to frame an aged manservant, definitely shabby, but conventionally clad. A substitute, perhaps. Shuffling and doddering, with watery, peering eyes and an ill-shaven chin that like the gate sagged on its hinges. His dubious manner and the unlit hall made her want to settle a tenuous doubt.

"Lady Wibbe—?" she ventured.

Instant alacrity as the butler stood aside for them to enter. Nervous, though, unless the trembling was palsy? As if mastering his duties he asked whether they would care to leave their wraps.

"Here?" Alison blinked round.

Evidently. He was opening a door just inside the entrance. It gave on a totally dark coat cupboard in which she could just make out a few dangling garments. David had peeled off his overcoat and was settling his black tie. (Thank goodness she hadn't made him wear tails!) As he stood there stalwart and foursquare the rather uncompromising cut of his jaw and the heavy bar of his jet brows seemed to be registering disapproval. The old man hung her broad-tail coat on a peg in the dank cavern, fumbling and pottering; but now with more assurance he was shuffling past a long flight of stairs towards a room on the left.

Odd she had not noticed the depressing state of this hall! Brown-papered walls, stained with ancient damp, revolting lincrusta and oil-paintings no self-respecting person in these days would give house room. The very parquet, nearly rugless, gritty from lack of polish. . . . She remembered that Sir Francis Wibbe was a prosperous K.C., that Cynthia's royalties had been pouring in. Of course crowds of people dress a place. It would explain her failure to be struck by this appalling taste; not, though, the penetrating cold, as of a house untenanted. A good thing she'd put on her long-sleeved velvet . . .

Suddenly, up above, someone opened a door, and into the musty chill surged a wave of warm, exotic fragrance. Alison Young knew that scent—Fortnum and Mason's bath essence, a guinea a bottle. A silken rustle on high suggested that the someone had paused by the balustrade to listen. What a time for a hostess to be just finishing her bath! Nine striking now from some wheezy, unseen clock.

The room into which their guide shut them had a stale, conserved warmth. They stared round ruefully. A dining-room?

And what a dining-room! Certainly Alison hadn't been in here before. She would never have forgotten this huge atrocity of a sideboard, this scratched, bulbous-legged table hogging most of the space with satellite chairs drawn up to it in long stiff rows. Not a flower anywhere; and why this funereal gloom? The colossal chandelier, all tarnished metal squirls and fitted unbelievably for gas, had only one burner emitting a choked, bluish flame.

David's eye was on her. She shrugged defensively.

"Don't ask me," she murmured. "Some domestic muddle, I suppose. Drawing-room not ready. It was a lovely big place, I remember, giving on a garden and . . . What's up?"

He pointed down at the table. "Holy snakes!" he grunted.

She saw a gigantic jigsaw puzzle, fully a yard square, showing a squadron of ships against a sickly blue sky.

All fitted together to the last squiggly bit, representing hours upon hours of patient toil. Funny for it to be here; but then so much was funny and—queer.

"Lady Wibbe's got a little girl," she whispered, and caught sight of her cousin's face. "Oh, David, don't look so glum! This is a party, not a visit of condolence. Though I must say they might have made up the fire." She chafed her hands over the almost dead embers.

Littered hearth; hideous black marble clock flanked by imitation bronze figures, horsemen spearing boars. The stillness! One would have expected some bustle somewhere. David, after swaying awkwardly from one patent-leather foot to the other, had picked up an old Tauchnitz book from the sideboard. A clinker rattled from the grate. Alison bottled her laughter. And then, soft steps descended the long, bare stairway just outside. At last! But how pattering, how indeterminate a tread for the corpulent, expansive Cynthia!

It wasn't Cynthia at all. A tall, flat-chested person was sidling in on them with a nervous, propitiatory smile; and she was certainly not dressed for a party. . . . Of course! The companion-secretary who on the former occasion had merged into the background. Some accident *had* happened, she was come to explain.

"How do you do?" With a flat giggle from sheer lack of ease the woman extended a hand like a dead sole, sent a flurried glance at David, and murmured, "I—I'm afraid I've kept you waiting."

"Oh, no! I expect we are early." Alison was dealing with this as best she could. "May I introduce my cousin Mr. Beddoes, from New York?" (She couldn't possibly recall the woman's name.)

"Americans?"

"Yes, didn't you know?" Alison was puzzled by the flicker of question and the almost palpitating agitation. "I've been here some time, but my cousin's just come over." Meeting only the same wavering and inane smile, she added, "Do tell me, have we come at the wrong time?"

"Oh, dear, no, not in the least!"

It was a hurried babble carrying no reassurance. She had dropped David's hand as though it were a live coal, and standing now in the circle of poor light was more clearly revealed. A spinster, undoubtedly, meagre and pinched in her brown uneven skirt all picked and snarled down the front, chocolate-brown spencer and shoes that had down-trodden heels. Hands damp from recent washing but still grubby. Of no definable age, though the lines in her unwholesomely pallid face might be premature. Eyes nearly lashless, pale green like gooseberries, one with a queer brown spot on the iris. Hair a frizzled, faded ginger, straggling in ineffectual wisps.

"W-won't you sit down?"

Amazingly she was drawing out one of the stiff chairs. Painfully ill-at-ease she apologized for the dimness and, stretching up, began to fiddle with the single lit burner.

"Let me," said David, but the flame refused to enlarge. They sat, Alison and David on one side the table, the woman facing them, and smiled at one another with mute expectancy across the vast jigsaw puzzle. To Alison the pieced-together ship seemed all at once quite sinister—which, of course, was ridiculous.

The woman spoke, desperately. Damp beads on her forehead.

"It's turned colder, hasn't it? November's such a trying month, I always think. I—I'm afraid you don't find it very warm in here. Shall I—"

Put on more coal, take them elsewhere? All she did was to glance dubiously at the dead fireplace, then towards the hall. Again ghastly silence, David clearing his throat. Oh, it was preposterous! Then in a blinding flash Alison got it.

"Oh! Is it possible we've made some quite idiotic blunder? I mean, Lady Wibbe. . . . Is this her house?"

Startled eyes goggled at her suddenly-scarlet cheeks.

"Lady Wibbe? Oh, I *see*!" A thankful gasp such as a fish might give when thrown back into the sea. "Oh, no, no!" hysterically. "Lady Wibbe's house is next door. I—" She giggled, "I thought *you* were Lady Wibbe. That is, I've never seen her, so—"

"How crashingly stupid!" Alison rocketed from her chair, excuses tumbling out of her. "That was my mistake. I said to your butler, 'Lady Wibbe?'—like that, you know, and he very naturally supposed—"

"So he did—tee-hee!" Poor creature, quite school-girlish in her relief. "Parsons is getting on, and—"

"My fault entirely! What simpletons you must have thought us! I am ashamed, getting you downstairs like this!"

They were stumbling over each other on their way out, a chaos of apologies.

"Oh, not at all!" chattered the woman in brown. "Most understandable on a foggy night—oh, most!"

"I kept looking for a turret."

"Yes, they have one too. So confusing. Can you see your way? This gas, very inconvenient. . . ."

She was as eager to be rid of them as they to be gone, yet trying so hard in her futile way to conceal it. Why those furtive glances into the pitch blackness above? Alison would have felt sorry for her if her own mortification had been less grilling; and if about the woman's spinelessness there hadn't been something—well, rather clammy, detestable. Maybe it was the house itself which created this frantic longing to get outside. Was there only the one person living here? No! This one would never use guinea-a-bottle bath essence. She smelled musty like the hall. Dropping their coats now, giggling at her clumsiness, gibbering remarks about the failing faculties of old family servants.

"No, no, we were to blame!" Alison found her sleeve as David started cramming her into the wrong one. "If I'd had an ounce of sense I'd have—"

What was that shriek from upstairs?

It rang sharply out only to be chopped in two—exactly as though a hand had been clamped roughly on the screamer's mouth. It was followed by brusque, striding footsteps and the soft closing of a door.

CHAPTER TWO
"WE HAVE A PARROT"

THE thing could not be ignored. Wheeling, David fixed a scowling gaze on the staircase. Alison, following suit, caught a sudden panic in the ill-matched eyes beside her. The woman in brown had given a gulp, and her face had turned a pastier hue, revealing every reddish freckle.

"We—we have a parrot," she explained with another vapid giggle. "Rather noisy at times. . . . Oh, not at all! Goo—good-night."

Shut into darkness. Almost pushed out!

Together they groped past the sodden laurel bushes. At the gate they paused, looking back.

"Was that a parrot?" asked Alison, with a shaky laugh.

No answer. David was staring hard at the blind windows above.

"Was it?" she jogged him. "I could have sworn—"

"Keep still!"

It might have been a woman's sob which had reached their ears. Now, however, the whole mist-blanketed house had fallen back into tomb-like silence.

Cars were crunching past, into the neighbouring drive. The dazzling headlamps had a steadying effect.

"May have been a parrot." Alison was recovering. "They do sound awfully human sometimes. Her face, though! Did you see it?" She shivered again, thinking of the ghastly ten minutes just terminated. "David, I don't like this, you know. That woman gave me the creeps—and the house! There's something horrible about it. Yes, all the time I was so

busy rationalising, trying to make it seem the same place I was in before
I . . . Oh, David, wasn't it just like a loathsome nightmare?"

David hadn't heard.

"What a fool!" she upbraided herself. "And yet, just supposing—"

"Supposing what?"

"Well, that something is wrong in there. Something they want to
keep covered up?"

"Come along!" He pulled roughly at her arm.

This time they were greeted by warmth, bright lights, comforting
festivity.

"Beet-red, of course!" muttered Alison, taking stock of herself in the
Empire mirror of the handsome bedroom into which she was shepherded.

Her swansdown hovered, but she returned it to her bag. Wasn't hers
the plain, out-of-door type, better left as it was? She did not value her
bloomy tan, coffee-hazel eyes or chestnut hair, though the latter rejoiced
in a natural wave and was still nicely gilded with the sunbleach left over
from last summer. Treating it as a bad job she wore it almost as short as
David's, brushed it till it shone and left it at that. It was even a wrench
to desert tailor-made and jumpers and get into evening-dress—though
she had to admit this bronze velvet wasn't so bad with her boyish hips
and square shoulders. A pity someone wasn't here to see her for once in
a way all nicely dolled up.

"Never mind, I'll make a good story of to-night's imbecility. He can
jeer at me. That may give him a thrill."

Through a happily-buzzing throng surged her hostess, a gypsy-queen
in rainbow chiffon and clanking bracelets.

"Oh, Lady Wibbe, such an adventure! Let me tell you what—"

"Do! One moment, though. You've met my husband?"

Firmly the authoress pounced on a small individual who formed
the nucleus of a group. She gabbled a few introductions and swam off
to welcome another guest.

"Hot punch, sherry?" Amiably vague, Sir Francis Wibbe cut short
what Alison was dying to pour out. "What's that, got into the wrong
house? Now that reminds me—"

No one, it seemed, wanted to hear. Bottled up, Alison escaped to join
David by the blazing logs. Lonely and taciturn, he was warming his back.

"I haven't told them," she shrugged. "There's not been a chance."

Moodily he handed her a Chesterfield. He had not, she noticed,
tasted his sherry. Maybe it was a mistake bringing him along. Already
he was looking bored.

Brave in blue taffeta, a small girl edged towards them. She was the daughter of the house, weedy like her father, but with her mother's snapping black eyes. There was purpose in the descent. She made a bee-line for Alison.

"Oh, Miss Young, I heard what you were saying! That awful house next door—what's it like inside? You actually spoke to the people? Tell me—tell me everything!"

Alison glanced at her cousin. He avoided her eyes and knocked off an ash.

"Well!" She laughed. "Thank goodness someone's interested. Here's what happened"—and she gave vent to her tale.

The Wibbe child sucked in every word.

"Crickets!" She gave a leap, clicking her flat silver heels. "Now maybe they'll believe me. Mums!" Swooping on her mother she tried to chain her attention. "You've got to listen to this, it's miles worse than I thought. Next door, you know. Now, Miss Young, tell it again, and don't leave out the parrot. That's the juiciest part."

"Parrot? Who's got a parrot? Beastly birds!"

"Just the point," said Alison dryly. "Have your neighbours got a parrot?"

"I really couldn't say. We don't know them, so—"

"Mums! You *know* they haven't. Wouldn't we have heard it? No, it was the poor woman who gave this blood-curdling scream. The creature who sneaks out with a market-bag just made up the parrot to account for it. I've told you they had the other one shut up. We've got to do something. We must! Will you ring up Scotland Yard? Because if you don't, I will!"

Cynthia Wibbe carolled gaily. "See, Miss Young? Penelope will write thrillers. Do forgive me, I must rush off."

"Oh, beast, can't you see it's serious?"

"Hush, Pen! Do you want your fortune told? Good! Then buzz off this minute to Daddy's study, get it over and up to bed. Yes, Miss Young, I've got hold of rather a clever woman. Cards, you know. Pen first, I've let her stop up for it—then a man. What about you, Mr.—no, don't remind me, Mr. Beddoes?"

Wavering, Penelope hissed into Alison's ear, "There's *no parrot*! If you don't believe me, ask Jinks—that's Mums' secretary, over there in the high-necked frock. She'll tell you things."

She skated from the room.

"Know what I think?" Alison addressed David, now her sole audience. "The woman we heard scream is a lunatic. She has to be restrained. Why, what's wrong about that?"

To her astonishment David had jerked away with sudden violence. There was no time to investigate, for bearing down on her was a callow author, hitherto dodged, whose gleaming spectacles proclaimed the fact that Miss Young, of Boxall's, was his meat. Alison was captured. When she extricated herself David had disappeared.

"American, aren't you?"

The old woman was seated at a green card-table in a small, book-lined room, a cone of light streaming down on her silver hair and the podgy fingers which were dexterously shuffling her stock in trade. David poised, vaguely antagonistic.

"Sit down." The voice was brisk, commanding. "Now, then, shuffle these yourself, and cut in three piles."

He obeyed, conscious of shrewd eyes. Rather unusual eyes they were, watchful under wrinkled lids.

"No faith in this, have you? Never mind, you won't be bored long. That's the worst of these gatherings, no chance to give any one a proper reading Let's see what you've done . . ."

Sweeping up the piles she began laying out a sort of cartwheel. She clicked her tongue.

"Dear me! Most curious. I hardly know what . . . Don't tell me anything, please!"

He had no intention of doing so. The fortune-teller knit her brow over the array and spoke with marked hesitation.

"Yes. . . . You're in business. Considering your age, you've made rather remarkable progress. That's excellent, only don't let it breed over-confidence. There are things you'll have to be careful about, yes, in the immediate future. Those three cards coming together in a row. Very awkward, that. I wonder if we can change it?"

With annoyance she stabbed at the knave of diamonds, king of clubs and queen of hearts juxtaposed near the centre. Doubtfully she continued:

"You're beginning a new venture. It promises well; but a false step will ruin it. I may as well tell you at once! You're far too hot-headed. Inclined to rush things. And you're too faithful for your own good. On the other hand, if you are too deliberate worse may happen. There's this, you see." She tapped the red queen with a plump forefinger, adding to herself: "It will just depend . . ."

"On what?" blurted David.

"I wish I knew! All these cards have a thick veil round them—like the fog outside here to-night. Have another try." She pushed him the pack.

When the new piles were cut, the old woman snatched them up greedily, spread them out and exclaimed irritably.

"There! They've done it again. I'm afraid it's no use."

Sure enough, here were the three fatal cards presenting the same order. With them was the diamond queen.

"Another one! Still, she's only a poor, weak creature. I don't think there's much danger from *her*. It's the club-king I distrust—well entrenched, you see; and the red knave, he's your real problem. . . . Do you know him? I think not. In fact, I question whether . . ." She stopped dead, a sort of convulsion agitating the grey lace over her bosom. "This won't do! I'm telling you nothing of the least use. I should help you. I must!"

"Don't bother," drawled David, getting up to go.

"Sit still!" It was a sharp command. "Listen: Whatever this trouble is, would it sound utterly mad to say it's cropped up since you left home this evening? That's how I see it—and it's very, very serious. Your fate and that of another person are balanced—like this." Her soft palms poised delicately in mid-air. "And here"—touching the heart-queen again—"is the other person. See," she cried eagerly, "how these evil cards press round her? She's hemmed in—un-get-at-able. Is she a total stranger? I can't make it out."

David leant forward, despising himself for his credulity.

"Where's this trouble? Here, in London, or—"

"Oh, decidedly! The water in your fortune's already been crossed." Frowning, she scrutinised the cards, then impatiently swept them aside. "They won't tell me anything more. They're like that sometimes. Oh, I could spin you a nice rigmarole! I won't, because I'm honest—and there's not time to read your hand. Quick, give me some object you've kept by you! Not your watch; I can see it's too new. If only I can give you some word of warning, of guidance—?"

Psychometry? More rubbish; but her fingers were clawing for the Phi Beta Kappa key he had half-drawn from under his coat. Changing his mind, he got out his wallet, and from it a worn and faded snapshot picture.

"Have this," he said gruffly and with shame. "It's been in my pocket for three years."

She seized the dim little picture, not looking at it, and pressed it tightly over her bosom. As she sat with closed eyes, swaying slightly, her commonplace appearance became almost eerie; but this, David told himself, was because fog had seeped into the room and was weaving a shimmer of gauze in the light playing down on her.

Suddenly a spasm crossed her features.

"Dead!"

David's brown hand gripped the table. Still with shut eyes, she seemed unaware of his movement. Her whisper went on, less certainly:

"No, perhaps not dead. Not yet. Better think of her as dead, though, for she is for you. Safer to believe it—I think. Odd, this." She was crooning in a curious, muffled tone. "I feel her near, very near. She can't be in this house. And yet why is it I can hear her voice calling for help? An American voice, like yours. Near—but so far away. For practical purposes she might be in China. Can you save her? I doubt it."

"Here!" said David dryly. "Aren't you simply tuning in on my thoughts?"

"Am I?" The eyes opened and stared anxiously into his. "It's quite possible, of course. In any case, I haven't solved your riddle. I can only give you this parting advice: Think, think hard before you act. Not that you'll remember," snapped the fortune-teller scornfully. "That's all, I'm afraid. And now, who's next?"

CHAPTER THREE
HEMMED IN

THE girl in the bed stuffed the sheet in her mouth and gave way to long shudders. What was this new feeling that mingled with her incredulous rage? It couldn't possibly be fear.

That was nonsense, of course. How be frightened of the person who was straining every nerve to get her well? True, the care bestowed on her had grown quite impersonal. Lately she was being treated as a combination of fractious child and public enemy; but that with her husband was inevitable.

Why blame Geoffrey for anything? Certainly she had disappointed him. Obviously, with his distaste for the unhealthy, he had become more and more detached. She, for that matter, had edged away from him, if for rather different reasons. As for his temper, flashing out like cold lightning, she had always known about that. It was much to his credit that he so rarely let fly at her. Her lying here week after week, getting whiter and more wasted, must be goading him to desperation. She was, in addition, no docile invalid. On the contrary, she was forever fighting against discipline. Just now must have been the last straw.

"Though why was it so frightfully wrong of me? I only wanted to hear people's voices after this age-long hell."

Tears sprang to her eyes. They could not know how she had pined for any outside contact, merely to restore touch with her lost world. And these people seemed to be American. Strangers—and now gone away.

"Only a voice in the darkness . . ." she quoted, and could not go on.

She was hearing again the eager, friendly tones—the first natural-sounding ones in . . . How long was it? She could hardly have said, time having become an immeasurable quantity. A moment ago she had forgotten she was ill, scuttled out of bed and, marvel of marvels, not stumbled once. Rushed into the dark hall, in only this chiffon rag of a nightgown. Would have plunged right into the visitors' arms if Geoffrey hadn't stopped her. It was that swift tiger's pounce that brought back her terror, illogical, but shattering.

She saw her husband now, taut and fury-like, as he flung out of the bathroom. Hot, fragrant steam surrounded him. It might have been the aura created by his own passion. Young, vigorous, with pale, blazing eyes and moist hair standing crisply on end, throat naked between the folds of his plum-coloured dressing-gown, fingers of steel fastening on her shoulder. . . .

She had screamed, but only once. Geoffrey's other hand had brutally silenced her. It was then her legs had crumpled. In the same moment, before she touched the floor, she had been bundled with rude force back inside her room, to be dumped, like a sack of potatoes, on to her bed.

"You blasted bitch! Have you lost your wits?"

Yes, Geoffrey had said those words—hurled them in her face, like vitriol.

It must have been her blank amazement which had checked him. Battening down his wrath, he had continued in a laboured fashion:

"Exertion, excitement—you know they're ruinous. Now, of all times, when I'm doing my damnedest to see you don't commit suicide!"

What on earth could he mean, and with that strange bitterness?

"Suicide!" She had repeated it curiously. "Are you really afraid of that? I wonder why."

Her own words had startled her. It was as though dim notions germinating in darkness had suddenly pierced the soil. They must have startled Geoffrey, too, for into his alien eyes had come an odd anxiety.

"Don't be literal," he had retorted. "Why do you suppose I'm spending all I can rake together to get you cured? Pigging it in a filthy old barn of a house just to keep you under the best medical attention? Think I wanted to close down my place, sell my hunters and—?"

"You couldn't afford to feed them," she had reminded with a shrewd flash, "or mend that leaking roof, either. I know I'm a drag on you; but as for giving things up—Geoffrey! Who were those two people?"

"How should I know? Blundered in by mistake."

"They were Americans."

"Oh? I'd have said Australians. Some putrid accent. Nothing to do with us, that's certain. If you have a set-back, don't say I'm responsible. And, God, don't sniffle! That at least you can control."

He had swung out, banging the door with such violence she had scarcely registered the small grating sound succeeding the jar. She thought of it now and, slipping across the worn carpet, tried the knob.

Locked!

Indignation and alarm made her dizzy again. Then, seeing the childishness of it, she began to laugh. How utterly silly! She didn't need locked doors to make her a prisoner. She was that already on account of her legs. Simply and stupidly they gave way. Now, of course, she knew why. The medical book Geoffrey had carelessly left by her bed with a marker between the pages hadn't remained with her for long, but quite long enough. Despite technical jargon, she had discovered what had so sedulously been kept from her.

Perhaps it was this revelation which had turned her so reckless. What could anything matter, since she was bound to die? At twenty-one her death warrant was signed, though execution might be considerably delayed. All this hateful treatment she was undergoing merely staved off a result ultimately certain—and this her husband knew. Himself barely twenty-eight, he was tied to a dead log of a girl whom in decency he must struggle to keep alive. Poor Geoffrey, his bitterness didn't surprise her. He was born to be untrammelled, a dragonfly in the sun.

To be sure, something might put a quick finish to her. Pneumonia? Her eyes strayed to the window, closed against the fog.

"That, I suppose, is what they're afraid of." She toyed with the thought of raising the sash, standing in the vile, clammy cold till she got chilled through. "No! My heart's strong, worse luck. They'd pull me round, sure as fate, and leave me more of a crock than I am now." Besides, she couldn't do it. Exhausted, she crept back to bed.

As the sleeves of her fleecy blue bed-jacket fell away she found herself staring in disbelief at two purple bruises, deep-dyed against her emaciated whiteness.

"Poor Geoffrey!" She murmured it again, as though the man she pitied had been a character in fiction. "I must have driven him wild."

Idly she wondered what he would do when she was finally out of the way. Marry someone else?

"No. That is, I can't imagine it. It's not that he doesn't want people round him—new ones, by preference. They make a better audience. It's double harness that galls him."

Geoffrey required no complement. Singularly self-sufficient, he withdrew almost disdainfully from any intimacy. The last thing he wanted, it seemed, was what she at one time might have given.

Queer, when she thought back to the star-glittering night when Geoffrey had raced her in his car along the hard sea-front with the wind rippling her hair and the smoke-blue Esterelles bewitching her eyes! She had been eager enough then to merge her own being in his—let it fuse in his white-hot flame. Only the flame had so quickly died down. Why?

She'd long ago given up trying to solve the mystery of that sudden black-out. Left with cold ashes, she had warmed herself with dreams of another love that might have been. One face out of a girlhood rudely curtailed had come again to haunt her—a face forever vanished—and yet only this evening, just now, it had sprung before her more vivid, more real, than her husband's.

Her aunt's counsel returned to her.

"Geoffrey may be brilliant and independent. Don't be misled. What he wants is mothering."

Mothering! He got it in a warm, wet deluge from the sister who from the days of her own cheated youth had worshipped and spoiled him. And how did he respond? Jibes—cruel disregard—using her as a safety valve when anything went wrong.

There, Evie was catching it again, out in the passage. Geoffrey was lashing at her, and Evie, poor simp, was as usual crawling back for more punishment. One would be sorry for Evie if only for one second she could stop being such a worm.

"Oh, God, she's fumbling to get in! Quick, let me pretend I'm asleep."

Too late. The lamp-switch hung fire, and in sidled Geoffrey's half-sister—eyes red, of course, likewise her nose, three inflamed spots in the face that was like the underside of a sole. Sniffing, she moved forward. Rolling her cotton handkerchief—why couldn't she buy linen?—into a damp, soiled ball, teetering slightly on her long, disgracefully-shod feet, opening and shutting her mouth in affrighted fashion.

"Well, Evie, dear, what is it?"

"So stupid of Parsons!" dithered her sister-in-law. "Geoff's wild at me. But how could I help them coming in? A man and a girl. Colonials, I think. And—oh, dear, I do try so hard to keep things absolutely quiet for you! You weren't upset?"

"No. Why should I be?"

"I—I didn't know." Evie stopped, stared anxiously, and seemed reassured. "Can—can I do anything for you? Tidy your bed, brush your hair?"

Horrors, what an idea!

"No! I mean, thanks awfully; but I've fixed my hair for the night. Now I'm going to sleep."

"So neat always," murmured the older woman admiringly. "How you keep it so I can't think."

"A perm's a perm while it lasts," observed the invalid with a dry glance at Evie's straggling wisps. "Look, Evie, was that all you wanted with me?"

"Yes, oh, quite!"

Still the spinster lingered and stared, nose twitching like a rabbit's, eyes strangely fascinated. She was always doing this, particularly of late, just as though . . .

Good heavens, it was true! Till this moment it hadn't seemed real. It never did about oneself. Evie, in imagination, was seeing a coffin covered with flowers—her own person in black. . . .

Evie in black? No, never! Not with that pasty skin and no make-up. It was a revolting picture. The girl doomed to die forgot her own fate and remembered only this poor, pinched, flat-chested slave who, whatever happened, would go on denying herself, suffering insults, having no fun.

"Evie! I've just thought of it. You know my green Henri coat and frock with the Indian lamb? Do have them—to please me. They'll only go out of style." Evie gasped and giggled nervously. "Me, Elizabeth? Oh, you can't mean that! Fancy me in your smart Paris clothes!"

"Why not? The colour will suit you. You can let down the hems. Here, let's have a look."

Out of bed Elizabeth darted shakily towards what courtesy called a dressing-room—unlit, freezing cold, with only bare boards underfoot. Frantic hands tried to stop her.

"Oh, Evie, do leave go! It won't take a second, and—"

"Don't, no, truly! Oh, if Geoff knew! You'll catch your death!"

Evie was half-sobbing in an agony of terror, but Elizabeth threw her off and began tugging at the huge wardrobe in which had been stowed wearing apparel, still good, thanks to advance fashions—lovely things Fanny had lavished on her, hardly worn, going to waste.

"Why! Where are they?"

From behind came a whimpered babble: "The—the damp was making them all mouldy. Geoff said . . . Elizabeth! You do understand?"

Understand! Fictitious strength ebbed away. Clinging to the heavy doors, Elizabeth wondered if the beastly film was again blurring her vision. She rubbed her eyes, stared harder. In the cavern of gloom all she saw was a bare steel rod and one scurrying feather.

So they had taken away her clothes. . . .

Chapter Four
OUT OF THE QUESTION

David had for some reason shut up like a clam. Was he worried about something?

Alison looked at him as he sat hunched over her hot gas-fire. He couldn't, she thought, be dreading this new job he had come over to take on. When they left Mecklenburgh Square this evening he had been chockful of confidence. Knowing her cousin like a well-thumbed book— hadn't they summered together till the last year, taken degrees from the same university?—she was at a loss to account for his abrupt change of mood. Unless . . . No, it couldn't possibly be that!

"Gosh, it's nice to be home!" Sinking luxuriously into the other arm-chair, she admired for a moment her soft beige curtains drawn against the dismalness without. "Not so bad, though, was it? Especially the fortune-teller—though I know you've no use for that sort of thing."

David failed to play up.

"By the way," she resumed carelessly, "Cynthia's secretary told me quite a bit about the people next door. They moved in just recently, after the house had stood empty for months. Took it furnished, just as it had been left by two stuffy old women who died. David, are you asleep?"

"The hell I am!"

"I see, not interested. Well, I am. There are three of them besides the old doddering servant. They arrived in a car which hasn't been seen since, so probably it was hired—two women and a youngish man; and one of the women was all muffled up and had to be carried indoors.

She's never once stirred out. Miss Dearling thinks, as I do, she's out of her mind. Did you say anything?"

Apparently not. Alison continued her disclosures.

"A doctor calls every day or so, but *no one else*. Yes, I mean it, literally. The Wibbe servants have remarked on it; and definitely there's no parrot. Apart from trunks, all they contributed to the house was—what do you guess?"

"Barrel-organ and a monkey," gritted her cousin.

"Fairly warm. A grand piano. Big to-do hauling it in an upstairs window. Miss Dearling says it sounds so odd to hear brilliant, quite professional piano-playing coming out of that tomb—often late at night. Bach, Couperin, sometimes modern incomprehensibles. Now and then it ends in a crash. Think the crazy one's a musical genius?"

"The one we saw is cuckoo all right," muttered David sourly. "What did you take her for, some sort of housekeeper?"

"Oh, no, David. She's a lady! You mustn't judge by her get-up. She had the right accent. You'll know it when you've been here as long as I have. I admit she struck me as queer and—well, rather slimy. Just like the house. But the man sounds all right. It seems he's tall, well dressed and good looking. In fact, it's my private belief Miss Dearling is developing a romantic crush on him—which may explain her vigilant eye."

"But," growled David, "she hasn't found out his name."

"David Beddoes, I do believe you took in every word she said! You can be irritating."

Yawning, she rose to rip off the cover from the divan which for this brief sojourn was serving her guest as a bed. David reached his pipe, only to fiddle with it broodingly. She turned on him with a sudden challenge. "What is it, David? Do spit it out."

"I'm wondering, that's all. Elizabeth Greentree. Have you ever run across her?"

Alison stared. "Little Betsy Greentree, you mean? No. Why should I?"

"Only that she married some Englishman. You being over here—"

"So she did. I'd forgotten. I'm not likely to meet her, all the same. She's years younger than I am. I knew her only as a kid running round Woods Hole in the summer. Have you had any news of her?"

He shook his head sombrely. "No one has. That's why I asked."

"No one? That's funny."

"It's true," David mumbled, teeth grating on his stem. "After her father's smash-up and death Fanny Rush carted her off to the south of France. As far as I can see, the two of them have vanished. That was over three years ago."

"So it was. I'm recalling it now, the big coming-out party, and right after it the plane accident. The papers were full of it. Goodness, I hadn't thought of it for ages! Nice child, wasn't she? Can't you see her in her little one-piece bathing-suit, streaking through the water—?"

"Like a dog-fish. Oh, I remember!"

"Not much like a millionaire's daughter. Shy, appealing, a tomboy, but somehow very feminine. I expect she'd blossomed considerably when she made her formal bow. Here! Seems to me you were invited to that debut-party. Did you go?"

Eyes averted, David gave a curt nod. "It was a mystery to me how any professional hostess ever got me on her list of eligibles. It was the usual unholy mob, of course—no air, rivers of champagne. Next day it made me wild to think of that rabble of strangers getting blind on the last gasp of the Greentree money. Nobody suspected; but what was blown that night would have kept Elizabeth for years."

"Did you dance with Elizabeth?"

"Four times."

"Well, well! You must have pulled your stuff. Was that the last you saw of her?"

"Not quite." David tugged at his dry pipe. "She cut a luncheon party next day and let me run her up to Westchester."

"I know, to Pilgrim's Haven," said Alison dryly. "We were all traipsing there just then, and eating little neck clams. Well, I'm learning things. Leading Nathan Greentree's one and only child astray and never saying a word! That takes some beating, I'll say. Did you propose to her?"

David flinched. "My God, what had I got to propose on, least of all to a girl I still believed was an heiress to millions?" He glowered another moment into the fire. "Coming home," he went on, "we ran into the extras about Greentree's death—and next day all New York was shouting about the bankruptcy."

"It wasn't suicide, was it?"

"Oh, no, pure accident. Twenty passengers killed. The wrong moment for Greentree, though. If he'd lived he might have pulled things round. Before the press had quieted down, Elizabeth and her mad hatter aunt had chased off to Europe. I dare say something was saved from the crash. Not a soul seems to know."

He'd been making inquiries, thought Alison shrewdly. It did not seem altogether strange to her, though, that Elizabeth had failed to communicate details.

"She can't have had any substantial roots in New York. Boarding school, summers in Massachusetts, a year on this side, if I remember rightly—all over at eighteen. New life now she's married, new circle of friends. Mrs. Rush, though—doesn't she write any one?"

"Guess again. They used to say that only on occasions did she send a cable when it suited her to turn up."

Alison thought back. Yes, Nathan Greentree's widowed sister was reputed to be off-hand, undomesticated, possessed by a passion for venturing off alone into remote corners of the earth. When she had played hostess at the summer residence she had reminded one of a fierce-eyed falcon straining at the leash.

"Who's the English husband? Damn! These slippers are red-hot."

Reluctantly, with more than a touch of shame, David dug from his wallet a worn newspaper clipping.

"Here's all I can tell you."

The *New York Sun*—two and a half years back! Alison shot a glance at her cousin, mentally shrugged, and began to read.

On June 16th, in the English Church in Paris, a marriage had been solemnised between Miss Elizabeth Ann Greentree of New York City and Mr. Geoffrey Edward Scarpath, only son of the late Rear-Admiral Scarpath, of Hampshire, England. The bride had been given away by her aunt, Mrs. Frances Penn Rush. That was all.

"Scarpath! Never heard the name. Colin comes from Hampshire, though. Shall we ask him?"

"Who's Colin?"

"Oh, David, wake up! My doctor friend. He's having breakfast with us to-morrow, so—"

"I see, the blond chap. A doctor, is he?"

"Of course—and if I'm getting up to fry bacon I've got to be turning in. Come, help me with your bed. . . . David, what made you start thinking about Elizabeth Greentree?"

"This and that."

"Liar!" Over the divan she faced him accusingly. "You can't fool me. It was something that happened to-night. What?"

"Oh, say, wash it out!"

Alison drew in her breath, nodding slowly. "You started acting this way in that God-awful house. That's why you were such a pain in the neck all evening. Well, what did you notice that got by me?"

"A book." He set his teeth.

"I saw. A Tauchnitz. You picked it up from the sideboard. Stories by Katherine Mansfield. Well?"

"I tell you, there's nothing in it. Can't be. . . . If you must know, it had E. G. scribbled on the flyleaf, and, under it, Cannes. That's where they went."

"Her handwriting?" Alison stood very still.

"Might have been. Hard to say. There was another little thing. Pages turned down." David wet his lips. "She did that. I used to row her about it. Of course, she was only about fourteen, but—well, that day in the car she told me how dippy she was about Katherine Mansfield."

"Rubbish! Thousands of people are—and just as many dog-ear their books. E. G.—why, it can stand for anything!"

"Oh, yes, I'm not taking it to heart."

Then why was he savaging his pipe? Alison buttressed her arguments. Think what streams of people went to Cannes. Most of them brought home Tauchnitz books, frequently passing them on to friends.

"Bilge, as you say." Still David did not look at her. "It was that scream got me going. When we hear the other woman is sick—"

"Ill, David! Sick's what you are when you lean over the rail. This is England. Do mind your manners. And listen, nitwit: Can you picture our pampered millionaire kid living in that ghastly place with all that musty-smelling furniture?"

"They took it furnished."

"But—a British admiral's son! It's too fantastic."

"Why? Is he God?"

"Oh—!" She gave it up. "No, David, that wasn't Elizabeth who screamed. It's simply out of the question." She paused. "David, my pet, did it sound like her voice?"

Gloomily he was depositing his watch and loose change on the table. She saw him wince, then shake his head.

"Of course," Alison sympathised. "Seeing that book put her into your mind. For that matter, how can we be certain it wasn't a parrot? Maybe it was one, just bought."

She bade him good-night and disappeared into the bedroom.

David yanked at his collar-stud. *"Hand over her mouth,"* he muttered. *"She wasn't allowed to scream again. If what we heard was a parrot, I'm a dod-gasted octaroon."*

Hung in space before him was a vision so vivid, so poignant, it cut into his very soul. He saw a brown-legged girl racing him to a raft that swayed and pitched on tumbling green waters. Now she had hauled herself on to the wet boards, laughing impishly back at him and shaking salt drops from eyes deeply blue. She had long water-blackened plaits clinging like eels to her shoulders. One was unravelled. She braided it up, holding a soaked ribbon in her teeth. . . .

"Hell and damnation! She's married—has been for two years. Can't I drop her out of my thoughts?"

He arranged his dinner-jacket over a chair, got into his pyjamas and viciously knotted the cord. Alison was right. It was sheer lunacy to imagine that unseen sufferer could have been Nathan Greentree's daughter, married to an English admiral's son.

Hand on the light-switch, he paused.

Why in God's name had the woman in brown started dithering when his name was mentioned?

For she had. That was something Alison must have overlooked. . . .

Chapter Five
THE NEW CAGE

ALISON dispensed the last drop of her superb coffee and moved the electric waffle-irons on to the hearth. Sunday breakfast was concluded, all but the washing-up, which Mrs. Marshall, the char, would see to in the morning; and her two guests, replete and somnolent, basked before the fire.

Colin Ladbroke stirred. "Ready to light up?"

She took one of his English gaspers because he offered it, though it was David's brand she preferred, and, bending towards a lighted spill, smiled into his steady, blue British eyes. He was wearing his oldest tweeds, smelling pleasantly of peat and tobacco. Conscious for a moment of the strong, light hairs on his wrists, she rejoiced that the somewhat driven expression—product of a new practice not yet paid for—had vanished from his brow. In this bit of home she had created he had learned to relax. The thought thrilled her, though she warned herself it might come to nothing more.

"There may be dazzling sun out of London." Dubiously she eyed the misted window-panes.

"Who cares?"

"Same here. No cross-country tramp yet awhile, unless David's itching to stretch his legs."

The divan was restored to order with its bronze and rose cushions. The fire shed a warm glow on Boxall's autumn list, gay in varnished jackets, Colin's chrysanthemums showed up handsomely against the beige carpet and covers. She jogged David with her foot.

"What about it, you?"

He was busy pipe-stoking. "Sour puss! Am I making a mess?"

"Don't growl at me. I'm merely asking you which you choose, to browse here or go rambling in Essex?"

"Too many waffles," he grunted, and returned to his moody absorption.

She remembered now that all during the night she had heard him threshing about in this room. Suddenly she remembered their conversation, and with suitable casualness turned to the doctor.

"Colin, do you happen to know a man named—what is it, now?—oh, yes, Scarpath. Some admiral's son."

"Geoffrey Scarpath?" Colin Ladbroke squinted at her a little curiously through an aura of smoke. "Vaguely, yes. He's from my part of the world. I overlapped him at Oxford, though he's probably unaware of the fact. Friend of yours?"

"Heavens, no! Only he married a girl David and I used to know. Tell us about him."

"Married?" The doctor seemed surprised. "I hadn't heard that. Still, he's younger than I am, and our lines never actually crossed. I'm Balliol; he's Brasenose."

"Explaining just everything, I suppose, to any one but barbarians!" Out of the tail of her eye Alison noted her cousin's rigid attention. "Go on, what's the crab?"

"Crab? Why, none."

"I gathered there was."

"Sorry!" Colin pulled thoughtfully on his briar. "What can I say about Scarpath? He's able, even brilliant. Rather unusually attractive. Possibly a spot unstable. Meaning to say he does a multitude of things more than average well, but seldom carries them quite through."

"What things?"

"All sorts. His tennis has got him into the Wimbledon semi-finals on two occasions. He's done one novel in the Evelyn Waugh manner.

He composes ballets and plays the piano, I believe, almost if not quite as well as many professionals."

"Plays the piano!"

"Oh, only for amusement." The doctor hesitated under the sudden penetration of two pairs of eyes. "As he does all the rest of it. I might even describe him as the perfect example of the gentleman amateur—England's curse. Which, of course, is only my vulgarian jealousy. I resent these lucky blighters who toss off achievements like soap-bubbles when I have to slog. I suppose, too, I've a bourgeois prejudice against leaving university bills to take care of themselves."

"Can that be done?" cried Alison, shocked. "Surely the admiral—"

"Young woman, you've a lot to learn! Many and many a middle-aged man is still paying off by driblets his Oxford tailor, wine merchant, and so on. It's a custom with the best people. In this case one hears that old Scarpath—a national hero, by the way—left his affairs in rather a filthy tangle. Young Mrs. Geoffrey has money, of course?"

Alison and David exchanged glances.

"No—or anyhow very little. Her father went bust, too. Why are you so astonished to hear Geoffrey Scarpath is married?"

Colin explored his pipe-stem with a pin. "Only because I haven't heard any one mention his wife; and as a rule his doings are pretty well publicised. Turn up any old copy of *The Bystander* or *Sketch*. You're almost sure to see him practising his spectacular back-hand, leaping on skis or seated in half-shadow at his keyboard. I'll ask my niece Angela about him. She moves in his crowd."

David spoke. "How does he get a living?"

"Now you're asking." Colin met the dark, glowering gaze. "Any point in knowing the answer?"

"Well, yes, in a way," Alison replied as David remained silent. "You see, last night—"

"*Christ!*"

David cannoned from his chair, disgustedly swearing at fingers which dripped stickily with maple syrup. As he tramped into the bathroom Colin jerked an interrogative head.

"Seems so," murmured Alison guardedly. "Old attachment—and I never suspected. Quick, let me get this over while he's away."

In rapid undertones she outlined last evening's adventure.

"Now you see what's eating him. He admits it's ridiculous, but he'll have no peace till he's made sure. We both thought it was a woman screaming. Of course, it's quite possible we were mistaken. Supposing we weren't, do you consider there's the remotest chance of its being Elizabeth Scarpath?"

The doctor scratched a reflective chin.

"Not one in ten million," he declared sanely. "Apart from the incredible coincidence, I'd call it beyond sill probability for a chap like Scarpath to have chosen the surroundings you describe. A small service flat in the West End is more his cup of tea. As for anything rum going on in that Hampstead house, I should even doubt . . . Damn!" The telephone was jangling. "Will that be for me just as I'm happy and comfortable?"

He had reached for the instrument, but Alison snatched it first.

"Egotist! If it is a patient I'll say you're not here."

"For God's sake don't do that! I've rent to pay."

Alison called a watchful "Hallo? *Who?*" She listened, her amazement changed to alertness. "Oh, I see, Penelope Wibbe! What's this? . . . Go on, you're kidding me."

"I'm not, oh truly, Miss Young!" A child's treble shrilled through the room. *"It's on a balcony right now—a huge, wicked green one, shrieking its head off!"*

"Well! Rather explodes things, doesn't it?"

"No, don't you understand? It wasn't there yesterday. I tell you, it's just come. I saw the freak of a woman putting it out, and she's terrified to go near it! Cook says there was a fearful row over there last night and—surely you see? They've got hold of a parrot simply to boost up a lie. They're showing it off so—What's that?"

David blocked the doorway, eyes smouldering like hot coals.

"We still may be wrong, Penelope."

"Wrong? Listen! The cage is brand new. That proves it, you see. I saw her taking off the price-tag. It is my business, I don't care what my mother says. I'm going to find out why not a soul but the doctor goes there, why the one upstairs cries but so quietly as if she's afraid of being heard, and—Oh, crumbs, I've got to ring off."

The excited clamour died just as David made a lunge. "Hold it!" he shouted, but the Hampstead receiver had shut down. He hovered, breathing hard.

"Sunday," mused the doctor. "Bad day for buying a parrot."

A pause. "That child's no fool." Alison spoke meditatively. "I wonder. . . . Would there be any place where you could buy a parrot?"

Colin shrugged. "Whitechapel, I dare say, but nearer than that— well, possibly in Camden Town. I seem to remember being dragged to an animal shop in that district, quite close to Hampstead, as a matter of fact, when my sister's young son kept tortoises and silkworms."

"But has this parrot been bought to-day? I don't see how we can prove it. Late yesterday would make all the difference. Oh, I can't think—"

She stopped, struck by David's expression. As though in a mirror she saw reflected all the queer, vague *wrongness* she had tried to dismiss as imagined. Bit by bit it came back into her mind—the listening Presence at the head of the dark stairs, the light dew of sweat on the woman's forehead when David's name was mentioned, above all the stammering terror in her eyes when the anguished cry had rung out.

David had taken off the receiver and was dialling a number.

"That you, John?" His tone was wooden. "Dave here. Still free for lunch? Right, I'll be seeing you."

John Fellowes, a New York acquaintance who was now domiciled in London. Alison asked no questions, but tactfully slipped into her bedroom. Something told her David was burning to talk this over with Colin, and that while she hung round he would not open up. She was right, for hardly had her door closed before he was broaching the subject of last night with painful bluntness.

"This niece of yours. Think you could sound her on this fellow Scarpath's marriage, and so on?"

"Of course. At the moment, though, I fancy she's away."

"Or any one who might have a line on him. I've looked in the telephone book. He's not there."

"I shouldn't worry, Beddoes. These people are almost certain to turn out total strangers."

"Yes. Then why the stampede to exhibit a parrot?"

"There's probably some mistake."

David's jaw hardened, his breath hissed in.

"I know I've darned little to go on. Same time—well, where is this place you call Camden Town?"

CHAPTER SIX
THE FEELER

DAVID peered into the shop. Narrow and dark, like a tunnel, it was lined to near the ceiling with wire-fronted cages, each of them occupied by some creature either feathered or furred. In fact, it strongly suggested the Looking-Glass Train.

Twitterings and munchings furnished the only sounds. David had picked his way for some distance over damp straw and rotting cabbage leaves before he discovered the proprietor, an elderly man tilted back comfortably in a kitchen chair before an oil-stove resembling red-hot organ pipes in a row. He laid aside his *Sunday Express*, fished a chameleon from his open neck-band, and got to his feet.

"No business to-day, sir. No harm 'aving a look round, though. Anythink particular you was wanting?"

"Parrots. Got any?"

"Parrots, eh?" The old man cocked an eye at David and rubbed the frosty stubble on his chin. "Well! We're a bit on the low side just at present. That chap interest you?"

He jerked a short clay pipe towards a dove-grey bird with rose trimmings. The sole parrot in sight, it hunched on an open perch, cracking a peanut.

"No? Fine bit o' colour. Not much of a talker, of course. Now, the green one I just got rid of had a rare lot to say for himself. And sing! 'Soldiers of the Queen, My Lads.' Learned it time o' the Boer War."

David shifted his feet. Two frail desert-mice, venturing their noses out of a lowly hutch, drew back, alarmed, while a spotted guinea-pig decided against sampling his shoe-laces.

"The green parrot. When did you make the sale?"

"Why, yesterday it was. Latish."

"Sure it wasn't this morning—early?"

A jovial chuckle. "Wot, on a Sunday? Blimey, sir, you don't know our regulations." There was a searching side-glance.

"Your shop's open, though."

"'Cos for why? Livestock 'as to 'ave its feed, don't it? Wotever day it is. I sits 'ere in the warm of a Sunday, has a look at my sporting news—"

"Listen!" David grinned and waxed confidential. "I don't want to make trouble for you. I might even do you a good turn. The fact is, I've got a bet on about that particular green parrot. If you tell me—strictly on the q.t., of course—that you sold it this morning—well, there'll be a pound coming your way. So what?"

He had heard that the gaming spirit was strong in the British of no matter what degree. He fancied he detected a warmer glint in the proprietor's eye which might mean sympathy, covetousness, or both; but the headshake remained stubborn.

"No, sir, yesterday. Sundays we don't part with so much as a packet of birdseed. Daren't risk it—that's flat." The shopkeeper spat into a heap of straw.

Beaten, David began a disgruntled prowl through the chaff-filled purlieus. Suddenly he drew up, kicking at an empty perch.

"Here! What's this? There's litter round that standard—and it's still moist, in spite of your tropical heat. Mean to tell me that mess hasn't dried overnight?"

The plaid waistcoat heaved again with chuckles, this time of admiration. The owner came closer and spoke in a hoarse whisper.

"You win, sir. Fancy you noticing a thing like that! Well, here it is, then: 'Bout an hour ago—young bloke in a car. No money was passed, though. I let 'im 'and me a post-dated cheque just to steer clear of awkwardness, see? My old woman wouldn't 'a' bin so trusting; but, there, I likes to oblige, and he was a proper gentleman, I'll back my judgment about that. All done in a wink, as you may say. Back he drives, old Joey covered over with the rug to keep him from squawking. Friend of yours, was he?"

Kept quiet on the journey. . . .

David's pulse gave something between a leap and a thud. He reminded himself that in a city of millions quite a number of persons might be seeking parrots on a Sunday. The description he pressed for was annoyingly vague—though it couldn't matter; he had never seen Scarpath. Other details interested him more.

"Tearin 'urry, he was in—catching a train, he said; but seems as 'ow his sister's parrot up and died on 'em larst night, and he didn't like leaving her to mope and fret, see?"

"Oh!"

David felt punctured. Possibly there had been a bird tragedy which he and Alison had imaginatively distorted. And then all at once he remembered an important item.

"Did he by chance invest in a new cage?"

"That's right, sir, so he did. Old one'd gone groggy. Poor brute 'ung his neck between the bars and choked to death, struggling. See that big brawss cage 'anging over your head? It was the mate o' that he took with him—and a big stock of feed."

"What's funny?" demanded David, for fresh mirth was convulsing the waistcoat.

"Why, sir, the questions I was arsked. Wot parrots was fed on, 'ow much, and the Lord knows wot, and whether old Joey was the lively sort wot makes a good noise. You'd 'a' thought neither 'im nor his sister knew a parrot from a pipin' bullfinch. Don't you go telling 'im I said so, though, will you?"

"I wonder," said David, "if it was my friend. Mind my having a look at that cheque?"

Thirty seconds more and David was striding towards the Camden Town Tube, making for Hampstead. At sight of the arrogant signature on the cheque his heart had flopped over. Indeed, he could hardly credit his spectacular luck, but now uncertainty was ended the knowledge that Elizabeth Greentree's English husband had deemed it vital to bolster up a fiction brought petrifying dread. How on earth could one *prove* that a certain cry hadn't been the death-shriek of an aged parrot?

As he shot underground, visions of what Scarpath and a companion might be trying to cover up became a searing torment. He told himself that a daylight view of the actual house would ease his mind, but this was not the case.

Across the empty road he stood looking at it. Summit View, it was called. He read the name in leprous black lettering on the gate-posts; but there was no view, unless from the rear, all in front being cut off by mangy cedar trees.

The Wibbes' dwelling, complete with turret, had been erected at the same regrettable period, but there the similarity terminated. In excellent repair, its door painted bright blue, it rejoiced in smooth lawns, tidy rock-gardens, a pergola and a brick-red tennis court. Darkness and fog had hidden all that, of course. Even so, would the blunder ever have been made if Alison had been wearing her glasses? David grew cold at the thought.

A car had purred round the curve of Heath Crescent, was halting opposite. The chauffeur had opened a door to let out the solitary passenger, and the latter, a man of advanced middle-age, in a handsome overcoat and dark grey spats, was trudging into the drive, carrying a doctor's black bag. David moved on a dozen paces, found a walled footpath running between back gardens, and in the shelter of its entrance prepared to keep watch.

The chauffeur was settling back in his seat to read a paper. All at once he jerked round and directed an astonished glance at the house into which his employer had vanished. David was doing the same, for the silence of the street had been rent by an ear-splitting screech. He saw the chauffeur craning for a better view and scratching a puzzled ear which told its own story. He himself, from his new vantage-point, could make out the origin of the sound—a parrot, poisonously green, behind bars of glittering brass. It was conspicuously placed on one of the little trumpery balconies on the Wibbes' side of the house. Till he had changed his position the cedars had concealed it.

Between this screech and the cry uttered last night there was not the slightest resemblance.

David thought of what the Wibbe child had shouted over the telephone. There had been a row. Which had got the mauling, Ginger-hair or the—the one who had been roughly silenced, the one who never went out—*who cried quietly, as if afraid of being heard*?

Setting his teeth, he forced himself to consider a less agitating matter— money. Had this fellow Scarpath any means? Darned little, by the look of this show; but if he didn't work—well, it stood to reason the old admiral, or Nathan Greentree, must have left something.

"It would clear everything up if I could manage a private word with Elizabeth herself."

Almost he decided to march boldly up, ring the bell and hand in his card. Then he saw he could not make a worse move. If Elizabeth was ill, there would be excellent excuse to turn him away. Those in charge knew him now and would draw fatal inferences. Better wait—send out a feeler.

Twenty minutes had passed, and now the doctor was leaving. David could hear him exchanging a few words with another man at the front door. It would be some satisfaction to get a look at this Scarpath, whose voice sounded all right, only a trifle supercilious.

David crossed the road casually. The doctor, emerging to view, was just hurling back a last irritable sentence to the man invisible on the steps behind him. "Rubbish, Scarpath! We've only the one iron-clad rule. Stick to it, don't go looking for trouble."

With a shock David felt his last lingering uncertainty stripped away. The name had come to him clear-cut, unmistakable.

Ruffled and petulant, the doctor got back into his car, paying not the smallest attention to the stranger strolling past. Letting the chauffeur tuck a rug over his knees, he leant back, closing weary lids. In another moment he had been bowled smoothly towards the Heath.

Doctor, car, chauffeur—all three conveyed the impression of sober affluence and respectability.

The house door had shut. Dead quiet again, except for the parrot up there, stuttering raucously in its brand-new cage.

"No business of mine," David reminded himself morosely. "Didn't she pick this fellow herself?"

Jealousy stabbed him. He knew that his own tennis-game, fair by amateur standards, would never get him into the sacred precincts of Wimbledon. Which, blast it, wasn't the point.

"Damned funny going all haywire because a couple of strange Americans happen to hear a scream. Hallo! What's this now?"

A piano, brilliantly played, in one of the upper front rooms. David stood listening. He rather prided himself on his musical appreciation, and it annoyed him to find no fault with the present performance beyond a hard nervous quality which the hyper-modern stuff being played might excuse. On it ground for several restless minutes, piling up agony of discord without one resolution. Then, without warning, the pianist's hands crashed down on the keys. Savage destruction—then silence, broken only by the parrot's steam-whistle rage.

Here is the note David composed in the writing-room of the American Club while waiting for John Fellowes to arrive:

"Dear Elizabeth,—I'm in London, but only for a few days. The job I've just taken will keep me mostly in the provinces. Is there any chance of seeing you and having a talk about old times? I'd like to do that, also to meet your husband. I got your address from a woman whose name didn't register. That's how I'm able to drop you this line.

"I spent August in Woods Hole. Some of the old crowd was there, but it wasn't the same. This club will find me. Hoping to get in touch with you one of these times,

"Yours sincerely,
"David Beddoes."

He read it over. No, he had said nothing to which any husband, should it meet his eye, could possibly object.

He sealed the envelope, directed it, dropped it into the hall-box. And now, what would come of it?

Chapter Seven
PROXY

Half a week had gone by, and still David had received no answer. Elizabeth might not be able to write, though surely in that case someone could do it for her. It hurt abominably to think she might not want to renew an old friendship. Her silence could be construed in several ways, all equally disturbing.

Alison could not be consulted. He was ashamed to tell her what he had done—not that her opinion would have been better than his own.

"It's this feeling of butting my head against a stone wall!"

Once again uncertainty was driving him nuts. He could no longer deny that Elizabeth's illness might be taking some peculiarly distressing form. Though it would still leave the parrot unexplained he even began to wonder if he ought perhaps to stop prying, particularly since an important suspicion had been squashed. By no chance could Elizabeth have been married for her money. Nathan Greentree had left precisely nothing.

"I ought to know," John Fellows had stated positively. "Wasn't my own father heavily involved in that crash? You can take it from me Elizabeth would have been serving at a ribbon-counter if her aunt hadn't rescued her. Seeming to indicate that Fanny Rush's investments weren't all of them affected. I imagine she saw Elizabeth married and called it a day. I don't for a moment suppose she's furnished an allowance. Those two never did hit it off."

John knew nothing of the Scarpaths and advised his friend not to get in a stew over a girl who had a husband to look after her and was probably okay.

"If I hear anything while I'm in New York, I'll shoot over a cable. Don't imagine I will."

Dr. Ladbroke had obligingly forwarded a line of inquiry to his niece, who was hunting somewhere or other. No reply had yet come. David, who had planned to get a lot of sightseeing into these few idle days, put in most of the time prowling the vicinity of Heath Crescent and calling at the American Club for mail—drawing nothing but blanks, till Wednesday evening.

By now David knew every crack and protuberance of Summit View's unwholesome exterior. He knew that no light would be visible in front, but that far round the right-hand side a faint thread of radiance marked the parting of drawn curtains till ten or perhaps ten-thirty. He hoped and believed this window, an upper one, was Elizabeth's, and acting on this assumption he now sneaked round the dank wall to crouch under an old lilac-bush and watch.

At nine o'clock he was rewarded. The curtains above were very quietly slid back, and in the rectangle of brightness he saw a shape, blurred through the intervening glass. Slowly, with infinite caution, the sash was being raised. The figure leant out. It was a girl—and her hair was dark.

His heart beat a muddled tattoo.

She peered, rubbed her eyes and peered again, as though her vision were misted. He saw her glance behind, nervously, and then stare once more out into the cold, dark night. Suddenly she stretched both arms out before her, longingly, as a prisoner might do. A shock went through David. Her loose sleeves had fallen back. He had seen her bare arms, mere wraiths, wasted to the bone.

"Elizabeth!" His whisper barely stirred the air. "Elizabeth—is it you?"

The arms dropped.

"Elizabeth!" he hissed again. "Look—down here!"

Her fingers gripped the sill. She turned, her little shapely head outlined sharply against the light behind. He stepped into the open, but she had gone. Up there someone was speaking, and Elizabeth—he'd have known her voice out of ten million—was stammering an excuse.

"It's all right, Evie. I just wanted some air."

Someone had come into the room. He dodged to cover as an unseen hand lowered the sash and closed the curtains, which remained drawn thereafter.

Still, he had seen Elizabeth, heard her voice, and got rid of one hideous doubt. There was no trouble about her sanity. At the same time he believed her to be utterly miserable. Just as she had disappeared he had caught a small gasping sob, and her tone to the intruder, apologetic, almost guilty, piled fuel on his consuming dread.

Thursday, as usual, he collected Alison at her office.

"Mind stopping in at the club? There may be something for me."

"Mr. Beddoes?" The inquiry-clerk roused. "A note has just this minute been left for you. Wait, maybe I can catch the gentleman!"

Indifferently David tore open the thick white envelope handed him. He saw a short, courteous message on club paper from an address in St. James's, signed—*Geoffrey Scarpath.*

"Elizabeth's husband. So now we'll find out."

"He's written you?" Alison stared at the enclosure thrust on her, and wheeling took stock of the young Englishman who, unnoticed, had brushed by them on the steps.*"Oh, gosh!"*

Skin prickling, David followed her eyes. The man now being accosted by the clerk was turning in slight annoyance. He had been about to join an elderly couple seated in a huge black Daimler, but now, after noticeable hesitation, he was murmuring apologies.

"Sorry, can't be helped, I'm afraid. I'd have liked to come back with you, but in any case I shall be seeing you at Newmarket?"

"Weather permitting." The man in the Daimler signalled that he quite understood, his companion—grey, angular and elegant—waved an affectionate hand, and the car slid away.

Scarpath, with the faint shrug of one facing a burdensome duty, ran lightly up the club steps. Inside he paused, directing a keen, unsmiling gaze on the two waiting Americans.

"It's good of you to bother with us, Mr. Scarpath." David spoke awkwardly, a ringing in his head. "The fact is, my cousin and I used to know your wife rather well, so naturally we'd like to—to hear more about her illness and so on."

"Of course."

Scarpath's sternness yielded to a smile of singular frankness and charm. To Alison it was as though dazzling sunshine had melted a thin sheet of ice. The pressure of his hand was brief and impersonal, but the great thing, she told herself, was that apparently neither she nor David was being associated with Saturday evening's event. As far as she could see the Englishman, with the unstressed ease of his caste, was accepting them at face-value—his wife's sometime acquaintances, boring perhaps, but persons to be dealt with courteously. *Noblesse oblige.*

Conscious of tension, David led the way into the warm, dusky writing-room, touched the bell and ordered cocktails. Scarpath's chary gesture seemed to imply that there might hardly be time for drinks, but David ignored it. Now his chance had come to form his own opinion of the fellow he meant to make a job of it.

"I'd no idea she was ill," he marked time mendaciously. "It's a big shock. Is she—well, bedridden?"

"At intervals, yes."

The other man, who had taken his stance on the hearthrug, bore scrutiny well. He stood level with David, an even six feet, and his good looks, of the fine sophisticated sort, were backed by supreme physical fitness. His build was slight. No flesh softened the whipcord muscles. Though essentially English in type he suggested that spitfire something found in first-class tennis players from the Continent. His clothes were a part of him, therefore right. It was Alison who noticed that the neutral-tawny tweeds matched his crisp, vital hair, and that the hair was cut short enough to reveal a head remarkably well-shaped.

It was his eyes which most intrigued her. Curiously pale, a frosty blue, they were exceedingly hard to hold. Glancing, attractive eyes—now piercing, now flickering off at a will-o'-the-wisp tangent. Summing the young man up, Miss Young of Boxall's made use of a newly-acquired adjective—"pukka." Whatever else Geoffrey Scarpath might be he was definitely that. In his presence all she had been thinking became gross impossibility.

"And you're not going to spend much time in London? Bad luck!"

"No," said David, "I'm off to Manchester on Monday."

Alison, in surprise, was about to correct this statement. Monday week was the date when David started in on his first assignment, but he was continuing firmly:

"That's why I hoped to get a glimpse of Elizabeth now. She showed you my letter, I suppose?"

"She asked me to answer it. Just now, most regrettably, she's unable to manage a pen."

The cousins glanced sharply at Scarpath, who had made the statement with grave reticence, but at this juncture the Martinis arrived. David lifted a glass.

"Accident?"

"Symptom." Scarpath looked away.

David's eyes burned. Alison smothered a gasp.

"Neuritis?" It was a painful hazard. "Or—my God!—not at her age *paralysis*?"

"Of a kind." Reluctant, Scarpath bent his gaze on the rug. "Intermittent, of course. It will get better. Also her eyes."

"Eyes!" David recalled Elizabeth's strained peering into the darkness. "What's wrong with her eyes?"

"Rather bad at present."

"How bad?"

"Don't, David!" implored Alison. "Can't you see—?"

Scarpath had faced the mantelpiece. Hands clinched, he turned back.

"At times," he jerked, "practically blind."

Chapter Eight
NO FLOWERS

THE cocktail spilled. Scarpath continued, angrily resentful, as though finding it distasteful to discuss a matter of this kind with strangers.

"It's an obscure trouble. Came on very gradually over a year ago, and took time to diagnose. Disseminated sclerosis. Does that convey anything to you?"

"Disseminated sclerosis?" David frowned. "No. It's rare, is it?"

"Fairly so. Anyhow, it's still extremely baffling. Oh, I know a good deal about it now," said Scarpath bitterly. "It's—it's neurological, you understand. Shows itself in oddly distressing ways. Fluctuates—and at the bad times, well, she can't see visitors. The first essential is to avoid all nervous excitement."

"Of course," whispered Alison.

Over the room hung a pall. There was a studied evasion of eyes.

"She'll be cured, though?" David challenged.

"Well—helped, at any rate. Or so one hopes. It's a chronic condition. Can stretch over a long period, even—" Scarpath paused painfully. "A lifetime. Age hasn't anything to do with it. Elizabeth was under twenty when it began."

Out of another dreadful silence Alison faltered, "But her eyes. Won't they get better?"

"Oh, yes! And other things, such as her present tendency to fall down."

Little active Elizabeth—darting through clear waters, racing sure-footedly up the slope to Pilgrim's Haven! Sensitive, yes, but oh, healthy to the core. . . .

"Why?" blurted David huskily. "I mean, what causes it—a germ?"

"No one seems to know. Some medical authorities cling to the theory that an elusive spirochete sets up patches of thickening in the spinal cord and other parts of the central nervous system, but I believe that view's out-dated. A predisposing cause may be an inherited weakness. My wife suffered two violent shocks simultaneously, you know—her father's death and a complete financial shipwreck—shortly before she married me." Scarpath moistened his lips. "I'm told she was always just a tiny bit unstable."

"Elizabeth? I never noticed it."

"No?" Scarpath glanced briefly at David's belligerent face. "I dare say not. What does it matter? We're all in the dark. It happened—and we're dealing with it as best we can."

"How?" demanded David. Alison squirmed over his deplorable manners.

"How? Well, by shutting my country house and bringing her to town where she can be constantly under a specialist's care. It wasn't necessary to take her abroad. Right here in London we have one of the world's best experts on nervous complaints—Guthrie Brodmart, of Harley Street. You've no doubt heard of him?"

They hadn't, of course, but to Alison the words Harley Street carried weight. What more could be said? It embarrassed her acutely to find David showing a tactless tendency to argue.

"You say these various troubles will clear up. Won't that mean she's cured?"

"Unfortunately no—because they'll return. She's unaware of that, naturally."

Once more the pregnant hush. David's persistence jarred across it.

"It's impossible to see her, then?"

"Quite. At least, now. By doctor's orders only the two of us are allowed in the bedroom. Yes," Scarpath answered the looks of searching inquiry, "my half-sister is with us. She's much older than I, an excellent nurse, and"—with light irony—"by way of being what is popularly termed a saint. She devoted years to my father's last illness, and she's doing the same for my wife. I needn't add she's happy to be helping."

"I see." David tried not to glance at Alison. "So a regular nurse isn't required?"

"Not at the present stage. All Elizabeth wants now is her treatment, which can be done at home, and absolute quiet. Eventually a nursing-home may be indicated, but she's fighting against it."

It was plain to Alison that Scarpath was being irritated by David's controversial tone, though he had remained unruffled. When he flicked his wrist-watch into view she took pity on him and rose, visibly suffering.

"It's all too frightful, Mr. Scarpath. Poor, poor Elizabeth! There seems nothing we can do except to send her our love and to hope that later on we might perhaps come and chat with her?"

"Later, oh, decidedly!" The frank, thawing smile flashed on her. "I'll let you know. You'll appreciate how at these bad times she herself is inclined to—to shrink from—"

"Oh, perfectly! Poor darling!"

"We must help her get over her rather morbid sensitiveness. At the moment we have to humour her or precipitate a crisis."

David was looking at Scarpath. "When I'm back in London can I get in touch with you just to inquire how she is?"

"Certainly, at my club. We discourage telephone calls to the house. They tend to upset her."

Scarpath bade them good-bye.

Two minutes afterwards David said heavily, "Well, shall we go?"

Side by side they left the club and made for Piccadilly. Neither had spoken, but now, as Alison was turning into a flower-shop, David pulled her back with a muttered, "Don't."

"What, not send a few flowers?"

He ground his teeth. "God, don't you see? We've got to watch our step, or we may make things worse."

"Worse for her? Don't be ridiculous!"

"Wait." He drew her along the pavement. "I'm not questioning Elizabeth is ill. Suppose, though, they're making use of her condition to keep people away from her?"

"David, do talk sense!" cried Alison hotly. "What possible reason—"

"Hold on. Notice how relieved he was when I said I was clearing out on Monday? As it was he took four days to answer my letter. I might easily have been gone."

"Nonsense! Candidly, I think we've let our imaginations run wild."

"Oh, yeah? Well, he nearly pulled the spell with me, too. Might have managed it only . . . what about the parrot?"

"Oh!" Alison smote her brow. She had entirely forgotten.

"Losing track, weren't you? Now then, pull up your socks. Elizabeth screams, because her husband goes for her. Who but her husband was likely to clap a hand over her mouth? The sister's terrified, tells the first lie that comes into her head. Scarpath hears, raises hell, but feels it advisable to—"

"I know, I know! But surely we're assuming such a lot."

"Are we? I say Scarpath has heard Elizabeth mention our names. That he may even believe we went there the other night on false pretences to spy the ground, so he's taking no chances. Can you imagine any other excuse for producing a parrot?"

"But I can't possibly see. . . . Didn't John say Elizabeth hadn't a cent? You talk as though this man were some sort of Bluebeard. Does he look it?"

"Oh, I saw him!" David's tone was grim. "And I still say he may have some reason for shutting his wife off from her friends."

Alison's brain revolved rapidly. A young man tied to an invalid wife, entanglements elsewhere, difficulties about divorce . . .

"I felt—yes, I certainly did feel he was keeping something rather unpleasant from us. Mental trouble perhaps."

He let go her arm violently. "No! That, I'll swear, is a lie! I saw Elizabeth—last night."

"Oh, David! You actually saw her? Tell me!"

A minute later she was dragging him across Albemarle Street and into the side entrance of the Berkeley.

"I'll ring Colin. Quick, David, you try and catch Fortnum's before it closes. Alligator pears—a bottle of Medoc!"

They met at Piccadilly Circus. Under Alison's arm was a book in a modernistic jacket.

"Geoffrey Scarpath's one literary venture," she panted with satisfaction. "Remaindered—so it didn't set the Thames on fire. I thought I'd like to—"

"Is Colin coming over?"

"Oh, yes, so we'll soon find out about this famous nerve-doctor. Gosh! I've forgotten his name."

"Don't worry, I've pelmanised it. More than that, I took down his car number last Sunday. That'll show if he's the right man. Telephone upsets her! What price piano-banging or the row of a parrot? Fine," growled David. "Oh, swell!"

They sprinted for a bus.

Dr. Ladbroke, nursing a bag of mushrooms, was waiting on the doorstep. Arrived in the top flat Alison set out sherry and vanished into the kitchen.

"Brodmart!" Colin raised his brows and emitted a soft whistle. "So they've got him, have they? Well, he's certainly at the top of the tree."

A buff overall hovered at the door. "Thank goodness!" Alison sighed. "Now, David, are you satisfied?"

"Hold on." David spoke cautiously. "What's this Dr. Brodmart like to look at?"

Colin considered. "Fiftyish, at a guess. Medium size, nondescript colouring, clean-shaven, figure slim but a trifle run to seed—"

David cut him short with a nod, waited till Alison had gone away again and then got down to business.

"I'd like all the dope on this disease. First, is it curable?"

Colin had grown grave. "Well! I may tell you that disseminated—otherwise multiple—sclerosis is extremely difficult to diagnose, that is in its early stages. A lot of mistakes have been made. I might even say that there's a tendency to use it as a sort of wastebasket for dumping purposes. Unclassified complaints are apt to go into it. Have you any idea just how far your friend's case has progressed?"

David supplied details as far as he was able. The doctor listened attentively and made guarded pronouncement.

"Sounds fairly typical—though I must warn you my own knowledge is almost entirely academic. The true cases we had in hospital were shunted elsewhere for treatment. Let's see: the trouble comes on roughly at any age between twenty and forty. In the beginning sight may be affected in varying degrees, even to relative blindness, though this as a rule clears up very quickly. It's a frequent but unreliable sign, because—"

"And the other symptoms?"

"Oh, too numerous to go into! One highly usual one is ataxia—meaning, of course, unsteady gait with a liability to fall down. Then there's the tremor, often of the hands. It could easily prevent holding a pen. Possibly the most characteristic feature is the ebb and flow of the symptoms. They flare up—die down; but recur. It terminates, generally speaking, in a long bedridden siege. Death, when it comes—"

"When! No if about it?"

The doctor looked acutely embarrassed. "I was going to say that the patient, growing steadily weaker, is more than likely to be carried off by some intermediary illness. As to treatment—well, quinine seems to give some results. It's what's being used now."

"You've dodged my main question. Do you yourself know of any permanent cures?"

"Well, no. Not when it's been the real thing." David walked to the window. Presently he broke the oppressive silence to ask in a low voice, "Tell me this: Can it injure the mind?"

"Certainly not. Never! Why, did Scarpath make such a suggestion?"

David did not reply. He was thinking deeply, one hand jiggling with the curtain-cord. When he spoke again it was in laboured fashion.

"Let's suppose that somehow or other I contrived to get a look in on—on Mrs. Scarpath. Could I tell if it was a genuine case of disseminated sclerosis?"

Colin began a protest, shut his lips and deliberated, frowning.

"Well, hardly, seeing the thing has many medical men stumped. I dare say there are certain indications, like signposts, you could watch out for."

"Such as?"

"The tremors—though both those and the dimness of vision *can* arise from a different cause. There's nystagmus, of course. That means a rapid, lateral oscillation of the eyeballs, very noticeable. And here's something: slurring of speech. Abrupt pauses between words—spacing, we call it— and groups of words run altogether. Also there's the ataxia."

David had taken out a notebook and was painstakingly jotting all this down.

"But!" Colin held up a hand. "Although you might notice every symptom I've mentioned it's even odds you mightn't see one of them. It would depend entirely on how you happened to catch her. Be certain of this: If Guthrie Brodmart's in charge, it's a bona fide case, with no hocus pocus attached to it. Brodmart has a big reputation at stake."

David put up his notebook. "Thanks," he mumbled and said no more.

That night, in bed, David went over matters thoroughly. However he viewed certain incidents he found the self-same paradoxes riding forth, jagged rocks out of the sea. In his tormented consciousness a single purpose was taking form. By hook or crook he had got to see Elizabeth—talk with her, judge for himself.

But how?

Every ruse that occurred to him savoured of Palais Royal farce—lovers disguised as gas-fitters, piano-tuners, hairdressers in order to wiggle into a mistress's presence. It might work, all the same, if a plausible role were chosen and the visit suitably timed. The sister went out every morning at eleven. The old butler looked a half-wit, and anyhow he hadn't seen the Saturday evening intruders in a good light; but Scarpath himself? It wouldn't do to risk failure. Success must come with the first shot, or else. . . .

"Hell, why didn't I think of it? Scarpath's going to Newmarket. What day will that be?"

He switched on the light and grabbed the *Evening Standard*. Here it was, front page stuff: POLE STAR LEADS FOR NEWMARKET. And the date? To-morrow!

Gosh, that meant hustling! Now, then, someone must have right of entry into that house—into any house. . . .

Of course—why not? He'd chance it and damn the consequences. Naturally he'd not breathe a hint of his intention to Alison or Ladbroke. They'd raise merry hell. . . .

Heath Crescent again. A still, grey morning, with silver rime on the pavements. In his hiding-spot David swung his arms and wondered if Miss Scarpath would make her sortie as usual.

Gates creaked on rusted hinges. He looked out, and here she was mincing along in her pinched brown coat—God, was it possible she was a blood-relation?—with the tip of her nose red from cold and a mock-leather marketing-bag dangling from her arm. He watched her disappear round the curve, then swaggered forth, hitching a pseudo tool-bag into prominence and tilting a shabby bowler—in his country a derby—farther over his eyes. These props, along with a crumpled old raincoat and a soiled muffler, he had raked together just now in a slum region called Kentish Town. He had omitted to shave.

The bell jangled. After some delay shambling footfalls approached, and now the old turtle of a servant, by daylight even dingier, stood blinking at him with watery eyes. Thus far there was no sign of recognition, but speech must be brief. This cursed American accent would give the show away.

"Telephone," mumbled David, a fag trailing from his lip. "Defect on the line. Can I test your instrument?"

"Just 'ere." The old dodderer motioned him inside.

The telephone, old-fashioned kind, was on a bamboo table at the foot of the stairs. Slouching to cover it, David depressed the hook, lifted the receiver and began conversational patter.

"All clear, sweetheart? See if you can ring me. . . . No good. Try again."

He mistrusted the "sweetheart," seeing this was England; but the old man, mercifully, was shuffling through a rear door. Not closing it, but one couldn't have everything. Now David strode to the front door and banged it loudly to advertise his exit. While the chandelier still tinkled he was taking the stairs in swift, soft bounds.

To left and right ran uncarpeted landing, on which abutted several doors, only one of them closed. He turned the knob, opened it a crack and whispered!

"Elizabeth? It's me—David Beddoes."

He heard a queer, choked gasp. Heart hammering, he pressed into the room. It was large, semi-warm, and revoltingly dismal, but he scarcely saw it, all his attention fixed on the small, solitary form which had sprung out of bed and was trembling midway on the floor. Emaciated, chalk-white to the roots of dark, trimly-waved hair . . . yes, it was Elizabeth, or rather what was left of her.

"Betsy!" Backed against the closed panels he swallowed a dry lump.

He might have been a ghost. She was clutching a little pale blue bed-jacket across her childish breast and gaping at him. Her mouth rounded in an O, her eyes were black with disbelief.

"David! You!"

She made a wavering rush. Her hands had just grazed his coat when the horrifying thing happened. Her legs crumpled, gave way. Down she slid into a heap at his feet.

CHAPTER NINE
EXCUSES

THE truth sandbagged him. In essentials, at least, Scarpath had not lied.

Sick at heart, he yet felt poignantly the pathos of that impetuous rush with its ignominious conclusion. Gathering her up into his arms he made a joke of her tumble. Her cheek was buried against his chest, she was laughing with a catch of hysteria.

"Steady! Is this what visitors do to you?"

Holding her close he could feel her whole feather-light body shaken with tremors. Only a few seconds, but already he had spotted two symptoms of the dreadful disease!

"How silly!" She was battling for control. "I—I do that sometimes. Put me down."

He carried her across to the wide, ugly bed, set her on it and placed himself alongside. Her violet eyes gazed back at him, and a tinge of faintest rose crept into her thin cheeks. She let one hand steal timidly along his sleeve.

"You!" She whispered it. "It's just not possible. Where did you spring from, David, and in those awful clothes?" She glanced furtively at the door.

He swallowed again, trying to grin. "I'm a telephone linesman. That's how I got in. Quick! Before we get going, how long is your sister-in-law likely to be out this morning?"

"Evie?" Her pupils widened. "How do you know about her?"

"Never mind, answer my question!"

"Oh, a good hour! And she won't come up here till she's cooked my lunch. David, you're the very first person from home—from anywhere—I've set eyes on in simply aeons of time! I write letters, no one notices. I've about grown to this room. Frightful, isn't it? And now you've come. I—oh, please don't mind if I blubber a little!"

Valiantly she blinked back the tears, smiling at him through a mist. David put his arm round her, felt her relax, then stiffen from him.

"Go on," she bade. "Tell me how you found out."

His eyes had never left her face. "Then you never knew I was in London?"

"Me? Why, how could I? You don't mean—"

"See here," David compromised. "You know my cousin, Alison Young? Saturday night she was taking me to a party in the house next door to you. We mistook the entrance and—"

"Oh, David, so it was you!" She was trembling again in painful excitement. "I was dashing downstairs, only—"

She had stopped with a gulp. He noticed the tremors; but not so fast! Surely there was normal reason.

"Go on," she begged. "What happened?"

"Oh, we just cleared out! I'd seen a book, though, with your initials in it and the word Cannes. Drawing a long bow I wrote you. That was six days ago."

"Oh!" She paused. "David, I never got it. Funny. . . . Never mind, they think they're doing the right thing. Did—did Geoffrey, my husband, answer for me?"

"Correct. Alison and I ran into him at the American Club just as he was leaving a note."

"I see."

She sat picking at the bedclothes—not overclean, he noted with anger.

"Then, I suppose," she murmured, "he told you about me. Everything?"

"He said you were ill. Not allowed visitors."

"Yes. Did he mention what was wrong with me?"

David wanted to hedge, but she had pierced through his hesitancy. "Of course he did."

A long, anguished pause, small hands gripped together. "Well, David dear, it's true. I've not known the truth of it for very long, but I do now. No good crying, is it? These things just—happen. It's worse in a way for Geoffrey than for me—because I shall get out of it. If I could set him free . . . but how can I? Not comfortably. So it just has to drag on."

Seared with sympathy and rage, David yet registered the thought, *She's grown up.*

"Look, Elizabeth," he blurted. "I had to find out the exact state of things. There seemed only this way of doing it. Doctors differ, you know. I want to know if you've had more than a single medical opinion?"

She laughed bleakly. "Oh, David, if you knew! Three doctors have had a go at me. I'm under a big specialist now, about the last word for what I've got. So you see?"

"Not altogether." He steadied himself against the blow. "How did it begin?"

"Let me think . . . it's so long ago. . . . Well, there was my tumble on the golf-links. Down in Hampshire, near Geoffrey's place. I put my foot in a rabbit-hole. At least I thought it was that, but the sprain never got any better. We all thought it was just a sprain. First we had the local doctor, then another from Southampton. And soon, well, other things started going wrong."

"What things?"

"My—my eyes." Her finger traced a circle on his sleeve. "Some days I couldn't see across the room. I get spells of this, bad ones, then it's all right again. Next, of course, it was my hand. This one." She looked down at her right hand, thin to transparency, as if it were some alien object. "It goes all cold and numb. I can't get a grip. I thought it was rheumatism. David, that house was so damp! I suppose I'd been spoiled by central heating. And the rain! Drip, drip—it never seemed to leave off. Grey sky, grey water. We were near the inlet, you know. I couldn't go out in those sloshing fields. I did so hate coming down plunk in horrible mud. So I just stayed in."

"Till when?" He was watching her closely.

"Well, till Geoffrey decided there must be more wrong with me than we knew, and got down this nerve-specialist. You see, the Southampton doctor believed it was connected with nerves, and who wouldn't have thought so? I was so *miserable*. Over being such a crock," she explained quickly. "It was something absolutely new, and of course it got me down. When a person's never had anything except scarlatina and measles . . . you remember the measly time, don't you?"

"Oh, yes! I brought you the *New Arabian Nights*, and you ruined it. So Dr. Brodmart came down. Then what?"

"Oh, he prodded me, took X-rays and tests. You know, all the usual stuff. He came several times, getting more and more solemn. It ended in them carting me up here. It was only two months ago, but it seems like two years. You see, I don't know any one, David! And if I did, I wouldn't be allowed to see them. All day, all night, with this ghastly cabbage wallpaper! Though if I'm to die anyway what difference can it make? None, I suppose."

This time the tears ran down unnoticed. David took her hand, held it tightly.

"You feel company would buck you up?"

"What's the use? I've got to have dead quiet. My doctor's terribly strict about that. As for the house, well decent ones carry big rents, and there isn't much money. As I keep saying, a thing like that can't matter when sooner or later I'll just peter out."

"Stop it!" he gritted. "Who the hell said you were going to die? I for one won't let you. So just you chew on that!"

There was gratitude in her glance. "Oh, darling David, how like you that sounded! It's true, though. I can't fool myself any longer. I read all about myself in a book."

"Book? You can't mean—"

"Oh, yes, a medical book Geoffrey left in here by mistake. I haven't told him. It's bad enough without that."

"You poor infant!" It was all he could say.

"Oh, don't start pitying me, please! I've got quite used to the idea now. I did rather want to go on living, yes, in spite of all, but—"

"In spite of—what?" David leant close. "Elizabeth! Were you happy?"

"Why not? I married the man I wanted, didn't I? I don't say it wasn't a scrap lonely down there with only county people, all thinking me a freak, but—"

"Cut that. I want the truth."

Quite suddenly her bravado wilted. She sank her head and gave way to a tornado of weeping.

"No! No! Oh, never, David, never! My fault, I expect, but oh, I did try!"

So now he was getting it. Blood surged in his temples, he was conscious of an immeasurable relief.

"It's all right, Betsy," he muttered, and put his arm round her, drawing her close. His head swam a little to observe that she no longer evaded his embrace, but his was a poor triumph, he told himself, one of which any decent man would be ashamed. Moved to the depths he fingered the little ragged ducktails of hair curling up from the nape of her neck, waiting patiently for her sobs to subside.

All at once a shambling step passed the door. Elizabeth sprang up, eyes black with panic. At the sound of a low chirrup she relaxed with a giggle.

"Only Parsons," she whispered. "Putting out the parrot."

Presently the slow tread retreated to the lower floor.

"Yes," she continued, "that's Evie's new pet. Someone's asked her to look after it—as though she hadn't enough on her hands! David, what's the matter?"

"Oh, nothing! You like your sister-in-law, do you?"

"Evie? Oh, quite! That is, she's all right, really, only she *is* rather what we used to call a wet. Fancy a woman of her age pottering for hours at a time over a jigsaw puzzle! There's no radio, I suppose she has to amuse herself somehow."

"She's kind, is she?"

"Oh, heavens, yes! Too kind. I sometimes wish she wouldn't fuss over me quite so much, but that's mean of me. David, you didn't imagine I—I wasn't getting considerate treatment, did you? Because that's too absurd."

"I'm glad," he grunted.

She drew in her breath. "I see. So you did think that. I understand now why you played this trick to get at me. Thank goodness you did! But you're wrong, oh, entirely! Every single thing that's being done is under doctor's orders. Poor dears, when they must realise it's a losing game...."

"So you pity them, do you?" he asked grimly.

"Pity them! Of course. It's perfectly beastly for them, and don't I know it! Geoffrey's nerves are all to pieces. I knew that Saturday night when he—" She bit her lip, scarlet with confusion.

"Go on," said David relentlessly. "We heard. What did he do?"

"You heard? Oh, David!" Struck dumb a moment, she seemed picking her next words with excessive care. "I don't wonder you and Alison got these ideas. I'd no business to go shrieking like a maniac. I was acting like one, heaven knows, rushing out like that in a thin nightgown, making for the stairs. I still don't know what possessed me, or why when Geoffrey made that grab—well, anyhow, you know the rest."

"Do I? All of it?"

"Why, yes, of course! Just what I'm telling you now. Geoffrey put his hand over my mouth and hustled me back to bed. He had to, I might have got a relapse. Really, David, you must believe me! Geoffrey may not love me. You can't force these things, can you? But considering all he has to put up with I'll say he's remarkably gentle, on the whole."

Her earnestness shook him. He remembered that Elizabeth Greentree had always been unusually truthful, for a girl.

"You say he doesn't love you. Did he, at first?"

"I thought so, certainly." She was speaking to herself. "And there wasn't any other reason for marrying me, now was there? None at all. I mean, he could have had heaps of girls with money. I was all swept away by the—the electric rush of him. In Cannes, you know. Fanny and I saw him win a tennis tournament. Oh, it was marvellous! Fanny fell for him with both feet, and—well, so did I. You'd have to know him better to understand. Let's see: yes, in exactly five weeks we were married. Most of that time I was frantic for fear he wouldn't propose to me—so that shows you how I felt about him. When he did, I thought all my problems were solved."

"Problems! So you and your aunt didn't—"

"Please, David! Fanny was so awfully good to me. Must I—? Oh, well, then, it's true, we were having rows day and night. Don't blame Fanny. Here she was, pining to be off by herself, but tied by her feeling of duty. Of course it made her irritable. I wanted to work, but she snorted at the idea. Said she'd as soon think of turning a caged canary out to fend for itself. Though I could have done something, David, I'm not quite a fool. So on we went, nagging at one another, till I was desperate. Then Geoffrey hove in view. Oh, dear, if you could have seen Fanny!"

"What's funny?"

Elizabeth wiped her eyes. "David, you would have laughed! She started purring, just like a cream-fed tabby-cat. Fanny, of all people, hauling me out to the smartest shops and plastering me with model frocks! Her sole effort at matchmaking, but she put her heart into it—poor Fanny."

Mirth had dried up.

"And now, of course, I hardly get a line from her. Oh, she doesn't know I'm like this! I've made Geoffrey promise not to tell her. I'd die rather than drag her back."

David steered back to what for him was the main theme.

"So you were both in love at the start. For how long?"

"I think," said Elizabeth dispassionately, "it lasted about three days. No, it was finished before that, only I wouldn't believe it. We had a wedding-breakfast at the Ritz in Paris, and directly afterwards Geoffrey and I saw Fanny off from the Gare de l'Est. As the train pulled out I turned to take Geoffrey's hand, and found him a little way off, looking at me. David, it makes me quite cold when I think of it. I might have been a total stranger."

For a second David did not speak. "Let's get this straight, Elizabeth," he said huskily. "Are you trying to tell me this marriage of yours hasn't been a real one?"

Red swept to the roots of her hair. "I don't mean that, David. Not literally. It would simplify matters, wouldn't it?"

"You're right, it would. Well! Go on."

She lifted her hands. "There's nothing to say. From that moment I never got over the feeling of being an outsider. Someone who got in his way and exasperated him. Every little thing about me was wrong—my clothes, my way of talking. . . . It made me so self-conscious! I used to lose my temper and fly at him. He got a little kick out of that, oddly enough, but not for long. He took to being away rather a lot. In six months I got ill, and that just put the lid on any pretence."

She caught David's arm.

"Why did he want me at all?" she urged. "I know he's fastidious and restless, but even so how can any man veer round so completely in just that little time?"

Hard brown fingers folded over her white ones. "Leave it alone," bade David. "Time's short, I've got to get it all in. Tell me this: Did your aunt make any settlement on you?"

"Fanny?" she laughed. "Goodness no! Haven't I told you we were at daggers drawn? Worse than ever at the last, though she did sniffle a little and pretend she'd caught cold. No, she had tried, you see, to make me accept an allowance, knowing, of course, that Geoffrey wasn't well off. I'd torn up the cheque, and she swore she'd never offer me another."

"Humph! Then it's got me beat. . . . Your husband, I mean. Can there, do you think, be some other woman?"

"To account for his change? I should doubt it, David. Certainly not among those Hampshire frumps. Some girl threw him over not long before he met me, I'm positive it was a relief. He's out nearly always now, I haven't a notion what he does with his time, but see here, if he wanted to get rid of me why should he get so upset if I run the least little risk?"

"Risk?" David scowled. "What sort—"

"With my health. That's Hampstead Heath out there, isn't it? Some days I'm positive it would do me good to ramble about on it a little, see people again and . . . couldn't I flop down on a bench if it was too much for me? I'm not to do it, and that's that."

"You've tried and been stopped?" asked David keenly.

"Not forcibly. Oh, Geoffrey did lock me in on Saturday evening, but he was just in a tantrum! I couldn't go out now, though, however much I wanted to. It's too perfectly silly, but—well, Evie's locked away my clothes!"

"What!"

"Hush! Only because I kept saying I meant to take that walk. They think it might kill me. I only tell you about it to show . . . David, why don't you laugh? Can't you see the scream it is, like these poor girls who get drugged and—"

"That'll do!" His voice was harsh. "Listen, Elizabeth: I hate like hell to shock you, but your being shut up like this is odder than you know. Do you realise it was your husband who bought that damned parrot, and why?"

"Geoffrey bought a parrot? David, you're nuts."

"Oh, no! He bought it early Sunday morning—to prove his sister was right when she told Alison and me what we heard scream was a parrot. It's being exhibited for that purpose. *Here, wait a minute!*"

He caught her as she dropped.

God, he was a fool! What right had he to deliver this knock-out?

Chapter Ten
SMOKE WITHOUT FIRE

"IT's all right." She whispered it with dry lips, her eyes purple in a paper-white face. "Tell me the rest."

At the close of his recital she sat pondering.

"I don't know, David. . . . Evelyn Scarpath's such a poor, conventional-minded softy. The mere thought of any misleading gossip getting started would just about finish her. I can't tackle her about this, now can I?"

"Fat chance if you did of getting the truth!"

"Well!" Elizabeth pleated her chiffon nightdress. "See here, David. Say what you're telling me is so, Geoffrey still couldn't have any wrong motive. Not possibly. Look at all the expense he's going to on my account."

"Says you!"

"Use your brain, David! Dr. Brodmart's bills must be staggering—three guineas if he bats an eye at you. Naturally we have to cut down on the trimmings, but—"

"Wait! Have you ever mentioned me to your husband?"

She flushed, embarrassed. "Yes, ages ago. It was when I used to romance about the men I'd known, to rouse a little jealousy, you know. There weren't so many. I may have worked you in overtime."

"Uh-huh! So he knew I was nuts about you."

"Were you, David? Oh, not truly?"

Pathetically eager, she was leaning towards him. Awkwardly he growled:

"You guessed all right—and you made him believe it. That's exactly as I doped it out. When my name was repeated to him Saturday evening he thought just the one thing—that I'd heard a rumour and was snooping round to substantiate it. Well, the parrot gesture shows he doesn't mean to have any one out of your past life muscling in on his game, whatever that game may be. If you're looking for more proof, why didn't he hand you my letter?"

Troubled, she shook her head.

"Stop, David! I know Geoffrey, you don't. Suppose some shocking tale had been spread about his treatment of his wife? I can understand his wanting to check it—yes, even doing this ridiculous, childish thing. He's got friends, you see." She paused, swallowing. "In a way I've brought this on myself. When I'm better I do get rather obstreperous; and surely you see what would have happened if I'd known you and Alison were in London?"

"Well, what?" he challenged.

"Why, I'd have given them no peace till I saw you. I might have worked myself up with excitement, and worst of all, what if you two, entirely ignorant of my real case, had started putting wrong notions in my head?"

As he might at this moment be doing. . . .

David held her eyes, masteringly. "Betsy, just answer me one question. Do you still love him?"

"No, David." She hesitated. "But I've got to be fair."

His blood sang. He squared his shoulders and let out a long, chastened breath.

"Okay. Maybe you're right about him. Now about this doctor. Is he doing you any good?"

"He can't work miracles," said Elizabeth simply. "I'm sure he knows what he's about, even if . . . Oh, David," she whispered, head bent, "I've never liked Dr. Brodmart! I can't."

"What's wrong with him?" demanded David suspiciously.

"Nothing." She spread her hands. "It's me, I suppose. I have this feeling he's two people—one almost too charming, the other all jumpy and bad-tempered. I expect it's his health. Some days he leaves me wondering if I hadn't better be ordering my coffin to avoid the Christmas rush." She gave a little, wistful laugh. "Christmas! It'll soon be here. Tell me, David, is Selfridge's all dressed up for it yet? Do country jays still block the sidewalk and yawp up at the electric news?"

"Just the same. Don't get side-tracked. After these treatments, do you feel better?"

"No, worse. They're pretty terrible, David, and when I'm knocked all to pieces is when they're supposed to do me the most good. I don't have many, they're too drastic, though it does seem as if I'm only just pulling up from one before . . . oh, let's not talk about it!" She shuddered.

David felt sick. He had lifted her right hand; was examining it. Understanding, she flexed her fingers.

"Much better now. So are my eyes—till next time. Oh, I shan't go absolutely blind! It's more a matter of not being able to move. Every morning I hop up quickly to make sure I can still manage it. I'm allowed to knit, because that's soothing, but with each jumper I make I ask myself, will I finish it?"

She crumpled against him. "Why, David, why must I go through all this? While I'm still able to enjoy things, why must I be penned up all alone with nothing to do? Last night I dreamt I was in a lovely, bright restaurant, eating my head off. With half a chance do you know what I'd do? Steal back an evening-frock one night, sneak down to the Savoy and have just one more dance with whatever man I could pick up. What if I did come down plop on the floor? They'd only think I was tight. . . . David, pet, am I shocking you?"

David was shocked, though not for the reason she assumed. In his unhappy mind he was hearing certain fatal words spoken by Scarpath and confirmed by Alison's friend: *It fluctuates.* This disease had periods of deceptive normality. At such times rigid restrictions would be galling to any one, to a girl of twenty-one simply hell. . . .

With a jar he woke to the fact that he had momentarily forgotten Elizabeth was suffering from an incurable complaint. He had been treating her almost as a well person. Damn it, could she have this illness at all?

He rallied her. "You and your pick-ups! Young Betsy, I'm the man you're going to step out with, and sooner than you think! No, I've not gone Christian Science. I just want to shake you out of this notion you've got about dying. Believe me, it's rot."

"Is it? I'm afraid not, David. I'd rather face things, you know."

"Inevitable ones, yes; but—well, you may as well have it. A doctor I've been on to tells me that a lot of bloomers have been made about this particular complaint. I say we don't have to accept Brodmart as the word of God. Why not get another opinion?"

He saw hope flicker, and lashed himself for raising it. Yet he had wanted to accomplish this very thing. He refused to turn back.

"I'd like to," Elizabeth faltered. "Only who's likely to understand my case better than Dr. Brodmart? They say he's about the best there is on my sort of trouble."

"You've only their word for it."

"Besides. . . . Oh, it's so frightfully difficult! I-I'm not up to making a fight. It'll be three against one."

He glanced at her shrewdly. "Leave it to me. I'll get hold of the doctor. When that's done, we'll find ways and means. See here, you're a free agent, aren't you?"

"Well—nominally." She shrugged.

"Of course you are. So you can have any doctor you like. The immediate problem is how to get word to you. If it can't be managed through the ordinary channels—Gosh damn! I've thought of a way!"

"How, David? Oh, whatever happens, I mustn't lose you again!"

Poor kid, she meant it. He had to remind himself sternly that she would be feeling like this about just any old friend who had turned up. . . .

"You won't," he promised gruffly. "If this scheme works I'll keep tabs on you regularly and—What's wrong?"

"Evie! She's outside!"

She mouthed the words, motioning him wildly towards a door at the side of the room. "Quick! She won't go in there." As David vanished she scrambled between the sheets and lay still.

Hardly had David shut himself into a disused, dusty dressing-room when in the room behind sounded a weakly-chiding voice.

"Naughty, naughty! You've been smoking, haven't you? Oh, so wrong of you, dear!"

His cigarette! What the hell had he done with it?

"Just one, Evie. I found it in a drawer. Need you give me away?"

"We-ell—perhaps not this once, but—My watch. Did I leave it somewhere? Oh, here it is. I must time the fish when I put it on to steam."

She was gone. Breath restored, David stole back guiltily.

"My gasper! Where was the damned thing?"

"There, burned to ash on a tray," Elizabeth giggled and pointed. "She's taken it. Oh, only to keep Geoffrey from rowing her if he came in here and smelled smoke! She's got the brain of a gnat. Now, talk fast. What was this bright scheme?"

"Cover those feet and I'll spill it."

Modestly she obeyed. Her toes, he noticed, were unspoiled as a child's, every small nail nicely pinked. The latter he regarded as a good sign.

Rapidly he whispered his plan. Eyes brilliant, lips parted, she drank it all in.

"Wonderful! Do you think she—"

"Why not? She's a nice kid, you know. Not so nice as you were, of course, but very quick on the uptake. If you've got the hang of it—"

"I was a beastly kid, David! All wrapped in cotton-wool. Won't I *see* you sometimes?"

"Certainly, but not yet awhile. Too damned risky. You'll be hearing, though, every day while I'm busy with my wire-pulling. Which reminds me: What's your aunt's address?"

"The last, that was months back, was Poste Restante Singapore; but oh, David, you won't write her?"

He glanced at her clouded face. "I'd like to. Isn't she your only close relative?"

"What if she is? I can't have Fanny fuming back half-across the globe only to find there's not a thing she can do."

"I'll be discreet." David rose, hoisting the tool-bag, which Elizabeth had had the wit to push under the bed. "And now, chin up! Maybe one dark night I'll do a little wigwagging from the next yard. By the way, did you know I was under your side window Wednesday night about nine?"

"You?" She gave a queer little gasp. "Then it was real. I thought I was—hearing things."

"You were; but other people mustn't hear them. Think your sister-in-law's in the basement? Then I'd better make tracks."

"Good-bye, David. Bless, oh bless you for the angel you are!"

She had slipped to the floor and with timid impulse was lifting her face. David wavered, stooped, and in brotherly fashion kissed her. Before either had become aware of the other's suddenly-warm skin he was out of the room.

Along Heath Crescent he strode, an unshaven ruffian whose exuberance might have claimed attention if any one had passed.

"*Oh, the world owes me a living,*" he warbled. "*Tol de riddle, tol de riddle dee. . . .*"

At the Wibbes' he made a movement to turn in, but checked it. No, the kid would be at school. On he tramped to the tube station, hardly at all bothered over the front door he had left not quite closed.

CHAPTER ELEVEN
ELIZABETH IS GAY

AT NINE that night Evie was still nagging at her problem. Was she right or was she wrong? She had never, she felt, been much good at deciding things. But Geoffrey! Ah, he would know. Tired though she was she had better wait up for him.

Perhaps, too, he would tell her a little about his day at Newmarket—what friends he had seen, who had invited him to lunch. Darling Geoffrey, so sought after, and by such really worthwhile people! Not people she was ever in the least likely to meet, but his sort, his world. He must sadly have missed these contacts during the first year of his disastrous marriage. Her heart glowed to picture him again in his natural and deserved element.

"Geoffrey always shines out in any company." She was taking her final, vague poke into the kitchen. "Even at six he *made* you notice him! Dear Father was so proud. Oh, why did he have to marry this unfortunate girl? So mad, so unwise. And now!"

Parsons, spectral in the dimness, was drawing a sodden cloth over the drainboard. Standing to attention, he fumbled tremulously with his white tie, conscious that in spite of alien tasks he remained as always the family butler.

"Shall I put a note in the milk bottle, miss? I'm sorry to say from the look of it we'll be wanting more butter."

Evie sighed. "I know, Parsons! Americans will have it at every meal. Her appetite was wonderful to-day. Not lowering the oven for the rice-pudding seemed not to matter. She ate every crumb."

Groping to assemble her vagrant thoughts she realised the bleared old eyes were still watching her for further orders.

"That's all, Parsons. Mr. Geoffrey will have dined; but oh, do be careful with his hot-water bottle! If it really leaks, take mine. Better lay out fresh pyjamas, the others will be rough dry, and you know how he'll hate silk that's been wet. Make quite sure you haven't left grit in the bath. Nothing so annoys him."

Parsons shuffled out.

Hand lifted to turn off the single, unshaded gas-mantle, Evie Scarpath hesitated. Here in the kitchen it was warm, and this week they had dispensed with the dining-room fire. The little stock of coal found in the cellar was nearly gone, Geoffrey stormed at the idea of ordering in more.

"I could do my puzzle on this big table." Rubbing her red knuckles Evie debated and shook her head. "No, if I move it I'll have to begin all over again. Better just take the kettle up with me, make myself a nice cup of tea and pop straight into bed."

A mouse scurried as she felt her way out of the sour-smelling darkness, but she was already back in her reverie. In fact she had been standing outside Elizabeth's door for a good two minutes before she awoke to why she was there. She set down the kettle and went in, blinking in the sudden yellow glare.

Elizabeth looked up from her book.

"Well, Evie!" It was a flippant greeting. "You okay?"

Really, Geoffrey's wife *was* pretty! Such a surprising colour to-night. American, though—which spoiled everything. So crudely direct, so lacking in all reverence—as Mrs. Levison-Crump had put it, and her judgments were always so apt. That short frock and tiny skull-cap Elizabeth had turned up in at the garden party, oh, hopelessly bad form with every other woman wearing a suitable long skirt and wide-brimmed straw. Rouged lips, painted nails . . . not true, of course, about the eyelashes. They *were* natural, after all. . . .

"My question to you, Elizabeth," Evie giggled. "You seem rather flushed. Oughtn't I just to make sure of your temperature?"

"Don't! I'm feeling fine, that's all. One of these days I may give you that shock."

"Oh, Elizabeth! You won't start begging to go out?"

"Beg? Not much! Oh, Evie, your expression! As though you expected me to walk roughshod over you and out into the cold, cold night in only a bed-jacket! This one wants a wash, by the way."

"Does it? Yes, perhaps. To-morrow I'll—"

"Oh, no! Bring along some Lux and I'll do it myself. Listen, do you know I can still touch my toes without bending? If you don't believe it I'll show you."

"*Get back, Elizabeth!* You don't mean to say you've actually been doing gymnastics?"

"That's right, I'm not keeping anything from you." Elizabeth eyed her sister-in-law shrewdly, but remained in bed. "Look, have you tried on that green outfit?"

"Not—not yet, dear. I didn't think you could really mean me to—"

"Since when have I said what I didn't mean? Better look slippy. I believe that's nice English for get a move on, isn't it? Hop!"

Evie gulped and scuttled away.

A little bee—David had put it there—buzzed in Elizabeth's head. Was Evie aghast at the harm it might do to stir out of this house, or because—well, for some other reason?

What other reason? A very simple one, possibly. Even for the invalid to *feel* like going out might augur recovery. Evie, poor soul, would prefer her to die.

"And why not? I don't blame her. That anyhow won't worry me. What counts is that she hasn't guessed for one moment that cigarette wasn't mine."

David, of course, couldn't be right. It didn't make sense. It was queer, all the same, about the parrot. . . .

Evie's own room was arctic. Never having been accustomed to a bedroom fire she did not dream of lighting the gas one now, but having put on the overhead jet stood beneath its flare in a troubled daze.

There couldn't be anything out of the way in Elizabeth's sudden transformation. Hadn't there been other periods of improvement, though all the time one had known them to be just the sputter of a candle before it goes out?

"Not like this one, I think. So gay, so—so *impudent*! In fact, almost well. Really I can begin to see what it was that attracted Geoffrey. I wonder—? Wicked of me, but—well, the other way did seem about the only happy solution. . . ."

It was the trickle of cold water on her instep which roused her. She set the lopsided kettle on the gas-ring, lit the blue rosette of flame under it, and fumbled, like a sleepwalker, for the big key hung round her neck, inside her blouse. She opened the ponderous wardrobe and surveyed its crammed interior.

Her own garments were few—a shabby skirt, the black gabardine bought for her father's funeral and still too good to discard, her best brown serge, its Liberty silk trimmings beginning to look grubby; but Elizabeth's! Surely no one girl could ever have wanted all this array.

Awkwardly she fingered them. Nice, jolly tweeds; un-English frocks of lovely, unfamiliar stuffs; fur coats, two of them, not to mention the dyed ermine cape; dinner-gowns *and* evening ones, some quite high-necked, others indecently backless but with little wraps to match, the crêpe and satin richer than one's wildest dream, and all, when touched, breathing forth a strange fragrance, dizzying, *evil*—like the Paris which had spawned them.

"Scent!" thought Evie virtuously. "Mother always said that good lavender-water was all the Queen ever used, and that no gentlewoman . . ."

Nervously she detached the green ensemble from its hanger. Certainly it was quite plain—and the hems would let out. A hot iron and a damp cloth. . . . Green was her colour—or had been.

She was worming guiltily out of her top clothing, to stand for a moment in a bagging wool vest, loose stays worn solely for warmth and brown, fleece-lined knickers, drawn over the knees into rotting elastic. The frock was harder to get on than she had anticipated, for thin though she was her hips had a deceptive span. The seams, though, had wide turnings, so perhaps . . . slightly drunk, Evie reached for the coat.

She had feared its shameless cut, but no, on her it looked quite different, while the grey Indian lamb—fancy, such common fur being fashionable!—framed her throat flatteringly. Maybe one fine day . . . oh, better save them for Hampshire! That's where she had friends, London didn't count. From what Geoffrey hinted the wait might not be very long. She turned before the long glass, preening herself—and suddenly heard a latchkey.

"Geoffrey!"

Up the long stairs he bounded, paused in her door and stood blasting her with fierce, frosty eyes.

"What the blazes!"

In an agony she explained. Really, really, it was all right! Her brother shrugged, sent another shaft which took in her unwonted flush, and began unhitching the field-glasses slung from his shoulder.

"Please yourself. You look a bloody freak." Blightingly he turned away.

Snubbed, Evie yet experienced a thrill. In denouncing for his own sister the sort of clothes his wife wore Geoffrey was in reality paying her a compliment. How coldly-dazzling he looked, fresh from the outer air—and how exactly *right* for a race-meeting!

She clutched at him. "Wait, Geoff dear! I—I had something to say to you."

"Oh? Get it over, then. I've got to change."

"Out again? Where?"

"What's it matter to you? Conisbroke House. Music."

"Lord Conisbroke?" Evie's eyes shone.

"See here, Evie, what the devil do you want? If it's cash, I'm stony, so you may as well—"

"No, no! It's—" Evie sank her voice. "It's about Her."

Her brother came close. "Elizabeth? Not worse?" he fired, but he too spoke in a whisper, apprehensive, accusing.

"No, better. Geoffrey, such high spirits! Not at first. It struck me after I had come in at twelve—and fancy, she finished all her lunch! I did notice—oh, quite likely I'm wrong, only I do know yours are Turkish and hers were always the loose American kind, such a mess in the teacups! This did seem different, but—"

Geoffrey was chained now. He had seized her by the shoulders.

"You mean you saw a cigarette in her room and of a new sort? She's not had any sort for months. How did she account for it? Answer, can't you?" He shook the cowering form.

"Said she'd found it in a drawer," chattered Evie, thrilled by the bruising clutch. "I did wonder, so I saved it. Look!"

There was no need to show him. Already he had pounced on the rosebud-painted saucer and was frowning down at its contents—a long, grey ash, broken from an inch of charred stump.

"Player's. . . . She may have bought a packet at some time and forgotten them."

"We've been through her things, haven't we? The colour she's got to-night! She—she's been doing exercises. Quite, quite amazing, when you think that at breakfast—"

"I didn't look in then. Here! Is she awake?"

"Oh, please, dear, don't say I told! She made me promise—"

"Oh, did she!"

He was at Elizabeth's door, peering cautiously in. All dark, not a stir. Pondering a moment he jerked back his shoulders and strode down the passage. "Get out my evening things. Quick!"

Off so soon, after barely gladdening her eyes. . . .

"Tails, dear?" she quavered eagerly.

"Obviously—and wash your hands before you start putting in the studs. God, I'm filthy! Run me a bath."

Evie scurried, in a panic lest the water had grown cold. Parsons, so forgetful these days; but no, he *had* stoked the boiler.

"Geoffrey!" Apologetically she hovered at his side. "I *did* do right in telling you? About Her, I mean."

"That? Oh, quite! Almost phenomenal your noticing. Shut that damned door! It's like a charnel-house in here."

Blissful as a spaniel whose master has patted it, Evie waited outside, braced to rush back the instant her brother made his exit to the bath.

Shut that damned door. . . . She gave a little gasp. Oh, dear, that was the other thing she had meant Geoffrey to know, and now, after worrying about it half the day she hadn't mentioned it after all! The front door—mysteriously left ajar. To be sure, the telephone-man had come and gone whole hours before, so how could it link up with—?

She decided not to speak of it.

"Geoffrey would only rave at Parsons for leaving the creature alone. Besides, it might just spoil his nice evening."

Conscience soothed—or nearly so—Evie prayed that this time she could work the pearl studs into the stiff shirt-front without leaving a smudge.

CHAPTER TWELVE

DAVID TAKES PEN IN HAND

WITH great firmness Penelope Wibbe shook her head to a fourth patisserie, although it was her favourite kind, squidgy with marron and oozing whipped cream.

"Nothing more, thanks. I've finished my tea." Smoothing her best winter frock she glared into space.

If Lady Wibbe had seen her daughter at this moment her thoughts would unwaveringly have sped to thermometers and castor-oil; but then parents are notoriously purblind, even those who like Cynthia conscientiously devour the small manuals of Freud. As for David Beddoes, seated opposite, he scarcely registered Pen's pallid intentness and rather pop-eyed expression; and yet it was he himself who in the past half-hour had accomplished the following:

(a) Lifted his guest to the dizziest pinnacle of her life.

(b) Displaced Clark Gable in the shrine of her worship.

(c) Caused a renunciation in essence symbolic.

Strange, Pen was thinking, that each of her great passions had meant silently-borne pain! This time, though, her suffering need not be barren. She had been co-opted. Let her purge her being of all selfish dross . . .

"Yes, Mr. Beddoes?"

"I was just saying, we'll have to watch our step. Think you can handle the job?"

"Oh, on my head!" In her ardour Pen relaxed into bluntness. "I mean, it'll be pitch dark. Who couldn't sneak over a wall that has shrubbery on both sides? You say she has knitting-wool she can let down. Tell her to make it double and weight the end."

"I wonder if she'll think of that?" David rubbed his chin ruefully. "I shan't be seeing her again, you know."

"That's so. Oh, she's bound to think of it! It's only for the first time, after that it'll be strong twine I've tied on to the end. She can hide that and the box under her mattress. I'll bet," Pen added darkly, "it doesn't get turned over often!"

Gravely, as man to man, they hatched their conspiracy to an obligato of Pen's private emotions. Yes, very lucky this was Saturday . . . *thick, black brows, nearly meeting, eyes that smouldered and snapped* . . . otherwise it would have been definitely necessary to cut net-ball, making difficulties with the Head and taxing inventive powers elsewhere required.

A beginning, of course, could be made to-night. *Lean, square-jawed, and oh, American! Old, too. More than twenty-five. . . .*

"To think I've actually seen her!" Decorously Pen sipped the last drop of her cold tea. "She looked lovely and so hopeless! Because, you see, this was only Tuesday, before you'd got in. I'd popped home for lunch, and as I looked up at those side windows there she was, little and pale, gazing out—like the *Lady of Shalott*; although"—in haste—"I don't read Tennyson now. She *is* a prisoner, Mr. Beddoes, and for some perfectly vile reason. Something awful is being planned. Why can't we act—I mean really act, before it's too late?"

David's brows knotted together. Simultaneously Pen felt a knife-stab in her breast.

"It's like this, Penelope. She says I'm all out in my calculations—and maybe I am. There's so darned little I know for certain. Only, in fact, that she's pretty desperately unhappy."

"Surely that's enough?" cried Pen, amazed.

"Is it? I do feel that in her present state of mind she can't possibly pull up. Same time, I'll have to know more before I can urge her to leave home. She'd probably refuse anyhow, and if she did skip out it might let her in for serious complications. No, for a little I shall just have to hold what your father would call a—"

"Watching brief." Pen nodded intelligently. "I suppose you're right, we have got to discover *why* they're doing this. There's no motive that I can see, though as a rule I'm fairly good. Much the simplest," she said calmly, "would be a divorce. Hasn't she any grounds?"

Startled, David met the unblinking black eyes. Then he remembered that Pen's mother wrote novels while her father was a distinguished barrister. For that matter, a course in Hollywood productions was not lacking in educative affect.

"If so, she doesn't know it."

"She!" snapped his partner in scorn. "Her husband must be followed, that's all. I'd do it myself, only he doesn't get up till I'm at school, and he's out so late at night only Jinks ever hears him come in. All he does is sleep there—practically. Know how I've worked that out?"

"How?"

"Why, what you said about the jigsaw puzzle being laid out on the dining-room table! No one uses the dining-room to eat in. There's your safe clue to a double life."

"Pen, you're a marvel. You've got something, or I'm a Dutchman." Brooding a moment, David leant forward. "Now, see here. One week from

Monday I'll be in Manchester. That means I'll be leaving matters entirely in your hands. Shoot letters along to the Midland Hotel. If you're in a hurry and have to ring my cousin, don't forget she's not yet in the know and will be apt to censure all this as officious meddling. That clear?"

Pen was scribbling in a notebook labelled *Bible History.*

"Midland . . . Manchester. Oh, perfectly! Didn't I promise to let her know if I did get on to anything? It would only be in case." Deftly she returned the notebook to the leg of her navy-blue knickers, sighed deeply, and got ready to depart.

"What's that?" It was chocolate truffles in a cornet. "Oh," she muttered, abashed. "You shouldn't; but thanks frightfully, all the same."

David had guessed that she would leap at his proposal as a trout to the fly, not that she would outstrip him, an efficiency expert, by heck, in practical suggestions. When he had whizzed her back to Hampstead he congratulated himself that from now onward he would have a finger on the pulse of what went on within the mouldering walls of Summit View.

In Gordon Square Colin Ladbroke was expecting him.

"Any news?" the doctor queried, busily mixing two gins-and-its.

"I'm going to tell you," said David, and dug straight into his subject.

After one startled stare his host's acceptance eased the strain.

"You've seen Mrs. Scarpath, then. Well, and your impression?"

It was a relief to find Ladbroke concentrating solely on the medical aspect. David gave a careful recital of all he had noticed.

"Weak as a kitten, of course. In no way questioning her husband's good intentions towards herself, but so depressed that it hurts to talk about it. At first, that is. And why not? Not only is she cut off; she's firmly convinced she's booked for a lingering death, and that no treatment can save her."

"My God! They've not told her that, surely?"

"Not in words. Partly, I think, it's been implied. What clinched it was Scarpath's criminal carelessness—call it that!—in letting her read a detailed treatise on her disease. Book left by the bed—and of course she lapped it up."

Colin slowly sank back in his chair. "And the marriage?"

"Total wash-out, after a week or two. Either the brute never cared two pins about her or changed at the start. There's little doubt all her letters are being held back. She's unwilling to believe it, though she knows mine didn't reach her. What do you know about this? They've removed every rag of wearing apparel, barring night-things."

Colin's eyes narrowed to pin-points. "Has she tried to make a bolt?"

"No, only talked about getting out. Say what you will, Ladbroke, I'm ready to swear that brother and sister are hell-bent on keeping her separated from any human being who might raise questions over her illness or its treatment. Not only that. Somehow or other they've got the doctor himself to back them up."

Dr. Ladbroke made dissenting noises. He did not like to mention the multitude of nervous sufferers who weave plausible fictions concerning themselves or the long and patient study it frequently took to sift the wheat from the chaff.

"But," he hinted, "you did actually see her stumble?"

"Certainly; but do we have to make a song about it? I admit it knocked me endways at the time. Afterwards when she told about her hurting her leg and all these months of lying in bed I got other ideas. Whatever the case, Ladbroke, the girl's racing pretty rapidly downhill. If nothing's done to stop her—"

"And her speech?"

"Perfectly okay. Ditto for the moment her eyes and her hand. She trembled, yes, like a leaf, but that wore off when she got over the shock of seeing me—and anyhow why drag in disseminated thingumbob to account for it?"

The doctor shook his head. "I warned you, you know, that this disease has spectacular ups and downs. I don't question her despondency, but the psychological factors you mention may be—probably are—purely a side issue.

"So far," he continued, groping for his pipe, "what I see is a deplorable situation, tragic in every sense of the word, but one which no outside person can hope to remedy. Don't forget she's in the hands of an unimpeachable specialist. I don't say she mightn't profit by another opinion. What I do insist is that no rival physician is going to take on her case without first coming to a clear and satisfactory understanding with Brodmart."

David glowered. "Hell! Are you trying to tell me she can't pick her own doctor?"

"She can, but what about the other doctor himself? Brodmart by hearsay is arrogant and touchy, a little god in his way. He happens to wield considerable influence. I can assure you most of us smaller fry would think twice about offending him."

David chewed the cud of his wrath. He had not realised the iron laws of medical etiquette, assuming that opposition would be confined to the Scarpath pair.

"See here, I've been doing some pretty tall thinking. Don't squash what I'm going to say, will you? We'll accept the fact that there have been off and on a number of characteristic symptoms. Well, then! Could Scarpath have induced them?"

Colin stared. "Fantastic! My good Beddoes, it would be beyond the power of any layman to do what you're suggesting."

"Why?"

"Sheer impossibility. Expert knowledge would be required, apart from the ability to obtain the necessary drugs, which would have to be administered with food—in itself an insuperable difficulty. No, no, wash it out!"

"We can't say Scarpath hasn't access to drugs."

For a mere second the doctor flashed a searching glance.

"Quite," he conceded, "but we're not speaking of dope passed from hand to hand in night-clubs. Anyhow I seriously doubt if even a physician could accomplish the desired result. Certainly it's unthinkable a fraud of this kind could be foisted on a man of Brodmart's experience without rousing suspicion."

David looked damped. The idea of Elizabeth's illness being a put up job had taken firm root in his mind.

"So what?" he argued defiantly.

"Well, this: One's forced to conclude that Mrs. Scarpath is simply entering into one of her approximately normal periods—in which case she'll be allowed to go out. If she keeps fit long enough one may dimly hope that even Brodmart is liable to mistakes in diagnosis. Time alone can show."

"Before that happens, she'll die."

Startled by the curt tone, Colin sat silent a moment. David went on, hammering his knee:

"One way or another, this is a frame-up. They don't mean to let her out of that cage, and if we don't act and that darned quickly, well, it'll be down curtain. I can't blame you for taking the conservative view. I'll just have to tackle the problem single-handed—somehow."

He got up, kicked at a footstool that found itself in his way, and strode about the room.

Colin felt sympathetic. He would have given much to help Alison Young's cousin, a decent chap if a thought impetuous; but really there seemed no way. "I suppose you've some plan?"

"No—yes! Get in communication with the aunt, of course, though it mayn't be an easy matter to track her down. I'm forgetting. Take a look at a Marconi night-letter I got this morning. It's from John Fellowes, a friend crossing to America on the *Queen Mary*."

"Vickers? Singapore? It's like code."

"John's code. I'll interpret. First item, he's run up against a Mrs. Abner Vickers who not only knows Fanny Rush—that's Elizabeth's aunt—but saw her in Singapore three months ago. Second item, Aunt was pleased as Punch over getting her niece so happily settled. Third, she said little about her own finances, though Mrs. Vickers got the idea they were none too flourishing. Fourth, Aunt herself looked sick and unfit to be buzzing off into insanitary wilds, yet buzz off she did—destination doubtful, probably Java."

David folded the cablegram and put it back in his wallet.

"Which," he said bitterly, "may explain why my cable to Mrs. Rush hasn't been answered. If I know the woman, she's disappeared without leaving any forwarding address."

Colin admitted it was unpromising. "Any other ideas?"

"There is one." Turning from a blind survey of a Degas drawing on the wall David showed a face dark red with embarrassment. "Divorce."

"Her suggestion?" In the doctor's glance there was a slight but noticeable dubiety.

"We never touched on it." David spoke gruffly. "See here, how in this city does one set about collecting evidence of the kind she'd require?"

"Now, there I can be of some assistance. I can put you on to a queer little fish who's by way of being what in your country you'd call a dick. Private one, of course. Wait, though! Are you serious about this?"

"Oh, no," said David dangerously. "Just beefing for the fun of it. Where does this sleuth of yours hang out?"

"His name," said Colin, "is Mortimer Bream. . . . It'll cost you something, you know."

"Can you name me one thing that doesn't? Go on."

Presently in a taxi David was entering a narrow street oddly entitled Great Smith which was situated quite close to the Houses of Parliament and—the driver pointed it out to him—New Scotland Yard. He wondered if this second landmark, so familiar to him in fiction, would ever come into his scheme. It was more than possible the money he was so eager to lavish on having Scarpath followed would be simply thrown down the drain. Not much money at that—only a two thousand dollar legacy drawing interest in the bank. Still, thank God he had it, for Elizabeth had none. If he squandered every cent, well, it wouldn't be done in self-interest.

"Or rather, I'm not thinking of it in that way . . . yet."

No, it was Elizabeth's life and happiness which constituted his sole urge. As for the rest . . .

A paralysing thought seized him. If Brodmart's diagnosis proved correct, *there would be no rest.*

CHAPTER THIRTEEN
PENCIL—PLEASE!

THE scheme was working without a hitch. That thirteen-year-old child whom Elizabeth had seen tearing about in a school tunic sloppily girt with a magenta sash was not only the true sport David had predicted. She was always on the dot, every evening at nine, to seize the cigarette-tin let down by a string, remove its message and send up another from David. Her warning hoot was such a creditable affair that Evie, on the single occasion she heard it, had instantly moaned, "Oh, dear, there's an owl!"

David's letters, long and satisfying, were bridging the gap of years. Often Elizabeth laughed over them. Always they brought a warm glow of well-being round her heart. She would have said it was altogether too late to be stirred by the knowledge that someone like David Beddoes had once been nuts on her and even now felt such keen anxiety on her account, but this it seemed was untrue. With death staring one in the face it was still possible to experience thrills—bigger ones, maybe, for being so humbled.

The letters she burned, the string and box she kept hidden far under the bed where rolls of dirty fluff proved that sweeping was infrequent. As the tin was Geoffrey's the finding of it would point only to Evie's carelessness. No, it was all perfectly safe.

Young Pen put in chits of her own. *"Do they feed you properly? Rub your tummy if you'd like something that won't spill."*

Odd their thinking she might be hungry. She was, ever since David's visit. Perhaps till then she'd been too miserable to realise how much of her strictly-edited diet was uneatable, but now! Really it did seem as if a good, juicy steak would put more vigour into her than this constant fish floating about in scorched milk. Evie, heaven help her, was no cook; and yet . . . no, she didn't dare take a chance.

"I don't half-like the way Evie's taken to popping in at odd moments—and besides, there's Geoffrey. . . ." The fact was, Geoffrey's recent attentiveness both baffled and disturbed. For long intervals she had seen so little of her husband that she almost forgot he was occupying the same house, and then, all of a sudden—

"Saturday he brought me these carnations. Sunday he actually had tea with me and laid Evie out for not giving me the Russian Caravan sort—as though she could possibly afford it! Last night he stopped in my room almost an hour, with that poor child freezing stiff outside. Does he guess anything? I wouldn't put it past Evie to have told him about the cigarette, but even so why couldn't I have hung on to a Player?" She knit her brow.

"No, it can't be that. If I didn't know him so well I'd almost say he was trying to win me back. What a joke! If I couldn't attract him while I was well, I ask you!"

She had seen him studying her, at the back of his oddly-fascinating eyes some feeling that might have been a wholly detached admiration all tangled up with resentment. It had been like that during the feverish days at Cannes—always the barbed sting, bent on destruction.

"That's Geoffrey," she decided impersonally. "He simply has to smash—rip to pieces. It's in every line of his book. It just manages to spoil his music. Maybe it's what keeps his tennis from being really great. I thought I'd married an all-round genius. Not that it would have made it any easier to—What *is* in his mind?"

She looked at the flowers Geoffrey himself had so exquisitely arranged. Flowers—just when she had begun for the first time to think seriously of leaving him. Oh, she had threatened flight to New York more than once, down there in Hampshire—knowing how idiotic it sounded with no money in her purse! Lately, though, she had sunk more and more under the yoke of her illness and the wills surrounding her. Escape hadn't seemed worth thinking about—till David made so many things appear possible.

Now, before the doctor came, she had better write her letter. She would tell him of Geoffrey's changed attitude, see if he had any views on the—

"Damn! What's gone wrong with my pen?"

The gold nib was bent double.

"Oh!" she raged. "Evie did that, knocking it on the floor. I'll have to use a pencil. There's one in my bag."

The pencil was gone.

Suddenly, with a cold shock, she recalled how her sister-in-law, prowling in softly after Geoffrey had said good-night, had caught her in the very act of hauling up her cargo. Evie hadn't seemed to suspect anything, merely closed the window and gibbered as usual about catching pneumonia, but what if she had told Geoffrey? He was quick-witted enough for two.

"If these things were done on purpose," muttered Elizabeth, desperately hunting her pencil, "it means they're on to David and me. Oh!" Kneeling on the harsh carpet she clapped a frightened hand over her mouth. "Is it true, then? Am I being kept a prisoner?"

If so she could imagine only one reason—to prevent her making mischief by telling persecution stories. Yes, it might well be that. That they believed at times she suffered from delusions. Well, she had for a little, after some of her treatments. She'd been delirious and raved, just as she was said to have done for half an hour when measles laid her low.

"If it's only that," she was pondering when a tap at her door sent her scampering into bed.

"Mind if I come in?"

To her utter amazement it was Geoffrey. She had supposed him still sound asleep, instead of which here he was at nine-thirty in the morning bathed, shaved, fully-dressed.

"Oh—it's you."

He was wearing the tweeds that so suited him, his tie and the silk handkerchief casually protruding from his breast-pocket matching as though by accident. As he came forward crisp and elastic his whole well-tended person exuded the faint, spicy fragrance which used to enchant her and now made her slightly sick. She contrasted him with David. Both men were tall, fit, strong. David, she thought, looked more rugged—not tigerish, in short.

Not happy at having to open conversation she asked, "Can you lend me something to scribble with? My pen's gone west."

"And mine's mislaid. What about this?" He fished up a slim gold pencil from his pocket. "Sorry! No lead in it. Well, you'll hardly be wanting it now. I came to tell you Brodmart's on his way. Are you shipshape? Evie's busy below."

"The doctor! As early as this?"

"He rang up to alter the appointment. There's a lot to get in, he's rushed off his legs."

She bit her lip, oddly shaken. Pen smashed, pencil missing, and now this untimely visit which might just unfit her for letter-writing!

"I see. Well, I'm such heaps better I don't expect he'll want to do much to me. Will he?"

"What's that?"

Geoffrey had crossed to the window—*their* window!—and was star-ing out and down. With purpose? Her heart stood still.

He registered her question and shrugged. "One would suppose not. As a matter of fact"—he lit one of the Turkish cigarettes made specially for him in Jermyn Street and puffed jerkily—"I was going to ask him about getting you out."

She could not believe her ears. "Oh, Geoffrey! You think I might be allowed to take a little stroll?"

He flashed a glance at her eagerness. "Well, better call it a drive. Remember your legs."

Elizabeth reddened in mortification. Only four days ago she had taken another tumble. Geoffrey didn't know that, of course.

"I'm much steadier. My headaches have cleared up, I can read even fine print. I've been thinking that maybe with just a little more to eat—"

There came a faint jangle from below. "That's Brodmart now. Yes, I'll mention food to him."

Tossing his cigarette into the grate her husband strode from the room.

Her pulse began its annoying flutter. Hope mingled with gratitude and with pangs of conscience. Geoffrey *did* want to get her well, though in all reason why not? Like this she was both a bore and a heavy expense.

He had spoken of a drive. Did that mean he still had his car? She had supposed it sold to defray some of these bills. It had been a nice car, an almost new Chrysler. How he had managed to pay for it had been one of many mysteries, but perhaps he hadn't. People tended inexplicably to trust Geoffrey. Often they made him handsome presents, happily called loans, and seemed to consider it a privilege. More, of course, during his bachelor days. There again she had hampered him. . . .

Feet tramped upstairs, but instead of turning into her room they passed along to the front. That was Geoffrey's door closing. So the confer-ence over her was being made a formal affair! Generally the doctor was too impatient for more than a hasty word on the stairs.

To-day *was* different. A premature visit, those two closeted together, Evie down in the kitchen getting her brother's breakfast. . . .

All David's alarms flooded into her mind.

"I've got to know what they're saying about me." She slid out of bed and across into the dressing-room. "Just to make quite sure I'm not imagining things."

Facing her was a locked door communicating with Geoffrey's domain—a big front room she had seen only once during one of its occupant's week-end absences. Vividly she pictured the air of luxury her husband had contrived to spread over the hideous mid-Victorian furnishings—pale Empire damask tucked cunningly over plush, books everywhere, most of them in the extravagant bindings Geoffrey loved to collect, and from the corner of the great black Bechstein piano a fountain of white lilac foaming up out of clear glass.

Pressed against the dirty panels she listened. Too bad! They were rambling about with the restless habit common to both, and only when one of them came near this door did his speech become distinguishable.

"Sunday?"

That was the doctor—and as he seemed to be echoing the word Geoffrey must have said it first. Why Sunday? Of course, the day suggested for her first outing. Geoffrey had meant it, then. She hadn't felt sure. . . .

Geoffrey's blurred tones, followed by a sceptical, "H'm, I should doubt that. How certain are you?" More argument from the far end of the room, and then the doctor again, quite distinctly:

"I see. Not very conclusive. . . . All considered, I wanted to let a longer time elapse. It's safer, oh, most decidedly! She's been rather alarming, whether or not you realise the fact. What's that?"

Geoffrey's next words were uncapturable, except for the end of a sentence: *"Four days."*

What four days? Elizabeth counted back, drawing in her breath. It had been exactly four days since David's visit! But Geoffrey had been racing that day. He couldn't build certainty on a cigarette she herself might have bought long ago when she had run out of Chesterfields. . . .

Close to her ear the doctor was grumbling. "Oh, I see, though mind, I hold you largely responsible. Feeling brighter she's bored. A little mild diversion—ever tried piquet? Damn it, man, do your share!"

So Dr. Brodmart thought Geoffrey was neglecting her. Oh, to have been able to catch her husband's low, urgent rejoinder! It had force, evidently, for the doctor was yielding, against his will, with a bad grace.

"Right," he rasped disagreeably. "But I'm warning you it's a risk. We've just pulled her through a rather frightening bout. If she goes under—"

"No!" Swift strides brought the word like a pistol-shot in her ear. "That mustn't happen, do you hear? I'm in your hands. Let her die and by God—"

"Tut tut!" testily. "Don't go pinning this on me, Scarpath. I've something at stake too—my reputation."

Dr. Brodmart gave his infrequent laugh. It jarred unpleasantly along the listener's nerves.

"Say no more," he continued brusquely. "And stop where you are. I'll go along in."

Elizabeth fled.

Back in bed she was conscious of quite a ridiculous relief. It was all right, Geoffrey didn't want her to die. The riddle of his strange violence could be examined presently, at leisure. Just now, with her arch-enemy about to descend on her, she must steady her heartbeat and prepare her smile..

Guthrie Brodmart came in.

"Well, Doctor! Has my husband been sounding you on my—my—"

"Getting some fresh air?"

He was warming his hands by the fire, and as the flickering flames cast light on his profile she was struck anew by his peculiarly jaded looks. For the first time a poor constitution and constant overwork seemed inadequate to explain a skin minutely puckered, like soft, ageing vellum, muscles that twitched and purple pouches under the eyes.

The eyes themselves had turned on her. Discerning eyes, a scientist's eyes coldly devoid of humanity. Suddenly she saw herself with their vision—a chronic, unreasonable invalid to be dealt with firmly. The trembling so nearly banished began all over again.

"Oh, yes," he answered cryptically and moved towards the bed. "Suppose we just examine into this wonderful improvement." He pinioned her wrist, sank exhaustedly into a chair and groped for his watch.

She shuddered a little, for his fingers had a dryness which made her think of a snake's scales. There was a slight tremor in them this morning, though their touch as usual was deft and sure.

"Now the tongue."

Oh, dear, the whole ritual!

"Humph! Eating well, are you?"

"As well as I can," snapped Elizabeth. "I could make a couple of nice lamb chops look pretty silly if they came my way."

Her new audacity drew a glance, but he only inserted the thermometer, corking her up. Something told her his decision was already made. When he frowned at the mercury her heart began to sink.

"Mustn't rush things. I'm glad to see, though, that you're just ready for another treatment. Good news, I expect?" He opened his black bag.

Panic filled her. She warded him off.

"Not now! Oh, no, no, I won't have it! That is—" She made a wild clutch at her dignity. "Surely it can't be necessary when I'm doing so well?"

All his suavity went. He straightened, exasperated, lips compressed to mark the extreme limit of patience, and as he resignedly thumbed the pages of a small diary she saw his temple squirm exactly like a Mexican jumping-bean.

"The correct date was last Sunday. I've postponed it, you see, and if I delay matters too long this better period will be wearing off."

"I'm such a wreck afterwards," she muttered. "Why can't you leave me as I am and just see?" Brodmart bent forward, ill-humouredly expounding, as to a singularly fractious child.

"Use your intelligence, Mrs. Scarpath. You dread this, I know, but a little temporary discomfort has to be borne for the sake of a cure."

"But will it cure me? Can you give me any guarantee?"

He had been carefully measuring drops into a glass. He set down the bottle with a click.

"Really! I must tell you I am not accustomed to such questions. If twenty years' specialisation on certain complaints doesn't command more confidence, you'd far better—"

Try someone else? Elizabeth prayed he would fly into a genuine huff and throw up the case; but already the mood was passing. No yielding in his eyes, he had picked up the bottle.

"Come now, let's not waste valuable time. Either you submit to the schedule or—" He paused, counting the drops—taking elaborate pains, she noticed. "Or this trouble will be fastening a permanent hold. No outings then, I promise you. It'll be bed or an invalid-chair for good. You've seen old people with palsy, half-blind, shaken to bits? In a short time that will be yourself—while," he added, "the five clinical cases under my care will have made splendid recoveries."

I'll not take it, her rebel self defied, but she knew that *ex cathedra* authority had prevailed. Young as she was maybe she did have a chance. New methods. . . . Geoffrey's book might be out of date. Possibly now she was stronger the dose wouldn't have its usual devastating effect. . . .

"All right. Let's get it over. . . . Ugh!"

She gagged over the nauseous, acrid stuff, snatched at the sweet-tasting water held ready for her. There, it was done.

She did not look at the doctor again, though she knew he was still out of temper by the sharp sounds as he replaced his paraphernalia. She muttered good-bye without turning her head. Tricked—yes, and beaten. She could not get rid of the idea.

Was it fancy that thus soon her head was beginning its buzz? In another ten minutes red-hot skewers would be boring into it. Darkness would close down, and the only noises heard would be generated by her own turbulent brain.

"It must be all right, though. Didn't he say his reputation was at stake? Naturally he can't afford to take risks with me. *Only supposing this wasn't so*," whispered a voice through the din in her ears, *"what earthly chance would I have?"*

Sweat had broken out all over her body. She had suddenly remembered David and her unwritten letter. She couldn't call out to Geoffrey and ask him for a pencil. That amount of effort would simply finish her. Quick, or it would be too late! Here was her paper. Oh, what could she write with?

Groping on the table she found her lipstick. In bright carmine she daubed two words: PENCIL—PLEASE!—underscoring them, and sealing the silly message into an envelope which she tucked under her pillow. The nice child would interpret—providing she received it. By the violent advance of symptoms such a result looked doubtful in the extreme.

Geoffrey was playing his maddening Hindemith—like barbed wire entanglements, lacerating her senses, but mercifully the music was receding farther and farther away. Geoffrey wasn't going out. That was queer. Yet she was not to be permitted to die. The very mention of it had shaken him—which was queerer still. . . .

In a room fast-clouding a parrot shrieked. At what? Oh, a rice-pudding, its grains of flint. A red spark glowed. It was the tip of a cigarette, but as she watched it changed into a fiery signal: *Danger*. And now she saw what danger it was—a rabbit-hole, but already she had slipped into it. First her foot, then her leg. Now her whole body.

Down, down, through blackness teeming and writhing with evil shapes. Deeper still . . .

She knew no more.

Chapter Fourteen
LIGHTS OUT

"Sawbones?" sang a young, patronising voice through Alison's telephone. "Angela here. Can you get into tails by twelve o'clock?"

"That depends," said Colin cautiously and waited.

"Suit yourself. I'll call round in case." The other microphone slammed down.

"Patient?" asked Alison from the depths of her arm-chair.

"My niece. I've been questioning her, as I promised, but—well, late parties aren't exactly my cup of tea." Colin glanced wistfully at his comfortable surroundings. It was peaceful here after a hardish day, more so since Beddoes had removed his irritating presence. He had rather hoped to go on sticking till his hostess saw fit to shove him out; but the girl opposite was raising her nice, unplucked brows with much the effect of a terrier cocking its ears.

"Thinks she means—him?"

"So I deduce. I can't see young Angela carting her uncle about for pleasure or self-profit. Is it worth it, I'm asking? I could ring her back and say No."

"You will not." Alison's hazel eye lit ominously. "Go to it, you sluggard, get an eyeful of Elizabeth's husband and tell me about it to-morrow. Look, it's after eleven now, I want to go bye-byes."

She hustled him on his way.

At something after midnight sharp honking woke the echoes of Gordon Square. Letting himself out, Colin discovered his twenty-year-old niece, blonde, confident and nonchalant, dropping ash through the window of an elegant new roadster.

"What is this binge? Who's throwing it?"

"Well, nominally Freddie Treddle. Climb in."

Angela threw in her clutch.

"Why nominally?" Colin covered her nude shoulders with a dislodged and inadequate silver fox wrap, chiefly because it was tickling his nose.

She did not answer, and he, feeling it safer not to distract her driving, held his peace. Recklessly they swooped down into Mayfair, parking behind a long queue of very sumptuous cars.

"South Street!"

"Right. Freddie's nest, when he's in it." Angela swept towards an entrance.

Treddle. That would be Mingo's heir. Amiable vacuity, plenty of cash. Colin remembered that Frederick Treddle had been one of Scarpath's makeweight coterie of sycophants at Oxford, so this was quite the old Brasenose touch.

As they stepped into a small lift which Angela punched into motion an uneasy suspicion took Colin. "I say, is Scarpath playing host?"

"Got it in one."

"Hold on, then. I ought to tell you I'm not precisely hankering to rivet his notice."

"Don't worry. You won't." Angela powdered her nose.

The house was an old one, converted into a few flats. The lift stopped opposite an open doorway, into which they penetrated unannounced and at once merged in a multi-coloured throng.

"He'll be in the dining-room," observed Angela. "Trail along, I won't introduce you."

Reasonably soon they managed to push themselves through the jam and into the host's orbit. Keeping in the background—though there was singularly little need—Colin scrutinised with interest the tall, well-knit figure dispensing drinks at a fine Italian table, marble above, wrought iron beneath.

"Darling!" Angela planted a ghost-kiss on Scarpath's ear.

"Oh, there you are, my pet!"

Hardly turning, Scarpath continued with his task, now shedding a brilliantly-vague smile, now throwing a word like a sop to the more importunate of his guests, but completely unconcerned with the uninvited individual in 1926 tails of whom some ten years previous he had once attempted to borrow five pounds.

"All's well," murmured Angela in passing. "Though what you're up to God only knows!"

Mayfair and the theatre, Colin summed up, casting an eye over the mob. Also a sprinkling of the more pampered artists. He saw Gross, the sculptor, picking his teeth of glazed pheasant, and alongside him the celebrated Burmese model, waist encircled by the thick arm of Adolphus Burt, the painter, while Lord Charmouth fed her sausages.

The girl's slanting eyes trained covetously on Scarpath. She pressed purringly against him, only to be dexterously eluded and handed champagne. Cyprian Rudge, surrealist photographer, squeezed Scarpath's hand. Again he withdrew, with a remark which must have been exactly right since it brought shouts of laughter.

"Geoffrey, my sweet!" A bedizoned dowager saluted him on both cheeks. "Peter's caught at the House—some wretched Three Whip—so I've brought Wogs. Do you awfully mind?"

"Of course not, Carlotta dear. Will you give him some food?"

Scarpath's manner was cool, delightful, admirably discreet. In an unstressed way it preserved aloofness. Perhaps that was the secret of his rather stupefying success.

In the larger room someone was playing the piano.

"Bernie Franks," informed Angela. "Lousy, isn't it? His own, of course. There, I knew they'd choke him off. He's giving them the Waltz."

A weird travesty rippled from the ivory Blüthner—discordant, mocking. It went well with the paintings on the walls, one displaying a headless torso propped in a rose-garden.

A few optimists tried to dance. Later Scarpath yielded to clamorous persuasions and performed portions of an unfinished ballet which owed a good deal to Stravinsky. In three feet of cleared space the Burmese girl did a burlesque of no small merit, Verity Bingham presented the imitations every one present knew by heart, and Madge Phipps crooned her current hit out of *Birdsong*.

It was perhaps two o'clock that Colin began to be aware of a migratory movement. Men and women, for the most part singly, were drifting away to some inner region, so that soon quite a number of gaps appeared on sofas lately crowded. He nudged Angela and put a question.

"Where? Well, I suggest the bath."

She seemed to know all the answers. Knew, and was not interested, for she had scarcely looked round from her job of remaking her face.

Colin explored. Here was a blue-quilted bedroom, filled with feminine wraps. Out of it led what should be a bathroom, and on the other side of the closed door he could hear the hum of voices. As he loitered the door in question clicked open just long enough to emit a stout, podgy-faced youth. Colin had a glimpse of packed figures, curiously absorbed. Then the door was pulled to from inside.

The podgy youth brushed past. Colin had noticed him earlier in the evening, struck by his sodden, grey pallor and dull irritability. There had come a marked change. The fat cheeks had colour now, the eyes had come alive, and every movement had decision.

Colin scratched his chin.

Returning to the fog of smoke he was met by the barking of large dogs and a deep-throated, somewhat raucous contralto voice. Apparently a late guest was making a spectacular arrival.

"Jane, of course," drawled a woman in a diadem. "The darling! How beautifully it's timed!"

Jane Boxe, Angela explained, though few could mistake the rake-thin caricature in severe black whose angles and grin drew full houses to the new Embankment Playbox at fifteen-and-six a head.

"Has her brace of duchesses with her, I see, not to mention the Alsatians, but—oh, God!—what's that other thing on the scarlet lead?"

The other thing padded forward, shivering and slinking. It was a cheetah, wearing a velvet coat, silver-edged.

*

In dank gloom Penelope crouched, eyes glued to a window which remained maddeningly and mysteriously closed.

For the past three nights this had happened. Did it mean better police-work on the part of the gaolers, or simply repentance?

"She can't be such a sop! Though if she is, I suppose it's as well he finds it out at once. I did think she had some spirit."

Pen shifted her position, her underneath leg having gone to sleep, and obtained a slightly improved view. Yes, there was the same dim light, the same deadly, ominous stillness; but she mustn't be misled into throwing a stone against the pane. As like as not Ginger-cat was sitting there now, watching the mouse-hole, keeping quiet on purpose. Knitting or something to pass the time.

"If she can knit. I'll bet if she does she makes the most awful mess. . . . What's this?"

Pen jumped and bit her tongue.

In the room above someone was moving about with a light, stealthy step. A faint ping sounded, as though a china basin had been moved, and then, without a word having been uttered, the hazed glow blacked out. Pen's ear caught the cautious drawing-to of a door.

Now, now was Elizabeth's chance. Would she snatch it?

Slow minutes dragged by. The dampness of the mould was soaking through Pen's tunic and ancient gym-shoes, right into her skin. She did a little arm-thumping, muffled a sneeze, and heard the clock in Church Row boom ten. No earthly good.

Getting her toe on the loose brick she hoisted herself on to the wall and slid dejectedly to her own smooth turf. This would have to be reported, of course. It would be safe to use the downstairs telephone since her parents were hearing the Busch concert at the Queen's Hall and Jinks, as usual, would be up in the spare bathroom washing out her undies—silly word!

But was she? As Pen let herself into the garden-room she found the fire going strong and Miss Dearling, drat her, calmly writing letters. Not a bit of use tiptoeing. Already the woman was wrinkling her brow.

"Why, Pen! What do you think you're up to? It's gone ten. And do look at your feet!"

"English essay," pattered Pen with the negligence of long practice. "Must see the moon rising. Got to describe it in fifty words."

"Moon on this thick night! Go on."

"I kept hoping it would clear. I'll have to try again to-morrow, that's all."

(Neat work. She'd prepared for the next time, just in case.)

Miss Dearling looked absent. Vaguely Pen noticed she was again wearing her best dinner-gown and was doing things to her hair.

"Well," added Pen, shovelling up a little brown coffee-sugar from the basin beside Jinks's empty cup, "I'll be off to bed, I think." She made for the hall.

It would have to be the upstairs extension, though Doris, worst of Nosey Parkers after her eight years' service, might be popping in any minute to turn down the beds.

"Pen," called Miss Dearling.

Pen turned apprehensively. Jinks had sounded rather too suspiciously careless. She was not looking up, either, but drawing neat squares on the blotter, which was her tiresome way when she had something unpleasant to deliver.

"Yes, Jinks?"

"Pen, you didn't happen to notice, I suppose, if there was a light in one of the bedrooms next door?"

Oh, damn!

"A light? Oh, a *light*! No, I don't believe I looked. Yes, maybe there was just one—very dim, in the back window."

Jinks nodded pensively, adding a few squiggles to her squares.

"A night-light," she murmured. "Such a pity, poor creature."

Pen glared. "W-what's a pity? What do you think it means?" Her voice had a husky note.

"Why, naturally, what can it mean except that the invalid woman is worse? I thought I told you the doctor had been coming twice a day and that none of them have stirred out of the house. I saw him under the portico this morning. Simply ashen, poor man!"

"Who?" barked Pen, bowled over by her own blindness. "The doctor?"

The secretary looked reproachful. "No, no, the husband. Or at least"—dreamily—"one assumes he's the husband. He can't be more than eight-and-twenty, if that. Tragic at that age to be burdened with a wife who's most evidently losing her mind. Though perhaps he won't be burdened with her for very long. I rather fancy this means the end."

In the throes of her panic Pen thought witheringly, "Gosh! I might have known it. She's fallen for the rotter."

The beds in her mother's room had been turned down. David, who all evening had stuck close to the telephone in the American Club, heard words which brought sweat bursting from his brow.

"And I, utter fool, never dreamed what was wrong!" chattered Pen. "Of course she can't write, she's desperately ill. What's that? . . . Oh, sorry, you were only swearing. Listen! *They've put out the light.* Oh, Mr. Beddoes, what do you think that can mean?"

Chapter Fifteen
CLOSE CALL

FOR three ghastly days David had been asking himself if Elizabeth still cared for her husband and meant to hold no further truck with a man who poured poison in her ears. It had looked like it; but now, tearing up to Hampstead in a taxi, he had a different and worse question to answer: Was this relapse his doing?

It was perfectly possible he had been playing with fire. Warned, he had refused to believe. Perhaps it was true that excitement might have fatal results. The fortune-teller, he remembered, had told him that he was too hot-headed. He remembered something more. When she had first pressed the snapshot to her bosom she had whispered the single word, *"Dead."*

He left the taxi at the Heath and approached Summit View on foot. All dark—even around the side.

For one horrible moment he saw crêpe on the door. It was only the inky bar of shadow cast by one of the cedars, but the illusion left him shaken in every limb. In that instant he had pushed through the gates, on the point of risking open inquiry, but in the nick of time he perceived the folly of such an action. What charge could he bring? None. Those in power held all the cards.

At intervals of roaming he returned, always to find the same unbroken darkness and silence. Finally he went back to Alison's flat to toss, not even undressed, a soul in torment, till day, and as soon as it was decent hare over to the club.

Here, at ten, Pen's report brought exquisite relief. The night-light had not been extinguished because illness had given place to death. The reason for the black-out, supplied by the old butler over the back wall to the Wibbe's cook, was that last night for the first time since Wednesday, the patient had been considered out of danger.

"She has been terribly bad again, but she's definitely turned the corner."

"Pen, are you sure?"

"Oh, absolutely! The piano's going now, Bach, with the soft pedal down, which proves it, you see. Thank goodness I could tell you this before you left for Manchester."

"If you hadn't I'd have stopped right here."

So he would have done, instead of catching the afternoon train in order to start work Monday morning. His first English factory inspection. To have cut it might have been an irremediable mistake.

In the middle of a man-sized breakfast he thumped his forehead.

"Great snakes, this has eased my mind in another direction! Here, let me get on to Bream."

In Great Smith Street the nondescript little detective listened and rubbed a thoughtful chin.

"I see, Mr. Beddoes. It does appear to alter the situation."

"Alter it? Why, it blasts it to smithereens! Whatever's going on, Scarpath is not trying to get rid of his wife."

"H'm, yes. Most reassuring. One might say he's had the opportunity and not taken advantage of it."

"Exactly. Then what *is* his idea?"

"Keeping her segregated, you mean? We can't prove that he is doing that. He may be acting in strict accordance with medical instructions. Or at most—"

"Well?"

"I was going to say, exceeding orders. Making them a little more drastic than is necessary. An abnormally jealous man, for instance, might wish to cut his wife off entirely from her former associates."

Though still secretly hounded by guilt, David snorted.

"If he's jealous, why does he neglect her?"

"You're thinking, I gather, of the South Street party."

"Not particularly. It's all down in your report. While she's living in squalor he spends his time floating from one wealthy hostess to another. If that isn't neglect—"

"Quite; but you may have noted I've not discovered him alone with any of these various ladies. In fact, thus far our hopes in a certain quarter have proved a total wash-out."

David frowned over the neatly-tabulated record of Scarpath's movements, beginning last Sunday with golf at a Hertfordshire club. There had been two dust-ups on an indoor tennis-court, one with a professional, the other with a man friend; one first night, followed by a look-in at a newly-opened night-club; one visit to an exhibition of African sculpture in King

Street, another to a Sackville Street tailor, and linking these activities a series of meals and cocktail gatherings scattered about the West End.

"Damn it, Bream, all it can mean is that the right woman's out of town. See here, this covers only half the week. From Wednesday Scarpath was sticking pretty closely at home, alarmed, one may suppose, by his wife's relapse. I admit none of it seems to match, but—" David thumped the innocuous report and thrust it from him. "The flat in South Street's your answer. Obviously, since you tell me he has free use of it, there's where we can expect him to conduct any sort of rendezvous."

"This flat," observed Bream, coughing, "belonged formerly to Mr. Scarpath himself. Did I mention that shortly after the admiral's death it was taken over on a weekly tenancy by Lord Mingo's son, the Honourable Frederick Treddle?"

"Oh, is that so?"

Weekly tenancy! It suggested that Scarpath could resume his bachelor haunt at short notice—if that meant anything. David wondered how many nights Scarpath spent in the place, and if Elizabeth had the least suspicion it existed. Who, for that matter, was supplying the money which Scarpath seemed to be squandering? Not this woman Gwen Boxe. Her reputation was well known—and besides she was a gold-digger herself. Yet the party Colin had been taken to must have run to big figures.

"By the way, have you any line at all on Scarpath's resources?"

Bream shook his head. Mr. Scarpath banked at Barclay's, but it was hopeless to attempt getting information every bank manager regarded as sacrosanct. Only Scotland Yard could elicit the facts, and then only in the event of a criminal inquiry.

David muttered, "I'm damned if I can spot anything criminal—yet. To all outward showing he's trying to get his wife cured, and worried to death when she's worse."

The detective's light eyelashes flickered very slightly. "Is it quite certain Mrs. Scarpath isn't due to inherit money?"

David met the tentative glance. "All I know is she has absolutely no such expectation. It's not easy, you know, to get behind her statement."

"And you still wish me to go on?"

"Like hell I do! Watch that flat. If you get on to any woman, wire me about it."

Bream's question troubled David. How the devil was one to discover whether or not Fanny Rush intended to leave her niece any money? John Fellowes, now in New York, had gleaned nothing whatever concerning Fanny's affairs. The lady herself had acknowledged neither the cable nor the explanatory letter which had followed it. She might at this moment be quarantined or eaten by cannibals. On the other hand she might merely be conducting herself along her usual exasperating lines. If she did take it into her head to come hiking back, could she get here in time to be of the smallest use?

It was a paralysing thought.

"And yet, how can I wire her point-blank, 'Have you made a will in Elizabeth's favour?' She'll jump to just one conclusion. I'm a dollar-chaser myself, trying for my own ends to separate the pair she and God have joined together."

In this as in every other direction his hands were tied.

All he could do now was to satisfy himself that Elizabeth, poor child, was really out of danger. A call on the Wibbes at tea-time secured him a few private words with Pen.

"Oh, Mr. Beddoes, she must be better! Isn't it a good sign that the doctor hasn't been there to-day?"

Luck brought him more comfort. As he was dodging back into the tube station a smart grey Chrysler flashed past, with Scarpath alone in the driver's seat—hatless, absently steering, his eyes chill and absorbed. Slung in behind was a pale rawhide suitcase, and next it a golf-bag.

Off to the country, evidently. A cold devil, blast him; but he wouldn't be going away if his wife were on the point of death.

The car was undoubtedly the one Bream had traced to a garage in this neighbourhood. Elizabeth had supposed her husband had let it go. One more deception, but just now it was of minor importance.

His load lightened, David returned to Bloomsbury and began throwing his own belongings into a bag.

Elizabeth opened her eyes. The room was dark, but less dark than the region she had at last quitted after horrors extending for she knew not how long. Weak as she was she doubted whether it would be possible to drag herself over to the window. Later on, though, the attempt must be made.

"I've got to manage it!" she muttered. "Oh, I must!"

"Manage what?"

The voice, not ten inches away, ran through her like an electric needle. She had believed herself alone, but all the while her husband was beside her, invisible in the gloom!

Though the hum in her ears was subsiding her heart started its frantic thumping and bumping. She would have to find some explanation for her odd speech.

"What's the time?" she croaked. "I've just waked up."

"Oh?"

The blurred shape moved. She felt she was being studied. Then the lamp snicked on, and despite the thick brown paper covering the dirty, fluted shade the sudden glare hurt her eyes. She closed them, but knew that Geoffrey was holding his wrist under the light. Knew, too, that he was chafing with irritation.

"Four-thirty."

He was weighing his announcement, all wrapped up, as usual, in his own interests. Maybe he'd let her unfortunate remark slide.

"Going out?" she inquired indifferently. It had just occurred to her that he might have been cooped up lately on her account, in which case his caged restlessness was understandable.

He was examining her again as she lay, flat and exhausted, under the covers. All at once the matter of his movements became vital. How, if he went on watching her, could she send her message to David?

She had roused his suspicions! Just that one casual question about his going out. . . . No, he hadn't noticed it. It was his own plans which occupied him.

"How are you feeling?" he asked. "More yourself?"

"Oh, I've skinned through again! I-I'd rather not talk."

She caught an explosive sigh. Geoffrey's hovering tautness seemed to relax.

"Of course. These treatments are pretty strenuous. It'll be several days before you begin the upgrade, won't it?"

He didn't expect a reply. His attention was already straying. He took a step away from the bed, stopped, and faced round.

"Oh! What was it you had to manage? If it's anything I can do for you—"

Elizabeth screwed her forehead. "Did I say that? I must have been dreaming. . . . Yes, I know, about Fanny. Maybe after all she ought to be told just a little. I must write her, when I'm able."

"Don't. I'm sending her a wire."

"A wire? Oh, Geoffrey, not a wire! Let's—let's talk it over."

She had raised her head. Back she fell, the world black gossamer.

"If you like." It sounded miles off. "Not now, later on."

She did not know if he had noticed her sudden collapse. As her head steadied she sensed his hesitancy and the sudden, brusque decision which swept it away.

"Better doze off again," he advised kindly, and coming back turned off the lamp.

Still for interminable moments he lingered, long after she had made her breathing even. At last a floorboard creaked, a gust of cold air sucked in on her, and then, very gently, her door was closed.

Oh, the unutterable strain! Muggy with sweat she lay listening to Geoffrey's quick strides to and fro in the passage, finally to the urgent clatter of his feet on the stairs. Not till a culminating thud assured her he had actually quitted the house did she strive to cope with her unreasoning terror.

She knew why he had stopped here so long. He had wanted to make sure she was really pulling round from her attack before deciding whether or not it was decent to keep an engagement. She had seen his overwhelming relief, none the less real because it was for his own sake, not hers.

Why, then, had it been so awful?

All she could say was that for twenty minutes, half an hour, she had been paralysed with fear. The darkness—shut in here with her husband—too weak to move. . . . Her brain still wouldn't work.

Even now the grey Erl-king, her childhood's bogey, seemed riding her down, his flying cloak spread in readiness to smother her cries. She was beating him—perhaps; but another time?

Four hours till nine o'clock. Should she be able to reach the window, let down her string?

With a stupendous wrench she hauled herself upright. As before, everything crumpled.

"They've not left me the power . . ."

It was her last despairing thought as consciousness ebbed away.

Chapter Sixteen
A RING AT THE BELL

"ALWAYS so level-headed till now," complained Alison, sorting silks for her darning. "I've never known David like this."

"Easy!" Colin went on with his perusal of an American illustrated journal. "Just say he's in love."

"You're telling me—and didn't it just have to be with a married girl? No, Colin, I don't like it. All this meddling about with another man's property may give him a tremendous kick, but it does have its dangerous side."

"If you're thinking of his qualifying as a co-respondent, don't worry. Mrs. Scarpath's an ill woman."

"Yes, I suppose there's no doubt about that now, is there? And for all we know she may still be fond of her husband. I've seen him, you know. He's plus-plus on the Come Hither and then some."

"Oh?" The doctor sent her a probing glance.

"Certainly." Alison's amber-rimmed spectacles trained on him for a mere second. "Doesn't your niece subscribe to that opinion? And all those duchesses and what-nots you saw fawning on him at the party? All very well you calling him a rotter—"

"My good girl! I've done nothing of the kind."

"Is zat so? Oh, no, what you've *said* has been all right. He behaved himself better than any of his guests, never got tight, seemed blissfully unaware that meetings were being held in his bathroom. And all the time you were telling me what a gentleman he was I've known there was Something."

She waited hopefully, but got no reply. Ruffling her hair she said crossly, "I must say I don't get it. Was there anything wrong in playing host for a friend who couldn't turn up?"

"Tush!" Colin went on with his reading.

"Mouse-trap!" She swept the newspaper from his grasp. "Is it or is it not the prevailing impression that Scarpath's a bachelor?"

Colin drew a resigned breath. "His intimates know he's married. It's generally assumed *(a)* that he got trapped by some impossible upstart; *(b)* has been living in hell as the result of her hopeless condition, vaguely thought to be mental; *(c)* is far too proud to discuss his private affairs. That satisfy you?"

"If he says nothing, how did this story get round?"

"Surely you know that dignified reticence will always build up a creditable fiction."

"I wonder if it is altogether fiction? Oh, not the upstart part, but—?"

Colin shrugged. "I myself heard Scarpath referred to half a dozen times as poor darling Geoffrey."

Alison remained silent till she had threaded her long needle. "Yet he must in the beginning have cared for Elizabeth," she said slowly. "For the simple reason that he can't have married her for money. As for the present state of affairs, we can hardly blame him for getting about among his friends, can we? Or for not having a job. That would damn about a third of your fellow-countrymen. What else was there? Oh, yes, the parrot! Well, if Elizabeth's finding an excuse for that why shouldn't we?"

"Quite. Should you have called her at all hysterical?"

Alison darted him a look.

"It would account for so much, wouldn't it? Colin, I just don't know. I never knew her very well, and she was only a kid. Her aunt's sort of loony. Oh, not seriously," she answered the doctor's alert eye, "but definitely eccentric. She must have got David's cable by now. It seems to me she's just washing her hands of Elizabeth—and that there may be a reason."

Diligently she attacked the heel of a stocking, while the man opposite thought less of her remark than of the burnished sheen of her head in the lamplight and the warm bloom of her unpowdered cheek. He remembered that she was the only American girl he had yet known who could walk. All the others yearned for a taxi after the first mile. Home-loving, too, despite the formidable pile of manuscript lugged from the office each evening; sympathetic, and—

"You're conventional, aren't you?"

"Me?" Alison bristled. "Why? Because I'm not celebrating the idea of interference between husband and wife? If that's your meaning, then I am. Funny," she mused. "I'd have said David was the really conventional one. He's got very strict views where womenfolk are concerned."

"You needn't apologise for him."

"David? I thoroughly approve. What makes me nervous is his knight-errantry. Happy Hooligan, you know."

"Happy—?"

"Now don't tell me you've never met Happy Hooligan! Look, that comic strip right under your nose. Every Sunday since before my time he's played Don Quixote, with a tomato-can for a helmet—and every Sunday, without fail, he gets it in the neck. Pick him up, you'll see."

The current adventure showed Happy remonstrating with a bricklayer who had just blacked his wife's eye. In the last square he was flattened beneath a hodful of bricks, the distressed lady having assisted in his demolishment and flung herself, starry-eyed, into her husband's arms.

"Topical, I must say." Colin excavated his pipe-bowl with a knitting-needle out of Alison's bag. "Yes, I conceive the possibility not only of Mrs. Scarpath's sticking to her husband but of Scarpath himself bringing a libel action. Beddoes may well be skating on thin ice. What seriously interests me, though, is how Brodmart is dealing with that case. Fat chance of finding out!"

"I know. Colin, can she get well?"

"I doubt it."

Alison sighed. "Poor David! He must have just caught her in one of her good spells. Will she ever get about?"

"Oh, yes, and for long stretches. The trouble being the thing will creep back again and in the end fasten a stranglehold, like the Old Man of the Sea."

With a shudder Alison tore off her spectacles. "Oh, what's the use? I'm desperately sorry, but there's not a thing we can do. I'm going to make some tea."

Both were on their feet when the bell gave a single peal.

"Damn and blast! That's the downstairs one. No, don't do anything yet. Let's see if whoever it is will just go away."

He consulted his watch. It was a quarter to twelve. Not that Bloomsbury considered this a late hour for a call. Too often a soothing tête-à-tête had been spoiled by some garrulous invader. He was glad Alison saw eye to eye with him on this subject.

They were standing close together, grinning a little guiltily, holding their breath. Colin's hand rested on Alison's shoulder. Its warm pressure sent a thrill of which she was slightly ashamed, right down to her toes.

"Want me to investigate?"

"N-no." She felt herself flushing ridiculously. "I expect it's one of those boys from the mews doing it for fun."

The ring was not repeated. Colin's hand slid lingeringly along her arm, found her fingers and held them.

"Oh, let's have our tea!"

Breathless, she broke from him, fled to the kitchen, and filled the kettle. As the gas sputtered she told herself a few solid home-truths.

"He can't think of marrying till he's making more money. That may mean years. I don't want this ending the—the other way."

Why not? She was twenty-seven, earning her own keep, answerable to no one. When her friends made these concessions she never cast stones.

"I suppose I am conventional. Or is it only practical? Anyhow I hate messing up a nice friendship which can last for—for something that always seems to me darned fragile."

And now, of course, she'd got to take care.

There was provokingly little need. When she carried in the Earl Grey brew Colin was prosaically occupied with her newspapers. She reminded herself that men's hearts seldom thumped after these little passages. His, she believed, was beating as calmly as usual. Still, it was good to know there wasn't going to be any awkwardness. She had torn away just in time.

"Try some indigestion-breeder?" She handed him American fruit-cake, moistly black, cut into chunks. "It came on Thanksgiving Day. Eat up. Don't you like it?"

"Wonderful. If you don't mind, I'd rather hunt myself a plain biscuit."

"Of course! Well, go forage. You may even find some mummified Brie. Mind the fish-heads. They're for the landlady's cat."

No awkwardness; but was it quite as before? Those dangerous moments had brought not strain but softening, as of a thaw in March. Alone, Alison asked herself if one ever did go back all the way. Somehow she hoped one didn't. She did not know that in the kitchen Colin was addressing rude remarks to a judgment suddenly grown sober.

He had been a fool to imagine this girl could be played about with. No, he hadn't even that excuse, since he had not imagined it. A damned good thing she was shoving him back into his place. He'd drink his tea and go home to bed. . . .

"It's bitter outside. Bundle up that neck."

"Sez you!"

"Sez me. Here, I'll do it." She gave a choking tug to his woollen muffler. "Now then, out you go. Don't take any bad cheques."

"I'll take any I can get," he said wryly, and made for the stairs.

Holding the door wide to light him on his descent she saw him pause and bend over.

"What's this? Looks like a bundle of old clothes. . . . I say, does your charlady drink?"

"My charlady! You know I don't have her on Sundays."

Alison pressed the light-button on the landing and hurried down to where he stooped midway the first flight.

"Oh!" A curious expression came into her eyes. "Colin," she whispered, "I do believe this is who rang my bell. What on earth—?"

Drunk or dead, the person inside the strange huddle of garments was limp as a sawdust doll. As Colin lifted the inert body to carry it into the flat the core of his burden had scarcely any substance, while the head lolled on his shoulder. Something dropped. It was a blue satin mule.

"Bare feet!" gasped Alison.

Each toenail showed a tiny red crescent.

"Whisky!" Colin eased his light load on to the divan. "No, stop—ever seen her before?"

The closed eyes had dark lashes, startlingly black against the corpse-like pallor of the face. The hair, too, was dark, and it was incongruously tidy. Alison knit her brow.

"N-no, never. That is—"

Suddenly she clutched Colin's arm.

"*Oh, my God!* It's Elizabeth."

CHAPTER SEVENTEEN
DELUSION

A CURT whistle roused her, but she continued to stare, first at the unconscious face, then at the crazy mixture of garments.

"She *is* unbalanced, Colin. That get-up—and coming here. What ought we to do, call an ambulance?"

He muttered something about the length of time Elizabeth had lain on those cold stairs.

"Help me, can't you? Raise her head." He had whisky in a tumbler. "It ought to be brandy, but—"

"Brandy? She's soaked in it now. Oh, don't you smell it?" Alison drew back, shocked.

His jaw tightened queerly. "Think I don't know? Yes, on second thoughts it had better be coffee. Quick!"

There was coffee left from lunch. She set it over the flame, feeling stunned and slightly nauseated. *Drunk!* Such a horror had never even dimly occurred to her.

She had heard of cases, but Elizabeth—! And now if she were to collapse and die, here in this flat?

Meanwhile Colin, working angrily and at top speed, had hauled the divan close to the fire and tucked Alison's blue taffeta eiderdown round the brandy-reeking form. Under its thickness his hand explored death-cold flesh between which and the weird outsize clothing lay only a wisp of chiffon. This was a hell of a business. Good thing he happened to be on hand, but even so. . . .

"Hurry up with that coffee!"

"Here it is," panted Alison. "Sugar?"

He left off chafing the small naked feet to ladle in big spoonfuls of the brown crystals and grit his teeth over the time they took to dissolve. His manner made her feel vaguely incompetent. To atone she raced to fill her hot-water bottle. Oh, Lord, what a mix-up! They hadn't bargained for this. . . .

Colin's judgment was baffled. This looked like a faint, probably from extreme weakness, but then there was the brandy. Much? Pulse not too bad, considering. Skin and bone, though, poor little devil. In no state to stand up to pneumonia. He would have to work fast. To hell with these Scarpaths! One way or another this was their doing. Well, one thing was certain, she couldn't be moved.

Here was the hot bottle. "Knees, not feet," he snapped, and Alison again felt corrected. "What's that? Oh, I see, the other slipper."

"It's hardly damp, Colin. That means she didn't come on foot. And I've remembered, too, about her clothes. Maybe it's true her own were taken away. But whose oddments are these, and how—"

He cut her short brusquely. "Hush, she's coming round."

They got a few sips of the coffee between the pale lips. The lashes stirred, and presently, propped against cushions, Elizabeth was staring dreamily outward. Alison frowned.

"But her eyes, Colin! We used to say they were exactly the colour of wood violets. Now they're black."

He silenced her again, but he also was bending forward, intently examining the enormously-dilated pupils, which covered every vestige of iris. They had a blind, questing expression as they turned from one face to the other.

Sick with dismay Alison breathed, "Oh, dear, she can't see!"

Elizabeth had heard. One transparent hand strayed to her hair as though to tidy a fancied disorder. Pathetic gesture! All the hardness within her melted, Alison sank on her knees and took the groping fingers in a warm clasp. She whispered:

"Betsy, child, it's all right. You're with friends—Alison, you know, and a nice doctor who's looking after you. Isn't it luck he was here?"

"Alison! Yes, of course." A pause, and then, all run together, "Please-forgive-me. Such-a-nuisance. Nowhere-to-go. . . ."

Colin's lips tightened. If what he heard was scanning, it was the very hallmark of the disease. To be sure this sloppy, slurred utterance might bear a more ordinary interpretation, as Alison obviously believed, for she was saying with slight stiffness:

"Ssh, Betsy. I wouldn't talk till you've slept this off."

"Sleep-what-off?" A puzzled frown, followed by flooding shame. "Oh!" Elizabeth covered her eyes. "Never-could-drink, you-know. I-told-Pen-it-was-too-much."

The tension broke. Hysterical with relief Alison caught Colin's eye.

"So it was Penelope Wibbe who gave you the brandy! Did she borrow this rig-out for you to put on?"

Of course it was so, thought Alison, smothering mirth. Who but the author of *Caravans* would own a Paisley wrap, a skirt from the Highland Industries, and this struck-by-lightning blouse?

"Stole it." Speech was more even as the stimulant took steadying effect. "She'd have come with me only it was so late I couldn't let her." The clouded eyes searched the room. "David. Isn't he here?"

"Gone to Manchester. Didn't you know?"

A crestfallen gasp. Elizabeth murmured distressedly something about Pen's handing her a note which it was impossible to read.

"There wasn't much time. Oh, what can you think of me, coming down on you like this?"

Two tears slid down. Alison put a handkerchief into the hand that was trying desperately to hide them and repeated, "It's all right," feeling it was most decidedly all wrong. This heap of misery dumped on her—what in heaven's name was to be done with it? Colin, utterly absorbed, was making no suggestion.

Elizabeth was speaking again—timidly, like a well-mannered child. Would it be possible for her to have something to eat?

"Anything—just a bite. I hate mentioning it, but—"

Colin roused from his reverie. "Right!" He said it with decision, strode into the kitchen, and beckoning Alison, closed the door.

"What's happened?" she urged in consternation, but he only asked where she kept the eggs and, bread-knife in hand, lit the grill.

"Here. Did the drink make her do this, or—?"

"It might, on an empty stomach. Unless I'm all out the girl's been half-starved."

"Oh—*Colin*! You mean she's deliberately not eaten? People do that sometimes, don't they?"

"Don't speculate, give me that milk."

He filled a small saucepan, and slicing bread spoke under his breath.

"I warn you, this is far from simple. Evidently she's just pulling round from a severe attack of some kind. It may be that for a few days she's been in no condition to take proper nourishment, though . . . no, it's too soon to form opinions. Can I have this blancmange?"

They found Elizabeth with a page of David's writing held tightly in her hand—clinging to it, as to a lifebelt, reflected Alison with fresh chagrin.

Here indeed was a nice kettle of fish. Since this afternoon she had known a little of what David had been keeping from her. Recalling what he had said about having seen Scarpath set off with a bag and coupling that flight with what seemed to her an emotional caprice she felt righteously indignant. Not for long, though. It was impossible to experience anything but pity over the way this poor child—absurd to think of her as a married woman!—was almost snatching at the food.

"Oh, that was too marvellous!" Elizabeth sighed as she finished the last crumb. "My sister-in-law . . . but maybe David's told you? Really not her fault. I oughtn't to criticise when she's been so good."

Colin squatted down. "When did you have your last meal?"

"When? Let me think. . . . I had some Bengers at six, only it was so scorched. . . . Before that—well, I can't quite remember."

"I see. So you've been unconscious, have you?" he asked quietly.

She nodded. "Delirious, I expect. I don't know how long. After my treatment, you understand. Oh, I'm getting over it now. I can hear all right, only there's still a sort of veil over everything. It's rather confusing."

"What made you come away?"

"What made—?" She was glancing first at him then at Alison with a cornered expression. "It's so hard to—David would have understood, I think. I—I heard my husband go off. I tried to get up, then I fainted. After a while I tried again. It seemed to me it was a case of now or—*never*."

The last was barely audible. She had gripped her hands together in an agony, and all her frail body was trembling. Gently wiping the sweat from her forehead Colin asked another question in the same easy, conversational tone. Had it seemed to her the one good opportunity to leave, while her husband was out of the house?

"Yes—because I knew I'd never live through another of these times. Oh, please don't get wrong ideas! They don't mean me to die. It's just that—" Her lips quivered to silence.

Alison telegraphed: "She's raving—obviously," but Colin's face was a mask, all his attention centred on Elizabeth's small, troubled features.

"They," he repeated. "Meaning, I suppose, your husband and sister-in-law?"

"And the doctor, of course. It was he who said I must have another treatment, or he couldn't take the risk. I heard him say he had his reputation to consider."

"Yes. And what about your risk, dashing out of a warm bed straight into the cold night?"

Helplessly she gazed back at him, torn between embarrassment and some anguish of fear. "I had to chance it," she said simply. "I'd rather die this way than—than like a rat in a trap. Oh, I didn't mean that! Not the way it sounded."

She had clapped a hand over her mouth and begun weakly to sob.

Colin signalled Alison to let her be. Together they watched her as she sank her neat dark head in the cushions, every wasted inch of her shaken by misery.

All at once she started up, casting herself on Alison with frantic appeal.

"I know what you're thinking," she cried, "and that I can't possibly stop with you. It was beastly of me to come, but oh, please, please don't send me back!"

Chapter Eighteen
DILEMMA

It had just struck two.

Alison's lips twitched a little over the garments spread on a chair and reeking strongly of public-house, but they straightened now into a rueful line.

"So what?"

Unhearing, Colin stared at the door behind which, muffled in all the woollies available, their charge lay slumbering.

"I'm wondering," he said, "whether or not to camp in the kitchen."

"Oh! Is it really as bad as that?"

"I don't know." There was heavy doubt in his voice. "We've put a little fuel inside her, but she was on those stairs a murderously long time. In her present state an attack of 'flu would finish her, like that." Softly he snapped his fingers.

Fear had sprung anew into Alison's eyes.

"There's plenty of fight in her, though. The fuss she put up over taking my bed! It's to-morrow I'm worrying about. I can cut work, of course, but—"

"Cut nothing. See here, first thing in the morning I shall send along a nurse."

"A nurse? What a brilliant idea! Can she take charge?"

"Entirely. It won't run to much, and Beddoes will insist on paying the bill. Will you ring Manchester and tell him?"

"David! And have him drop everything to come skating back? No, Colin. At least—" Alison hesitated. "Let's say nothing till to-morrow evening. She may be much better by then. Besides, what about her husband?"

"Quite. There's a worse problem to be met." Colin rubbed his chin.

"Colin, he can't have gone away for long. When he does come home and finds what's happened—you see?"

"Oh, yes, I see." He still eyed the door.

"I mean, this is too horrible a responsibility for you or for me. She's explained nothing, has she? Not one little thing. So we're still completely in the dark as to the real situation."

"You've seen what her body's like. That's real enough," he muttered.

"Yes, but this disease. Wouldn't that account—? I'm only saying that if she's got those confusional attacks you were telling me about and anything should happen to her while she's under my roof—?"

His hand had closed mechanically on her arm. Suddenly the grip tightened till it hurt. The violence startled her. Never before had she known him exhibit such feeling. She glanced at him curiously, but his remark when it came seemed addressed to himself.

"See here," he jerked. "This case has been handed me, so to speak. I hate like blazes to pass it up. I won't pass it up! I'm going to—"

"Not treat Elizabeth yourself? Oh, Colin, after all you said to David about medical etiquette and—"

"I didn't say treat her. Simply keep her for a bit under observation. I'm not a neurologist, but if she's willing, where's the harm? In essentials it's much the same as rendering first aid to a street casualty. Or if it isn't, I'm damned if I care!"

She studied the grim determination of his jaw. "Well! So long as you aren't landed in a mess."

His breath hissed inward. "Brodmart! We'll have to keep it strictly hush-hush, of course. Will they guess where to look for her?"

"First shot out of the locker. She hasn't a friend in London except David and me. It may take a little time to locate me, because, thank God, I'm not in the telephone-book. How long," Alison faltered uneasily, "will you be wanting for this observation stunt?" He brushed her aside. Eyes oddly brilliant he was getting into his coat.

"Good! It's settled, then. You'll have the nurse, a reliable one, and I'll call round after breakfast and give her instructions."

With a pat on her shoulder, oh, wholly perfunctory, he was gone.

All at once Alison felt too weary to drag the cover from the couch. Colin's interest in her seemed to have evaporated. She stood dully in the centre of the room where less than three hours ago every nerve had tingled at his touch and asked herself wherein she had failed. She had certainly shown herself incompetent, a dumb blockhead while he did everything. She might even have been at the start a little uncharitable— though Elizabeth, poor child, had been her friend, not his. But was it that?

She crossed to the door and looked in on her guest.

Elizabeth was sleeping soundly, the blue quilt in a hood round her head, the gas-fire lending a delicate flush to her now tranquil face. How lovely she looked—wistful, appealing, and so *young*! About fifteen in this warm dusk. No wonder David had lost every atom of critical judgment. Men were like that, whatever their brains. Colin might kid himself that his interest was purely professional, but—

"Gosh! I'm not by chance feeling *jealous*?"

She who despised pettiness in every form couldn't, she hoped, be such a crawling worm.

She scribbled the milkman a note ordering extra cream, butter, new-laid eggs. In bed at last, pretending not to miss her hot-water bottle, she muttered firmly, "Chicken. Grapes—big hot-house ones. Oranges. Yes, and flowers."

Certainly flowers. God alone knew what wrath might come toppling down on them, but for the present let this unhappy sufferer find some comfort and cheer.

The nurse, broad-hipped and hearty, was on the doorstep at eight. It was a job to prevent her rousing the patient and subjecting the latter to the washing process, but the strong touch prevailed. Alison explained that Mrs. Greentree—it had been agreed to call Elizabeth that—was a nerve case and that Dr. Ladbroke had insisted she get plenty of sleep.

"I see. Well, just as you say."

No imagination, evidently, but that was an advantage. Alison prayed that the friendly relations between Mrs. Marshall, the char, and Nurse Badger would continue as well as they had begun. The two at any rate shared one weakness—tea. They were drinking it now in the kitchen while she, feeling slightly fagged, lingered as long as she dared over her bacon and eggs. She had wanted to see Colin, but she was forced to abandon the hope.

Her usual Monday lay ahead. How she was going to bring her faculties to bear on agreement clauses and what-not was a problem, but bread-earning had to go on.

There was one nasty jolt.

"Look, A. Y." Her colleague, Hartley Matfield, thumbed a document lately handed into his cubicle. "Since when have we collected an author named Scarpath?"

"Who? Oh, Lord, give it here! Gladys"—to a befogged secretary—"this top sheet'll have to be retyped. For Scarpath put Scathling, Peter G. I am a fool," babbled Alison, for H. M. was watching her closely through his owl-spectacles. "I had this novel on my desk and I simply dictated the wrong name."

"*Plate Glass.* Yes. Any good?"

"M-m-m. . . . Well, rather dazzling in spots, thin, you know, rather unfinished. Say, H. M., would you awfully mind scramming? I'm up to my ears."

Red ears, commented the retreating glance. H. M. pondered a little on the instructions he had heard A. Y. issuing to the telephone girl and drew private conclusions. If she was so averse from having her home telephone number divulged was it because people ringing up at night might be answered by a man?

"One did answer the other evening—darned late, I'll say. Scarpath! Well, well, you never can know."

Aghast to find that even kind, dull Gladys was shooting little rabbit-glances over the noiseless Remington, Alison took a stern grip on herself. If Geoffrey Scarpath did track her down to this office, and how easily he might, why, the entire staff would be buzzing, and if the truth came out business would certainly suffer.

She could not believe that Scarpath would simply let things drift. Whatever his feelings towards his wife he could hardly leave her straying about, ill and without money. Oh, if only Mrs. Rush were here to take charge! But the woman herself might be lying fever-stricken in some South Sea hole.

The telephone! Alison's mouth went dry. This, she thought, would be Scarpath.

Stodgily young Gladys was saying, "It's your cousin, Miss Young, calling from Manchester."

Oh, damn! Alison jammed the receiver to her ear.

"David, you prodigal ass, why this expense? . . . What's that, you've had a wire from Pen? . . . Listen! I can't talk now, but it's all right. Got that? All right. I'll call you at eight this evening. Goodbye!"

She cut off, though he was still bellowing, grabbed her coat and fled to lunch.

David, of course, had gone berserk—just like Elizabeth, into whose veins some of her aunt's crazy blood must have strayed. And what about the Wibbe child, shunting an invalid off at dead of night to a flat which might have been closed for the week-end? She, too, was mad. So was the whole world.

Except Nurse Badger, who, reached from a call-box, gave a cheery report. The little patient had eaten ever so toppingly and was now tucked up for a nap. Yes, the doctor had been. He'd stopped more than an hour.

Well, and why not? Alison sat stoically on her emotions. Colin would want much more than an hour to make any decisions. There had been no disturbances—yet. The luck, of course, couldn't last.

The next post brought Pen's explanation, with Personal underscored in very black ink. Pen had tried to telephone, but had got only the engaged signal.

Guiltily Alison remembered that last evening she herself had quietly removed the receiver. So it was not Pen's fault.

Pen, it seemed, had collected a message daubed in lipstick—proving, she pointed out, that all writing materials had been taken away. No choice had been left her. Elizabeth had been planning to escape as soon as the house was quiet, with clothing or without. So Pen had simply raided a chest for warm garments, met the fugitive in front and, having gingered her up with a tumblerful of liqueur brandy sent her off in a taxi.

A postscript said, *"They were killing her, Miss Young. I hope you don't mind."*

Killing her? Strange that the victim herself didn't question her family's good intentions. . . .

If Elizabeth did die, how could her husband benefit? Alison mused. Only, it would seem, by being free to marry someone else. Maybe the other woman was a Roman Catholic who could not bring herself to marry a divorced man.

"Rubbish, he can't be a murderer! If he wanted to be, how could he possibly get away with it? The doctor would suspect. And now—! I must say Elizabeth has taken about the worst conceivable course, making this bee-line for David. I don't know that I blame her, but what will our family say if David is cited as a co-respondent and I have to give evidence in court?"

David would be back again at the end of the week. And Elizabeth, according to Colin, could not be moved.

CHAPTER NINETEEN

THE CABLE

From attic to basement Evelyn Scarpath roamed, twisting her red hands.

How could she know where her brother had gone, or when he would return? Questions made him so cross, and lately he had lashed out at her for no reason at all. When he did come home—to-morrow, the day after?—woe would be on her head. She would have to meet him with the news that Elizabeth, his wife, had flown.

Flown where? It could scarcely matter, seeing that in only a silly cobweb of a nightgown she must instantly have caught a fatal chill. Parsons had mumbled something about her having been picked up in a dying condition and taken to a hospital, but this, it seemed, hadn't happened. She had vanished completely, just as though the frozen pavement had opened and swallowed her, dimmed eyes, scarlet toenails and all.

She, Evie, would be blamed. Geoffrey, in his rage, might even kill her, but she was long past caring, able only to pray in cowering anguish for the onslaught to come.

And now the cablegram. Assuming it meant tidings of Elizabeth she had torn it open before she grasped her unpardonable sin. The message was for Geoffrey—and she had read it. Maybe he'd be too upset over the bigger fault to pounce on her for this.

"Now, of all times!" she moaned. "Elizabeth run away, Geoffrey where I can't possibly reach him. What shall I do, what can I say?"

She had come out into the dank portico, still clutching the flimsy envelope in her hand, her weak eyes straining into the dusk. All day she had been doing this, never with much hope of seeing her brother appear. Now he believed immediate tension to be over he might stay away for several days. In the ordinary way she'd have been glad, for his sake, but now . . .

Suddenly Evie gasped. Geoffrey!

He was turning in at the gate. There was caked mud on his plus fours, he looked as though great draughts of country air had put new zest into him. Evie took hold of the flaking column by her side and began to whimper and shake.

"I couldn't help it," she mouthed. "So quiet, not a sound—just slipped out while I was asleep—"

Sodden with weeping she cast herself on his breast, felt him stiffen to stone. Into the house he thrust her, pinioning her with a grip of steel.

"Damn you! What's this you're telling me?"

"Elizabeth, Geoffrey, last night. Oh, I know it's incredible! We didn't think she could move. In her night-things, like a mouse, down these stairs, out this door. T-that's all."

She saw him, unmoving, a shadowy blur in the unlighted hall. Not a muscle had stirred, but—bewilderingly—she heard his breath exhale in a long, explosive sigh. How little she understood Geoffrey! She had expected to be riven by the lightning of his wrath, instead of which, after the first shock, he seemed inexplicably relieved.

"Oh!" Absently he flicked a match and lit the chandelier over their heads. "Go on. What else?"

Now she could see him clearly she noticed that his features, though still pale, were set in dangerous control. Every crisp hair seemed to bristle, his eyes, ice-blue and expressionless, probed into her soul.

She poured it all out—the empty bed, undiscovered till morning, the total uncertainty as to when or where Elizabeth had gone, her own efforts and Parsons', all to no avail.

"So you did ring the police?"

"Oh, yes, Geoffrey! She hasn't been seen."

Motionless again. That meant his brain was working hard.

"What's this?"

Gaze swerving, he had swooped down on the cablegram she had momentarily forgotten. Unmindful of her newly-babbled excuses, he was running his eye swiftly along the strip of printed words, absorbing the heading, the signature at the end.

He wasn't stone any longer. He made her think of a coiled, taut spring. Still staring he smiled, bitterly but with a forewarning of action. The next moment he was striding to the telephone, setting a finger on the dial.

"Upstairs," he ordered curtly. "Shut your door till I call."

Evie slunk aloft, clinging to the rail.

Geoffrey couldn't be *pleased* this had happened? Really there was no making him out. Oh, no, not pleased! That was out of the question. Ready, though, to cope with what she had supposed a paralysing débâcle. So the load was off her shoulders.

For the first time this terrible day she remembered the parrot, shivering and unfed on the front balcony. Geoffrey couldn't mind her just taking the poor bird in. It was as she tiptoed along that she caught her brother's opening words, down there at the telephone:

"Seeing a patient, is he? Well, get him here at once."

Of course, the doctor. She did not attempt to hear more. Perhaps, thought Evie, tending the parrot in her cold bedroom, this might offer quite the happiest solution. Elizabeth—first ill and now mad—had brought only trouble. Far better for them all if she were simply to die through no one's fault but her own. Very likely she would, and there would be an end of it.

She heard Geoffrey come up, go into his own room, and begin flinging things about. Forgotten about her, she supposed, and she had just realised that she had taken no nourishment since her early cup of tea.

Timidly she was just creeping forth with the purpose of boiling herself an egg when she heard her name called and went scuttling to reply.

"Why, *Geoffrey*!"

Like a fish yanked to land, she gaped at what confronted her—cupboard stripped, a helter-skelter of suits, silk pyjamas, books and music piled on the bed, and in the midst of the confusion her brother working like a beaver.

"Evie." He scarcely turned. "How would you like to run down to Hampshire? That is if any one there will take you in."

Hampshire! Her lashless eyes glowed.

"Oh, *yes*, Geoffrey! If I can be spared. Dear Mrs. Todd-Bryce has said she'd have me any time, that is—"

"Right! I'm leaving, so you'd better go too."

The question, what about Elizabeth, hung on Evie's lips.

"I see." Her brain whirled. "But Parsons—the house?"

"They won't run away," said her brother grimly. "That'll do. Now help me pack up."

Alison let herself into her flat to find curtains drawn, a room warmly aglow, and a great many flowers. She remembered buying chrysanthemums—there they were, very handsome, alongside the grapes and tangerines heaped in the black Wedgwood bowl—but not the pale blush roses, ruinously expensive at this time of year.

Colin's, of course. His tribute to Beauty in Distress. Very sweet of him.

Suddenly weary, she dragged off her coat. While it was yet in her hand her eye was drawn to the opening bedroom door, and rivetted by the timid, weirdly-attired figure hesitating on the threshold.

"Elizabeth! Oh, you poor little shrimp!" Laughter took her. She sank to the sofa, wiping her eyes.

"She made me put it on." Elizabeth doubled her hostess's blue quilted dressing-gown round her pencil-thin body. "Do you awfully hate my wearing your things?"

It might have been Pen Wibbe apologising with her best company manners. Between gusts of mirth Alison shook her head.

"But what are you doing out of bed? Chase back this minute, or I'll spank you."

"Oh, no, Alison, didn't your doctor friend tell you? I'm to sit up for a whole hour. I'm marvellously better, you know. Give me those, please." She reached for Alison's coat and hat.

"You wait on a great hulk like me? Think again. I can't believe this, Betsy. Sit here, let me look at you."

Alison pulled her guest down beside her, touched the soft cheek with a protective hand. Poor Elizabeth—and to grudge her a few roses. . . .

"I've had to borrow your comb, Alison, and powder, and—well, everything. Why are you looking at me so hard?"

"Was I? It's the change, I suppose, from last night. Why, you've actually got colour!"

"I know. You're thinking it can't possibly last. While it does, though, I do wish you'd let me do just a few little things for you. It wouldn't seem quite so bad, shoving in on you like this, eating your nice food—"

"Was it nice? Could you eat?"

"Did I eat! Oh, darling Alison, don't mind if I sniffle. So heavenly, all of it—but I won't go on using your bed. I'm going to sleep in here, where David slept, anyhow after to-night. We're changing over the sheets."

"Oh, are you? Look, who's giving orders, you or me?"

Alison had reached a cigarette. Elizabeth lit a spill, explaining with firmness that Dr. Ladbroke wanted her treated not as an invalid but as an ordinary person.

"Besides"—her brow furrowed—"I've got to begin thinking just how to get myself off your chest. If I'm worse again there's always a hospital, or—"

"Drop it, Betsy!" Alison also was firm. "Will Colin let you smoke? I can see you're longing to."

"He said I could now and then. . . . Oh, how wonderful!"

Elizabeth drew a grateful breath of smoke, kicked off her mules and sat curling wool-stockinged toes to the fire.

"Your country stockings," she murmured ruefully. "Can you smell that divine chicken? You see, I'm ravenous again. Now if only David were here—" She stopped, scarlet with shame. "Well, he'd enjoy it, too, wouldn't he?"

It was time, Alison decided, to tackle the subject of David. She told Elizabeth that Pen had wired him, that he was displaying unruliness and mustn't be permitted to do anything rash and perhaps fatal, like dashing back to London.

"It might lose him his job. You do see the danger?"

Elizabeth looked aghast. "I hadn't thought—oh, he couldn't be so silly?"

"I don't know. I'll be ringing him at eight. I don't suppose any one has rung you?"

At this very instant the telephone pealed, striking terror to them both. Elizabeth, white as a sheet, was trembling as she had done last night.

"Nonsense! That's probably David now. Keep calm while I answer."

"It—it may be someone else. . . ."

David it was. Elizabeth's colour flowed back. Alison whispered, "He's had a letter from Pen now. He means to rush down by the next train and get back to work in the morning. Will you deal with that proposition?" She handed over the receiver.

Elizabeth issued stern commands.

"David, if you do I'll never speak to you again! Don't you realise? I'm feeling fine. Up for dinner. Alison's spoiling the life out of me, I'm eating her out of house and home. I—what's that?" Guiltily her eyes met Alison's. "Nothing happened, David. I—I'm horribly ashamed. . . . No, nothing, nothing at all. . . . I can't spit it out! There's nothing to spit. . . . Money?" Elizabeth's hand gripped the instrument rather tightly. "No—and that bothers me, David. I mean—well, I have got a pretty good ring I can sell. We can go into that later when—but just when will I be seeing you? Friday! . . . Good-bye."

He was swearing, but before he was cut off Alison caught what sounded suspiciously like "darling"—a word David never used with its current casualness. She looked at Elizabeth, sitting upright, starry-eyed, and put a question to her.

"Is it really true, Betsy, that nothing happened except what you've told us?"

"Absolutely. Did you think I'd gone crazy? Maybe I was for a little while. It was a feeling, a . . . something terrible here." Breathless, she touched her breast. "All hedged in, helpless. . . . No one's to blame."

"Well, relax. I'm going to get rid of my Fleet Street grime."

In the bathroom Alison met the nurse, coat on in readiness to depart, there being no sleeping accommodations for her, and in her hand a fingerbowl of snowdrops.

"Well, Nurse, you've done wonders. Aren't you pleased?"

Nurse Badger beamed. "Sweet she looks, doesn't she? Fancy her trunks missing the boat!"

With a jolt Alison recalled her hasty fiction and played up to it. "What she was wearing had to go to the cleaners. Never mind, she won't need much till she's able to get about. More flowers! Dr. Ladbroke has been nice to her, hasn't he?"

"Her? Oh, I see, you've not seen the card that came with them. It's here under my arm."

The florist's envelope was addressed to Miss Young. On its enclosure was written, "To A. Y. Always the best." Alison felt as tipsy as though she had drank three cocktails in quick succession. Now, of a sudden, she was as hungry as her guest.

To be sure she could not help noticing how Colin, when he dropped in for coffee, had eyes only for his patient. She followed him out on to the landing, but he was not to be drawn.

"Don't ask me anything—yet. I admit she's astonishingly better, but haven't I told you her disease is subject to rather amazing ups and downs? What we're seeing may be only the natural upcurve—hastened, of course, by happier conditions."

"Oh! Then you yourself can't possibly tell—?"

He lowered his voice. "Frankly, I can't. My experience thus far has been limited to the very advanced cases brought into hospital. I didn't want to upset her to-day by too many questions. To-morrow, provided no hitch occurs—"

"Hitch?" His tone filled her with apprehension. He motioned her to accompany him down the stairs. "Scarpath's back," he whispered. "I thought you'd better know."

"How did you find out?" she asked quickly.

He explained. David's detective had been watching the house.

"And now a rather odd thing's happened. Scarpath got back late this afternoon, stopped about an hour, and left again with a lot of bags which he piled into his car. He drove to Harley Street—yes, to Brodmart's consulting-rooms. After a short time he continued his journey to South Street, the flat where the party was given. That's all Bream could report."

"What on earth is he up to?"

"God knows! We can be sure, though, he'll try at once to get in touch with his wife. Keep back, I'll have a look-see."

Thin sleet was driving in at the street door as Colin pushed it cautiously open and peered into the dark square. He pressed Alison's elbow.

"There! See that grey car?"

It was parked near the gates of the old Foundling Hospital, its head-lamps streaking a glistening path over the wet pavement. The driver, whose gaze had been trained on the windows overhead, ducked inside, started his engine, and slid dexterously away. Colin nodded, hissing in his breath.

"That was Scarpath right enough. Keep the chain on your door, and if there's any rumpus get through to me. Not worried, are you?"

"Well! I don't quite see what he can do. . . . Colin, is that nurse quite trustworthy?"

"Badger? Oh, I think so! I've told her the patient is to see no one, and on no account to take telephone-calls. That's for the day, and at night, well, you're in charge."

"If he gets at Elizabeth," said Alison doggedly, "it'll be over my corpse. . . . I still can't quite make it out, all the same. Last night seems to have been just some sort of brainstorm—don't you think?"

Colin shrugged. In the gloom she saw his jaw take an obstinate line.

"Was it? Be that as it may, we're going to hold on to her for the present, with our eye teeth. Yes, if I'm jailed for it. Now get upstairs."

In his second-hand Austin he sat for some minutes, stationary, staring out into the dark. He wondered if he was turning visionary.

"If it's true," he muttered, "Scarpath couldn't manage it alone. It can't be true! And yet, damn it, where are the symptoms? They do vanish, admitted, but like this, overnight, to find the lot of them na poo . . ."

That, of course, was the infernal nuisance of it. With not a single sign to guide one, how was it possible to make a diagnosis? Not one, except perhaps—

He swore and smote his thigh a resounding blow. God! Why hadn't he thought of this before?

Chapter Twenty
THE LECTURER IS LATE

THE idea just come to Colin was wild enough to be dismissed on the spot. Not only wild. It amounted to a species of high treason, so that if he considered it at all it was because of the impression the girl herself had made on him—reasonable, restrained, utterly anxious to be just.

He had offered her ample opportunity to make accusations. She had done nothing of the kind—and this inclined him to credit her every statement. She was suggestible, naturally—who wasn't?—and with peculiar justification, since in her case there had been not one dissenting voice to cast doubt on her illness.

"She's *had* to accept certain views. Those in charge have seen to that . . . unless there's some feature not yet apparent? She was nervous as a cat when I let her walk across the room this morning—afraid of stumbling; and stumble she did, but I rather fancy it was the right leg that gave way. I'll just look into it."

In doing so the following day he heard a queer story, though he warned himself not to attach too great importance to it.

"Funny, wasn't it?" said Elizabeth. "I mean about never locating that rabbit-hole again. I thought I could lead my husband right to the place, but there was no hole there, only a little smoothed-over dip."

"Filled in, probably, and returfed."

She shook her head. "We called the old man who looks after the golf-course. I still feel hot to my ears when I picture the way he and Geoffrey looked at me—just as though I were some poor, drivelling idiot. I began to wonder if just possibly I'd dreamed the whole thing."

It had, he suspected, been the first of many incidents to shake her self-confidence. Hinting that the old man might have been protecting himself from a charge of negligence he asked which knee she had twisted, and learning it was the right-hand one tried a little gentle tapping and kneading.

"Does that hurt?"

"N-no . . . yes, that does. You see, it never would get really strong. As Dr. Brodmart said it couldn't have been a simple sprain."

"Yes. Had you stumbled at all *before* the accident?"

"Once," she admitted. "Not for very long, only then it was my ankles that used to turn. It was directly after my father's death, when I wasn't—well, exactly happy with my aunt. I thought it might come from my being so horribly depressed."

"Why not? It's a very usual result of that sort of thing."

Colin spoke absently. The decision he now had to make was one for which he alone must shoulder responsibility. Not only that, if he backed the wrong horse he—and in a minor degree David and Alison—would inevitably be involved in a damaging scandal.

Fully alive to the risk he put his suggestion. It was rather frightening to see the light it brought leaping to Elizabeth's eyes.

"Could it be that?" Her breath almost forsook her. "Oh, Doctor Ladbroke, *could it*?"

"I don't know. Don't start building hopes on it. Let's say it's an avenue worth exploring and leave it at that. I think if to-morrow's a decent day and you go on making this good progress I might trundle you out for an hour. Now let's talk about Hampshire, it's my part of the world, you know. Let's see, weren't you near Lymington?" He handed her a cigarette, lighting one for himself.

It was not easy inducing her to open up on her married life. He felt sure that each of her abrupt halts marked a sore spot in her memory. She was frankest on her failure to fit in with her surroundings, a fact for which she was ready to take most of the blame.

"It might have been better if I'd had longer to play games. As it was— oh, I was all wrong, my upbringing, everything! Too shielded, too. . . . What," she appealed scornfully, "can you expect from a girl who's not once in her life ordered a meal or looked up a train?"

"Well, you were only—was it nineteen?" soothed Colin, knowing his country people. "And breaking into a closed circle does take time."

"It was more than that." Elizabeth hesitated. "Don't laugh at what I'm going to say, will you? I myself loathe a person who says she's not wanted. I always think it must be her own fault. But—" She spread her hands. "Well, here it is: My aunt didn't want me. I just got in her way. Hampshire didn't want me—"

"Go slow. By Hampshire don't you mean your husband?"

"Well, yes." She hurried on. "And now, what's happening? For the third time I'm being a nuisance—crowding in on Alison, who's practically a stranger, costing her money, upsetting her comfort and her life—"

"Steady!" He laid firm fingers on her arm.

"But it's true, isn't it? No matter what an angel she's being. I've simply got to move on—somewhere, somehow. I won't be a sponge! Can't *you* get me off her hands?"

"Not in those."

He had pointed to her weird combination of dressing-gown, ribbed stockings and shabby blue mules. He got the laugh he was aiming for, and while the tension was eased talked her into a more sensible frame of mind. Presently he coaxed more details of her illness. . . .

Was he by raising her hopes committing an unpardonable sin?

Home in his own flat Colin weighed the question seriously and with concern. Nine out of ten colleagues, he knew, would condemn him utterly, and his own conservative judgment agreed. It would have been another matter if the man on this case had been of less eminence than Guthrie Brodmart. Since it was he—

"I'd be crackers, no less, to go pitting my opinion against his. If I mean to go ahead, I must simply find some fellow who deals with the C. N. S., get the girl to him, and . . . but whom can I trust?"

Barham was a back-number. Henderson was good, but pretty certain to carry tales to headquarters, as would various other specialists—indeed all of them. Except . . . what about MacConochie? He, definitely, offered possibilities. He mustn't, of course, be deliberately approached. His interest must be roused during casual conversation. Yet one couldn't waste time. . . .

"MacConochie!" Colin was rummaging through the cards on his bedroom mantel, having remembered a medical lecture the hairy Scot would almost surely attend, if only to jeer. How Mac was hated! "Business methods, tactless tongue—it's all my eye. He gets results. . . . Holy smoke, it's to-night!"

He stared at the date and still harder at the name of the speaker. This was a bit of unforeseen luck. Things, he felt, were moving almost miraculously his way.

Late in the afternoon he looked in again on his patient. Even more encouraging than a perfectly normal pulse was the fact that he discovered her deeply absorbed in the latest *Vogue*. It was the nurse who, sneaking after him on to the landing, imparted news he had expected but which none the less disturbed his balance.

"It was while she was asleep, Doctor. I kept telling him he'd rung the wrong number and that there was no lady named Scar . . . Scar—?" Nurse Badger looked her question, but Colin returned a blank gaze. "I can't just remember the name he said, but anyhow I'd a rare do choking him off."

"I see. Did he say anything more?"

"Only that the lady might be calling herself something different. Ever such a nice voice he had, but—well, after what you told me I never mentioned a word of it to Her."

"Quite correct, Badger. I don't want Mrs. Greentree upset."

Now the move had been made he saw more vividly his own precarious position. He was treading in the dark, perilously close to a live rail; and yet—

"Only terror," he reflected, "could have driven that girl from under her husband's roof. Let that justify what I'm doing—and the rest can go to hell!"

The Royal Institute Hall promised to be crowded out. It always was when Guthrie Brodmart, M.D., F.R.C.P., gave one of his infrequent addresses. Tonight's paper dealt with recent progress in the diagnosis and treatment of disorders arising out of the central nervous system—a timely topic which the speaker, considering his standing and royal patronage should know something about. Not often did invitation cards append the warning: *Doors will be closed promptly at eight-thirty, after which there will be no admittance*. It hinted that Guthrie Brodmart, in his own estimation at least, was too important a personage to be annoyed by late-comers.

In the ante-room Colin kept watch on the steady stream of doctors, young and old, shabby and prosperous, who pressed towards the entrance. Some had wives with them; all seemed too anxious for seats to exchange more than a bare greeting. Presently a rich burr smote his ear. His shoulder was seized in a punishing grasp, and turning he beheld Angus MacConochie, sparse red hairs on end, face fiery from bad shaving and diabolic good-humour.

"Weel, now, Ladbroke! Paying homage to the big wigs, is it? I trust ye'll not be above keeping company with a Sans Culotte like meself."

It was a lusty shout. Colin, as he responded, saw disapproving glances directed at the broad ploughman's back over which villainously-cheap broadcloth strained at imminent peril of splitting; but here and there he read a subcurrent of envy.

"Come along, then," roared the nerve-specialist cheerfully. "We can't have yon door shutting in our faces."

Elbow gripped, Colin found himself thrust into the fore ranks of the procession.

Seated, MacConochie expanded, as for enjoyment, and one of his dull black studs burst with a little *plop* from its frayed buttonhole, allowing a side-view of hairy chest where his shirt-front—pockmarked and grey from inferior laundering—buckled outward. He paraded his watch.

"Eight-thir-rty. Aye! And what's gone wrong with our speaker?"

There followed, indeed, a tiresome delay, during which shoptalk continued its polite buzz but boredom was beginning to seep through dutiful respect. Almost a quarter of an hour had dragged by when a slight, immaculate figure appeared on the platform and tumultous applause accompanied its progress to the high-backed throne next to the chairman.

Brodmart made benign acknowledgment. In the hush that followed robust scorn rumbled audibly at Colin's side.

"Why not kiss his hand and have done wi' it? Will ye speir yon wee cock, strutting and swelling! Och, weel, he'll be crowing noo—showing the likes of us puir bir-rds just how 'tis done."

The chairman had risen and was pausing for complete silence. His remarks, a thought more fulsome than was customary on these occasions, were suitably brief, and now Guthrie Brodmart stood forward, gathered eyes, and began to read.

Chapter Twenty-One
THE GLIMMER

IT WAS a neat, scholarly paper whose somewhat general character and scarcely-technical wording drew rasping comment from Colin's companion.

"Stepping doon to us, ye see. And what sort of audience does he take us for—secondary pupils, requiring instr-ruction in common hygiene?"

Undoubtedly it went down well. Heads nodded in confirmation, flattering titters and even joyous guffaws greeted occasional sallies of a wit academic but able; but none of this interested Colin half so much as the man himself. Suave, incisive, self-assured and at moments scintillating—yet how altered! In a purely physical sense, that is. The leaden tint of his skin as the footlights beat pitilessly upon it—the fine, crisscrossed wrinkles—the facial muscles playing unseemly tricks. . . .

"Bad!" The rival specialist wagged an enormous head. "Mark my words, Ladbroke, yon chappie's riding for a fall."

Towards the end eyes a little too bright were losing their lustre. Gestures grew jerky, a nerve on the temple twitched under its dry sheath. Released from the strain, the lecturer seemed hardly able to bear the press of congratulations. He disposed of his admirers almost querulously and bolted from their midst.

Outside in the street a chauffeur was holding open the door of a shining black coupé. Colin saw Brodmart duck into it, the astrakhan facings of his coat-collar turned shelteringly high. There was a final glimpse of him, sunken in a corner with closed eyes and a look of drained lassitude. A corpse—only corpses don't twitch. . . .

"Aye, he's made it, but only just!" muttered MacConochie darkly. "Interesting. . . ." He watched the coupé drive off.

Colin said, "What about a drink at my place? My own bus is here, round the corner."

"Is it, noo? I'm not so wasteful of the petrol. Weel, a sma' drappie's wanted after the mush we've been swallowing. We'll have a crack by your fire."

In Colin's sitting-room MacConochie fulminated anew. New discoveries, whoosh! What was wrong with the man that he couldn't say right out that he wasn't on to anything fresh?

"Brodmart's no worse than the most of us. 'Tis a bad sign when a fellow like him starts high-hatting men of his own ilk, as he was doing this evening at dinner, just as if we were the ordinary fry. Means he's losing his grip and knows it. Aye, that's what it is."

"Would you still rank him at the top?"

Grimly MacConochie observed that a reputation once it was wound up kept going of its own momentum for a considerable time. However, his red-brown eye gleamed with a challenge, which Colin promptly took up.

"So you've been dining with Brodmart. At his home?"

"No, no, d'ye think he'll be wasting social favours on me? Restaurant in Piccadilly. Small dinner got up by our honourable chairman—five of us nerve-men passing compliments to one another, ye know the kind of thing. I was fir-rst to arrive, Brodmart came along on my heels never kenning I was aboot. And that," declared MacConochie, sprawling back in his chair, "is how I chanced to speir—weel, what I did speir."

"Such as—?"

"Mon, he was streecken!" The brawny Scot thumped his knee. "Shaking—drooling—tie under one ear. Oh, a sight to make you weep! Down he falls on a seat in the lobby, taking peeps at the swing-doors from behind a newspaper he can't hold steady. Jumps up, sinks down again, mops his face—me watching him, ye see?

"Weel, then, a pair-rson stops outside. Out pops Brodmart, like a Jack-in-the-box. Catches hold of the pair-rson, man or woman it might have been, I can't tell you that. Back he dives, alone, and straight into the gentleman's lavatory. Henderson turns up, then Barham, then the chairman. We're waiting for our Martinis when Brodmart joins us. And the transformation!"

"How do you mean?" demanded Colin, chained.

"Not the same mon," declared MacConochie with emphasis. "Spick and span, all pulled together, at the top of his form—in the space of five, or at the most we'll say seven, minutes."

The speaker stared meaningly into the other man's eyes, then gulped his whisky with malicious zest.

"I see. So that's your idea, is it?"

"And what might your own be? The colour of him—!"

"It's some time since I'd seen Brodmart. I must say his appearance gave me rather a shock."

"Soft, puckered skin, dry as a snake—nerves jumping all over the place. . . . Didn't you see for yourself he can't harness himself for any stretch of time? Mark you, I've had my suspeecions this twelvemonth and more. To-night's business confir-rms 'em."

"The old story, I expect." Colin spoke with caution. "Overdriven, can't sleep, possibly a few domestic tangles—"

"Aye," wagged his guest portentously, "but it's my private opeenion there's more in it than that."

"More?"

"A vast deal more. Doctor Guthrie Brodmart's bitten off a bigger mouthful than he can chew, what with his town establishment in a vairy expensive quarter, two lads at Eton, wife that tricks herself out like a royal duchess *and* a thumping big country place which I'm told is grand, though I've not set eyes on it meself. Why has he turned his nose up at the knighthood that's been offered him? Only because he's set his cap for a peerage—and *that'll* cost him a big wallop!"

MacConochie muttered that he would not be standing in Brodmart's shoes, not for all the Birthday Honours the King could bestow. Brooding, he roused at Colin's next question.

"Morphia? No! It's cocaine. At the start careful doses, only vairy occasionally. Presently bigger ones—and so it goes on. One of these fine days he'll over-reach himself. They'll find him dead—yes, with creditors howling like wolves round the door."

"You didn't, I suppose, catch sight of this person Brodmart went out of the restaurant to meet?"

"No, no, male or female 'twas only a blur through the glass."

Meditating, Colin remarked that it was about the last thing he would have conceived.

"What I'm wondering is, just how far a habit of this kind would affect professional judgment. Could it, in your opinion, be responsible for a faulty diagnosis?"

A mountainous shrug. "Oh, no! You couldn't blame that on the drug."

Quick to note that MacConochie's manner implied a damning reservation, Colin refilled his glass and settled back in his own chair. He was thinking, he said enigmatically, of a patient who had just come under his eye.

"She is said to be suffering from multiple sclerosis—in the early stages, you understand. Strictly speaking I shouldn't be venturing to treat her at all, but there are circumstances—"

"Aye?" The specialist cocked an eye.

"Frankly," said Colin, "I am struck by what appear to be very glaring contradictions. It is in certain respects a very complicated case. If I might just outline it to you—?"

"And why not?" demanded MacConochie largely. "I'll be richt pleased to hear."

Soon the north-of-Tweed man, whom further whisky seemed only to render the more clear-headed, was asking pointed questions and weighing the answers with pursed lips. For a time guarded, he declared that he would obviously have to make a personal, possibly a prolonged, examination before committing himself; but on a few details he was dogmatic if not scathing, and at one moment he sprang out of his seat.

"Doctor," he roared. "The patient's being murdered! Have ye the least doobt?"

"Oddly enough," replied Colin, "a most definite doubt. Not only is there no visible motive, but I've good reason to believe—but wait, let me finish. . . ." At the close MacConochie was no longer listening. Risen again—though remembering to drain the final drop of his toddy—he was fidgeting up and down with a deeply corrugated brow. Presently he towered above the younger man, motioning him to silence.

"Say no more, Doctor. Just you slip the little lady along to my rooms—unoffeecially, see?—and I'll look her over. Ye say she's no money. Weel, then, there'll be no charge. It's entirely between friends." MacConochie waved a flail-like arm. "No need," he continued, "to ask who it is that's been butchering her case. We'll name no names, but just keep our little consultations strictly private."

It was what Colin had been angling for. He had guessed that MacConochie, niggling over pennies, might propose this generous act, and not wholly to score off a rival. His thanks were swept aside. Already the big man was thumbing through a pinched little diary and suggesting Saturday morning for the first appointment.

"Can't make it before. I'll be in Edinburgh, delivering two lectures. Saturday, twelve-fifteen exact. . . . Now, then!" He thumped Colin's white waistcoat. "Gang just as ye're ganging. Make sairtain aboot the thing ye've mentioned and mind ye bring me the report."

Though a fine rain was falling he declined with indignation Colin's offer to drive him home, considering it a braw nicht for a guid pair-r of legs. Off he set with great strides; and as he reached the far side of the square a long grey car which had been stationed a few doors away crawled tentatively after him. It looked very like the one that had been in an adjacent square the previous evening.

And supposing it was? It was a bit difficult to see just what Geoffrey Scarpath could accomplish by his spying.

"He might attempt to prove his wife is mentally incompetent, of course; but could he get away with it? Not much."

Again, the following afternoon, Colin saw the grey Chrysler. This time it appeared in Queen Anne's Street at the exact moment that Elizabeth was being conducted forth from the offices of a well-known Swedish manipulator. Fortunately Elizabeth took no notice of the car or its driver. She was too full of her new, panting excitement.

"Only one little go at me, and I've walked all this way without a single stumble! It can't be true. That is, I'm so terrified to believe."

Unaided she climbed into Colin's Austin. Colin, tucking the rug round her, said non-commitally that Svendsen was almost unique in his method and had certainly put right a number of obstinate cases. Out of the tail of his eye he watched the grey car slide forward, only to turn into Harley Street. Instantly he realised that there was one thing Scarpath could do, and that in all probability he was deserting his wife's trail to accomplish it now.

The moment Elizabeth was safely housed, Colin went back to Queen Anne Street for a private word with the Swede. As he had expected Svendsen had just received a telephone-call from Dr. Brodmart, who had issued a bald statement.

"I see. And what did you say to Brodmart?"

"That I knew my rights and my business." The manipulator eyed him steadily. "I reminded him that I did my six years' medical in Vienna before ever I took up my present line."

Aware of Svendsen's qualifications, Colin had known there could be no harm arising out of ignorance as had lately occurred when an osteopath had started mauling a knee-joint in reality tuberculous. He had guessed, too, that Svendsen, standing apart from the ordinary faculty, need not fear intimidation.

It was hard now to keep a tight rein on his own jubilance. He warned himself it was far too early to be sure, that he might yet be confronted by other symptoms. Still, whatever the future held, his patient was almost visibly putting on flesh, showing each day greater stamina and strength. Thus far, except for the weak knee, he had found nothing wrong with her. Even her hovering fear was fast disappearing. Svendsen had said she might begin walking a little after another treatment. She would have the nurse as a bodyguard. Round that quiet Bloomsbury Square. . . .

Perhaps it would be wise to have Bream keeping an eye on them. He would ring Bream now.

Bream, as it happened, rang him.

"Yes, Doctor, I thought you'd better know that Mr. Scarpath has taken to watching your flat as well as Miss Young's. He's done nothing else of the smallest interest to us."

"See here, Bream, were you following him last night shortly before seven-thirty?"

"Yes, along Piccadilly. I lost him, but only for about a couple of minutes. It was in a bad traffic jam. Where? Well, more or less opposite Gatti's restaurant."

Gatti's. . . . That was where the neurological brotherhood had dined. After a moment's reflection Colin spoke cautiously. When he had done a low whistle came over the wire.

"You'd like me to look into this matter?"

"Well, if it turned out to be true one theory might appear slightly less fantastic. But be damned careful, won't you? Between ourselves, Bream, we're treading on extremely rotten ice."

"H'm—yes. It might mean a freeze-out for you, Doctor?"

"Quite so, and in time to prevent any good being accomplished. I'm simply shutting my eyes to the personal danger, but it's there, and it'll affect others besides myself."

Once more Colin attempted to reason things out. A man—dared he say two men?—would not play a game of the kind he envisaged unless for substantial stakes. That being so they would not give up readily. No, they would make an organised effort to finish what they had begun.

Well, Brodmart, tipped off by Scarpath, had tried to put the fear of God into Svendsen; Scarpath himself was spying intermittently on certain persons' movements; but was this all? It seemed insufficient, if the stakes were really large. So possibly they weren't. Yet, to view matters from another angle, what had either of these men to fear? At most the showing up of an error in diagnosis. Damning, yes, but by no means criminal.

"If it had been any other disease but this!"

There was only Elizabeth's own word for what had been done to her by way of treatment. No exact information as to drugs or quantities, nothing at all which could not with authority be contradicted.

"And here's the other big crab: *Every* solitary symptom she's exhibited could have arisen from a different cause. I've seen it happen, oh, scores of times!"

The knee seemed the one feature about which certainty could be reached, though even here one dared not jump to an immediate conclusion. . . .

Elizabeth, no longer requiring Nurse Badger's arm, rounded the corner of Mecklenburgh Square.

Her small excursions had been extended till now, on Friday afternoon, she had actually been as far as Oxford Street and back. Crowds, buses, shop-windows enchanted her. Walking again! And no word, oddly enough, from Geoffrey. It would seem he didn't intend to interfere.

She was living solely in the moment, buoyed to the skies by delirious hope. Maybe after all some ghastly mistake had been made. She mustn't think of it too confidently, in case she got a horrible jolt. She'd think of David instead—David, who would be arriving back from Manchester this very evening.

He had been her idol for so long! She remembered the days when she, the shy little rich girl, had let him take splinters out of her feet and tell her what books to read. It was true Geoffrey had eclipsed him, as the dazzling full moon wipes out a remote star, but after the first cold shock back her thoughts had flown to David across the Atlantic. David, probably married to someone else by now. Only he hadn't been. Whatever happened, nothing could ever rob her of the bliss that had been hers when he burst, all shabby, brown and dynamic, into that drear Hampstead bedroom. . . .

Nurse Badger was looking back.

"What's wrong? Forgotten anything?"

"Well, just my *Evening Standard*. I did rather want to see if my horse had come in, but I can get a copy later on."

"Oh, get it now! There's a paper-shop, we just passed it. Here, give me the key, I'll go ahead."

"But the stairs, ducky!"

"Nonsense, didn't I manage them this morning without any help? Run along, you'll catch me up."

"Righty-ho, but take it easy."

Nurse Badger turned towards Guilford Street, and Elizabeth, still day-dreaming, embarked on the first flight. She was thinking that she mustn't kiss David again. Technically speaking she was still a married woman; and besides there was this cursed matter of her health. In fact, there were two gigantic problems to be solved before . . .

"And how do I know he isn't just sorry for me? He *used* to care. It doesn't mean he still does."

The top landing was dark. Head swimming a little from her climb, she groped for the light-button, and found her hand tightly pinioned.

Her first reaction was a shrinking terror, her second brought a glad cry. "David! It's you!"

No answer. The figure in the dusk began to take shape as a faint odour warned her sickeningly of her blunder.

"Geoffrey!" she mouthed, and all the blood in her body stopped circulating.

CHAPTER TWENTY-TWO
TOUCH AND GO

SHE thought, *"I won't faint! I mustn't. This was bound to come. Get rid of him, that's all."*

Quietly, with reassurance, he was speaking to her.

"I've had the devil's own time finding you, Elizabeth. Can't we go inside and talk this over?"

Voiceless, she shook her head and planted herself desperately against Alison's door. Geoffrey did not insist. She could see him now, almost clearly. Was it fancy that he looked drawn, altered, less glacial?

"Please go," she managed between parched lips. "I—there's a nurse with me, you know."

"I saw her. All the same, my dear, this situation has to be discussed. I can't expect reasonable behaviour from you in your present state—and I'm quite prepared to shoulder most of the blame. Still—well, you are my responsibility, Elizabeth, and, as it happens I care for you rather deeply."

"You—!" She stared at him, utterly incredulous. "Don't make me laugh, Geoffrey. Just—just go away."

She felt his eyes on her.

"You don't believe me?" He shrugged. "Not surprising, I'll admit. You have made it a little difficult for me, haven't you?"

The irony of this left her speechless again. As for the first time she found herself noting his easy, well-pitched voice, his fastidious Oxford accent. Just as though he handled every syllable with sugar-tongs, wearing—no, not kid gloves, but a very smart, clean buckskin pair. . . .

"No fault of yours, I dare say, if you began holding me off rather a long time ago; and not wholly mine, perhaps, to be unduly sensitive about—

atmospheres. I suggest we call quits. After all, whether you realise it or not, I *am* the same man you married."

"Oh, I know!" cried Elizabeth sincerely. "Exactly the same. Geoffrey, I've always wanted to ask: Why did you marry me? Don't bother about my feelings, you can't hurt me any more. Just tell me, Why?"

"God knows!"

He had brought it out with such bitter honesty that she felt some of her former respect for him return. Now, now, he was taking off those gloves!

But was he? His next words made her wonder. "Ask any married man that question. If he's frank, he'll give you the same answer." He drew in a long breath. "Attraction," he said, "isn't a thing one can analyse."

"Did I really attract you, Geoffrey?"

"You can't doubt that, I think. Why else—?"

Yes, this was so. Her old puzzled feeling came back. Her husband continued with effort:

"You still attract me, Elizabeth. Very much so, I'm afraid. It's this illness of yours—a cursed business! Never mind, let's forget it. We were getting you cured. The rest, I believe, would have righted itself. Now, of course, when I find you removing yourself from serious medical attention and messing about with God knows what manner of quacks, I'm bound to protest. Would you expect less of me?"

She edged from him. Oh, what was keeping Nurse Badger? It was her first unguarded moment, and Geoffrey had found it. . . .

Uneasily she muttered, "But I wasn't getting cured. Now I am, you see. I—I can only suppose Dr. Brodmart has been making a mistake."

"Brodmart?" He laughed. "Don't be childish, my dear. A man of his calibre, whose text-books on the central nervous system are—"

"What do I care about his text-books? I've never liked him—no, never!"

"Oh, I see!" Geoffrey lifted his arms, let them fall to his sides—the old, familiar gesture of scorn. "He's honest, of course. He doesn't pay many compliments. I gave you credit for more intelligence. Naturally I wanted you to have the best. Is it the drastic measures you complain of? They were necessary for a time, but that phase, thank God, is over."

In the dusk she turned startled eyes on him. "You mean I wasn't to have any more of those horrible treatments?"

"Not if you took reasonable care." Suddenly he hurled at her impatiently, "Don't be a little ass, Elizabeth! Surely you've grasped the fact that all this wonderful improvement is due simply and solely to that last rather shattering dose?"

She gasped. Such a thing had not once occurred to her. Geoffrey must believe it, she thought, or he wouldn't have lost his temper like this. It was the old, flashing irritability she understood so much better than she did his conciliations. Shaken, she gathered together her defences.

"And if it is so, Geoffrey? I still won't come back to you—if that's what you expect. I'm *free*—free! Can't you see the difference that makes in my getting well again?"

He too had collected himself. "Of course," he said reasonably, "I've no intention of hampering your liberty. Very soon now you'll be able to enjoy life in your own way. I was looking forward to a few theatres, to having you meet my own circle here in London; only, as Brodmart says, it won't do to rush things. This is a critical juncture. If you start overdoing it now and getting excited, well, don't be surprised if you land back in a rather more trying state than before."

She had begun to tremble. Flattened against the door she hardly took in his next speech till the words *"flat"* and *"Mayfair"* captured her attention. Tardily she realised that the awful house was a thing of the past.

"But Mayfair, Geoffrey! How can you possibly afford—"

"Haven't I generally been lucky?" He smiled. "This flat's been lent me for six months. There it is, with a lift, all waiting for you to walk into it. We'll have a nurse at first—this one, if she suits you. Evie, you see, is back in Hampshire."

"Evie—?" She tried to beat her way through the confusion.

"Cracked up. Finding you gone was rather a shock."

Poor Evie! "I never thought—" Elizabeth swallowed. "And—and the doctor?"

Geoffrey explained that Dr. Brodmart had very naturally been annoyed, but that he had agreed in the interests of the case to set his personal feelings aside.

"You didn't think, either, about the terrific risk you ran of getting pneumonia? Still, Brodmart sees, as I do, that you'd hardly have done this insane thing on your own initiative. In short," said Geoffrey dryly, "that your American friends are well-meaning but rather misguided. Here's another aspect:—You can't very well think of saddling yourself indefinitely on a woman who has her living to earn and only this limited space to share?"

She muttered swiftly, "Oh, I can't! Only—"

"There, don't upset yourself. Let me talk with this Miss Young. I'm positive she'll take the sensible view. She can fetch you along this evening and see you comfortably settled in your new quarters, which I'm bound to say are extremely pleasant."

"No!" She fended him off. "Not that. Whatever you say, I'm not coming back. Could you send me some clothes?"

"I see." There was a subtle alteration in his tone.

"Then the real obstacle, I take it, is this man Beddoes."

"I've not seen him," she denied hurriedly. "He's not here."

"But he will be." Geoffrey's lips took a contemptuous curve. "Well! And may one inquire what you and he propose doing? Because you are still married to me, you know."

Hotly she cried, "But you can't want to hang on to me, Geoffrey! You wouldn't. Would you?"

"I've no wish to divorce you," he said clearly. "And I may add you can't divorce me."

"Oh, can't I? I'm American. There's always Reno if—if I can't manage it here."

She had a fleeting consciousness of having scored—yes, despite scant knowledge on her part, despite the fact that till this moment Reno had never entered her head.

"Oh?" His manner became uncannily detached. "And Beddoes, I suppose, will provide the funds. . . . Yes. I would then enter counter proceedings. You realise what that would mean?"

Steps on the stairs. Were they turning into the lower flat?

"If you don't," said Geoffrey evenly, "perhaps Beddoes will enlighten you. Think it over. In the meantime, here's my new address."

The nurse was puffing up the last flight. Geoffrey pushed a card into Elizabeth's hand, turned, and ran down.

Badger peered curiously. "What, still out here in the dark? Oh, dear!" It was a smothered cry as her patient slumped at her feet, a small, shuddering form.

In another minute Elizabeth lay on the Chesterfield, bright lights weaving a haze, Badger busy with smelling-salts, excuses, questions.

"Who was it, duck? Did he give you a turn? What about a wee drop of brandy?"

"Just a—a man. Wrong flat. I—I guess I'm not quite so strong as I thought I was. Let's have our tea."

Left alone, Elizabeth found her heart pounding to suffocation. She had crumpled again—as though to prove Geoffrey the oracle he always had been. One moment laughing at her own fears, the next—

"Stupid fool! What can he *do*?"

That, she knew, wasn't the point. It was his *sureness* that had the inevitable effect of shrivelling all her confidence. Was her foolhardiness racing her pell-mell into disaster?

Reaching the new copy of *Vogue* she made a test of her eyes. To her exquisite relief the print was still decipherable. Her hand, too, was functioning quite ably; so just possibly that tumble on the landing meant only panic. She looked about her. Security—warm fire—David coming to-night. . . .

David! The dam broke. Weakly, miserably, she began to cry.

Once again she was seeing herself with her husband's uncompromising vision. She was a deluded little fool, placing her trust in a young doctor who, however kind, admitted having no first-hand experience of her ailment. She had rushed far in advance of even his encouragement, leapt headlong to conclusions perhaps utterly false. Suppose it was true her recovery was the outcome of Dr. Brodmart's treatment? How was she to know?

Tea steadied her. She had dried her eyes and recklessly dabbed on powder before Alison arrived with Colin Ladbroke in tow; but neither of them was fooled.

"Overdoing it a bit?"

Overdoing it! Geoffrey's own words. The nurse was signalling from the doorway. Colin motioned her out, sat down by the sofa and asked, "Well, what was it?"

"Geoffrey." Her voice shook. "Out there, waiting—in the dark. Oh, don't blame Nurse Badger, please! She got hung up in the paper-shop and—"

"I'll settle with her," ground the doctor, while Alison looked stern and dismayed. "Well, what did your husband say?"

Omitting only the bit about the divorce she repeated the conversation. Tenseness came over both her listeners. After a dead silence Alison stole into her bedroom. Elizabeth struggled on.

"He—he gives Dr. Brodmart entire credit for my—my being as I am now. He says if I'm not terribly careful I'll—" The sentence dried up. Gripping Colin's hand convulsively Elizabeth whispered, "Is it true? Will I get like that again, lame, half-blind, all the rest of it?"

Her eyes supplicated him. Colin saw, or thought he saw, with pitiless clarity what had been happening; but how to answer her?

"In my belief, no." He spoke slowly. "I've told you—haven't I?—it will want more time before we can decide absolutely. Let's waive matters till to-morrow, after the other specialist has seen you. Shall we?"

She had seen him battling for a reply.

Head bowed, she said, "About this flat Geoffrey's taken for me. I can't possibly go on staying here, that's understood. I think maybe I ought to make up my mind before—before David comes. You see?"

Thus far Colin had spoken no derogatory word of the Brodmart regime. It would be unwise, very likely slanderous, to utter that word now. Leaning forward he took both her hands firmly in his.

"Tell me this one thing: Do you want to go back to your husband?"

Her head dropped lower. Tears spilled on his knuckles.

"Quite! Now I'm going to mix you a cocktail—and if I hear any more of this nonsense, I'll throw up the case."

When he had handed her the drink she sent him her small-girl smile, chastened but not wholly conquered. Taking a second glass into the bedroom he closed the door and spoke briefly, to the point.

"You see, Alison? Scarpath, damn him, has overthrown all our good work. As she is now it's touch and go whether she goes back to him."

Alison turned from the open wardrobe where she was inspecting her dresses.

"If she does—?"

"Yes. Well, in that event, I should doubt very seriously if we ever set eyes on her again."

Their eyes met. Alison grew cold down her backbone.

"Colin, what can I do? I'm fond of the child. She must realise it's been a joy having her with me. Is she still in love with him then?"

"God, no! Don't you grasp it? Scarpath can and does make assertions not one of us can possibly refute. Later, perhaps, but not now. It's the cursed time-element—as he thoroughly appreciates. It gives him a strong hand."

For what? She wanted to ask, but as she hesitated Colin came closer to her and whispered, "Badger, just now. How can we know Scarpath hasn't got hold of her? We can never be sure."

"Couldn't we tell her the truth? No, I suppose you daren't risk it. I must say it was funny leaving Elizabeth alone all that time."

"Darned funny!" His eye lit dangerously. "She's worked with me before. I'd have sworn she was straight, but—and yet if I change nurses now shall I draw a safer one?"

One of those annoying little pangs shot through Alison. Never before had she known Colin Ladbroke so deeply stirred. She felt he was counting on her, that she mustn't fail him.

"Don't worry," she comforted, and as she spoke she selected a blue, patterned chiffon and detached it from its hanger. "Yes, with a few pins this ought to do. . . . Listen, Colin: There may be just one person who can tip the scales against Geoffrey Scarpath. Thank goodness he'll be with us this evening."

"David? Yes, let's hope you're right. We'll leave matters to him."

Chapter Twenty-Three
DAVID WINS

At ten-thirty David burst in. Riding roughshod over Alison he stood with dropped jaw.

"Gosh! And I thought you were kidding me." Elizabeth's cheeks were wild roses. Her eyes exactly matched the cornflowers of the last summer's frock Alison had managed to put on her, and while she was still only a wisp there was already a hint of rounded contour visible beneath the fluttering chiffon.

"Kidding? Just you give me another week of Alison's good food. I'll burst all her seams."

He had been holding her hand in a vice-grip. His gaze, dark and brilliant, devoured her, but for that matter Colin's had been doing much the same for the past two hours.

Elizabeth grew self-conscious. With slight primness she pulled away. Colin, as though a spell had broken, said good-night in the passage, adding, "Pack her off in half an hour. Tell your cousin to come round to me."

"Wasn't I right?" Alison challenged. "About David, I mean."

Moodily he shook his head. "That girl's a Puritan. Don't you see it's exactly on account of David she may rush back to her hearth and home?"

"Oh! So you think Scarpath may have said something about David and that she doesn't want us to know?"

"I'm sure of it. Whatever it was, it shocked her worse than all the rest. Oh, we won't get it out of her, but just let her get one small attack of conscience and she'll wreck every chance. And that," Colin muttered grimly, "is what it means to be a free agent!"

"I'd better warn David." Worried, she went back.

There was, she decided, no immediate danger of her cousin's getting out of hand. At one end of the hearthrug David squatted on his thick suitcase, merely feasting his eyes on Elizabeth who, with her ankles modestly veiled, occupied the distant corner of the sofa. Up he sprang, made a lunge for the whisky set out for him, and burst into song.

"Oh, the world owes me a living . . ."

In his ardour he deluged Alison with the siphon, treating her to a rub-down with a rather grimy handkerchief. He then took a pull at his drink, smacked his lips and indulged in a little shadow-sparring. Letting off steam. It was a pity to puncture such complaisance. Clearly, though, David ought to be told.

"Betsy, does he know?"

"Know?" David wheeled. "Know what?"

Scarlet, Elizabeth twisted the thin platinum band which had been missing from her finger since the night of her arrival. That it was back again, along with a big square sapphire hitherto kept on the dressing-table, struck an ominous note.

"You tell him," said Alison, and disappeared into her room. Perhaps in her absence Elizabeth might bestow a fuller confidence. She would know then how to deal with things.

Her forecast was wrong. How, thought Elizabeth, could she mention her horrible blunder about Reno? She'd rather die than have David realise . . .

"Found you!" With hardened jaw David sat down on the Chesterfield. "How the hell . . . never mind, let's hear about it."

He listened, black-browed, to the halting recital. "Here! Is that the lot?"

"Yes, David. Oh, don't glare at me like that! He was awfully reasonable, you know. I—I began to think what a fool I must have been, running away like that for no real excuse, forcing myself on Alison when my proper place was—was with my husband."

"Husband! That swine?"

"Oh, not a swine, David! I may not love Geoffrey, but—"

"You're scared blue of him. Look at me and deny it."

"Was I? Remember, I never said . . . David, I told you at first that Geoffrey was doing all he could for me—all any one could. You must see he's the only person who has the right to—to keep me. Here I am, not a penny to bless myself with—"

"So that's it! Well, you listen to your uncle." He clamped tight hold of her hands, just as he had done that grey morning in Hampstead. "I've got a nice wad of cash by me—no, sit still!—and seeing it's a matter of—" he gulped down the obvious words—"of your entire future happiness, well, it's yours, that's all."

"Me take your money? Don't be silly." Her lips set in a stubborn line.
"But a loan, girl, a loan!"

She laughed bleakly. David grew irritable.

"Look here; if you weren't scared, what made you break loose?"

"How do I know?" She screwed a button on his sleeve. "Listen, David,
Geoffrey can't possibly mean me any harm. What would he get by it? It's
for my sake he's moved into this nice flat. He even means me to have a
nurse and—"

"What made you break loose?"

Goaded, she burst out, "Because I didn't dare take any more of that
medicine! Last week I came so near dying I thought . . . but the bad treatment's finished now. I didn't die, did I? On the contrary I got better, much
better. So how can I say the stuff they gave me wasn't right?"

Checkmated by her argument he got up, took a turn about the room.
Coming back he stood over her.

"You've answered my question, anyhow. You loathe this man like
poison. Well, you're not going within range of him again. If you refuse
to take help from me—Stop! Is that the ring you spoke about selling?"

"Take it." She slipped the big sapphire into his hand. "It's quite valuable, you know. I always knew Fanny couldn't afford to give it to me. Don't
you think it might raise just enough to see me through a few months?"

"Certainly, if you don't hate parting with it. Meanwhile, though, how
about five pounds advance?"

"David, put that wallet away! I—I might let you lend me five shillings."

Disgustedly he handed her two half-crowns. She treasured them
humbly.

"This will do beautifully till you sell the ring. Will you be back again
next week-end?"

He roused. "Gosh, no, haven't I said? My next job is here, just out
of London—a rubber-band factory, family-owned, going to pot. You'll
be sick of the sight of me. I'm hunting a room close by, and I'll be here
every evening, if Alison doesn't shove me out."

"Oh, David, what fun!"

She hoped she wasn't looking too deliriously glad. Funny! With David
here those moments with Geoffrey seemed only another bad dream.

Mortimer Bream was waiting at Colin Ladbroke's flat.

"I suppose," he said tentatively, "you still haven't any news of Mrs.
Scarpath's aunt?"

"Not a whisper. The woman may be dead."

"And her money?"

"Mrs. Scarpath has always understood that the little her aunt could leave was earmarked for some exploration fund. That seems to be the impression among Mrs. Rush's friends, though her lawyer in New York has never executed any will, and has no information on the matter. See here, is it a fact Scarpath has settled into this South Street apartment?"

"Just as I wrote you," said the detective. "He's engaged two servants, and his sister is off the map. There's nothing fresh to report, except that I have managed to scrape acquaintance with Dr. Brodmart's chauffeur and learned two small and possibly worthless items. The first is that Dr. Brodmart attended Admiral Scarpath in his last illness. So he has been known to the son for some years."

"How did the admiral die?" demanded David. "Not that it's important, I suppose, if he left only debts."

"The trouble seems to have been mental," declared Bream with a cough, "and in consequence very carefully hushed up. To be sure the admiral was eighty and due for a break-up."

David weighed this and shrugged. "And the other item?"

"Well—" Bream glanced sideways at their host. "Dr. Brodmart has been plunging rather heavily on the stock market. The chauffeur believes he was badly hit by the de Larch crash, and that this may be what is affecting his health and his temper. At any rate the doctor appears to be suffering from heart-attacks, the last occasion being Monday at about eight p.m., when he had an alarming collapse in his consulting-rooms. He refused to allow one of the other physicians in the building to be called, simply lay on a couch, looking like death. Mr. Scarpath happened to drop in. Ten minutes later Brodmart came out entirely himself and got into his car. Matheson says he has lately been subject to these astonishing ups and downs, and that you can usually tell when an attack is coming on. He gets extremely strung-up and peevish."

David jerked an exasperated hand. "All very well, Bream, but where the hell is it getting us?"

"I know, Mr. Beddoes. With the main line of inquiry I've had not the smallest success. If there's a woman in the case I've seen no sign of her. In fact, now Mrs. Scarpath is safely under your cousin's protection, don't you feel I am merely wasting your money?"

Colin interposed quietly. "Suppose you repeat what you saw last night up at the Hampstead house."

"Last night?" David's eyes lit.

"Yes, that. Sorry, I'd forgotten. Well, then, I followed Mr. Scarpath back to Summit View at something past midnight. Directly he'd disappeared into the house there came a most blood-curdling screech. A moment later Mr. Scarpath emerged with a parcel about a foot long, and this he carried round to the rear. It was the body of a green parrot. I dug it out of the dustbin at two this morning. Its neck had been wrung."

David felt slightly sick.

Tormented, he sprang up, crossed to the window, and pushing back the curtains stared unseeingly out into Gordon Square. Bream had spoken to him twice before he took in the question.

"Call this off? No! At least—" David considered with knit brows. "Well, take a vacation till this other nerve-specialist has seen Mrs. Scarpath. If anything criminal's afoot, I dare say he'll be able to spot it. Afterwards, we'll see."

When Bream had gone Colin asked, "And now, how did she strike you?"

David's gloom vanished. "How! Ladbroke, all I can say is that somehow or other you've worked a miracle. Why—"

Colin shook his head. "I've done next to nothing, old man. In my opinion it's just that she's been given a chance. I want to believe that, anyhow," he muttered.

"Oh, I understand," said David quickly. "I'm not trying to pin you down as to whether or not she's really got this disease. Let your specialist fellow do that." He turned towards the door.

"Stop, what's the rush?"

"Only to get myself a room before these hotels close up."

"Don't bother. You can doss down here, if you don't mind a little discomfort, and frankly I'd like to have you at close range during the coming week."

"It's darned decent of you." Gratefully David sank down by the fire. "By the way, was it your idea making these inquiries about Brodmart?"

"It was." Hesitatingly Colin reloaded his pipe. "I must tell you my private hunch depends very largely on the belief of a highly-prejudiced rival—yes, Angus MacConochie, who is undoubtedly itching to oust Brodmart from his tinpot pedestal. Even if it should prove correct it may not touch any vital issue."

"What is your hunch?"

"Wait. When you last saw Mrs. Rush was she in fairly sound health?"

"Cast-iron. She looked good for another thirty years of globe-trotting. Say, what's the idea?"

"Full of energy, was she?"

"Fanny Rush? If she had to sit still five minutes she'd burst a blood-vessel. I never saw her try."

"I see."

David glanced sharply at his companion, but Colin let the subject drop. "Yes . . . well, about Brodmart. . . ."

CHAPTER TWENTY-FOUR
SOFT NEST

A LONG boat-train was snaking into Victoria Station. The lone occupant of a first-class carriage, already on her feet, cleared a peep-hole on the misted pane, twitched manfully at her somewhat cavalier hat, and tapped with impatience.

Gaunt and purposeful, in her late fifties, she had the sort of handsomeness which, though ravaged by hot suns, ocean gales and a lifelong disregard of facial remedies, still manages to survive. Her piercing eyes, arched nostrils and defiant chin put one in mind of an exceedingly wild hawk.

"Should have come by air," she muttered. "Didn't like turning up pea-green and limp when I've so much to tackle. Besides, an old woman's bad enough, but a frowsy one—"

Was she frowsy? Anxiously she peered into the mirror, thrusting a stray wisp under her hairnet. Just in time, for doors were banging back to reveal a sea of strange faces.

"Porter! All those."

She waved towards the collection of canvas-covered bags and turned her back. It was an aggressive back, softened now by the slightly out-of-date Persian lamb coat dangling loose on it; and for the moment her eyes had lost some of their fierceness and become incongruously wistful as they searched the crowd and found no welcoming response. She told herself she ought to have wired again from Paris; that even Geoffrey could hardly be expected to meet every boat-train. Still, her weather-beaten face fell noticeably as she strode towards the customs' benches, where under the R's her single steamer-trunk was being dumped.

"Fanny!"

She spun round, saved by a shepherding arm from a barrow of luggage. There, smiling down on her—yes, down, for all her five foot nine inches—was her nephew, as frostily clean-cut as she remembered him.

Relief swept over her. Only a mind innately suspicious of the opposite sex could have harboured those recent doubts.

"Well, Geoffrey, here I am."

Her gaunt cheek tingled. She had never grown used to being kissed. To cover her awkwardness she gave his arm a rough squeeze, and, submitting to the protection she would have brooked from no other man, she proceeded to make her usual short work of the customs.

"Nothing," she snapped.

The officer took one look at her and chalked a discharge. She was heading for a taxi when Geoffrey steered her instead to a shining grey car.

"Oh! Yours, is it?"

"Yes, thanks to you. And now—?"

"Savoy. Well, why not?"

"I was wondering," said Scarpath diffidently, "if I couldn't put you up. I'd like to, you know."

Warily she answered, "I don't want to intrude." What she really meant was that she preferred the freedom of a hotel.

"I'm all alone, as it happens." Sweeping deftly into the Buckingham Palace Road he took no heed of his companion's swiftly-turned head. "Suppose I just show you my place? That is, if you're not too tired."

"Tired? Bah! It's only eleven, and I snatched forty winks on the boat—mostly upside down, I'll admit. Where is this place of yours? Mind, I don't promise to stay."

He smiled, circling the palace and shooting up into St. James's. Then his face grew grave.

"By the way, Fanny, what brought you here?"

She cocked a droll eye. "Grouse. Isn't it the season?"

He chuckled, questioning her no more. She on her side remarked that London looked much the same dismal, badly-run city she had always detested, and held her peace till they had stopped on the far side of Piccadilly and Shepherd's Market. Fanny got out, too late realising she was being assisted. She cast an eye about her, grunted, "Hum, Mayfair," her tone that of grudging approval, and tramped into a small, lighted lobby.

Geoffrey, she thought, must be managing quite ably on the allowance she had contrived should come to him without his wife's knowledge. She had known he could be trusted to install Elizabeth in suitable surroundings, that the dreary, insanitary house she had heard about was all wicked fiction.

"Elevator, I see. Does it work?"

Once, for three hours of hell, she had been trapped in one of these minute, amateurish bronze cages. The memory had formed the basis of nightmares ever since. However, no accident occurred, and now, holding open the door—how fine his head was, etched against the ivory wall!— Geoffrey was ushering her into an interior softly carpeted, really warm for England, and aglow with discreet lamps.

A large, yes, a handsome room! Fanny fumbled for an eyeglass suspended on a black ribbon.

"Well?" Geoffrey was removing her fur coat.

"Very nice," she said gruffly. "Adam mantelpiece. Genuine? Looks like it. Don't care for the pictures, but I dare say they're good. I'm glad you don't go in for modern furniture."

The sofa, with upcurved ends, would be English Empire. Faded mulberry and ash-green—excellent combination. Log fire—Elizabeth's books and a brocaded bag of some needlework she must have been attempting—flowers. . . .

She herself rarely if ever bought flowers. In the abstract she scorned the type of man who for his own pleasure chose and arranged arum lilies and misty gyphsophila with such skilful taste; and yet, by a paradox born possibly of her own masculine bent, she made an exception of Geoffrey. In her eyes whatever he did was bound to be right.

"Humph!" said her glance. *"The girl hasn't much to grumble about, that's certain."*

Her brain boiled with questions. Ought she to begin on them now? She had noted the little lace-covered table drawn close to the fire. On it Geoffrey, after a brief disappearance, was depositing a silver basin. As he lifted the lid she sniffed, and her hawk-eye lit.

"Oyster-stew? So you remembered."

"Eat first," he commanded. "You must be starving. Afterwards—well, we can talk."

He had even procured the right crackers. Down she plumped in a petit point chair, crumbled a handful into the hot, creamy mixture, and fell to with appreciation.

Geoffrey was untwisting the gold foil from a bottle of her favourite Pommery—indeed, the one brand of champagne she would touch. She observed how he splashed a little into his own glass before filling hers to the brim, and reflected that wretchedly few of her own countrymen had ever heard of this courtesy. Grimly she wondered if Betsy, tiresome child, realised what she had got.

"Well, Fanny dear?"

His glass grazed hers. Above the two rims there was a quiet, intimate communion of eyes which sent a thrill along Fanny's battle-scarred veins.

"Well!" She sighed and sipped her champagne. "Yes, it's pleasant to see you again, Geoffrey. But now"—her backbone stiffened—"where's your wife?"

He set down his glass. "It's a longish story."

His contours had sharpened. Not, she thought, to disadvantage, though she mistrusted the new bitterness of his eyes and the effort it was evidently costing him to speak. He was so intensely reserved. It was one of the things she most admired in him.

"Long or short," she encouraged, "let's get on with it," and waited, for still he was sitting there, gravely silent, gazing on the fire.

Suddenly frank he leant forward. "Fanny," he said, "if I believed in such nonsense, well, I'd call your coming here now a—an answer to prayer. Haven't I always said you and I didn't need to send cables?"

"Tchah!" Red like dregs of old claret crept into her weathered old cheeks. He was handing her a dish.

"What's this? I can't touch anything more, I—" It was cold grouse, delicately garnished. "Oh! Well, I can hardly refuse that, can I?"

Again their eyes met.

"Just another proof," he said lightly, "of our mutual mind-reading."

She attacked the plump bird, using her fingers on the leg with the unselfconsciousness of a duchess; and all the while, his face in shadow, he studied her, weighing every blunt gesture, the anxiety quivering beneath the surface of her strong, tanned features, her defiant grimace when his examination grew too acute, her pleasure in his notice. When she pushed back her plate and took a cigarette from the crystal box at her elbow he was ready, gold Dunhill aflame.

"Coffee?"

"No! No coffee."

He did not insist. Flinging aside the cushion placed at her back, she stuck her old, expensively-cut brogues out towards the fire, took a few jerky puffs, and set her jaw.

"What," she demanded, "do you know of an American named Beddoes?"

Scarpath glanced at her, then away. "Very little." He spoke without emphasis. "I have met the man, but only once." Pausing, he added, "Elizabeth has mentioned him fairly often."

"Oh, has she!" Fanny also paused, to ask tentatively, "Well, and would you call him a gentleman?"

Very faintly Scarpath shrugged. "It's so hard to know, isn't it? With Americans, I mean. Educated, I should say."

Fanny Rush reddened uncomfortably. "I see, a person. Yes. Well, this person, of whom I've no recollection whatsoever, has had the gross impertinence to cable me—and to write. I won't say his communications have had anything to do with my return. Actually I was already on my way back when I picked them up in Singapore. Was it wise, though, to keep me in total ignorance of—of certain matters?"

"Was it? I wonder. I think"—quietly—"you'll have appreciated my reason."

Furtive but grateful she flashed him an eye. "Yes, yes, we know all about that! Here's the cablegram." She fished it from her bag. "Says nothing, you see."

"Quite." He glanced at the brief form. "I suppose," he ventured, "you wouldn't care to show me the letter as well?"

"Torn up. Now and then," explained Elizabeth's aunt simply, "I give way to an impulse of that sort. The contents so enraged me. . . . Never mind, I can give you the gist. Did I know my niece was seriously ill? That she was penned up, yes, practically a prisoner in some beastly, dilapidated old barn on the outskirts of London, cut off from the world and desperately unhappy? Next—oh, better have the whole of it!—that in the writer's belief her case was being wilfully and cruelly misconstrued. That if she died it would be unpunishable murder. There! And now, what about this farrago of nonsense?"

Her challenge was less that of a woman old in disillusionment than a child's. It sought reassurance, and was confident of getting it. With all her fierceness Mrs. Rush looked for an instant amazingly like her young niece.

"Quite," said Scarpath again, and nodded with a ghost of cynicism. "I'm afraid none of this bowls me over, Fanny. Which broadside shall I handle first?"

"Betsy's health, of course. She *has* been sick?"

"Very; though she's now virtually recovered."

"What's wrong with her?"

"I'd prefer you heard all that from Guthrie Brodmart. You're familiar with his name, of course?"

"No, no, why should I be? Some specialist, I imagine."

"Rather a celebrated one. He made one mistake, I'll admit—the Hampstead house. Not that he or I could foresee the violent antipathy Elizabeth would conceive for it. Or," Scarpath added slowly, "for himself, which has proved still more unfortunate. Naturally she has been influenced—is being influenced now. I should have said, perhaps, that she is recovering in a *physical* sense—almost in spite of herself and her American friends, with whom she has elected to stay."

"Geoffrey, what are you trying to tell me?"

Scarpath drew a long breath.

"Suppose," he said, "we begin at the beginning . . ."

CHAPTER TWENTY-FIVE
BRAKES

BACK in Alison's dark living-room, David hovered for a moment above a small, peacefully-slumbering form.

Here—in safety. His hand itched to touch the little trim head nestling on the same pillow he had savaged through so many haunted nights, but an upsurge of tenderness forbade the risk. A-tingle from Elizabeth's nearness and his own exultant feeling of proprietary rights he picked up his bag and crept away, reaching the street just as a clock struck two.

"Mine," he told himself. "Always was, always will be—but even if I'm too optimistic, she's never going back to that cold-livered scoundrel."

Never more firmly than now had he believed in his lucky star. Hadn't it landed him a job older and more experienced men had been clamouring for? Not in Chicago, not in Mexico or Hong Kong, but here, in London, where it had steered him within three days to Elizabeth's own home. In addition it had introduced him to a decent medical man who shared his views as to her condition. Now it had provided him a whole week during which he could keep her under his own eye. He must remember these things and not lose faith if Elizabeth's divorce looked hard to nail down. Sooner or later Scarpath would be caught bending. Then—oh, boy!

No, there could be only one of two motives actuating Scarpath's conduct. If it didn't hinge on money, then it must involve a woman . . . unless it turned out to be some abnormal quirk in the man's nature which the law couldn't handle?

Somehow David felt it might be this. Although he furiously spurned the thought that Elizabeth could not secure legal freedom back it crept like a slimy toad. He remembered that while there had been no open act of cruelty, like wife-beating, the victim had screamed as in mortal terror, and even now began to sweat and shake at the mere mention of her husband's name. He thought of the emphasis she kept laying, as if to reassure herself, on Scarpath's anxiety to preserve her life. Wrongdoing there had been—who could deny it?—and yet from first to last there seemed nothing whatever to get a grip on. Some misshapen persecution, hinting at—madness?

No! Geoffrey Scarpath wasn't mad, he was sane. He knew to a cold certainty just what he was doing, if others didn't. Was his lying low now simply an additional sign of a deep, underground game? He'd been pretty successful as it was, working his plausible doubts into Elizabeth's mind.

"Oh, what the hell? We've got her, that's the answer. As far as more harm is concerned, his gun is spiked. I've talked sense into her, and to-morrow, when she's seen Ladbroke's pal, we may be able to settle the whole business."

He was striding through Bloomsbury's chain of squares, all empty at this hour and in the dank gloom as like as beads on a string. Only an occasional dim light showed in the boarding-houses that called themselves hotels, footfalls echoed from one square to the next, and the mangy enclosures, whose peeling plane-trees dripped moisture on the sodden mold beneath, looked eerily like graveyards. A region of the dead, with just a single survivor, tramping towards bed.

No, two survivors. The other was in a car.

A whale of a car, too, from the deep hum of the engine, which David now vaguely realised he had been hearing in his wake for some minutes—slowing tentatively at corners, spurting forward only to hesitate again. Now at last it seemed to mean business. Sure of its direction, probably. David had forgotten his fleeting interest when the dumbfounding thing happened.

It might have been the dull bump of the tyres against the kerb which prompted his backward glance. Perhaps it was the hot breath of the radiator, big and steely, as it bore down on him. Certainly all within him repudiated the notion that any driver in his wits could be steering bang out of a normal course to wreck himself on—

Christ! The black Juggernaut was upon him. No escape from the solid, grinding wheels supporting a two-ton weight—not a split second to vault the area-gate into which he was driven.

The gate yielded. David hurtled head foremost down stone steps while above him the monster car cut an arc, bumped back over the kerb and roared out of the square.

Knocked silly, David staggered to the street level.

Gone! He sprinted some distance after the receding hum, gave up, and limped back to glare down upon the wreckage of a once-strong suitcase—cut in twain, squashed to flinders, as *he* would have been. Not a nice job for the undertakers.

A six-foot constable paced towards him.

"Little accident, sir?"

David boiled over. "Accident! Great Christopher Columbus—when a car jams on its brakes and runs slap-bang on to the sidewalk?"

"You don't mean pavement, sir?"

"I stand corrected. Pavement it is." Gritting his teeth David pointed. "Take a squint at those tracks."

The constable was staring with disbelief at the duck-egg swelling luridly on the young man's temple.

"Now, now, sir! Didn't you just take a header into that area and—"

"And sit on my suitcase till it hatched? Use your brain, man, use your eyes!"

The officer bent over. Sure enough there ran the faint parallel tyre-prints, circling up over the kerb, grazing the area-railings, just missing the lamp-post beyond. He scratched his chin, got out a worn notebook and wetted a stumpy pencil.

"Hum! How much did you see?"

"Why, all of it! If that gate had been latched—"

"All! You saw the number of the car?"

"Number, my foot! And me ten jumps underground? No—and I couldn't make out the driver, either. He was on me, I'm telling you, it was over in a second, and the lamps blinded me, but whoever he was he was out for my blood."

"Could you say what make of car it was?" soothed the constable, passing over the last statement.

"Hell, no, can't you see I'm an American? There are umpteen British cars I'm not familiar with, and this was one of them. Black, stream-lined, a deuce of a long bonnet, silver doodah with wings in front—and a fat lot of good that'll do us. This I do know, it'd been snooping after me right away from Mecklenburgh Square, stalking me. I only noticed it because of the way it kept slowing and picking up speed. I think now—yes, I'll swear it—the slight braking was what gave me the warning."

"Drunk," observed the constable, but he might have meant it for the witness.

"Drunk? Not much. I saw him aim straight, like dart-throwing. It was sheer calculation, and damned good driving."

Perhaps it was the words "dart-throwing" which brought a keenness into the ruminant blue eyes. The constable unpocketed a torch and began examining the tracks, which had passed right across the new grey pull-over Alison had just knitted and a bundle of Elizabeth's letters, mashed to a pulp in a mess of toothpaste.

"Dunlops, I think. I'm afraid it won't get us far. See here, sir, have you any reason to imagine some party has designs on your life?"

The bruise was beginning to throb. Summoning his faculties, David opened his lips and closed them again. Scarpath's car was a Chrysler—and grey. As for the face behind the glass, it had been but the dimmest of blurs. He was merely assuming it to have been a man's. The last thing he wanted just now was to raise a hue and cry which would achieve nothing except the dragging of certain names into the public eye.

"Well, hardly. I'm practically a stranger in London. No, better let it slide."

The policeman picked a stick of shaving-soap out of the gutter.

"Shall I get you a taxi, sir? Right! Then we'll load all this stuff in. Hot bath's my advice, and raw beefsteak, if it's handy . . ."

Chapter Twenty-Six
PERFECTLY CLEAR

Fanny blinked dazedly round and let her tousled head sink back on her pillows. It was coming back to her now—the long talk with Geoffrey, and afterwards the sudden feeling of age and utter weariness. She hadn't meant to stay, only the temptation of this room with its sprung mattress, hot-water bottle and soft openwork blankets had been too much for even her iron independence. She had grunted a curt "Good-night," and just flung into the warm nest her nephew, with his usual forethought, had prepared.

This news about Elizabeth! Some of it had been a devastating shock. As for the rest—

"Might have guessed it," Fanny muttered. "She's her mother's child, harum scarum and spoiled. Nerves, pah! It's managing she needs, and I'll see she gets it."

Sickness was one thing, chopping and changing another. Having got the husband of her choice—far better than she deserved, incident-ally!—why on earth couldn't the girl spend the rest of her days in humble thankfulness instead of casting herself after some worthless young hood-lum from the Woods Hole period? True, Geoffrey hadn't dwelt much on this feature. Fanny blessed his reticence even while a prudish heat burned in her hard old cheeks at the thought of what it undoubtedly covered.

"He shows his breeding if she doesn't. Twice her brains, an artist every inch of him, but we don't find him kicking over traces from pure selfishness or—this I can never forgive!—spinning wicked tales just to gain sympathy. She must be daft."

Odd! There were times when, looking round her, Fanny felt herself almost the one sane, perfectly-balanced person of her acquaintance. It made her fume with irritation, though of course it carried a great responsibility.

Soft sounds issued from the bathroom. In the doorway appeared a staid woman in a crisp morning-uniform. So this explained why fresh undergarments were spread on a chair and the confusion of the dressing-table put in order.

"Awake, are you, Madam? I hope it was right not bringing you tea."

"Quite right." Fanny, who couldn't abide early tea, grimaced as she hoisted herself; but the twinge was only rheumatic, thank God! "I'll have it presently with my breakfast."

"Tea, Madam?" The maid seemed taken aback. "Very good, Madam. The master thought it was coffee."

Fanny wavered. After all, just for a treat. . . .

"Coffee, by all means, I'd prefer it." She appraised the woman and found her comfortingly plain. "Do you sleep here?" she asked bluntly.

"Oh, no, Madam, I come in by the day, and so does Lubbock. He does the cooking and valeting."

A most suitable arrangement, thought Fanny as the maid produced a pale blue bed-table and slipped out, at least while Elizabeth was away. Aglow from her bath and a ruthless pommelling with a vast, warmed towel, she nodded again to herself. Men always cooked better than women. The coffee wouldn't be up to the oyster-stew, this being England, but—

"But it is!" she marvelled.

Yes, what she sipped was real American coffee—and with cream, not disgusting hot milk. Nathan's negro chef couldn't have surpassed it—or the iced orange-juice, or the kidneys and mushrooms piping-hot under their silver cover.

Papers by her tray. Unfailingly thoughtful, Geoffrey had provided her with the *Daily Mail*, a pictorial tabloid, and the new *Geographical Review*. As she ate she glanced at them, skidding blind-eyed over some European uproar—politics had never impinged on her horizon—scanning the ungainly photographs of a young peer's wedding, and becoming absorbed in an article on Patagonia, a country she seemed somehow to have overlooked. Well! Let her straighten out this muddle and she would see. . . .

For one moment she let her hawk-eye rest on the pleasing room round her, the room whose glazed blue chintz and bright mirror glass was being spurned by its intended occupant. It was nice to realise that she, Fanny, had made all this comfort possible; nicer still that once Geoffrey had yielded to persuasions there had never been the slightest feeling of strain. Graceful acceptance was a rare gift.

"But I'm generally a pretty good judge of character. I was right about Elizabeth, and doubly right about him."

Her suit had been beautifully pressed. Erect, the same swashbuckling hat aslant over her eyes, she made a sortie into the other room she only dimly remembered and found Geoffrey waiting for her with visible restlessness. As he asked how she had slept he looked her up and down, searchingly, her lean knuckles lightly retained in his clasp.

"Quite certain you're all right?"

"And why not?" Grimly coy she changed the subject. "Now, then! What about this doctor?"

"He's calling here any minute. It meant cutting an appointment, but he appreciates the—well, the urgency."

"Humph!" said Fanny, and the specialist went up a notch in her estimation. She would have thought less of him if he'd had a free hour at his disposal; but that he deferred to her claims was a proof of good sense.

"Well!" She took a cigarette because Geoffrey offered it and stood tapping it against a bony fore-finger. "I'll see him, and then get straight on to Elizabeth. Either she marches back here or else into a sanatorium—which all along would have been the wiser solution. Never mind, what's done is done, and I don't anticipate the least difficulty in coping with her. Just firmness." Fanny squared her jaw. "It shouldn't take long. In fact, I might even make the sailing for . . . but I'm a little undecided. I must call in at the American Express."

"Intrepid Fanny!" he teased. "Still planning to die in your boots?"

"Certainly. Saves bother."

"I'm not so sure," he said slowly. "Though I must say you seem rather more fit than when I last saw you."

"Oh, I'm holding out!" She tossed her head, glanced warily at him and hesitated. "Geoffrey. Did you wonder why I had already started for England when those lying accusations reached me?"

"Well?"

"I knew, you see. Out there in Java. I felt you drawing me to you. There! Are you laughing at me?"

For one telling second his eyes held her embarrassed ones.

"And I knew you'd come," said Scarpath simply. "When I got your cable I—I rather cursed myself."

A strange emotion surged over her. No longer ashamed, she poured out her uncanny telepathic experience, totally unconscious of post-embellishments. The mysterious rapport of kindred minds, defying space, making possible the receipt of a message all the way from the fog-bound island in the north to the tropic one half round the globe.

"So distinct, Geoffrey. Your voice, no mistaking it. Oh, I pooh-poohed it at first, but after the third time, well, I just sprang out of bed, roused the boys, and began packing my—Was that the bell?"

Stiff-backed again, Fanny breathed hard while the doctor was shown in. "Dr. Brodmart?"

She liked his clever, scientist's eyes and his simple, man-to-man address, with no hint of soft-soaping—also the surreptitious glance bestowed on his watch. Hating delays on a par with uncertainty she made straight for the point. Could he in a few plain words give her the truth about her niece?

The doctor bowed his head, staring gravely down at his dark grey spats.

"I'll attempt to do so, Mrs. Rush. Understand, it's by no means easy."

For some moments Brodmart spoke deliberately, using incomprehensible terms and, as by afterthought, translating them. Awe was instilled into Fanny. She schooled her fly-away brain to what she conceived to be close attention, and at the first pause broke out with relief.

"So you honestly consider the treatment has been successful?"

"Certainly." The hooded eyes met hers. "But only if she takes no undue liberties at the present moment. That, I am much afraid, is what she is inclining to do, it may be with dangerous results."

"Wait! You tell me this disease has, or did have, a physical basis. Yes, yes," for Brodmart was raising an expostulatory hand, "I quite realise every disease must have, but that's not the point. What I'm asking is, How far can we attribute her present behaviour to actual illness and how far to—to—well, natural flightiness?"

The doctor pursed his lips. He glanced at the questioner, then away.

"A difficult problem to decide. I might almost say that you, Mrs. Rush, could answer it as well or better than I. Think back a little to the period Mrs. Scarpath spent under your guardianship. During that time did you find her complaining of indisposition without apparent cause? Bursting suddenly into angry tears, conceiving violent and inexplicable antipathies?"

Fanny gave a start. Why, this was pure mind-reading! Vivid in her memory were the pleas of eye-strain, silly backaches and what not that had made her niece such a trying companion. A girl of nineteen giving out after only four galleries of the intensely-interesting South Seas Exhibition, yet the same afternoon tramping by herself all the way from Cannes to Juan-les-Pins! Nonsense, of course—and then the ridiculous wrangles, the out-and-out rudeness to Nathan's old friends who wanted to comfort her, the weeping behind locked doors . . .

"I knew it!" Fanny bit off the words. "Hysterical."

Dr. Brodmart again raised his hand. "Not that it lessens the difficulty—as I need scarcely point out to a woman of your understanding." He looked squarely at Fanny. "Bear in mind, if you can, that quite possibly your niece is at times virtually unable to discriminate between fact and fantasy. I beg your pardon?"

He paused, but Fanny had merely snorted.

"While from the first this unfortunate weakness has proved the worst obstacle to a cure it nevertheless calls for great forbearance. At this highly critical juncture—well, I wonder just what to suggest?" Placing dubious fingertips together, Brodmart continued, "Adverse influences, of course, must be eliminated. Perhaps some tactful persuasion . . . the exercise of a strong, guiding will . . ."

Fanny was not quite clear as to when the doctor took his leave. Long before he had ceased speaking something like a giant buzz-saw had begun to grind and jolt viciously in her brain. Suddenly she became aware that she and Geoffrey were alone, and that Geoffrey was repeating a question.

"Plain? Oh, perfectly so! There's nothing the least strange about it, except that it should happen in my family. Now, then, what's that address?"

He scribbled on a card. Her hand opened and shut to seize it. A mad flame danced in her eyes.

"Lunch is ready," he reminded her. "And another thing; this happens to be Saturday. That means you'll run into these other Americans, who, of course, have had only Elizabeth's own distorted version." He handed her a glass.

"What's this?" Fanny tapped her foot. "Take it away."

"Nonsense, my dear, it's mostly fruit-juice. Seriously, don't you see it would be better for all of us if you waited till Monday and caught Elizabeth alone?"

Her eye swerved on him. "Beddoes will be there, will he? Well, who cares if he is?"

"I care," said Scarpath. "Very much. In fact, quite apart from not wanting you to undergo a harrowing scene, I have two tickets to the Haymarket for this evening, and I'd like you to feel fresh to enjoy it. Now be a good girl. Will you tuck into bed and rest till time to change?"

"Rest! With this thing hanging over me?"

"You must, Fanny. I insist. After this fiendish journey—" Scarpath hesitated. "I didn't mean to tell you what Brodmart said to me as he went out. He thinks—well, that you ought to go slow on the excitement."

Her foot stopped jiggling. She gave him a long, cryptic stare.

"Doctors don't know everything," she retorted. "Still, perhaps you're right about the nap."

"Thank you, Fanny!" He patted her hand.

Dusk had fallen when he peeped into her room. The glazed curtains were drawn, from the hump under the covers issued a satisfactory snore. He let out his breath, straightened his shoulders, and quitted the flat.

It was some ten minutes later that a taxi-driver in South Street was hailed by a woman of slightly demented appearance. He didn't altogether care for the way she was brandishing the umbrella, which had a hefty ivory handle, pointed at one end. Powerful old girl, too. However, once inside, she did nothing more alarming than to prod him in the back with the ferrule each time there was a hold-up.

"Allez, allez!" shouted Fanny, a little hazy at the moment as to what country she was in.

She chewed at her reindeer gauntlets. The buzz-saw was still making a noise in her head, loud as a road-drill. The red lights turned yellow, then green.

"Just my luck," ground Fanny, "to have picked a half-witted chauffeur. Well, thank God, I'm cool."

Chapter Twenty-Seven
QUICK CURTAIN

THE appointment with MacConochie had been cancelled. The specialist, while in Edinburgh, had come down with 'flu.

"Rotten luck." Colin was helping Alison get tea. "It means more worrying delay. Oh, I don't think Mac's not playing straight! He's keen as mustard."

Alison laid down the bread-knife. "Look, Colin! Are you seriously suggesting any other doctor could have been got at?"

"Got at? Oh, no, nothing quite so crude in our profession. Same time, it would prove a damned sight more deadly," Colin muttered to himself.

"How deadly? I don't understand."

"No? Then I'll explain. Suppose it was any nerve-man but MacConochie. He wouldn't so much as look at Elizabeth without first shooting off a kid-glove note to Brodmart, full of apologies and compliments. He'd be too afraid of giving offence, maybe losing out on a dinner invitation. As for a general practitioner, he would simply decline to see her at all, once he knew she was Brodmart's patient. You see why, of course?"

"Not quite. Why would he decline?"

"Say he does take on the case. Well, one fine day some patient of his will be wanting Guthrie Brodmart's opinion. Brodmart makes the examination, gives directions, then asks, 'By the way, who is your medical advisor? Jones! M'm . . . I see. . . . Well, if I were you, I'm not sure I'd continue with Dr. Jones. Robinson, now, round the corner from you, is a man I can thoroughly recommend. Take my tip, try Robinson.' That's all. The trick is turned."

"Beastly!" she blazed.

"Is it? It's above criticism. Nothing's been said. But it won't end there, oh, by no means! Brodmart will take care to drop hints in all the right places. A shrug will suffice, or a nastily-polite snigger. Before you know it, Jones will find his patients fading away. Word has got round that he's a dud. He may have to sell what's left of his practice, sneak off to some provincial hole and start all over again, at the bottom of the ladder."

Alison's colour had mounted. "You're Jones," she whispered. "Oh, Colin, hands off!"

"Hush!" He glanced at the door.

"Think she'll hear? Or David? Those two are in a blissful dream. Oh, dear, suppose Brodmart's found out—petty-minded prig!—and it's already too late to keep him from stabbing you in the back? And I, yes, I, hauled you into this. Oh, what can I do?"

"This," he murmured, and kissed her.

It was a full moment before she felt the drainboard cutting into her back.

"Silly! That oughtn't to have happened. Leave go." She pushed him blurredly away.

He touched her warm cheek impersonally. "Just like a nice, ripe peach."

"Peach! Here, get busy with that kettle. Haven't our two lovebirds got to be fed?"

"Lovebirds. . . . I can't see any too hopeful prospect for them. Can you?"

"Is it Betsy's health you mean, or her husband's refusal to free her?"

"I was thinking of the latter."

What had he meant by that kiss? Nothing—*evidently*. An impulse—and even now he had gone back to the important subject. . . .

"Yes, why is Scarpath taking this attitude? So dog-in-the-manger. Colin, it's—queer."

"Too damned queer." He frowned.

"I believe you've got some idea about it. Have you?"

"Not one I can prove. God, the whole thing's fantastic! This stalling, this seeming casualness—"

Colin shut his lips tight. "No use. I'll have to know more."

Alison came close. "David's close shave last night. Do *you* believe that was Scarpath's doing?"

"Don't know. Seems a spot improbable, doesn't it?"

"Unimaginable. Why, it would have been cold-blooded murder! It would argue he was jealous. Or wouldn't it?"

"Again I don't know."

"It wasn't his car," she reasoned.

"Oh, that! Nothing's simpler than to borrow someone's car from a quiet place and return it or else leave it for the police to find. If you killed your victim no identification would come from him; and you'd take good care there weren't any witnesses. It would want skill and nerve, but Scarpath's got both."

"But Colin, how could Scarpath have known David was back? No human creature could have told him he was even expected."

"Badger could have told him. That's why I got rid of her to-day."

"Oh!" Alison gasped. "I see. . . . How horrible to have all these suspicions!"

"Better have them now than when it's too late," he said grimly. "Now Elizabeth's up and doing, your Mrs. Marshall will be all the protection she'll want during the day. At least"—his brow furrowed—"we'll chance it like that for a few days."

He took her arm. "Don't forget, let her go on thinking David ran into a lamp-post. It's safer than having her upset."

In the living-room conversation had flagged.

"Well," said Elizabeth, "you collected your mail, bought new B.V.D.s, which you'll freeze in, heaven help you, and looked at second-hand cars. Was that all you did after you trundled me home?"

"All." David busied himself with his pipe. "Clock struck one. Fellow serving me made a grab for his hat and left me cold. That's old England, I guess. I'd found something, too. Wait till you see it. It's own cousin to Mehitabel, but it goes."

"Mehitabel went." Her eyes grew dreamy. "Remember that chicken we ran over outside Mount Kiscoe?"

One awkward spot skidded past! Damn it, he'd got to think up a good lie! Any moment she'd come out with the question he was dreading. If it killed her to borrow or to sponge—

"Whoopee!"

The other couple had joined them. Crumpets hot and buttery poised over their heads.

"Three each," snapped Alison. "After that, toast your own."

They wedged round the fire, and Alison dispensed tea. "Easy girl to amuse," declared David, motioning towards Elizabeth. "Take her up and show her Selfridge's. She goes goofy with joy."

"Not cheap, though," flashed Elizabeth. "You had to buy me ice cream soda *and* a hot fudge sundae."

"Yes, but at that I saved on the deal. Another ten minutes in the toy department and you'd have had to walk home."

No, thought Alison, it was all right. It must be. Geoffrey Scarpath couldn't be the devil they were trying to picture him. Selfish, yes; equivocal, oh, decidedly; but nothing worse. . . .

Elizabeth was giggling and poking in the crevice of the sofa.

"You didn't see what I bought. Look! Can you bear it?"

David stared. "My God, a mouth-organ! Girl, you can't play the thing."

"Oh, can't I? I'm out of practice, of course. I know, I'll try *Shenandoah* and see how it goes." Fitting the mouth-organ to her lips she ground out the tune.

"Away, you rolling river," crooned David's basso profondo. "Swell, keep it up."

Three of the party had misted eyes. They were back in Woods Hole. It was night, their feet dangled over the edge of the long, jutting pier, and beyond them stretched the Atlantic with the moon making a silver track across the waves and the salt-breeze mingling with stale fish and the scent of pines. Sometimes Elizabeth, from the big white house, had slipped along to take her place with the student company. . . .

"Give us 'Happy Days,' Betsy. Think you can?"

Now Colin added his rusty baritone, the combined din nearly drowning the accompaniment, though Elizabeth was labouring hard, quite literally warming to her work. She had slid to the rug, where the roasting fire made her cheeks flame like a peony. For once her hair had strayed moistly from its tidy waves and clung in wisps to her forehead and neck. She felt, indeed, slightly intoxicated with her success. Dimly she realised that David's right arm was buttressing her back, but what of it? There were two chaperons present.

"Louder!" urged David. "Let's try that harmony once more. Now, then, from the start. *Happy days are here again—*"

It was the final sweep of his left hand which sent Alison's cigarette flying and Elizabeth on her face, to lie panting with hilarity. The chorus had ended in a wild and disorderly scramble, legs intertwined, cover half off the Chesterfield.

Colin alone had heard the bell. He had gone out and come in, and now was clearing his throat.

In the centre of the room stood Fanny Rush.

Chapter Twenty-Eight
THE SAPPHIRE

Alison, on all fours as she pawed about for her cigarette, gave one petrified look and staggered to her feet.

"Mrs. Rush! Oh, do forgive me, I—"

"*Fanny!*"

Elizabeth caught her breath. As she rose, something snapped. It was neither more nor less than the safety-pin anchoring Alison's skirt round her slimness, but that she didn't know.

"Fanny, oh, Fanny darling!"

Laughing and sobbing, skirt dropping disgracefully off her, she ran for her aunt's embrace.

The embrace didn't materialise.

"Get them out," cried Mrs. Rush in a choked voice. "I'll speak to you alone."

Her umbrella—yes, the old, diehard umbrella with the whale-tooth handle—swept an imperious arc. For some reason it failed to achieve its purpose.

"But, *Fanny*! Don't you remember Alison, Alison Young? This is her home. Oh, surely you see—"

"Out!" Fanny's eyes glittered. "It's you I want, not this rabble. Tell them to go."

It was a nightmare moment—Alison clutching frantically at her dignity, David beet-red and fumbling with the tie that had migrated under his ear. It was Alison who spoke, one hand flattening back her boyish crop.

"Please, Mrs. Rush, hadn't we better make this a general discussion? Elizabeth—well, she's not up to much yet, you know."

"By what I've witnessed," said Fanny harshly, "my niece seems perfectly equal to hearing what I have to say to her. That is, if she's sufficiently sober to take it in."

David moved forward. "Don't get this wrong, Mrs. Rush. I'm David Beddoes. If you've had my letter—"

"Your turn will come later. Get out."

"No!" Alison stood her ground with polite firmness. "We'll none of us get out. Not till you've heard what Dr. Ladbroke thinks about Elizabeth's illness and—other things. Now, won't you sit down quietly and let us explain?"

Fanny's eye rolled round. "I've no wish to discuss private matters with any of your shady associates. Is that plain?" She tapped her foot.

A gleam in her eye, Elizabeth refastened her skirt-band. "Please go," she whispered. "All of you. No, really, I'll be all right."

David was muttering darkly, but Alison, with a last rueful glance at the littered tea-things, pushed him into the cold passage. Colin followed, closing the door.

"What's this?" blazed David.

"Idiot! Need you ask? She's seen him. Of course."

"My God!" David's fist beat softly against his bruise.

"And," murmured Alison dryly, "she's taken our little binge for one hell of a petting-party. Well, there it is. It can't be helped now. Hadn't you two better smooth up?"

In the bathroom David snarled, "So now we know. If the old Tartar didn't answer my letter it was because she's been in touch with Scarpath all along and had her mind thoroughly and systematically poisoned. Did he know she was coming? Is that why he scrapped the house and set up this new place?"

Colin looked grave. "We can take this much as established: Now she is here he intends to make use of her."

David swung round from the basin. "Ladbroke, if she manages to talk Elizabeth round, can we count on you to back us up?"

"It's as well, Beddoes, to face the position. Brodmart will swear his patient was due to improve, and that I'm merely taking credit for what he's been doing all these months. In actual fact," said Colin to himself, "I've done almost nothing. It's the food, fresh air and the happier mind that are working the cure. Provided it is a cure."

"But her knee, damn it! What about her knee?"

"Yes, there's that. The trouble being that the word of a masseur carries little or no weight with the regular faculty. She's got to see MacConochie!" Colin's hand clinched. "Even if she goes back, that appointment must be kept . . . if possible."

"But I won't let her go back!" It was Alison, from behind.

"Now you're talking," grunted David, but Colin shrugged.

"Quite. And what's your plan? Drugging, forcible detention? This free agent business, you see, happens to cut both ways."

During the taut silence Alison thought, *Colin's right. If Elizabeth decides to go nothing whatever can stop her.*

"I shall simply tackle Mrs. Rush," she declared resolutely. "After all, she must have average intelligence, and in her own peculiar way she was kind to Elizabeth. At least I can destroy any beastly notion she may have about David."

"I wonder?" Colin raised his brows. "No, on the whole, I think I ought to deal with her. The calm professional touch—"

"Oh, yeah?"

Alison whirled him round towards the mirror. He gave a startled stare at his ash-strewn tweeds and the smear of melted butter the last crumpet had left on his chin. As he grinned and began washing Alison clamped down on him.

"No, Colin! This is our responsibility—David's and mine. Will you go right away home and keep out of it?"

"Yes—when you throw me out."

"Oh," she moaned. "Why bicker? I can't think of anything except what may be going on in that room."

With one accord they tiptoed back into the passage. Elizabeth's voice, near breaking-point, came through to them.

"Fanny, dear Fanny, if you only *knew* how I've prayed you'd write or something! I'd begun to think you'd simply gone right out of my life."

"Write? I did write. A long letter, only the other day—"

"Four months ago," rasped David, drowning Elizabeth's reply. Mrs. Rush's retort came sharply.

"Rubbish! You never troubled to answer my letters. I've heard regularly from your husband, so there's no good blaming it on the post."

"I know!" It was Elizabeth again, eager, defiant. "Doesn't that prove what I'm trying so desperately to make you understand? No one's had my letters. I haven't had theirs. Surely you see it's—well, funny?"

David wrenched at the doorknob. "Let me get through! I'll tell her something a darned sight funnier—"

Colin dragged him away. Slowly he withdrew his hand from his trouser pocket and dark with fury stood listening to what had now become barely audible.

As a matter of fact, Elizabeth's strength was going. She and her aunt seemed to be moving in particularly vicious circles, getting nowhere. With the feeling that she was attempting to drive nails into steel she tried once again, patient but trembling, to make Fanny see.

"I tell you, I was shut in. I wasn't getting nearly enough to eat. Then they took all my clothes, so—"

"You can sit there and admit such a thing was necessary?" Mrs. Rush's glance was suddenly shrewd.

"Oh, Fanny, *please* don't misunderstand! Here's the point: In a little while I'd have been dead. Yes, dead and buried. Instead of which—well, look at me now!"

Fanny refused to look. Already her hawk-eyes had shown her a girl in positively rude health—certainly rude spirits. Thin, of course, but so were all other young girls with this modern craze for slimming.

"Enough!" she snorted. "I quite expected this concoction of lies. Save them for your disreputable friends. You've had proper care, you're benefiting by it. And now—"

"Now—yes! I'm seeing another big specialist, just to make absolutely certain there's been nothing the matter with me. I would have gone to him to-day only he's ill, in Edinburgh, and . . . Fanny, are you taking *any* of this in?"

Fanny took a firmer grip on her umbrella. "Why your husband should want you back," she said succinctly, "passes my comprehension. He does, that's flat, and he assures me that on no account will he consider a separation. Are you coming with me, Elizabeth? Tell me plainly, yes or no."

"Why?" Elizabeth twisted her handkerchief mutinously. "I just don't get it. It's not as though Geoffrey loved me. He doesn't, not one little bit."

"Pah! Why not say outright you're infatuated with this ruffian Beddoes? It would be more decent than casting infamous aspersions on the English gentleman you had the good fortune to marry."

"You've said it! I married Geoffrey—not you. How can *you* know the sort of husband he's been? Why, I have to pinch myself to realise he is my husband! That part of it was over so long ago—and it wasn't so terribly good, anyhow," Elizabeth muttered.

Instantly she saw her mistake. A dark, embarrassed flush had overspread her aunt's cheekbones.

"That will do!" barked Fanny. "I don't wish to go into what was probably your own fault."

I knew it, thought Elizabeth. *Her marriage didn't take so well, either. That's why she's so hard on me.*

Fanny was battling for control. The buzz-saw was confusing her, but she stabbed her question again, "Well, are you coming?"

"No! No! If you'd heard one word you wouldn't want me to come. I'll never go back to Geoffrey—never."

"Think carefully," warned Fanny, and the mad flame quivered in her eyes. "Let me remind you I can make things extremely unpleasant for you."

"Aren't you doing that now? Oh, Fanny, and I was so glad to see you—so ready to love you! I've always been, you must realise it, yet you come asking me to walk straight back into a—a death-trap!"

Purple in the face Fanny shouted, "Have you gone stark crazy?"

"No," flared Elizabeth. "But I think you have."

David heard her, with clearing brow. "Good kid!" he applauded; but Alison felt less sure of results, for the bullying incoherence which followed seemed vaguely ominous.

Suddenly, without warning, the door crashed back with a violence which sent flakes of white showering like snow from the ceiling. For one instant what might have been an elderly Valkyrie on the warpath towered in their midst, glaring through them with glazed eyes.

"Wills can be changed," ground Mrs. Rush. "A stroke of the pen. Let that show her!"

She stormed out of the flat. David made a lunge.

"Stop! Here, Mrs. Rush!"

"Beddoes, for God's sake, *not now!*"

David stood still, breathing heavily. His two confederates looked pale and shocked, as though a hot hurricane had swept over them. All at once he tumbled to what Colin had meant. It was not merely that Elizabeth's aunt was in no mood for sane reasoning. It was her words about a will, quite unconsciously spoken aloud. No, not intended for an audience. As far as the visitor was concerned no audience had been there.

God, had Elizabeth heard?

Apparently not. Striding into the room David found her upright beside the rumpled Chesterfield, her gaze as sightless as her aunt's, but her anger fast ebbing, and with it her strength. He put his arms round her. At first she seemed not to notice. Then she fended him off.

"I'm perfectly all right," she whispered. "I—I think I'll sit down."

He sensed the change in her manner, and guessed it had come from things her aunt had been saying. Very childish her attitude now as she sat hunched, her head resting on her knees, and yet subtly she had grown older, more mature. She dabbed furtively at her eyes, lifted her face and tried to smile.

"That's that. Joke, wasn't it?"

Alison answered soothingly. "It was. Feel like telling us what happened?"

"Oh, yes! Of course." The voice was toneless, reciting a lesson. "Well, she got David's letter. On her way back, in Singapore—"

"She was coming anyway?" David demanded.

"So it seems. Don't ask me why. Geoffrey, though, was the attraction. That's quite natural, she's always adored him, like every one else. He knew, so he met her. Last night."

The quickly exchanged glances, at first blank then calculating, passed Elizabeth by. She continued in the same cool, dead tone:

"She's stopping with him now. Of course she's had his story. And, just to make it all quite authentic, she's had Dr. Brodmart's."

Colin nodded, sharp flame in his eyes. "I see. So she wouldn't accept yours?"

Elizabeth spread her hands. "She wouldn't listen. She never heard. Oh, I told her everything, but she's like that, you know, once an idea's wedged in her mind. I can't say I altogether blame her. Between them those two haven't left me a leg to stand on. I'm a liar, that's all. Well! She laid down the law to me. I'm to go back, finish my treatment, do exactly as Dr. Brodmart says. And if I do or don't, Geoffrey will hold on to me like grim death."

All her false composure splintered. "Oh, don't you see?" she sobbed wildly. "Geoffrey's the injured one. I'm simply a—"

"That's enough!" David silenced her. "Now just let go."

It was significant that she did her weeping not on his shoulder but discreetly, into her own lap. Presently she signalled them to leave her, and this they did, to hold another conference in the passage.

"No," murmured Alison. "Her aunt hasn't said a word to her about a will. Should we tell her?"

"Not just yet, I think." Colin spoke slowly. "Though, God, what an eye-opener!"

David said, "Anyhow this will's going to be reversed. Thank the Lord for that!"

"Is it?" hesitated his cousin. "Mrs. Rush may veer round."

"That's so," glowered David. "She's so entirely under that scoundrel's thumb. Oh, what the hell? We've got Elizabeth. Nothing else can matter a damn."

"David," said Alison curiously, "what were you going to tell Mrs. Rush?"

His brooding air left him. He dug a ring-box from his pocket, opened it and flashed on them a square, dark blue stone, set in platinum.

"Call this a sapphire? Guess again."

"Not an imitation? Oh, David, don't try and persuade me Nathan Greentree's sister would give her own niece a—"

"Put your own theories to it. Three jewellers have examined this, and the verdict is unanimous. What you see is a reconstructed stone, value five pounds."

Chapter Twenty-Nine
THE HAWK IS SNARED

AT SIX-THIRTY Scarpath returned to find his guest in her fur coat and slightly ridiculous old hat, pacing the floor. On the verge of going out. So he was just in time to stop her.

"A lawyer," she croaked. "Where can I get one?" His puzzled expression brought an angry stamp. "Lawyer! Solicitor, if you like. Surely in a city of fourteen millions—"

"Now, Fanny? But it's Saturday afternoon."

"Saturday, Saturday!" Her arms menaced heaven. "You'd say the clock had stopped and everything with it. All those bee-hive offices in the Temple closed. I've driven from end to end. In fact, I've just got in. Haven't you got a lawyer? Get him here. I'll give him double his fee."

The young man's eyes had not stirred from her face. "Is it so urgent?"

"Urgent! Certainly it is. I've seen Elizabeth, and her precious Blooms-bury crew. I'm washing my hands of her once and for all. I mean to cancel my will."

With stiff fingers Scarpath lit a cigarette. He let a mouthful of smoke remain imprisoned for fifteen seconds, and now it trickled forth from lips that had gone grey.

"Sit down," he begged quietly. "What about a sip of brandy?"

"Brandy? I've had it, all that's good for me." She jerked her head towards the decanter on the table. "No, no, I can't sit."

"You must." He pressed her firmly into a chair. "And now, you might just tell me about this rather wretched experience."

"Understand," said Fanny obliquely, "there need be no difference where you and I are concerned. I should like to go on doing little things for you, Geoffrey—if you will allow me. It's my will I must alter."

He made a gesture of pained reticence. "I know nothing about that, of course."

"Certainly not. Why should you? Neither does Elizabeth. I've never seen fit to gabble about my affairs." Her face brightened. "I've got it! I'll cross to Paris in the morning, have my own lawyer, Macadam, draw me a brand-new will. Will you wire him immediately and tell him to see me on Monday at ten sharp?"

"Of course. Have you his private address?"

"Private fiddlesticks! Rue Auber will reach him."

"Not sooner than we can telephone." Scarpath laid his hand on her arm. "Seriously, Fanny dear, all this frantic rushing about can't be very good for you. Can it?"

For the first time she looked at him. "Geoffrey, I've something to say to you about my—my health. I was saving it for a surprise. Can you guess what it is?"

"No. Not bad news, I hope?"

"Far from it! Do you remember how I said that doctors don't know everything? Well, then! Believe it or not, those giddy turns and so on didn't mean high blood pressure. Not a bit of it. The English doctor in Singapore made me give up coffee, and since that moment I've never looked back."

As she changed for the theatre Fanny felt her mind immeasurably relieved. She had poured her whole sordid and humiliating experience into Geoffrey's ears, and although Elizabeth's point-blank refusal to return had dealt Geoffrey a horrid blow it had seemed to draw him even closer to herself.

Also, as she had foreseen, Geoffrey had been overjoyed to know that her life wasn't likely to be cut short at any moment. It warmed her heart to think of the sigh which had followed his first incredulous start, and the little, teasing push he had given her as he murmured, "Wicked old humbug! Keeping me on the rack."

"I knew," she mused complacently, "he'd decline to accept anything from me. His pride wouldn't let him, now this has happened. I suppose I'll have to make some small provision for Elizabeth till she's legally separated; but after that let her marry this Beddoes. My money will go to a worthier object."

She had always earmarked Bob Rush's fortune for an exploration fund, at least till Nathan's financial collapse. Now "The Robert and Frances Rush Memorial Subsidy for Geographical Research" was a realisable dream. Her conscience was clear.

Surely it wasn't wrong to feel another glimmer of compensation? From now on she might look forward to some delightful times with Geoffrey himself.

"Yes, let me attend to this will business, and once that's over try and persuade him to join me somewhere on the Continent. Patagonia can wait. The poor boy will be very downcast. Winter sports in Switzerland may take him out of himself."

Scarpath studied his features in the beautiful old Venetian mirror that hung over the Adam mantelpiece.

Odd to find oneself looking precisely the same! Cats were like that, of course—always the same, unchanging mask. Once an English girl, rolling in money, had shrieked at him that he had a cat's eyes, a cat's mouth, and a damned cat's mind. She had said that the utter impossibility of knowing what went on inside him was driving her mad. Well, there were advantages . . .

He wondered if Fanny would simmer down after a good meal at Boulestin's, a carefully-selected wine. Slowly he shook his head. The woman was like rock over this Paris plan. She was determined not to waste a day in carrying out her infernal project. She had actually stood over him while he dispatched the wire to Macadam. In the morning she would be off.

His hand clinched. To think that last night matters had been all but accomplished! They were ruined now and by a bloody fluke which no logical forethought could have reckoned upon.

Ruined?

His gaze, turning, rested on the decanter. It was nearly full, Fanny having taken only one small glass. Considering a moment, he picked it up, carried it through into his bathroom, and returning rang the bell. When the man-servant entered he was holding the decanter up to the light.

"Lubbock, when was this filled?"

Lubbock stared. "I never touch the stuff, sir! Why, the smell alone turns me. I—"

"To-day, wasn't it?"

"This morning, sir—full right up." Lubbock eyed the almost-empty decanter and muttered that it didn't seem possible. "Shall I fill it again, sir?" he asked awkwardly.

"Don't." Scarpath spoke shortly. "Oh, by the way. Mrs. Rush will be leaving for France by the ten o'clock train. Don't give her coffee for breakfast. She tells me she shouldn't take it, on account of her blood pressure."

"Yes, sir. I understand."

"Have you laid out my clothes? Clear up, then go."

The odour of brandy still clung in the mauve-grey bathroom, but the fragrance of bath-essence in the water already filling the bath soon dispelled it. Seven o'clock. Scarpath was back in his bedroom, lifting an ivory microphone and dialling a Welbeck number. Presently, in response to a querulous voice, he was issuing instructions, over-riding protests, turning a deaf ear to questions.

"Eleven-fifty, here," he repeated. "Make it to the dot."

Humming softly the gigue from the Bach suite with flute, he fingered the studs Lubbock had inserted into his dress-shirt. Valuable pearls, these, the gift of the fiancée who had flung a less valuable—and unpaid for—ring in his face. Thus far he had managed to cling on to them. Something had always cropped up in the nick of time to prevent his selling them, or his piano, or his car. . . .

Something always cropped up. . . .

He pulled open a drawer in a lovely old transfer-decorated commode. Before him lay carefully-ranged socks, silk on the right, medium wool in the middle, heavy-ribbed golf stockings on the left. He chose the thickest of the latter, not disturbing its position, closed the drawer, and let his eye rove over the room.

In the corner, on a shelf under the shell-top of a niche, stood a crystal ball the size of an orange. He lifted it from its ebony stand, weighed it meditatively, and put it back.

When he was dressed he again summoned Lubbock, bidding him leave a few sandwiches in the drawing-room.

"Whisky and lime-juice, *but no brandy*. Got that clear?" To himself, carefully avoiding the man's glance, he added, "I've asked my friend Dr. Brodmart to drop in for a moment or so after the theatre. It's about the best I can do."

"Madam's waiting for you, sir. She seems fairly all right."

Scarpath slid into the overcoat Lubbock held ready. "No damned radio on the floor below. Does that mean the other tenant's gone away?"

"For the week-end, sir. Your scarf, sir."

Some four hours later Scarpath and his guest re-entered the flat.

"Fanny, you're shivering. Don't take off your coat. I'm going to fetch you some brandy."

She opened her mouth to object, but Geoffrey had vanished into the dining-room.

"I very seldom touch this, you know," she explained as he came back with a glassful of brandy. "Thank you. I do feel I may be catching a slight chill."

"That settles it. You can't cross to-morrow."

"Nonsense! I'll stay in my cabin, and French trains are always super-heated. Can't you see I'll not be able to draw breath till this affair is dealt with?"

"Dear Fanny! As usual living up to your name."

"Just so. Well, you must humour me, that's all. And now about our little jaunt to Switzerland. You've not given me a definite answer. No counter attraction here, I hope?" She cocked a suspicious eye.

Scarpath's smile held a faint irony. "No, no counter attraction." He paused. "It's been a blow for Beddoes, hasn't it? He pays a detective to dog my footsteps and draws a completely negative result."

Fanny blew up. "Wicked! An unforgivable outrage! If only I'd known about it before this afternoon. . . . Why, this alone proves her relations with the man. Would he go to such scandalous lengths if—"

"Laugh, Fanny, as I'm doing." His hand slid into hers. "Really, my dear, one must see the thing with detachment and appreciate its absurdity." He bent to make up the fire.

"Don't do that on my account, Geoffrey. I'm getting straight into bed."

"Right. Why not have a hot bath first? Do that, and then when you're nicely tucked up I'll bring you along hot lemon and a couple of aspirins. Will you promise to call out?"

"I'm not used to being coddled," she grumbled, looking tremendously pleased all the same. "Very well, if you insist."

More than ever like a ruffled hawk, her ancient sables huddled about her neck and the tail of her old black velvet tagging behind, she shivered into her room.

When she had gone Scarpath spent a few minutes in Treddle's electrically-fitted kitchen and a lesser time in his bedroom, where he replaced his evening coat by a dressing-gown of plum-coloured brocade, tightly swathed. Thus attired he brought the silver tray containing the steaming lemon drink and aspirin bottle into the drawing-room, and unstrapping his watch laid it face up on the mantel.

Eleven thirty-nine. He watched the small hands register two age-long minutes, and then, with his tray, walked steadily to Fanny's door.

He tapped lightly. "May I barge in?"

"No, keep out!" The reply came thickly from the bathroom beyond. "I'm brushing my teeth."

The removable ones, evidently.

"Don't be silly, old dear."

Chuckling affectionately, he placed his burden on the bed-table, and approached the partly-open door, through which, only a few feet distant, stood Fanny's tall, shapelessly-garbed figure. Her back was turned, the mirror which would have given her his reflection was dimmed over by steam. A curious frostiness in his eye, he noted the ragged rat's tail of iron-grey hair straggling downward over her wadded satin robe. His right hand stole to the bulge in his pocket, felt about and fastened a grip.

"Don't get a worse chill," he advised, and as he said it he stepped forward on to the warm, marble floor.

CHAPTER THIRTY
THEORIES

THE ring at the bell sent Elizabeth trembling again. Was this Fanny come back? A gruff Cockney voice and a series of thumps emboldened her to peep into the passage, where her three friends grouped bemusedly round a heap of luggage just dumped at their feet.

"My wardrobe trunk!" she gasped. "My suitcases. But why?"

"Why not?" shrugged Alison, but her tone was puzzled. "You should have had them before."

"But I didn't. Do you think Fanny's responsible? She can't be. There hasn't been time. Does—does it mean Geoffrey's given me up as a hopeless job?"

David handed over a bunch of keys. "Better open things up and look 'em through," he advised dryly.

"Well—" Alison hesitated, glancing at Colin.

"What else can it mean? It's a relief, I must say. Let's unpack and clear this elephant trunk off somewhere. It can't stop here, can it?"

"And I can't stop here either." Scarlet, Elizabeth bent over the Yale lock. "They both know that, of course. I'm pretty handicapped without money."

"You're nothing of the kind," Alison was warmly protesting when David cut in decisively.

"Girl, who says you've no money? Right now I can get you four hundred on that ring."

"Four hundred *pounds*? David, it's not true!"

"Oh, yeah? I'd have mentioned it sooner only I was hoping to get more."

Lest her face betray her Alison sped into the bedroom to clear space for Elizabeth's wardrobe. Colin followed, pushing the door to with his foot. She whispered, "Well, he's done it. Of course she'll insist on sharing expenses with me, but I can just quietly hand it back to him."

"With that independent spirit of hers," he answered, "it was about the only solution. This is a critical moment, and so long as she felt under obligations there'd have been imminent risk of her going back."

"Would she if she knew her sapphire had been stolen and a worthless stone put in its place?"

Colin's shoulders went up cynically. "Could it be proved the substitution didn't take place in America when the ring was originally bought? And if she did believe her husband had done it she'd probably argue that the proceeds were devoted to her medical expenses."

"Damn!" Alison stuffed an armful of her less desirable garments under the bed. "You're right again, I suppose. Still, I can hardly imagine Mrs. Rush, once she grasps the situation, will leave her one and only niece utterly stranded."

"Why should she ever grasp it?" he asked pointedly.

Silent a moment Alison objected, "Scarpath has had the decency to send along her belongings. Surely that means capitulation?"

He did not answer. Elizabeth's voice floated through to them.

"I can sell my mink coat, David. See, Blue River skins, good as new, worth a lot of money."

"And credit," David growled. "Hang on to that with your eye-teeth."

Laden with frocks he burst into the bedroom. "For the love of Mike don't let me down!" he hissed. "It's working like a charm. Ladbroke, is she up to a cinema?"

Coming out of a reverie Colin said, "Best move possible. Take her to see 'Snow White,' while we do the Marx Brothers."

"Whoopee!"

Later that evening Alison, in the Café Royal, remarked, "It's no good saying it now, but was it altogether wise to send those two off alone?"

"Part of the cure," Colin replied simply. "You see I'm trusting David not to overstep the mark."

"It's Mrs. Rush I'm bothering about. She's convinced they're having an affair. What if Scarpath's spying on them now?"

Colin shook his head.

"No?" She took a sip of her foaming Pilsner. "You must admit it's positively spooky the way that man seems to know all our doings. Who, in the first place, gave him my address? Not the office, and Cynthia Wibbe's never heard of him. Hard as it is to believe he tried to murder David last night, I keep thinking about that car."

"Well, anyhow a trick of that kind can't be tried twice."

Her usually clear brain felt muddled with obscure conflicts. One corner of it thought how odd it was that the burning question of just where she and Colin stood with regard to one another was continually being pushed into the background. Much safer—perhaps.

Glancing sideways she saw that Colin's brow was still heavily lined.

"Look here, why are *you* more worried than you were? Don't lie to me, I began noticing it from the moment Mrs. Rush rode rough-shod over us muttering to herself. I must say she looked capable of—"

"Of getting a stroke?"

Alison set down her glass with a click. "Goodness! Is she likely to do that?"

His shoulders went up. "Possibly less soon than Scarpath may be hoping."

"Oh!" She sat perfectly still, her hazel eyes widening with comprehension. "So you believe that may be his game."

Colin shook himself angrily. "He can't be such an ass! The notion did just occur to me when the woman in the *Queen Mary* mentioned how seedy Mrs. Rush was looking in Singapore a few months ago. She's got high blood pressure, I'll swear it, and she may, at that period, have been recovering from a slight attack. On the other hand, I'd say a subject of her age and stamina was calculated to withstand a number of attacks—go on living, in fact, for fifteen to twenty years."

"Dr. Brodmart's seen her," Alison reminded. "Doesn't that make the theory rather chimerical?"

"Chimerical! Exactly." Colin rumpled his hair.

Carefully Alison dug out her cigarette. "Colin, will Elizabeth ever collect evidence for a divorce?"

"Never. Not unless Scarpath is willing."

He said it with such energy that she felt slightly startled. So, she reflected, it's like that; but she did not say it aloud, for the one time she had tried to sound Colin he had declared that he had neither knowledge nor interest concerning Scarpath's morals.

"Well! And if Elizabeth simply won't make it up with him? Supposing her aunt did die and leave her money, he couldn't touch a penny of it. Of course, the money may have been left to them jointly with a provision against separation. What about that?"

"Let's deal with known facts," he said dryly. "Take this gesture of the clothes. Carter Patterson brought them. My idea is they were meant to arrive before Mrs. Rush's visit. What sort of impression would it create—did it create—for Mrs. Rush to find her niece dressed like a charity orphan? It might have given Scarpath a black eye."

"Tut, Fanny wouldn't notice what Betsy was wearing."

"Most women would. Scarpath, with his subtlety, would think of that detail. I contend this capitulation, as you call it, was a gallery act. If so, what's up his sleeve?"

"I'm no mind-reader. Are you?"

"I'm trying to be. I say he'll do his damnedest to prevent his wife's consulting another specialist. Mrs. Rush has now reported that this very thing is being contemplated, and whether or not Brodmart saw me at the lecture-hall with MacConochie, Scarpath trailed MacConochie away from my flat. Brodmart, too, will be dead against having his mistakes shown up. If a false diagnosis has been given he'll be the one to take the rap."

"And if the diagnosis was right, it'll be you." She let this shaft penetrate, then added. "Right or wrong, Dr. Brodmart may have given his opinion in good faith."

Colin mopped his brow. "There's not a vestige of hysteria in her." He hammered the table with his fist. "And equally, not a solitary sign of dissem—" He pulled up with sudden panic. "Don't quote me," he muttered. "I was wrong to say that."

"Assuming you aren't," she gave him back steadily, "the alternative seems to be that Dr. Brodmart is a dope addict and a—"

"Good God, mind your step!" He glanced round in alarm.

"No one's heard." She swept an eye over various long-haired and comatose persons in their vicinity. "Anyhow, can we prove it?"

"It'll be a messy job proving anything," he said despondently. "And I strongly suspect that whatever we prove that poor girl will still find herself matrimonially tied."

The same grim thought had been present in Elizabeth's mind at intervals during the raptures of the cinema. It had kept her left hand buried deep in the folds of her mink coat and her head upright, even though the cheek on David's side burned in sympathy with the bronzed one that drew constantly nearer, and every nerve in her body quivered on the brink of a frightening bliss.

It was harder still in the home-going taxi. The broad shoulder beside her was a magnet it required all her will power to resist. Three years ago, she thought, she wouldn't have had to battle so fiercely. Yet only this afternoon, how revolted she had been by Fanny's slanderous assertions!

For her own safety she prayed that Alison had come in, but no, the flat was in darkness. Then, when David had put on the lights, she saw with relief he was going to be practical.

"Sit down, Betsy. Now listen to me. It seems pretty clear your husband doesn't intend to release you without a struggle. That's according to English law. I find, though, you can get an American divorce, I believe, in Paris—that is if you want one."

She had gone a little pale. He looked at her as she sat cross-legged on the hearthrug in her soft blue Angora frock, the rich mink framing her slenderness. Then he moistened his lips and withdrew his gaze.

"There's this about it," he continued awkwardly. "The kind of divorce you'll be able to get won't free you in this country. I mean, you couldn't marry another British subject."

"That won't worry me," said Elizabeth.

David's pulses leapt. "Good! I hoped it wouldn't. That being so there's only the financial side to consider. If the four hundred gives out maybe you'll think of something else you can sell."

An elfin eye flashed on him. "My virtue? I might get fifteen and six for it, don't you think, on one of my good days?"

Her levity jarred him. He was reminded of the fact that the barelegged kid he had known had in three years' time penetrated, though only for a few steps, into a sophisticated world. Her husband's world. In one and the same moment he was jealous, enraged and curiously excited.

"That's not funny, Elizabeth." Blood hot in his face, he seized her roughly in his arms. "I . . . Look here, once this is over you're marrying me. Or am I a poor nut to hope it?"

"David! Oh, *please—*"

His lips had captured hers, the muscles restraining her were like iron, and for a space all her resolutions turned to water. It was true, then, David Beddoes loved her. She belonged to him, all of her—his to use, cherish, command.

There was a full minute of swimming ecstasy before she managed to fight free.

"No!" She was on her feet, wildly pleading. "Don't ask me anything—yet."

"Why not?" He loomed over her dangerously. "You're well, you're going to cut loose. Here, what's wrong with it?"

She backed from him round the sofa. A lump moved in her throat.

"Everything, David. I feel well, I feel fine, but . . . how do I know all that trouble won't come on again?" Her head sank, she picked at the fringed edge of a cushion. "I don't even know for sure if I can—cut loose. Till it's all smoothed out will—will you swear not to do this again?"

He breathed hard, but the sofa—and wisdom—lay between them.

"I swear," he muttered, and walked to the window.

The spectre had returned. She had nearly forgotten the page of inexorable scientific terms Geoffrey had left by her bedside, but now every damning sentence seemed branded in her memory. Who was she to think of love and marriage, overhung as she still was by the shadow of an incurable illness?

From the window David spoke, wooden, contained: "Okay, Betsy. I can wait."

Chapter Thirty-One
QUICK WORK

As SCARPATH re-strapped his watch a bell pealed through the silence. He strode to the door, opened it, and found Brodmart on the threshold.

"Just in time. She's had that stroke a moment ago."

"What!"

Brodmart backed against the closed door, all the fussy annoyance wiped from his face.

"I don't understand," he muttered. "We hadn't bargained for this, you know. Why have you got me here?"

"To sign a death certificate," snapped Scarpath. "That's one of your functions surely?"

Brodmart's jaw sagged. His skin grew more leaden, and one hand groped at an immaculate winged collar.

"Death certif—" He could not finish the word.

His starting eyes had fallen on the other man's dressing-gown. All up the front it was splashed with what seemed to be water.

"Well, what are you waiting for?"

Scarpath dragged at his arm, but it was no longer flaccid.

"No! I'll sign nothing. *Nothing!* Do you hear?"

"Oh? Better view the body before you decide."

Brodmart searched the contemptuous eyes and went a sicklier grey.

"Where is she?" he quavered.

"I'll show you." Scarpath pushed the older man towards the spare bedroom. "You were here when it happened, of course. We were having a drink together when we heard the fall and the cry, dashed through, and found—this."

Brodmart stared into the steamy bathroom. He did not move, and his gaze for long moments was glued to the half-filled tub.

The water was still warm, opalescent with soap. It partly covered a nude body, whose sightless eyes glared at the moist ceiling. Strands of grey hair lay plastered on the forehead, two kneecaps protruded, and round the neck had gathered a small crimson pool.

Scarpath was watching not the body but Brodmart.

"Simple enough," he murmured. "She turned giddy and struck one of the taps. The brandy may have helped. Smell it?"

There was a furious contraction of the physician's brow, but his gaze remained riveted. At last, with mechanical method, Brodmart began turning back his cuffs, blindly handing over a pair of platinum links into Scarpath's keeping. He had spoken not a word. Only when the dripping corpse had been hoisted and laid full-length on the bath-mat did speech return.

"What devil possessed you?" he accused venomously. "There was no need, no—"

"Stop. Did you bring your bag?"

"It's in the car. Hold on, I've not promised—"

Scarpath was already sprinting from the flat. In the street below he panted to the chauffeur,

"Hawkes, the doctor wants his kit. Yes, an accident, possibly serious. Don't wait, he'll go back by taxi."

The car moved away.

"Well," said Scarpath, in the bathroom again, "Hawkes is gone, and if he's questioned—which he won't be—he'll know the right answer. Here's all you'll want, but don't begin till you've got your lesson by heart. Are you listening?"

Broderick was on his knees, turning back the soaked hair from the base of the skull.

"I wasn't here," he said mutinously. "I've had nothing to do with it. . . . Well, go on?"

Scarpath hammered his words home. "You were here. Your own chauffeur will swear it. You came because I telephoned you. She'd had a slight attack in the late afternoon. Just enough to make me anxious. I couldn't keep her in bed, she insisted on going to the theatre with me, but I knew it would be suicidal for her to travel to France to-morrow morning, a project only you, in a semi-professional capacity, might have prevented—"

"Prevented! Why on earth should we want to prevent—"

"France." Scarpath leant over. "Paris. Her solicitor. She was changing her will."

Their eyes crossed swords. Understanding tinged with hate came into the doctor's expression.

"You had influence. Why didn't you dissuade her?"

"And plant suspicion in her mind that would wreck the whole scheme? She'd stolen a march on me, you see—called on my wife to-day instead of when we'd planned, got into a state of mind where it was impossible to cope with her. She had to be stopped. It was that or total loss. God, you fool, aren't you grateful to me?"

Scarpath mastered his rage. More evenly he said:

"I got a lot out of her. They are calling in another opinion. It was to have been done to-day, only by a streak of luck it's postponed. Let her get into MacConochie's hands and where will you be?"

"MacConochie! I knew it."

Brodmart collapsed to a quivering jelly. The probe he had automatically extracted from his bag tinkled against the marble floor.

"Yes," said Scarpath, eyeing him. "There'll be shouts and cheers when you're found guilty of malpractice. Wait, you'd better have a shot."

Disappearing he returned in a moment with a packet of bicarbonate of soda, from whose lower end he fished an envelope so thin as to seem merely a part of the inner wrappings. This, too, contained white powder, indistinguishable from the bicarbonate. He found a hypodermic syringe among the doctor's equipment and with deft speed performed a few operations.

"Been going it heavily, I see." His lips curled as he noted the thickly-dotted forearm into which Brodmart, with loathsome eagerness, was stabbing the needle. "Now, then, get yourself in hand. We've plenty to do."

The bathroom was cooling. Where mist had spread mirror-glass walls were showing open patches intercepted by glistening streaks. On three sides they reflected the distasteful scene—two conventional Englishmen, with a naked corpse between.

It was an hour later that Scarpath laid a fresh log on the drawing-room fire, sank with relief into the petit point chair, and poured a couple of stiff whiskies.

"Well, and where's the difficulty?"

Brodmart turned with a snarl. "Difficulty! There speaks the amateur. Cremation it's got to be. That's forced on us, but don't you realise what it entails?"

"A second death certificate, of course. Well, surely you can wangle that?" Scarpath paused. "You'll have to, won't you?"

The hooded eyes glared. "How? Crude, bungling . . . why, it stinks of foul play! Instead of consulting me—"

"No post-mortems, please! No, that's not meant to be funny. Can't you get it through your head I've pulled us both out of a tight corner? I've saved the pieces, not once but twice. Now it's up to you. What about it?"

"They won't accept just any physician's signature." Brodmart paced the room, a man trapped and goaded. "If not a police surgeon, it has to be some man of unimpeachable standing—on the register, no black marks. That sort's not easy to intimidate."

"Who's mentioned intimidation? Fractures do occur accidentally. You found the body, so there's no shadow of doubt it was an accident. Think! Among your vast collection of bootlickers, isn't there someone who will be flattered to see eye to eye with you? Yes, flattered. That's the idea. . . . Good! You have thought of him. I knew you would."

The driven specialist had paused. He was stroking his chin.

*

John Barkstone, gaunt, harassed, and suffering from a neglected chest cough, deposited his carefully-brushed bowler on a red lacquered commode.

"After you, Doctor," said Brodmart, with suave courtesy, and indicated the door facing them.

The room they entered was luxurious, fragrant with flowers and bright with wintry sunshine. Barkstone seldom saw any interior on a par with it, and as he thought of his shabby Paddington house and of the warm, chauffeur-driven sedan which had been sent to fetch him here his faint envy was tempered by gratification that he and not some more prosperous colleague had been approached. He remembered that more than once Brodmart had sent him a well-to-do patient, and he told himself that all the talk of the specialist's high-hatted smugness was the backbiting of jealous minds.

A young man moved forward gravely. His fresh complexion showed a slight ashy tinge, but his bearing was composed.

"Mr. Scarpath? How do you do. I was a great admirer of your father."

Scarpath shook hands. "A drink, Doctor?"

Barkstone conscientiously declined. "After, if I may. I suppose it's in order for me to view the body?"

"Certainly, Doctor," replied Brodmart, but he motioned Barkstone to a chair, explaining that he would like to outline the position a trifle more fully. He waited till their host had handed cigarettes, then placed his fingertips together and resumed with quiet candour.

"I was not, you may have gathered, in professional attendance on Mr. Scarpath's aunt. Having just arrived in England she had no medical adviser. She was, however, in such obviously bad shape that Mr. Scarpath confidentially requested me to see her and offer some friendly and tactful counsel—this in his opinion being the only way in which the somewhat headstrong lady might be induced to take proper precautions. I did see her, yesterday morning. I formed a serious conclusion and urged her first to take a complete rest and then to get in touch with Groves. Are you following me, Doctor?"

Barkstone, though actually engaged in drawing comparisons between his own reach-me-down suit and his companions' excellent tailoring, maintained an air of intelligent attention. Certain well-worn references rang a bell in his brain. When he caught the words "our common middle-age foe," he promptly murmured, "High blood pressure?" and saw he was right.

"Suicidally high," emphasized Brodmart. "Inveterate traveller, excitable, typically energetic and difficult to curb. I myself noted slight giddiness and traces of tongue-thickening. That is why I persuaded her to get into bed, but it seems she refused to stop there. Feeling better she got up, went out, and stubbornly insisted on accompanying Mr. Scarpath to a theatre. Am I correct, Scarpath?"

Scarpath gave a reticent account of the behaviour which had led to his telephoning Dr. Brodmart a second time.

"I hoped he might argue her out of that Channel-crossing. She wouldn't listen to me, though she was looking pretty rocky, and to crown it all was complaining of a chill."

"Which may account for her imprudent recourse to brandy," put in Brodmart delicately. "She took rather a lot, you said?"

"Half the decanter," admitted the young man with reluctance. "I'd hidden it, but she dug it out again last night."

Dr. Barkstone made deprecating sounds. The picture was coming clear.

"Well!" continued Brodmart. "I arrived here directly after the return from the theatre, took her temperature and incidentally her blood pressure. I then laid down the law, though it seems doubtful if she took it in. Once more I ordered her into bed, meaning when she was settled to administer a hot drink and aspirin, possibly a mild sedative—about all one could do at the moment. Mr. Scarpath and I sat here talking. Evidently Mrs. Rush had elected to take a bath, for the next we heard was a loud thud and a splash. Naturally we rushed in. There she lay in the hot water already unconscious. A heavily-boned woman, she had struck her head with such violence as to incur fracture with, it would appear, intercranial haemorrhage. Restoratives were of no avail."

"Quite. Most unfortunate." Dr. Barkstone coughed. "She had, of course, expressed her wish for cremation?"

Scarpath quietly flicked ash into a vase of lilies. "Often. Even yesterday, as it happens. Didn't we touch on the subject yesterday morning while you were here?" he inquired of Brodmart.

"She did, yes. Your wife, if need be, can be consulted for confirmation; but I think you mentioned some letter in which Mrs. Rush stated her desire?"

"Oh, yes!"

Scarpath searched on a writing-table and had the letter in his hand when Barkstone, with a polite gesture, stopped him. As two persons, one a relation, and the other Dr. Brodmart himself—here Barkstone inclined courteously to his colleague—had heard the wish verbally expressed further proof was unnecessary. It remained only to take a look at the body and append his signature to the form.

The bedroom showed a blue dimness. Brodmart pulled back the curtains, the better to reveal what lay shrouded on the bed.

"I think," he said calmly, "that death must have been almost instantaneous. Do you share my opinion, Doctor?"

Dr. Barkstone did not immediately reply. He was gazing down on the features, which showed no discoloration. Now he was turning the head, parting the stiffly-dried hair at the back and examining the skull injury. His eyes when he lifted them held a startled expression.

"Eh? Oh, er, yes, Doctor! Decidedly." Hesitating, he folded back the pale-blue sheet and, in silence, extended his observations. "Quite." He spoke absently. "I'd say the fracture merely hastened what was probably inevitable. All this congestion, badly-taxed heart . . . Yes. And now, if I might have a wash?"

Ten minutes more and he had quitted the flat.

"Of course," muttered Scarpath. "I said you'd have him eating out of your hand."

Slumped in his seat, Brodmart dabbed a streaming brow. "Barkstone's no fool," he retorted. "See his face when he found that hole?"

"What of it? He can't make difficulties without involving himself. Not now we've got his signature—and the cremation will be over and done with before *The Times* can print any announcement. For the rest, hasn't this given us exactly what we wanted?"

Brodmart sprang up mulishly. "This ends it, Scarpath. I'm wiping the slate clean. I'm cancelling appointments, do you hear? Two months retirement in the Canaries is my programme. So reckon me out."

"Two months? You're an optimist. No, Brodmart, get this clear: once MacConochie gets a look in you're washed up for good. Which is it to be—bullet through your brain or saving your reputation with a fat bonus thrown in? Earlier, too, than you were banking on. Only a matter of probating the will."

Brodmart wheeled. "And having found you fallible on two counts," he jarred, "how am I to know there'll be enough in this to warrant further risks?"

"Just thinking of that?" Scarpath spoke cuttingly. "I can only repeat I had my information straight from the horse's mouth—in other words the solicitor's clerk. A bottle of cheap champagne, and he spilled all the details. That was in Cannes. Well, we can't play about. Shall you throw up the sponge?"

Brodmart winced. "Edinburgh," he mumbled, licking his lips, and glancing towards the telephone. "I can just make certain about this 'flu attack. If it should finish the bounder off . . ."

"Use a call-box." Scarpath was watching him.

"Yes, yes—obviously." Brodmart sank back into his chair. "Well, let's hear it. No nurse at the moment? I see. Well, what do you propose?"

Chapter Thirty-Two
ONE MORE RIVER

Elizabeth lifted blank eyes from the letter in her hand.

"Alison, it's Fanny. Do see what she says."

Bolting her coffee and knotting her scarf, Alison made a grab. Her brows shot up.

"Goodness, this is a Christmas packet! We certainly never expected this. After all, though, she is your aunt. Going to play up?"

"How can I do anything else? Oh, damn! I do wish poor Fanny didn't put my back up so dreadfully. I could be so fond of her, especially when she overwhelms me with kindness and—and generosity." Elizabeth snuffled and felt for her handkerchief.

"Crying?" Midway the wild hunt for gloves and reading-glasses, Alison turned a suspicious eye. "Or did you go and catch cold on yesterday's drive?"

"Only a tiny bit. Now, don't start badgering me, I adored getting into the country, and I'm feeling perfectly grand. It's just that—"

"Gargle, then, and keep in the warm. It *is* marvellous news, we'll thrash it all out this evening."

Alison crammed a last bit of toast and marmalade into her mouth and dashed out, chewing. She herself was rather bowled over by Elizabeth's letter, though by the time Colin rang her up she had more or less worked out the explanation and along most satisfactory lines. Having made sure her secretary was out of the room preparing mid-morning tea, she informed Colin that the problem was all solved.

"Mrs. Rush must have a good heart, you know. She's climbed down beautifully; but the big bang is that *Scarpath's given in about the divorce.* So what?"

"Given in!" There was a flabbergasted pause. "Wait. Does it mean he'll furnish grounds for—?"

"He'll be a dirty dog if he doesn't. That part's not very plain. Anyhow, Mrs. R. hasn't said beans about her will, but she does mention making some financial arrangement for Betsy. So that's all hunky dory, too. Well, why don't you shout?"

"Wait," said Colin's voice again, and this time it sounded strained. "Is Elizabeth all right?"

"Perfectly, except for a bit of a sniffle. Why—? Oh, you mean you've got a full day, and can't look in on her! Mrs. Marshall is there, we haven't really got any more worries, have we, now this letter has come? I'll tell you later why I think Mrs. R. has come round."

"Tell me now."

"Why, I think Mrs. R. will make a new will, splitting her money up between E. and G. Wouldn't that explain G.'s sudden complaisance?"

Another silence. "Yes, perhaps." Colin rang off.

"Whew!" exploded Alison, and attacked her work with fresh vigour. She was only just realising how for ten days or more the various perils of Elizabeth's dilemma had been weighing her down like a millstone.

Elizabeth, meanwhile, had read her letter three times, always with the same sensations of bewilderment; though wasn't it truly like Fanny, blowing violently hot or cold but at rock bottom rather magnificent?

Here in part was what she had written:

"Geoffrey has convinced me. My peacemaking efforts will be wasted, so, although I bitterly deplore what has happened, I will simply do my best to make both of you happier. Separations, I am told, can be managed quietly. I hope this is true.

"Funds will be provided you, but for the present don't expect me to hold another personal interview. The fact is, after yesterday's scene I had rather a bad giddy turn. I hadn't wanted you to know this, Elizabeth, but since your father's death, at least three doctors have warned me seriously about my blood pressure. While there may be no immediate cause for alarm, I am at last realising I'll have to go slow and not get over-excited."

Scales had fallen from Elizabeth's eyes. She thought of her aunt, unwilling to breathe a word of her condition lest those about her, most of all her niece, try to regulate her conduct. Poor Fanny, irritated by sympathy, spurning advice, Spartan to the finish. All in character—and she, Elizabeth, had never seen.

"Geoffrey has convinced me." Yes, it had taken Geoffrey to soften Fanny's anger and turn her from enemy into friend. That meant he was being decent, and reasonable, too. It was hard not to feel grateful to him.

Mrs. Marshall was clearing away breakfast. Elizabeth sprang up and began helping her, only to be waved away.

"What, miss, and you in your pink finery?" Mrs. Marshall had never quite digested Elizabeth's married status. "You run along and get into something warm. Got a cold coming, haven't you? Well, then, you'll have a boiled onion for your lunch. It's what I always give Mr. Marshall. He gets colds something shocking."

"Onions? Oh, no!" Elizabeth went cherry red, and hugged her velvet négligée about her. "That is . . . yes, of course, whatever you say."

She was thinking of what had taken place in this very spot last night. David had sworn there would be no repetition, but it was herself she couldn't altogether trust. By all means onions. They might stiffen her resolve.

Changed into a wine-red jumper frock, she considered her trans-figured fortunes. It was harder than ever after Saturday's humiliating scene to accept Fanny's favours, yet how not accept them, at least till she was certain of being well? Her misgivings came back. If this aston-ishing recovery proved only another deceptive flash in the pan, then it was good-bye to David, to life, to everything. Freedom from Geoffrey would be an ironical joke.

Still, it was getting impossible to believe she ever had suffered from that nightmare disease. Daily manipulation had resulted in her being able to walk anywhere without a stumble; no kindred symptom had reappeared, and now other obstacles had removed themselves she refused to quail before the chief one.

"One more river to cross. It looks like the Mississippi at Memphis, but maybe when I walk right up to it I'll find it's nothing but a creek. Or no river at all, just a mirage. One More River. . . . Where's my mouth-organ?"

She ground out the negro spiritual, drawing courage from its harmon-ies. There came the sun. How warm it shone! One of Alison's nice cushions was ripped. She must get her workbag and mend it. What was that tucked down in the sofa corner? David's pipe, the stem bitten nearly in two. That told a story.

She stopped playing and pressed the pipe against her cheek. She might some time to-day slip out and buy a very superior new one—have it as a surprise for this evening—that is, if a woman's choice in pipes could be trusted. She wondered if the fine weather would last till three-thirty, that being the hour when Mrs. Marshall propped her feet on the second kitchen chair, covered her face with a newspaper and indulged in a snooze.

Scarpath stopped his Chrysler round the corner from the Old Foundling gates. Mists were gathering again, and very soon December gloom would be settling down, thick and damp. A bit awkward for him if Elizabeth had not stirred out to-day. No great matter, though, with *The Times*'s notice still not inserted and MacConochie not due back till the end of the week.

Savouring his cigarette, he let the smoke trickle from his lips in a thin spiral. He took another whiff, inhaled deeply—and sat forward, eyes intent on the small figure just coming into view.

Yes, it was she. Wearing her mink coat—luck that hadn't been sold!—the fur-edged hat he had selected for her in the Faubourg St. Honoré, and trimly-buckled brown suède shoes, American style. She had been to the hairdresser's. He would scarcely have recognised her with her cheeks rounded out and this new spring in her step.

What the devil was drawing her back? Oh, the flower-barrow at the corner. She was acquiring russet chrysanthemums and a big bunch of dyed beech-leaves. The coster was wrapping them up. He slid out of the car, and by the time she had toiled up the three flights of stairs had his finger on the bell-button. She was humming a tune. As she saw him it died in her throat, but this time there was no shrinking start. She came forward with a dubious smile.

"Geoffrey! Would you like to come in?"

"Can't stop." Short and sharp he brushed her invitation aside. "It's your aunt. If you want to see her alive, then come along with me, now."

"Fanny!" Elizabeth went white. "She's ill? Oh, Geoffrey, it's not possible!"

"In a nursing home. Conscious, but only just. Asking for you. Otherwise I shouldn't have intruded. Well, will you come?"

"But—but—" She had remembered the blood pressure. "I was a little anxious, but this! I can't take it in."

She had dropped her bundle and her latchkey. Picking them up he unlocked the door and with a brusque movement thrust the flowers inside.

"Of course it's a knock-out. She had a stroke in her bath. I've rushed her into a first-class place, but her speech has practically gone, and I'm afraid there's not much chance she'll recover." He looked at his watch. "Can't you make up your mind?"

"I . . . oh, Geoffrey, I'll come! Just let me explain to Alison's servant so they won't be—"

"Rubbish, I'll have you back before your friend is home, or if not, you can ring up. Call this woman, quick, if you must, though I warn you—"

Elizabeth pushed through into the living-room, where tea was laid before a bright fire, then on to the kitchen. A kettle was simmering, but there was no one to greet her. Mrs. Marshall must have done what she called popping round to the dairy or the grocer's. She was not in the flat.

"She's gone out, Geoffrey. Can't I just telephone Alison?"

He frowned. "Here, scribble her a line." He jerked his gold pencil at her and started down the steps.

Elizabeth tore a corner from the white paper round the flowers, and scrawled a few words. *Fanny dying . . . Her fault, perhaps. If only she'd humoured her . . .*

"Hurry!"

She banged the door and caught him up. After all, if they did find her gone they couldn't feel worried now. Fanny's letter had put a stop to all that.

Geoffrey was already in the car. Roughly impatient, he flung her a rug and started the engine. He must, she thought, have a genuine fondness for Fanny. It meant that somewhere in what had seemed to her a block of blue ice there was one warm, human spark. It must be so, since nothing substantial could be got by this frantic rush to Fanny's bedside. What other reason—?

None whatever that she could see, and his face, when she stole a side glance at him certainly wore a look of controlled suffering.

"Did you have Dr. Brodmart?" she asked.

He shook his head. "Not his line. A man called Groves."

Vaguely this relieved her. "She wrote me, you know. Or didn't she tell you?"

"Wrote you? No, she said nothing. I knew a letter had been posted, just before she had the stroke." Geoffrey paused. "How did her writing strike you?"

"Well . . . I did think it was a tiny bit wobbly. Not much. I certainly never imagined . . . It's here in my bag, only you couldn't read it in this light."

He was not listening, sternly intent on negotiating tramlines. The feeling that she was being regarded simply as a piece of luggage Fanny had asked for lessened the awkwardness she might have experienced in his company. Making no further effort at conversation she began to take note of their movements. The nursing-home must be farther afield than she had supposed, though as London for the most part was an untracked wilderness to her a bus labelled Highbury Barn carried no message. They seemed to be making a vast number of turns, whizzing from wide, cheap thoroughfares ablaze with red and blue neon lights into dark suburban areas, all unfamiliar.

Rain was falling. As the screen-wiper made its first sweep she uttered a cry of recognition.

"Why, that looks like Hampstead Heath!"

"Yes, and we're nearly there. The home is in Highgate."

Elizabeth nodded. Nurse Badger had mentioned Highgate as a favourite region for nursing-homes, quieter than the West End.

"By the way," said Geoffrey suddenly. "Have you had tea?"

"Yes, thanks," she answered, astonished at the mark of consideration. "I went to Fuller's in Regent Street."

He said no more, but began with frowning concentration to examine street signs almost indecipherable in the gloom. There were large villas about them now, curving irregular roads and tree-lined gardens, dank and dismal in the rain. Except where the headlamps blazed a trail little could be distinguished.

All at once Geoffrey pulled up with an angry jolt.

"Blast!" he swore. "Serves me right for trying a short cut. We can't get through here. Look behind, will you? Tell me how far I can back."

They were in a narrow turning walled high on both sides, a lane separating back gardens. Just ahead, round the angle which had hidden it, were a charcoal brazier and a pair of red lanterns where the pavement had been torn up.

Elizabeth craned her neck through the window, the sleety drizzle in her face.

"About ten yards, then turn left." Backward they crawled. The red glare was hidden again. "Mind the lamp-post. A little more. . . . *Oh!* What was that?"

In her right arm had come a sharp, stabbing pain. A furrier's needle left in her coat and taking all this time to work through? She had known of its happening, but as she clutched her arm, Geoffrey's hand thrust itself into her open mouth, gagging her.

Only for an instant did the grotesque thought penetrating her mind lend her a wild-cat's strength. She was conscious of a fierce struggle, of steel rivets clamping her down into her seat, and of an insidious torpor that slurred through her veins.

Far away she heard the hum of the Chrysler's engine. It ebbed, it dwindled, the passing of a demon express. Now it was gone.

CHAPTER THIRTY-THREE
EVIE IS WANTED

UNDER the choked gas-burner Evie fiddled once again with her beloved ship-puzzle. B-r-r-h! This room was an icebox. Parsons had not only failed to light a fire, he was not in the house at all. Never mind, Geoffrey wouldn't be long.

As to what had been happening, she hadn't the dimmest idea. Only this sudden, bewildering telephone-call from her brother, bringing her up to town to do some strange shopping at Harrods' and lug her purchases here to the house. A cold, empty, echoing house. Why, if she hadn't remembered her latchkey she wouldn't have got in! Five o'clock of a sleety December afternoon, huddling here in her coat, waiting for enlightenment. . . .

Down there in Hampshire her eighty-year-old hostess would be seated in a cosy arm-chair before a blazing red fire. The velvet curtains would be drawn, and Moffatt, the tall parlourmaid, would have brought in the tea. Pikelets to-day. A new jam sandwich, *and* yesterday's currant cake. Mrs. Todd-Bryce would have spoken severely if no uncut cake had appeared at her tea-table, and for visitors, of course, she always had two.

Wistfully Evie pictured the perfect ritual of the past week. Now she would have been listening to the Children's Hour over the radio. Presently dazzling copper jugs of hot water would be carried up to the bedrooms and snuggled under wool-worked cosies, as in mother's time. Dinner next, beautifully served; then Miss Milligan patience, and at ten sharp candles and bed. Yes, it had been a life replete with amusements and devoid of rude shocks. She had longed to continue it, but—

Was that Geoffrey?

Flurried, Evie sprang up and ran into the hall. Her brother was just striding in, a limp burden in his arms. Evie's mouth fell open.

"You—you've found her. Where?"

Not answering, Geoffrey deposited what he held on the dusty parquet. Only then did Evie grasp the fact that her sister-in-law was unconscious—fainted, or . . . no, she was breathing. Geoffrey stooped for a cursory examination, straightened, glanced round.

"Alone, are you?"

"Oh, yes, I can't think where Parsons . . . Geoffrey, how—" Evie gulped. *"She's wearing her mink coat."*

It did not enter her head to do anything about Elizabeth. She was still staring, goggle-eyed and stunned, when a curt question roused her.

"Oh, yes, dear, everything! There's the parcel, by the stairs. Two nurse's uniforms, a—"

"What did you say to old Todd-Bryce?"

"Why, what you told me to say. That my sister-in-law was still in the nursing-home, dangerously ill, and—"

"Yes. It will be true in another hour." He consulted his watch. "You understand, don't you, we've got to hush up this past week."

"A whole week! I can't . . . Geoffrey! Has someone been keeping her?" Evie whispered.

"Call it that," he said curtly. "Better not pry into it."

Dingily-red, Evie edged away from the figure on the floor. She was remembering the backless evening-gowns, the painted toe-nails—and then, in a flash, the rough telephone mechanic. Every shoot of compassion withered. She felt physically sick.

Geoffrey had lit a cigarette. Now, his hands on her shoulders, he pulled her round.

"Listen, Evie. You and only you can help me cover this damned business up. It's Brodmart's suggestion. He's being a real friend. You did have some nurse's training, isn't that so?"

"Me? Oh, yes, Geoffrey, ages ago, and I don't know if—"

"Right! Then get into one of those uniforms—yes, now, as quickly as you can manage it. Don't argue, it's our only solution if we're to avoid a nasty scandal. Brodmart will tell you all you need to know, it won't be much. Here's Brodmart, I'll let him in."

As she had not heard a car, the doctor, out of breath and with melting ice on his upturned collar, had evidently come by tube. Geoffrey had motioned her towards the stairs, and the two men were holding a whispered conference, curiously ignoring the crumpled form at their feet. Evie had lugged her bulky parcel to the landing when Geoffrey sped after her, cut the cord with his little gold knife, and hauled out the two night-garments—one of nun's veiling, the other of thick Jaeger wool—which it seemed were designed for Elizabeth and not herself.

"There! Now carry on."

Evie collected what remained, and in her frozen bedroom struggled into her new and unaccustomed attire.

All so strange, so upsetting! Panic at the thought of how on earth she was to behave before qualified nurses without disgracing herself made her weak; but, of course, if Geoffrey expected this of her that ended it. Her numbed fingers had a job wedging the bone studs into the stiffly-starched belt, but at last it was done, and her cap, a lovely winged one, such as she had found so becoming before the Armistice cut short her happiest dream, rested for a moment on her head till she folded it in paper to preserve its crispness from the rain. How nice she had chosen mauve uniforms! Just as though she had known they were for her.

"Ready?" called the stern voice of her brother.

"Yes, dear, coming!"

She had fallen into a daze, trying to recall some of the things the Red Cross sisters had taught her—the proper way to make beds, dipping the thermometer in a glass of water. . . .

"Lock these up." Geoffrey threw a heap of clothing on the floor. "Mind you bring me the key."

She noticed he kept the beautiful mink coat slung over his arm.

When she scuttled down two stretcher-bearers were coming in at the front door. "Gently," grunted Dr. Brodmart, easing the limp figure into place and making it into a mummy with blankets. The gas! Evie ran into the dining-room to extinguish it, and last of the little procession followed out into the horrid darkness and slush.

By the gates a huge white ambulance was pulsing. Its lighted interior was almost a small room. Curtly polite, the doctor signalled her to mount the steps. Then he got in and closed the door.

"My brother—isn't he coming?" faltered Evie, a queasy feeling in her stomach.

"In his own car."

Perched stiffly on her folding seat, Evie heard the ambulance grind ponderously on its way. Dr. Brodmart, also seated, passed a clean white handkerchief over his face, tucked it in his pocket, and glanced once at the shapeless cocoon on the stretcher against the wall. His hand trembled oddly, but his voice when he spoke again was even and rather like a schoolmaster's, dogmatic and precise.

"Listen carefully, Miss Scarpath. Here is what I shall expect you to do . . ."

Round the curve of Heath Crescent came Penelope Wibbe, dragging listlessly on her return from school. She was dangling a disreputable attaché-case, and her woven sash, unknotted, impeded her steps. Rehearsals for the Christmas play had kept her late, and even the once-coveted role of King Herod had no magic to gild an existence all at once grown stale and unprofitable.

A week ago she had vibrated in the centre of real drama. Now she had been shoved into the wings and the safety curtain had descended with a bang. She had helped her protégée out of peril to safety; she had enjoyed the rapturous notes and the beautifully-bound *Marco Polo* which had come by this morning's post, but this awful flatness! It was getting her down.

Oh, well, what could one hope from reality? Villains never turned out as promised, and that was that. This one apparently was just letting things slide. Presently one of those discreet, undefended divorce-suits would come along without even the thrill of being called as witness to cruelty. Might as well face it. She, the heroine of a week, was just Pen Wibbe again, playing net-ball in the mud, yawning over prep.

Pen stopped dead in her tracks. Why, what was an L.C.C. ambulance doing, drawing away from the house next door? Some dull road-accident, obviously. There weren't even any watchers, but then you couldn't expect this blankly-respectable street to scare up a crowd. All she saw as the big white hulk moved past her was a smart, grey car, bang opposite the gates. Since there was no use trying to get a peep inside the ambulance's curtained windows she might as well turn her attention to that.

A man was dumping a fur rug or something into the rear seat. Stepping back he bumped into her. Good God, it was the brute himself!

Pen's breath deserted her, but not her wits.

"That ambulance!" she blazed. "Who's in it?"

It might have been the pistol-shot suddenness of her question which produced the stunned silence. He didn't know her from Adam, evidently, but he was taking her all in—banded school-hat, draggled sash, knee muddied by its contact with Betty Barnes's lacrosse stick in the passage.

His stern scrutiny relaxed. "My old servant," he answered amusedly. "Tumbled off a ladder and managed to smash his thigh. Any objections?"

"Oh," gulped Pen, a punctured balloon.

In her whole life she had never felt sillier. Indeed it was mortification alone that kept her shoe-button eyes boring into him with bellicose intentness and barred from her features every vestige of softening. She racked her brain for some remark that would make retreat not quite so ignominious, but she was still planted there facing him when his queer light eyes slid impatiently from her gimlet glare, and a lithe movement left her alone on the pavement.

In her ear a door slammed. A second more, and the grey car shot away into the rain.

Chapter Thirty-Four
GONE

OVERTAKING Alison in Mecklenburgh Square David learned of Fanny's astounding *volte-face*.

"Well," he said slowly. "For crying out loud!"

Alison remarked that he seemed less pleased than might have been expected. He commandeered her manuscript-case and walked on for ten yards in complete silence.

"So Scarpath's shown the white feather, has he? Good, I thought we'd got him stymied." Brooding another moment, David blurted out, "All the same we could have wiggled along without that damned Rush woman's patronage."

"Go on!" jeered his cousin. "Who do you think you are, Mussolini and Hercules rolled into one? I see. You just can't abide having Elizabeth staked by any one but your almighty self."

"Conceit, you think? Oh, hell, maybe you're right. Somehow I'd have liked it better if—"

"If she went on being a poor stranded orphan?" Alison melted. "Oh, my pet, that's not conceit. It's sheer, crawling humility. Listen! Don't you realise that if Elizabeth takes you it will be all for love and your glorious Sex Appeal, which even your own cousin can detect when she doesn't feel like sloshing you?"

"If!" he underscored, and then: "How do you work that?"

"Baby! Because, if I'm any judge, her aunt will stop this allowance the very minute Betsy marries again. She'll make her new will in favour of Geoffrey Scarpath—and *that's* why he's taking this unselfish view."

David brightened. "By George, you may have hit it at that! Gosh, I could eat a horse. What's for dinner?"

"Steak and kidney pudding—with mushrooms. I rather believe Elizabeth's made us a butterscotch pie."

"Swell doings!"

As they climbed the stairs David said, "I never told you how that fortune-teller at the Wibbes' party predicted all this, that is in a rather hazy way. She was wrong about one thing, though. She said I was damned hot-headed."

"Well, aren't you?" Alison fitted her key into the door.

"Balls," said David loftily. "I've had the sense to take prompt action. If that's ruined anything I can't see it. Where's Elizabeth?"

They were in the living-room, looking round.

"In the kitchen, I expect." Alison disappeared, returning at once with a puzzled expression. "Gone out," she announced, "before tea, while Mrs. Marshall was having forty winks. She's not made the pie."

"Out? Why, hang it all, it's after seven!"

"Oh, it's this cursed rush-hour, she's stuck in a taxi, that's all. Maybe she found there was no nutmeg or . . . I begged her not to stir out, she had a suspicion of a cold, but I suppose when the sun came out she—"

Alison's voice trailed away. From the passage she spoke again. "Why, she must have come in! Look at these flowers."

David scowled at the moist bundle. "What's this, a note?"

Together they read the hurried scrawl. *Fanny's dying in a nursing-home. Geoffrey's taking me there now. Quite all right, I'll be back for dinner.*

"Dying!" Alison paused. "I wonder if she had a stroke? The letter did mention something about high blood pressure and—"

"Why didn't Elizabeth ring you up?"

"Maybe she did try. My line was hectic all afternoon. Let's ask—"

David was already hammering Mrs. Marshall with questions. The answers were the same. She herself had popped out for fresh cream, being absent not above ten minutes and confident of spying Mrs. Greentree as the latter returned; and coming in she had failed to notice the flowers lying in the dark on the hall table. That they had not been put in water seemed a plain indication of Mrs. Greentree's haste.

In the living-room David knit his brows blackly over the triangular scrap of paper. "Nursing-home. That means sanatorium, I take it. She doesn't say where."

"Idiot, she didn't know where. Can't you see she hadn't time to think properly? You don't when your aunt's dying."

"Where's that damned letter?"

"Mrs. Rush's letter? It should be round about. I'll look."

Alison rummaged, but the pages of thin blue note-paper had disappeared completely.

"She put it in her bag, of course. David, what's the matter with you?"

"That devil called for her. I don't like it, that's flat."

"Oh, nonsense! He may be a devil, I don't say he's not, but you can't call him a fool. Who but a fool would start luring his wife away on false pretences when she's got three huskies like us to protect her?"

"I'm not so sure." David went on staring at the note. "We haven't got anything definite on him, have we? We might have in a few days, but as matters stand there's not a single damned thing to hang your hat on. We can't prove they made her sick on purpose, that Scarpath's ever known there was a will in his wife's favour, or—well, I put it to you, supposing we nabbed him now what charge could we bring?"

Their eyes met. Alison fiddled with the chrysanthemums.

"Oh, David, I know it's all right! It'll be simple as pie to find out if Fanny really is ill, where they've taken her, everything, only it won't be necessary, because Elizabeth will be turning up any minute." She threw off her coat. "Now what are you up to?"

"Dialling Colin." He tugged busily at the numbers.

"You won't get him." Alison crossed into her room. "He's had one hell of a day. Mix yourself a drink, act as though you had two ounces of brain."

Colin was ushering a baby into the world. There was no telling when the job would be finished. Leaving a message, David looked at his watch. After all, it wasn't so late, considering.

At nine Alison brought in the steak and kidney pudding, set it on the table, and carried it out again. She cleared the ash-trays of half-smoked Chesterfields and filled two breakfast cups with extra strong coffee.

"Do keep away from that window!" In her irritation she overlooked the fact that she herself had been hanging out in the rain pretty frequently. "Why on earth are you putting on your coat?"

That was so. Why was he? David dialled Bream's number, getting no reply. "What's Scarpath's Mayfair address?"

"South Street, wasn't it? I know it was where Colin went to the party. Elizabeth had a card, but she threw it in the fire. Wait, won't your detective friend know?"

Back at the window David ground his teeth. Of course Bream knew, but a fat lot of good that did if Bream was on the loose.

"Pipe down," Alison begged. "Even supposing Betsy was away all night, would there be any reason to tear our hair? There's no point in hurting her—none. And her aunt *is* dying."

All night!

David couldn't think, still less settle into a chair. Reason might support Alison's contention. It had no power to stem the ghastly rushes of fear.

It was close on midnight when Colin came in. His British composure was a help, but quite suddenly Alison found herself abandoning her role of comforter.

"You see, Colin, it's not a bit like her to leave us in doubt. If she hasn't telephoned does it mean she's being prevented?"

"Prevented, yes; but I don't know if we need draw bad conclusions. The nursing-home may be out of London. On the way back Scarpath may have had a breakdown in a difficult spot. Or again an attendant may have been told to ring you and simply neglected the order."

David had thought of a third contingency. "Suppose," he muttered, "she's fallen back under that fellow's influence?"

"In what way?" Colin's eyes narrowed.

"About herself, about him. The one other time he had a go at her didn't he nearly convince her she'd done a risky thing in breaking off the Brodmart treatment?"

Colin returned the glowering gaze steadily. Quite true, Scarpath represented the solid body of opinion he as yet could not authoritatively contradict. During the past week of improvement nothing had actually been said to discredit the honesty of Scarpath's intentions. There had been nothing to say.

"He's got her all to himself again," urged David. "We've kept things dark for fear of upsetting her. He goes and knocks her flat with this news about her aunt. What if she goes haywire, believes she's getting a relapse and puts the blame on us?"

"She'd hate us to know," said Alison heavily. "Colin, can it be that?"

Colin said hesitatingly, "Let's give her a little longer. If she's not back in an hour—"

"Yes, what?" The cousins spoke in unison.

"Well, we can't go far wrong by informing Scotland Yard."

"Why fool about?" fired David. "Let's do it now. You've got a pal at the Yard, why not get through to him?"

In spite of his impatience it was easy to interpret the odd conflict in his eyes. By to-morrow, he was thinking, he might be calling himself a fatuous ass.

"It's a little difficult to define our position," murmured Colin, picking up the receiver. "Whitehall 1212? Inspector Headcorn, please. . . . Out of London? Then connect me with the Lost Persons Department."

What followed was unsatisfactory. Wasn't the appeal decidedly premature? Hundreds of these messages were handed in, and in a high percentage of cases the missing individuals turned up almost at once. Unusual circumstances, eh? Such as—?

Colin hung up. "You see?" He shrugged. "She's *with her husband.* That cancels us completely. Did you notice the drop in temperature when I mentioned Scarpath's name? The admiral was a popular idol. You can't explain a thing like this in a few sentences, and if you could—"

"I get it," gritted David. "We're confounded mischief-makers—or worse."

"Quite. Shall we try Bream again?"

The detective was still absent. There was the South Street flat, of course, where inquiries could be made regarding the nursing-home; but Colin was disgusted to find he had taken no note of the number on the one occasion he had visited the building. David had already canvassed the telephone-directory without discovering any town number for the Honourable Frederick Treddle, and Angela, it seemed, had flown to Paris with her usual bland casualness as to hotels.

"Come along," said Colin dubiously. "I dare say I'll know which house it is. If there's a servant in residence we may at least collect some information about Mrs. Rush."

Telephoning had wasted so much time that it was nearly two o'clock before the two men reached South Street. The various converted houses had all been closed for the night, and the one Colin believed to contain Treddle's flat seemed deserted.

"There's bound to be a porter." Colin kept his finger glued to a bell-button. "It will be something to discover if and when Mrs. Rush was removed."

"If! You think there may be a doubt?"

"I don't think at all. Look, we've roused someone."

A frowsy man peered up the area steps.

"No, sir, I'm not the porter. 'E's 'opped off to Brighton, won't be back till to-morrow some time. Wot was it you was wanting?"

The deputy, an uncle, knew nothing except that a note had been left at his lodgings late Sunday afternoon asking him to mind the house. The tenants being all absent the porter had snatched this convenient moment for a breather.

"Lady took bad? It's the first I've heered on it."

David was pulling at Colin's arm. "Let's get back," he urged. "She may have come home."

But no, Alison's headshake blasted this hope. Three in the morning, and Elizabeth still gone.

Chapter Thirty-Five

AN OPENED WINDOW

In dripping gloom the ambulance turned into a semicircular drive, curved to a doorway and stopped. Dr. Brodmart got out, and as he set foot on the gravel the house door opened wide and in the pathway of bright yellow light a woman in black peered expectantly outward.

"Doctor, is it you? I've only this minute got in, but you'll find everything quite ready. Will you bring the patient in?"

She had the pinched lips of a martinet and an air of rather passé elegance, artificial pearls visible between the fur facings of her coat and a picture hat of black velvet atilt on her fluffy dark hair. The doctor shook hands, noted the eagerness of welcome in her very luminous brown eyes, and murmured a few words.

"The admiral's son? Oh, I didn't realise!"

She directed a pleased glance at the private car which was drawing up alongside the ambulance, and another, even more approvingly interested, at the young man now gravely approaching.

Dr. Brodmart became business-like. "We must get her straight into a blanket-bed, Miss Baldman. You're giving us the three rooms, I hope?"

"Oh, certainly, Doctor! Just vacated, wasn't it lucky? You did say you were bringing your own nurse?"

"Yes, yes, here she is. She used to work with me, now she's just back from abroad. Miss Tompkins."

Miss Baldman bowed with distant condescension and took no further notice of the angular woman sidling into the light. She waited till the stretcher-bearers manoeuvred their burden out of the ambulance, then turned inside and led the way to the upper floor.

"Unconscious?" She whispered it, glancing back at the muffled form on the stretcher.

"I've been compelled to administer morphia," said Brodmart curtly. "Are these our rooms?" He waved his gloves towards a group of doors, the central one open to reveal a buff-clad nurse. "I see. In that case you and your own nurse may leave us. I'll have a word with you presently in your office."

"If you're sure I can't be of any assistance, Doctor?"

"If I want you, I'll ring."

In her cosy room below Miss Baldman removed her hat and her pearls, arranged a snowy organdie coif on her head and jerked round her neck a black ribbon laden with a large silver cross. Behind a screen hung a mirror. In an anxious flutter she studied herself, toned down the matinée-going rouge on her thin cheekbones—very few complimentary tickets these days!—and decided it was better to keep on her black satin dress, since it had originally come from a good place and showed its age less than the workaday serge.

When Dr. Brodmart joined her she had tea ready before a cheerful fire, serving it in the fine old cups she had jealously guarded. The great man looked shockingly seedy—much changed from her last glimpse of him six years ago. So many of the big doctors were run off their legs and never took the rest which would have put them in condition.

"Well, Miss Baldman, and how are you making it?"

Brightly she smiled. "Oh, so-so, Doctor! Not quite full up just now, and naturally not over-staffed. I have the usual bother with young nurses, so independent these days, especially the incompetents. I expect you had that in mind when you brought someone you knew was reliable?"

Brodmart eyed her closely. Dyed hair; getting old, haggard with the struggle of hiding it—or from something else? Heloise Baldman—a rural vicar's daughter who many years ago had flourished in Bulstrode Street till quarrels with her partner, another neurotic spinster, had led to her flouncing out of the luxury establishment and setting up on her own in this remote and cheaper quarter. For a time he had sent her his less affluent patients, but flaws in her régime had made him withdraw his patronage. . . .

"Reliable, yes." He was answering her question. "Miss Baldman, as you know I never discuss my cases. In the present instance, however, I feel bound to take you a little into my confidence."

For a few minutes he spoke in a reticent undertone.

"I see," murmured the matron tactfully. "Most tragic. Poor man!"

"We must, you understand, avoid scandal."

"Oh, dear me, of course!"

"That is why, as a mark of friendship, I am giving the case my own personal attention, and why I have placed the unfortunate lady here, instead of in the West End. We must have no interference from the persons who are responsible for her getting into this state. Should they by chance discover her whereabouts and make nuisances of themselves will you know how to deal with them?"

"Leave it to me, Doctor!" The thin lips snapped together. Then, half-expecting a snub, Miss Baldman ventured, "Is she at all likely to recover?"

He ignored that. It did not surprise her.

"I'll tell you this: she tried to throw herself out of the ambulance. That's why I had to inject morphia, by main force. Unbalanced as she is we can't have a strange nurse being told fantastic stories or it may be offered bribes. I shall want Tompkins's meals carried up."

"But the night-duty? Can she manage that?"

"If not, I'll arrange."

Catching the relief in the over-brilliant eyes, Brodmart set down his cup, leant forward, and spoke in almost an affectionate manner.

"We must not lose touch again, Miss Baldman. Forgive me if I'm treading on delicate ground, but is it a fact you're in danger of closing down?"

Her taut smile quivered. "So that's what they're saying," she said in a choked voice, battled a moment, and then let the flood of her woes gush forth. Her partner's malice had hounded her for six years. A lone woman, too proud to beg favours. . . .

"There, there," soothed the doctor kindly but with impatience in his eye. "We all have our difficult times. Now I shall be seeing something of you shall we just go into matters and decide what can be done?"

"Oh, Doctor, how good you are!"

Her fine eyes swam, she made an emotional grab at his hand. Brodmart patted her convulsed shoulder, rose, and stared down at his slightly-splashed spats.

"Yes. . . . By the way, is your oxygen-tent in working trim?"

"Indeed, yes, Doctor! You shall have it at once."

"Bring it here. I'll take it up myself."

Hectically, in a good humour which astounded the one resident nurse, Miss Baldman prepared the evening meals, ate her own boiled egg, and when the trays had gone up carried a small basin of hot water from the basement kitchen to her office to indulge in the luxury of manicuring her nails. At the foot of the wide stairway she paused, listening. All silent up there—not a single cough as yet, so the morphia hadn't worn off. A long case? Never mind if it wasn't, it had brought back the personage who promised to prove her saviour.

Triumphant, she re-entered her sanctuary, unlocked a cupboard hidden behind the screen, and poured herself a tiny glass of port.

"Then I'm to stop in here, Geoffrey?" asked Evie, her puzzled survey of the tidy bedroom returning uncertainly to her brother's face. "Just go through when I'm wanted?"

"Certainly. Brodmart told you, didn't he, there'd be little or nothing for you to do? Now, then, eat your dinner. When you've finished, set the tray in the passage, and if any one's there *don't* hold any discussion. Got that perfectly clear?"

"Y-es, oh, quite!"

It was a belittling thought that after all she was not expected to fulfil many functions, but it did ease her of a frightening responsibility as well as—yes, a shrinking distaste. Doing things for Elizabeth now would have gone terribly against the grain. Perhaps Geoffrey didn't want her to hear the infamous disclosures the unhappy girl might babble in her delirium. His face as he left the room was very stern.

The house was strangely quiet considering its size. For long stretches there was no sound at all. That was why Evie noticed the raising of the window-sash in the adjoining room, and just afterwards the faint squeak of wheels, as though the bed were being shifted.

The slight noises beyond the green wall didn't interest her. She ate the last spoonful of her nice baked custard, laid the final prune-stone on the side of her plate, and wished vaguely for her jigsaw puzzle.

Chapter Thirty-Six
THE AMBULANCE

ALISON turned jadedly from the telephone. She had informed her own office and David's factory of acute 'flu.

"That's done. So now we can both stick round in case she does ring up or . . . David! Do stop this caged lion act, it's driving me nuts. Surely it's something to have nailed your detective?"

"Nailed him, yes, but why doesn't he get busy?"

"Give the man time. It's only nine o'clock now." Only nine! Already the day seemed a year.

"She walked with him down to the car," said Alison significantly. "You heard what the landlady said. She saw them, together, going out, getting into the grey Chrysler, driving off. You see? Whatever notion you've got, Elizabeth did go of her own accord."

"I'm not disputing it; but afterwards?"

The telephone rang. David jumped for it.

"Oh, you, Bream! Yes, what?"

Bream had just seen the South Street porter, home from Brighton by an early train. It was true Mr. Scarpath's relative had been taken suddenly ill. It had happened late Saturday evening, and on Sunday afternoon she had been removed in an ambulance. Both servants, now dismissed, had supplied the information. Mr. Scarpath had also gone away, the inference being that he intended staying somewhere near the nursing-home in which his guest had been placed.

"The servants may know where he is," said Bream, "but it's going to be a job to locate either of them. They were engaged through a *Times* advertisement, didn't live in, and the porter doesn't know their names or their present addresses. Our best card will be the ambulance."

"Can you find out where it went?"

"Easily. Every such journey has to be recorded at the London County Council Ambulance Depot. I'm off now to the Central Hall."

David put down the microphone. "So that illness wasn't a hoax."

"Exactly! I said it couldn't be. Now I feel better. Don't you?" Alison sent her cousin a sharp glance.

"Not much. It still doesn't give us a line on this silence. Supposing she's patched things up with her husband, what the blazes can be done about it?"

"Here's Colin," said Alison uneasily, and ran to let him in.

Colin weighed their news in judicial immobility. "So," he remarked slowly "Scarpath's got rid of his servants."

"Why not? No one's at the flat. He may be going abroad or God knows where once this is over. The point is, there's no fake about Mrs. Rush, so—"

Alison looked from one face to the other, startled by their expressions. She seemed to have exploded a bomb.

"Christ! If he takes his wife with him?" muttered David, his face twisted.

Colin said quietly, "He can hardly do that, I think. Not while the aunt's life is hanging in the balance. I'm still thinking of those servants— of what light they might be able to shed. There's not much chance of finding them, I'm afraid."

Theorising was sheer waste of energy. Ill at ease, they waited for the report on the ambulance.

Shut in a red telephone-booth Scarpath savagely fished back pennies from the slot. He had been thus engaged for half an hour, and still the Hampstead telephone went unanswered.

Back he strode through the cold morning mists, let himself into the nursing-home, and mounting the stairs tapped three times on the middle door.

Brodmart peered out. "Well, what now?"

Scarpath stepped inside, pushed the door to and said, "You'll have to carry on alone for a bit. I sent the old fool off to Watford. He's not back, evidently, so now there's nothing for it but to hurry along to Hampstead, lie in wait for him and the second he turns up pack him off for good. It's that damned child from next door. She doesn't guess anything, she can't, but if she saw him pottering about when he's supposed to be in hospital—"

"Why did you say it was your butler?" snarled Brodmart, livid. "Here am I, sacrificing valuable appointments to seal up every cranny and you leave a door wide open for any one to walk in!"

He wiped the sweat-beads suddenly sprung on his forehead and glanced towards the bed. Scarpath followed the movement of his eyes, shrugged, and remained impassive.

"Can you suggest a better lie? There was no telling how much she had seen. Parsons was the only person in that damned house. I naturally assumed he'd come home late last night, in which case I'd have caught him now and got him quietly off the premises and back to his sister's while the girl was at school. Don't get in a stew, Brodmart. These Wibbes are completely ignorant, the secretary's my ally. It's she, you know, who got the Young woman's address out of her employer's book and handed it to me in the High Street. I only came along to let you know why I'd have to disappear."

It took only a few minutes to reach the Chrysler and not above twenty to spin down into Hampstead; but once inside the house Scarpath was in for an all-day vigil. He was forced to cancel a luncheon appointment at the Berkeley and stay the pangs of hunger on mouldy bread and a remnant of stale cheese. While light lasted he watched the street from behind dusty curtains, strewing the floors with cigarette-stumps till his case was empty. Once it was dark he stuffed certain garments into a fire-place, touched a match to them, and when the ashes were cold conveyed them in a scuttle out to the dustbin. The inaction and discomfort told on his nerves to a greater extent than the uncertainty about Parsons. It had been a mistake not to secure the Watford address. It simply hadn't entered his head to ask.

Towards seven o'clock the old man stumped harmlessly in with a tale of crippling lumbago which Scarpath cut short.

"That'll do. I shan't be wanting you for a while. Throw your clothes into a bag and get back to your sister's."

Actually it was as well that Parsons had delayed his return till darkness had set in. The servants next door might otherwise have noticed him and mentioned the fact. It was with considerable satisfaction that Scarpath dumped the butler and his dilapidated Gladstone bag at Baker Street Station. There was no open door now.

Turning northward he found himself longing irritably for a bath, a decent meal, civilised company. He would relieve Brodmart now, of course, but perhaps later on—?

"Summerdale," announced Bream, gathering eyes. "Near Reigate. You won't find it there, Mr. Beddoes," for David was flopping through the telephone-directory, "and you can't get the number from the Reigate exchange. Summerdale, let me add, doesn't appear on the list of registered nursing-homes."

"Non-existent?" demanded Colin suspiciously.

"I don't say that, only that under the given name I've not been able to find it." Again Bream rounded the circle of taut faces. "I've not interviewed the ambulance-men. They're out on another job. It was Mr. Scarpath who telephoned the order, though. He spelled the name Summerdale most distinctly, and stated that in case there was any difficulty in locating the home a nurse from the establishment would be making the journey and could furnish directions."

"A nurse!" Colin grew alert. "And was there a nurse?"

"Apparently, though the porter himself didn't see her. Mr. Scarpath sent him to Piccadilly for cigarettes, and when he got back the ambulance had come and gone, Mr. Scarpath with it. He thinks in the rush and worry Mr. Scarpath forgot the cigarettes."

Dryly Colin asked, "Anything more?"

"Both servants knew about the nurse—and they knew all about Mrs. Rush's sudden attack late Saturday evening. Mr. Scarpath's man told the porter, giving the unforeseen event as the reason for his master's breaking up his domestic arrangements so soon after settling into the flat. He confided that the American lady drank like a fish—"

"*Mrs. Rush?*" Alison gasped. "Oh, is that why—"

"—and," continued Bream woodenly, "that the stroke occurred while a well-known doctor, friend of Mr. Scarpath's, was actually in the flat giving advice on her condition. On Sunday morning a second doctor was called in consultation. The ambulance was then ordered, and just before it arrived, about five in the afternoon, the nurse made her appearance. The servants heard her but didn't get a glimpse of her. Mr. Scarpath let her in, showed her straight into the bedroom, and she was still busy with the patient when they were handed their week's wages in lieu of notice and allowed to get away.

"That's all I've managed to collect," said Bream. "Except this: The housemaid, not having been able to get into the visitor's bedroom on the Sunday, came back this morning to clean up. The porter, who let her in with his key, had a look round and noticed that Mr. Scarpath's clothes—and the lady's—are still there. They haven't yet been removed, although there's been no message on the subject."

Out of a dead silence Colin asked if any one had seen the ambulance drive off.

"The house itself was empty just then but for Mr. Scarpath, the doctor, the nurse and the patient. Someone in the street may have noticed it, but before inquiring I thought it better to see if you couldn't help locate this Summerdale. Then there's the question of the doctor. The porter did see him, and he was the same who paid the late call on Saturday. From the general description I'd say he was Dr. Brodmart. Isn't it possible that Summerdale is some new, ultra-private nursing-home patronised rather exclusively by Brodmart and not known to the general faculty?"

"We'll soon find that out," said Colin curtly, and dialled Brodmart's consulting-rooms.

A chill woman-secretary informed him that Summerdale was not on the doctor's books and that the doctor himself was taking a few days' complete rest. She declined to say where. From Brodmart's Park Street home an austere butler confirmed the latter statement, thought that his master had gone to the country cottage, but refused categorically to supply the address. Mrs. Brodmart was on the Continent.

Hard lines round his mouth, Colin issued orders. "Bream, get anything, no matter what, relating to that ambulance!"

"I'll go with him," said David, and reached his hat.

In South Street Bream plied methodically from door to door and at last struck oil. A parlourmaid, near the corner of John Street, had been posting a letter when she noticed an ambulance and someone on a stretcher being lifted into it. She had seen a gentleman whom she had taken for a doctor and with him a nurse in a winged cap, her uniform partially concealed by a brown coat, but they had climbed quickly inside, and it had been too dark to make out their faces.

"Can't you recall any other details about the nurse?"

The parlourmaid said, "Well, only that she was tall and slim. When they come down the steps to the pavement she seemed to me a bit taller than the doctor."

"Tall or short," exploded David, "where the hell does this get us?"

"A long way, I hope." Bream drew him tactfully away. "Nurses, you see, can generally be traced."

"Oh!"

Slightly cheered, they hurried back to find Colin still on the telephone making futile attempts to discover Dr. Brodmart's country retreat.

"It's a dark secret. The exchange has orders not to divulge it, and out of twenty colleagues I've not found one who has ever known where the place was."

"Gosh, you don't for a minute imagine Brodmart's really there? If he was you wouldn't get any change out of *him*. Here, get busy with this nurse. We know there was one, she was seen. Bream says you can find where she came from. Is that so?"

"Easily, I should think."

With fresh confidence Colin set his finger on the dial. In an hour's time he had given up and was looking thoughtful and depressed. No nurse from either a hospital or a nurses' register had gone to a home called Summerdale, in Surrey. The woman seen by the South Street parlourmaid was as much a mystery as Summerdale itself.

"Sounds like a disqualified person. Not that I can see Brodmart employing a nurse of the shady class, it would be running too big a risk." Colin tapped the table. "There is, of course, one other possibility . . ."

"What?"

"Well, that it wasn't a nurse. Someone dressed in nurse's uniform. She was taller, you say, than Brodmart. How many persons were seen getting into the ambulance?"

All at once David saw. "God! It was Scarpath himself?"

Alison protested. "Nonsense, David! Colin, Mr. Bream, you can't seriously believe—?"

"It will be exceedingly difficult to prove," answered the detective with a cough.

Difficult to prove! Even in her sleep she was hearing those words. . . .

"But how would they *dare*?" she argued weakly. "They'd know that when Elizabeth failed to communicate with us we'd start a hunt for her *and* her aunt."

"That's been allowed for, I fancy." Colin spoke to himself. "Why make a clean sweep of those servants if not to prevent them being questioned?"

"Then there is a weak spot!" David barked. "Damn it, there's got to be!"

"Possibly." Colin glanced at Bream. "I'd say they are counting on keeping it covered for a sufficient time—after which, of course, it won't matter."

David's pipe fell in pieces. Alison picked up the dry bowl and the two fragments of bitten stem and laid them tidily on an ashtray. Her whole ordered, integrated world was crashing round her ears.

"If I could get a word with Inspector Headcorn," began Colin hesitatingly.

David dragged him roughly by the arm. "To hell with your inspectors! I'm making tracks for the American Consul. If he can't do anything, I'll collar the Chief Commissioner of the police or the Home Secretary or . . . what's wrong with that?"

"Try, by all means. I'm only thinking of something Headcorn said to me just recently—that unravelling a crime was child's play compared with preventing one."

"True," said Bream quietly. "You'll find the law can't move hand or foot till a criminal act is really committed."

"And in this instance," muttered Colin, "the act won't so much as smell of crime. I can guarantee that."

David shouldered on his coat. "There's still the fellow who drove the ambulance. Or"—darkly—"will he have been squared?"

Bream looked slightly shocked. "No, no, Mr. Beddoes! You forget you're not in your own country. Leave the man to me. I'll go back now to the Central Hall and camp there till he comes in."

It was late afternoon before Bream returned. He had questioned both ambulance-men, whose story was as follows:

Arrived in South Street, Mayfair, they had been met by the gentleman who had ordered the ambulance and by the doctor in attendance. In an upper flat a patient previously swathed in blankets and seemingly unconscious was placed on the stretcher and conveyed down the stairs, the doctor fussing along to supervise the transference.

The doctor, from a rather vague description, might have been Brodmart, though this was by no means certain. When the men were in their seats they were told to wait for the nurse who was to accompany them. They had not yet seen her, as she had been making ready her patient's bag, but Mr. Scarpath went back upstairs to hurry her up, and presently she appeared, alone, and climbed into the ambulance. Beyond the fact that she was rather tall and thin the men had not noticed her.

From Reigate onward there had been some confusion. They had got down into the Surrey hills, among winding by-roads, and after some delay and a number of false turns they were halted in a lane where the doctor, anxious to avoid another swing-round in a limited space, offered to explore a little on foot. In the pitch darkness the nurse had lost her bearings and was afraid they had missed the right turning.

In about five minutes the doctor came back with the command to drive ahead. Round the next bend was the nursing-home—a large house with an ivy-covered lodge and a longish avenue through what appeared to be well-kept grounds. Light streamed from an open doorway. Under the doctor's direction the patient was carried across a handsome lounge and upstairs to a bedroom prepared for her reception. This ended the job, except that the doctor, after conferring behind scenes with the busy matron, produced two bottles of Bass along with a moderate tip.

"Did they notice anything out of the way?" demanded Colin.

"Nothing at all, barring the fact that they did not actually catch sight of any of the personnel. They hardly thought of this till I mentioned it. You see, the doctor had gone ahead and been admitted. That explained the door being left open. Often at that hour an entire staff is occupied with evening meals and preparations for bed. The place was luxurious, but so are a lot of these expensive establishments. There was a smell of ether hanging about, and one of the men noticed a tray of bandages in the upper hall. It was admitted," added Bream with a neutral cough, "that the whole house seemed extremely quiet."

"A nursing-home should be quiet," said Alison. David, with fixed eyes, was hunting the flaw.

"Can these fellows find the place again?" he asked suddenly.

"Whether they can or not," said Bream, "isn't the immediate question. We'll have to produce a police order before either of them will be let off duty to make the attempt—and I, unfortunately, haven't the power to obtain one. Possibly you or the doctor here could manage it?"

David cursed savagely. "God, Bream, don't you realise what Scotland Yard, yes, and the American Consul too, thinks of me? I'm just a rotten adventurer, trying to skin an heiress out of what's coming to her. Hands off! That's what they're saying to me. I've a damned nerve to show my face, I—"

"Shut up, David! You know Colin warned you."

"Let him have the whole of it. If Scarpath's taking steps to safeguard his wife and her aunt, it's because of the trouble I've been making. He's her lawful husband. He's had her under a top-notch specialist and—oh, damn your police order! Why can't this chauffeur do a little night-driving? I'll pay him what he wants. Lead me to him, if he loses his job I'll—"

The tirade ceased abruptly. The telephone was pealing.

"No, David, let me." Alison snatched off the receiver, jumped, and held it two inches off from her ear. "Pen! Please, not quite so loud. . . . No, Pen, she's not with us. Not here since . . . what's that? An ambulance? When? Where?"

Deafening clamour had broken out over the wire. The child up in Hampstead was gabbling shrilly about a butler, Scarpath, a broken leg.

"Give it to me!" David's eyes blazed, but Alison clung on, drinking in the excited words.

"It was a lie, Miss Young! I'm telling you I trailed the old man there from the tube station only a minute ago, and there was nothing wrong with him, nothing! Oh, don't you see who they'd got in that ambulance?"

CHAPTER THIRTY-SEVEN
DAVID SEES RED

A SECOND ambulance—and it had been seen to leave Summit View, in Hampstead, some twenty-six hours ago. Interest in the first ambulance evaporated. Like a hurricane David swept Colin and the detective before him to the Central Hall Depot.

The man at the desk was getting bored with the bombardment of questions. Sarcastically observing that his department wasn't an information bureau, he dragged forward a ledger.

"Here you are, then. Call received by telephone at twelve a.m. yesterday. Name, Parsons. Address, 3 Heath Crescent, N.W.3. Patient to be conveyed to 127 Garibaldi Road, Crouch End. That's up north of Highgate."

"Parsons is the butler," muttered Colin. "I wonder if the Wibbe child saw some relation on his way to inquire and took him for the butler himself?"

David shook a stubborn head. "I know that kid," he rasped. "Now, then, how do we get to this Garibaldi Road?"

The trio pored over the G's in the directory and in the same instant swore. There was no road of this name—no, not in the entire London area.

"Who took the message?" demanded Colin.

Grudgingly their informant went to find a brother employee, who appeared, wiped crumbs from his mouth, and repeated the facts with one slight addition. The person ordering the ambulance had admitted some uncertainty as to the nursing-home address.

"He said the doctor would know, and if a mistake had been made he'd ring up and correct it. Well, we've not heard from him. It's no fault of ours if the name in our book is wrong."

The first official said, "Why don't you get on to 3 Heath Crescent and ask?"

"You try," David blasted him. "Let it go. What we want is the fellow who did the driving."

"Clocked out. Gone home."

Those in charge, more than ever recalcitrant now that an error had been pointed out to them, balked over furnishing names or addresses, but at last these were looked up. The driver, Edward Hollis, and his companion, Alfred Wilkinson, both resided in outer London, the one at Wandsworth, the other in Bethnal Green. Miles from Westminster, both of them—and naturally unreachable by telephone.

"Far apart, too." Colin shrugged as they regained the car. "We'll try Wandsworth, I think. Bream, are you coming?"

"It's better to split forces, Doctor. I shall try to discover where Dr. Brodmart is hiding. We can communicate via Miss Young."

"He's right," murmured Colin as they drove southward along the river. "It's the time element that may beat us."

"Time!" David paused to yell at a heavy dray which was blocking their course. "You've said it." He forced composure. "Tell me this: Will she still be alive?"

Colin nodded, his face gone slightly grey. "Yes."

"Because till her aunt's dead there's no good killing her?"

"There's another reason. Understand, I'm obliged to count Brodmart in on these doings, and therefore to view any coming step from his angle. Elizabeth can't die from disseminated sclerosis. You see why, of course?"

"You mean we'd force an inquiry."

"Exactly—and the p.m. would show not the stated disease but narcotic or other poisoning. No, her death has got to be contrived in a way calculated to rule out the remotest suggestion of foul play."

"Suicide?" David's throat was dry.

"I think not. Don't ask me more. My ideas aren't worth tuppence. I believe, though, that a small margin of time will be wanted for preparation. Anyhow," said Colin under his breath, "we won't waste another moment over Mrs. Rush."

Edward Hollis occupied the upper portion of a tiny brick villa wedged between others as like as dingy peas in a pod. He was not at home, having gone to the pictures.

"What cinema-house? Ah, now you're arsking!" Mrs. Hollis gave a dubious sniff. "Like as not 'e's cycled right along to Clapham, or else over the bridge to Walham Green."

Since it would be hours before Hollis would turn up, they decided to hunt Wilkinson, only to find after miles of traffic-struggle that Wilkinson had quitted Bethnal Green to spend the night in Ilford—exact quarter unknown. Back to Wandsworth, to park outside the Hollis abode. At midnight the ambulance-driver hove in sight, riding a suspiciously-wobbly bicycle. He was a powerful chap, red-jowled, alcoholically truculent.

"Oo's wanting Ted Hollis?" he demanded. "And it'll be Mister Hollis to you blokes, see? Stand 'way!" Unsteadily he swept off the hands which intercepted his progress. "Carn't an 'ard-worked bloke get inside his own 'ouse when he's wanting 'is night's rest?"

During the next few minutes windows went up, sympathetic neighbours counselling Ted to stand no nonsense; but Mrs. Hollis had opened the door, and through it the rioters swayed. In stuffy darkness there came a crash. As gaslight sputtered, Hollis was discovered prone and senseless on the narrow stairs, his wife in a greasy flannelette nightgown bending indignantly over him.

Colin got his breath. "He's struck his head against the newel-post, that's all, except that he's had a drop too much. I'm a doctor, Mrs. Hollis. Will you help me sober him sufficiently to answer one or two questions?"

"Questions!" The woman glared. "Ted! Wot's this 'ere lot up to? Shove 'em out, d'yer hear?"

Edward Hollis lay like a felled ox. God, another hold-up!

Mrs. Hollis turned hostile. "Want me to call the perlice?"

"I don't advise it." Colin laid a hand on her arm. "See here, Mrs. Hollis, we don't mean trouble for your husband. Be reasonable, you can't lift a fourteen stone weight, and he'll catch his death lying here. Suppose my friend and I get him to bed?"

Mollified, Mrs. Hollis allowed them to hoist Edward to a top bedroom, where he sprawled, breathing stertorously.

"I said 'e'd got a fat tip over that larst Monday job," she wailed. "Bin blowing it, o' course. Not that you can 'old it against 'im this perishing cold weather."

When she retreated Colin said, "It'll be an all-night session, I'm afraid. If we don't stop by him till he's able to talk there'll be another whole day wasted before we can nab him."

"Able! The swine's faking. Stop if you like, but I tell you he's been fixed."

"I shall stop, anyhow. Is it too great a strain for you?"

"We're getting side-tracked, Ladbroke. Look, you can manage alone, can't you? I'm itching to get back."

"Push off, then. Any particular scheme?"

"No. Well—Scarpath, you know. He's left his clothes behind, hasn't he? Wouldn't it be about now, when the building's quiet, he might sneak back to do a change?"

"I see. Well, possibly; but if you attempt to trail him, don't let him spot you. It'll mean throwing away a good chance—if not worse."

In his stampede for action David was in the street before he took in the final words. Even now he thought of them only briefly, his entire attention centred on how at this dead hour to transport himself to the West End. The underground had ceased operating, no vehicle of any description was in sight. Eventually he found a tram. It conveyed him to Lambeth where the first taxi-cab materialised, and in another ten minutes, bidding the chauffeur wait in a side turning from South Street, he was looking up at a row of curtained windows.

His pulses leapt. Through two pairs of curtains percolated a faint glow.

In the dark street there was no sign of the Chrysler. Afraid of missing his prey by searching the wrong parking-places he slid into the entrance, flattened himself against the right-hand wall, and prepared to wait for the man upstairs to emerge.

As the slow minutes passed he wondered if Scarpath intended to sleep at the flat. He doubted it, since the last thing Scarpath could wish was to be accosted by his wife's friends. That he was here at all argued in favour of Colin's belief, for if immediate murder was contemplated or had just taken place Scarpath would be too occupied to bother about a change of linen. Actually there had to be two deaths—first the aunt's, then Elizabeth's. Staggering that with so much suspicion afoot . . . but did Scarpath realise Fanny had unthinkingly spilled the beans about her will and thus furnished the key to the whole plot?

David considered. It was not necessary for this to be known. Quite apart from it those involved were in no position to court inquiry into sudden deaths. It ought to stop them—and apparently it did nothing of the kind. Colin was right, then. The deaths when they did occur would pass for natural ones.

Therein lay the terror that froze. *It was all doped out.*

Find her—find her now, before it was too late! The idea pounded in his head, making it nearly impossible to go on hugging the cold wall and rivet his gaze on the wired glass beside him, watching for the descending brightness of the lift.

It seemed to him now that perhaps it was not Scarpath up there. It might be Treddle, or whatever his name was, returned. Softly he stamped his feet to rid them of numbness, and unable to continue the suspense made a movement to see if the lights still showed. It was exactly then that the unguarded door banged back, pinioning him in his niche. As it swung into place again he saw Scarpath striding past.

Whether it was the unheralded blow or the sudden sight of the man himself, cool, shaven and immaculate, about to elude him he never quite knew. Red mist swam before him. He lunged, gripped his enemy by the arm and hauled him violently round to face him.

"Where is she? What have you done with her?"

Scarpath betrayed only a momentary start. In silence, detachedly, his ice-blue eyes levelled their gaze while the brain behind them seemed deliberating whether to grant a reply. It came, with frigid contempt.

"By her I suppose you are referring to my wife. Is that so, Mr. Beddoes?"

"You know damned well it is! Where is she? And her aunt, for that matter?"

The pale gaze veered. "I rather anticipated this, Beddoes. Do you seriously imagine I shall tell you?"

"Oh, you'll tell me, if I have to choke it out of you!" David thrust with his full weight and pinned the other man against the wall. "Where's Elizabeth? What's happening to her?"

Scarpath's face changed. It was as though swiftly and venomously a snake had uncurled to strike.

"You have the effrontery to expect an answer? Good, here it is. My wife is suffering total collapse—the result of your damned interference. If she dies, as she may do, you can thank yourself. Certainly I've placed her where you and your charlatan pack can't get your clutches on her. Now, you bloody fool, clear out!"

David had a sensation of staggering. For one sick instant he forgot everything except the weird vanishing-tricks disseminated sclerosis was known to play and that he had yet to prove any hoax had been perpetrated. He knew now that the dim dread of this very débâcle had been hovering in his mind. His hold loosened. The pale, alien eyes had not wavered; and yet what was this expression he had caught? Nothing to be grasped. Odd that in a flash he should see a monstrous black car roaring down on him out of the peace of a Bloomsbury square. . . .

"Stop!"

His fist landed on Scarpath's chin. Singularly well-matched was David's thought as he and his adversary grappled, swayed, and of a sudden slithered on the ice-filmed steps.

"Come, come, what's this?"

Over them loomed a blue-coated constable.

"Sorry," laughed Scarpath. "It's this beastly ice."

The constable looked mildly on as the interlocked bodies separated. In a black rage David saw Scarpath rise, give a flick to his trousers, and join the big guardian of the law.

"My fault for dashing out. By the way, what's the time?"

"Just on three, sir. Nasty slide that was."

On the pair strolled, the officer playing a torch beam into each dark area. Now was the moment to make a charge; but what charge?

David had been the aggressor. If those at the top refused credence to his tale . . . He'd be run in for street brawling, that was all. Wiped off the board. He had foozled badly—and Scarpath knew it.

"Good-night, sir."

"Good-night."

Scarpath was ducking into a mews. An engine whirred. Doubling round to his taxi David said, "Trail the grey Chrysler!" and cannoned inside.

There was a brief delay in starting, and during it the grey ghost shot westward towards Park Lane. Red lights intervened. When they flashed green no Chrysler was in sight.

Chapter Thirty-Eight
THE NURSE

EDWARD Hollis roused. Tea like ink was being forced on him, and a strange gentleman was firing questions.

He groaned. "Highgate job? All oke that was. 'Orspital nurse, doctor one of the big pots by the look of him. Wotcher after, mate?"

"The address of the nursing-home. There's no such street. Can you find it? I mean now."

"Me? Gawd 'elp us, it's gorn six! I've got to report."

"Here's your coat. You're coming with me. Listen, Hollis! I know you never heard of Garibaldi Road. You were shown the way and—"

"Strewth, governor, 'owdyer expect me to find the bleeding plyce again? Way up the top of Crouch End it was. Wot with the dark and the rain—"

"Of course. That's how you caught the chill. Oh, I'll see you don't get in a jam! You'll have your panel doctor's certificate and a fiver for your trouble if you show me the house. Now, hustle!"

"A fiver! Coo, sir, I'll 'ave a try."

Street-lamps still burned as through pockets of raw fog they drove northward. Once Colin halted to telephone. What David told him was a worse blow because of certain details Hollis had now communicated. He did not upbraid David. Poor devil, he himself was realising that his foiled strategy last night might hurry matters to a conclusion. Scarpath's coolness argued that the fellow-schemers knew themselves on safe ground. What they did not know, of course, was that the Wibbe child had seen the butler before he was spirited away.

Miles north, in Highgate, Colin stopped at an underground entrance. Wreathed in dirty mist the two Americans dived forward, Mortimer Bream in the rear.

Alison gibbered, "Oh, Colin, I had to come! May I squash in?"

They piled into the car.

It was now seven-thirty, the visibility poor. Only Hollis had had any sleep, and the faces of the others looked pinched and heavy-eyed. Onward they bowled, coughing as the fog rasped their throats. Bream, tightly wedged between Colin and their guide, related what he had gathered from Brodmart's garage-proprietor.

"The doctor is away. He's given his chauffeur leave of absence while the big car is being decarbonised. Occasionally, it seems, Brodmart goes down alone to his cottage, though the place is regarded as closed in the winter time. There's a caretaker who looks after him. This time he went by train, Sunday afternoon, latish." Bream paused. He added, "The cottage is somewhere in the Surrey hills."

Three heads turned sharply.

"Meaning," said David, "it's where they took Mrs. Rush?"

"It's an idea, isn't it?"

Colin nodded. "It fits in. I thought of it when we heard how Brodmart left the ambulance and went ahead by himself. That would have been to make certain the caretaker was off the premises, put on lights and so on. Yes, to get Mrs. Rush there if for only an hour would be an excellent way to muddy the trail."

Bream had still not been able to obtain the telephone number of the cottage.

"Only the police can force that sort of information, and in view of your message just now—"

"Right, this matter's vital. It's true that light on the subject of Mrs. Rush might give us some leverage with Scotland Yard, but . . . Hollis, have we gone right?"

"Stop a bit, sir." The red-faced giant squinted round. "Yes, there's the Alexandra Palace a-standing out over there. I'd say we're getting fairly warm. I know it was a long stretch t'other side of Crouch End, but by night these 'ere roads are pretty much of a muchness, and abaht 'ere we did a bit of doubling in circles like. The doctor hisself wasn't sure. He'd always depended on his chauffeur."

Useless to hurry Hollis. If on Monday evening there had been a definite attempt to bewilder him his clouded wits must be left to sift things out.

His bloodshot eye brightened. "See that red pillarbox, sir? Bear left. It should be the second turning . . . or will it be the third?"

It was neither, nor was it the fourth or the fifth.

"Stalling," ground David in Alison's ear. "The bastard knows all right, but he's leading us a goose-chase."

The same idea was taking root in Alison's mind. The third degree methods of her own country were horrible to her, but she understood when David began muttering about trussing men up, keeping them awake for days on end, and torturing them into admissions.

"It's no good," she whispered. "They don't do that here."

"They ought to do worse to me."

Then she saw. Of course, David had muffed up a heaven-sent chance. By now they would have found Elizabeth, succoured her, instead of which by going all out for Scarpath he had let the dodger slide like an eel from his grasp. Time that was precious was being squandered in random prowlings. It might even be this wasn't the right quarter of London at all.

"Hold 'ard!" A hand like a York ham slugged down on Colin's knee. "Not seen this road, have we?"

"Gambetta Road? Only four times, I fancy."

"Wot, that big Guinness poster?"

"We've passed twenty at least."

"Not with the seal we haven't. *My Goodness—My Guinness!* Why, sir, that's wot took my mate's eye! I remember him saying as 'ow the sight of that there good ale wasted on a seal . . . I've got it, sir! Wot we've bin seeing was t'other end of the road. Get into it. Go slow."

Hollis scowled through the mist. They crawled past blank spaces, cleared for rebuilding. Three cheap bungalows in a row. A market-florist, a forlorn tennis-court, then a hairpin bend. Another empty gap. A scarecrow house bearing a To Let sign. Beyond it—

"Stop! Them's the gates, round balls on top. And blime, if there ain't the brawss plate we was told to watch out for!"

Dimly the brass plate glimmered at them. David read, "Blythedale Nursing-Home." His heart turned over. A half-moon of gravel, circling up to a huge stuccoed house, like a mice-nibbled wedding-cake. Doorstep freshly chalked, spotless curtains at the windows, net below, casement cloth above.

"Beddoes, for God's sake sit tight!"

Scarcely pausing, Colin drove past a second bend. Here Bream got out, took the cardboard box he had been nursing, and went back on foot.

An acid lady in black answered his ring. She wore a snowy coif, and on her breast a silver cross.

"Well?"

"Mrs. Talbot Greene, Madam. I was asked to deliver this fruit."

Dark eyes swept him calculatingly. "Greene? We've no patient of that name."

"No Greene?" Bream looked abashed. "I'd have sworn that was the name. Ought to have written it down. Would you mind telling me who the lady is who arrived here late Monday afternoon by ambulance?"

"Smith." The matron's thin lips barely parted. At once annoyance tightened her face. "At least, we did have a Mrs. Smith arriving at that time, but as it wasn't Mrs. Greene—"

"Yes, yes, I must have come to the wrong nursing-home. There's another one near here, isn't there?"

"Three," snapped the woman in black and closed the door.

Quick though the movement he had caught a glimpse of a nurse, stocky and buff-clad, just mounting some stairs.

In two minutes he was back at the car.

"If Mrs. Scarpath is there they're calling her Smith. I didn't risk any more questions. We mustn't rouse suspicion. It looks a thoroughly reputable establishment."

"Reputable! Obviously. What did you expect? *David*, sit down." Colin frowned. "It's got to have surface conventionality, otherwise it couldn't possibly succeed. Cover—and the safety that goes with it. The matron may not know it's a false name. If the nurse belongs there you can be sure anything the least dubious will be kept from her eyes . . . though it's a puzzler to see how."

"The nurse," said Bream softly. "She'll be our best card."

"Provided she's genuine. First we've got to satisfy ourselves this *is* the right place."

"Not arf it is!"

Hollis's assurance was a shade too eager. Colin looked at Bream. It was David who cut in.

"If we hang about a little we may see Scarpath himself—or his pal."

"It's worth trying," agreed Bream. "Stop in this spot. I'll take the other end of Gambetta Road."

At ten o'clock no one at all had emerged from the nursing-home. Bream returned to say that every upper front window was tightly closed.

"Empty, I should imagine. If Mrs. Scarpath is inside, she's where we'd expect her to be—at the back, well away from the road. Here's a plan. The mist is clearing, we'll have to take care not to be spotted." Bream outlined his idea.

Something to do! David shot from his seat, Alison following, for after the South Street fiasco she felt her cousin couldn't be trusted on his own.

"Go back," he snarled.

"No, David, I'm coming too. Colin, do you mind?"

Making a circuit so as to avoid passing the house they sneaked into the abandoned premises adjoining and creeping to the farthest corner of the party wall scaled over into the Blythedale grounds. These were deep, narrow and untended, containing a mouldy summerhouse and little else. The only cover was a clump of ragged laurels fifty yards from the house. Here Alison crouched low, David beside her, to spy on the rear windows.

David grunted, "That was easy, anyhow. It's a safe bet no one comes pottering back here in this weather. There's no excuse to—*Christ*! Get down. . . ."

They ducked flat on their stomachs. Bearing down on them was a raw-boned grenadier of a woman who that instant had made her appearance up basement steps.

When she came closer they realised that the pail she carried was destined for the cinder-heap almost behind them beyond a tangle of dead raspberry canes. On she stalked, like doom. She would have to pass within twenty feet. One turn of the head—but she did not turn. Her burden dumped, she was standing away from the rising cloud of ashes, pensively gazing over the rear wall. Still with no glance towards the laurels she dusted her red hands on a calico apron and stalked back to vanish indoors.

"Whew!" Alison sat up. "David, can you see?"

"Plenty, but that's not saying much."

The house had three floors above the basement, from which came the only sounds—a clatter of crockery and now and again a sharp voice giving orders. Above, the cracked and stained façade enclosed a complete silence, though the middle windows, unlike the front ones, were all open—the outer two sashes lowered a hand's breadth from the top, the central pair stretched wide to the raw wintry air.

"That middle room—or will it be two rooms?—is being aired." As Alison murmured it she fumbled in her coat-pocket and brought forth opera-glasses. "The chances are it's just been vacated. Keep your eye on the end windows."

Ten minutes, and Alison's teeth were chattering with cold. David squirmed, cursing under his breath.

"What did I tell you? This ambulance-fellow's been bought. He means to string us along, play us for the mugs we are and collect five pounds out of it. I know the breed."

"I don't think she can be here, David."

"No, nor within ten miles. Keep her right in London? They're not mugs, if we are."

"Wait, though. It's the merest fluke we found out it wasn't the butler in the ambulance—or that there was a second ambulance at all. By their count the very centre of the West End would have done just as well. And then Garibaldi Road. See how easily you might confuse it with Gambetta Road, if you wanted to mislead and get by with it? They had to furnish an address, so . . . *oh*, David, look!"

There was no need for the nudge. David also had seen.

The sash on the right was being timidly raised, and a woman's arm, white-cuffed to the elbow and mauve cotton above, shook out a yellow duster. No vigour in the action. Ineffectual, it had a haunting, irritating familiarity. Now a capped head came into view. The face was pallid and vacantly staring. Round it straggled tendrils of gingery hair.

Alison pinched David convulsively.

"Oh!" she breathed. *"See who it is?"*

CHAPTER THIRTY-NINE
SHOES

"Sure it's the sister?" Colin demanded searchingly.

"Hell, no, it's just our idea of a joke. Well"—David's grimed fingers twitched—"what's holding you?"

"Get back in the car." With a weather eye out, Colin spoke, low. "Right, Beddoes. The sister's there, acting as nurse, but—! You think, do you, we can just barge into that house and snatch Elizabeth away?"

"Watch me. Damn you, leave go!"

"One minute. Hollis, here's your fiver. Go buy yourself a drink, we shan't want you any more."

When the passenger had taken himself off Colin laid down the law, quietly but with weight in every syllable.

"Get this into your skull, old man. We can't walk in. We'd have to gate-crash. Well, the first move of those inside will be to call the police. Did you notice there's a police station almost directly behind? While we're breaking down doors the law will be down on us—*on their side.* Will our being locked into cells hinder this plot or assist it?"

"The police will see her. God, man, it's what we want!"

"Do we? Think again. How much medical understanding do you expect from an ordinary policeman?"

"I don't get it," said David stubbornly.

"Get this, then. There'll be nothing to see but a patient desperately ill and apparently receiving the best attention. She can't answer questions. I doubt if she can speak."

"But the fraud of a nurse—"

"Fraud? Miss Scarpath may easily have had nurse's training. Thousands of all sorts did during the war. It's quite sufficient that she's being sponsored by Guthrie Brodmart, who may argue that especial circumstances make it wise to employ a relation. What do we gain by revealing her identity? Time—the one thing our criminals require, in order to contrive a perfectly natural death."

David's mind was beginning to refunction. Colin fired his last shot.

"Here's another point. In the state Elizabeth's in the disturbance we'll create will probably finish her off. She won't stand up to a shock."

"You win." David brushed an arm over his eyes. "Well, what do we do?"

Bream hesitated. "Doctor, shall we risk another appeal to the Yard?"

"No. What support have we got? Scarpath was under no obligations to furnish the true facts to an inquisitive child who accosted him in the street. He has only to claim it was in his wife's interest to conceal her whereabouts to earn full justification for telling a lie. Who are we to refute him? You should realise by now we're in no standing—or worse."

"But two disappearances! Can't we bring him to book over the aunt?"

"Not if she's dead."

Alison jumped. "Dead! Colin, what makes you think—"

"It's my belief she died in South Street. That she was dead when she was removed. A borrowed flat, remember. The owner might dislike a death occurring in it, hence the excuse, if wanted, for staging a deception. Nothing actionable, eh, Bream, in depositing the body somewhere else prior to burial, or in juggling a little with the death notice?"

"Not in the least," affirmed the detective. "You'll find death notices are frequently undated. They appear when and how someone chooses to insert them in the papers. This much is certain, no patient called Rush has been admitted to either a hospital or nursing-home. Doctor, mightn't the Yard stir itself to the point of securing another expert opinion on Mrs. Scarpath?"

"Eventually, perhaps. Not soon enough. If it was, what would be seen? Two minutes warning would suffice to clear the decks of everything suspicious. Try to understand it won't be possible with safety to the patient to attempt any prolonged examination. And it won't be considered necessary. Ordinary illness—unmistakable symptoms, dealt with in the approved way, but already advanced to a crucial stage. Is that clear to you? Expert or not, a physician's sole chance will be to get into that room *without warning*, and within a very limited time."

David's eyes burned. "How limited?"

"It can't be done till the middle of the night. I daren't postpone it another twenty-four hours."

"Now we're getting places," burst from David. "Catch them red-handed—beat hell out of them!"

Colin said steadily, "It may mean that, of course. Bream, can we count you in? Thanks, we may need you. Yes"—he drew a deep breath—"we must risk it, that's all."

Alison alone grasped his meaning. "Colin! If nothing's discovered, what about you?"

"Me? Oh, up the spout!" At sight of her dismay his grin vanished. "Look," he whispered sternly, "this is my funeral, understand?"

Miserably she quailed. He was right, she couldn't argue the point, but to be struck off the rolls at the very outset of his career! The thought that she had dragged him into this affair returned. In the tumult of the moment she cursed the night their paths and Elizabeth's had crossed; and then, swiftly, she cursed herself. Here on the frayed edge of London the girl she had befriended and grown to care for was imprisoned, help-lessly driven towards death. Against that stark fact no other danger could be allowed to weigh.

She had been staring blindly along the dismal reaches of Gambetta Road. Suddenly she jerked forward.

"Colin! Here's the charwoman we saw in the back garden. Why not speak to her?"

The three heads turned to study the battered figure trudging philo-sophically towards them. At close range the woman was handsome—a mature Trilby with her stalwart proportions and the man's hat rakishly perched on her head. Her frieze coat, too short in the sleeves, was fastened across her chest with a safety-pin. She was lugging a string bag.

Colin stopped her. "You work at Blythedale, I think?"

The woman nodded a debonair affirmative and cocked an eye.

"Good, we'd like a word with you. There'll be something in it for you, of course. Can you suggest a quiet pub?"

"Green Dragon," she answered promptly, and as he opened the door climbed in with perfect aplomb.

"One moment. Any chance we'll run into the gentleman whose wife is at the nursing-home?"

"Wot, the toff? Not 'im. The George'll be more his style."

In a few minutes the party had commandeered a corner in a fuggy, ale-smelling atmosphere. Sarah Glover, as the charwoman was called, voted for a pint of bitter and proved willing to talk.

"How long? Oh, getting on for six years! Plyce is run down now, all I get is three half-days a week, and then like as not I 'ave to wait for my money. There's only a few fires, not but wot there's a rare lot of scrub-bing and polishing."

"How many patients are there at present?"

"Gorn! Only your Mrs. Smith. We'd an appendix, but she went 'ome yesterday."

"Then who exactly is in the house?"

"Well, there's Matron, o' course, Miss Baldman she is, and there's Mrs. Smith's doctor, and 'er husband—and 'er own nurse wot come with 'er. And we've still got Broughton, that's our nurse, though she don't get a look in, not even on night-duty. Maybe we're keeping 'er for show. She says to me this morning, 'Glover, you may get the sack, but I'm to be a fixture. Business is picking up.'"

"Is it?" Colin signalled the barman for another pint.

A massive shrug. "'Ow'm I to know? I bin looking for bailiffs. Now Matron's singing 'Ark the 'erald Angels down in the kitchen and talking abaht central 'eating and lifts."

"Have you seen Mrs. Smith?"

A bright eye trained on Colin. "You're a doctor yourself, ain't you? Thought so. Well, then, I 'ave seen her—wot there is to see. It's not much, they've got her muffled up like a corpse, and I can tell you this, I'm shoved out o' that room before I've arf done my mopping. Friend of yours, is she? I'm sorry to 'ear that."

David stirred. Colin kicked him under the table.

"Go on, please. Is she conscious?"

"Shouldn't think it. Twice I've bin in, cleaning the grate and that. Both times she never moved, and now she's begun to cough. Deep down, a nasty, 'orrid rattle. I've heard too many of that sort not to know wot it means. She's in good 'ands, o' course. One of the big nobs, Matron's pet we used to call 'im, only he give us the go by for donkey's years till now."

"They are in the back of the house, are they?"

"That's raht, three o' our best rooms they've got, 'er in the middle. Cawn't say much for the nurse. Doesn't seem all there, the way she just stands about gawping. Pardon, Miss, did you speak?"

Alison asked if it was usual for a doctor and a relative to take up their abode in the nursing-home. Sarah Glover smacked her lips judicially as she replied:

"Now and again I've seen it 'appen—only, o' course, when the patient's far gone and there's money to be wasted like. Matron says this 'usband's all wrapped up in 'er—wot a pity it is, young people and all. She was mentioning as 'ow the oxygen tent wouldn't be long wanted, and we needn't get in any more cylinders. It's funny abaht that, though. . . . Mind your foot, Miss!"

Dislodged by David's fierce grip of the table the string-bag had tumbled to the floor. Sarah Glover picked it up, brushed off the sawdust, and in full view proceeded to re-wrap a lumpy parcel which had fallen loose.

"This'll show you."

She placed on the sticky table a pair of small, brown American suède shoes.

"Matron just 'anded 'em on." Busily she polished one of the buckles. "Not big enough for 'er, but they'll do lovely for my Beetrice. Gawd, 'ave I said somethink?"

Overcome, she stared at the dark young man who had left the group and blundered through the swing-doors to the street.

"Go after him," Colin said swiftly to Alison. Sick with horror, she obeyed, Bream in pursuit. To Sarah Glover he said, "No, but you're going to say something now." Sinking his voice, he demanded, "About the oxygen. What did you notice?"

Bream and Alison between them had got David in hand when Colin joined them in the car.

"I *think* he's subdued, Colin. Hadn't we better get him away quick?"

"We'll do that. I hadn't banked on those shoes. Listen!" He was whispering as he wiped the dimmed windscreen. "It's all as I expected, down to the n'th detail—nursing-home a respectable derelict, matron fawning on Brodmart for his patronage, probably completely gulled as to what she's abetting. Better face up to it. Delaying things till to-night means a touch and go gamble, but rushing in now—well, can you make David realise those blighters will win hands down?"

"Mr. Bream's doing that now, I think."

They listened. The detective was saying. "That will be the size of it, Mr. Beddoes. Either they'll get her away God knows where or simply race matters through. The latter may wreck their own game, but which is more important to us—punishment or life-saving?"

Alison got a glimpse of Colin's face. It had gone a dirty ash-colour, though his voice had remained steady.

"Is it—do you think already it may be too late?" Her voice stuck in her throat.

"I don't know." His answer hardly moved his lips. "Food's what we want. We'll hunt a restaurant right away from this neighbourhood and settle our procedure."

Bream continued to the Central Hall. Colin returned home, dropping Alison and David at Mecklenburgh Square for what was to prove an endless afternoon. It was when Alison brought in tea that she found David, cavernous-eyed, cleaning a second-hand automatic.

"God, why didn't I drop her a hint?" He fitted cartridges into the clip. "One word about the will, even about the sapphire, might have put her on guard."

"David, it wouldn't. Don't you see how Fanny's letter counteracted anything we might have said?"

"I let her walk straight back into the trap."

"We all did, then. Here, give me that gun! Didn't Colin insist neither you nor he was to go armed?"

From the Central Hall Bream rang Colin.

"You hit the nail on the head, Doctor. There was a third ambulance, ordered on Sunday evening, to call at a house called Welton Hanger, near the village of Crow's Hill, Surrey. From that place it conveyed a woman's body direct to the crematorium at Golders Green."

"Crematorium!"

Colin grabbed his unopened *Times*, ran an eye along the Death column, and after a sharp exchange with Bream, bolted back to Mecklenburgh Square.

Grimly he thrust the copy of *The Times* into Alison's hand. "So now we know."

The item leapt forth: *Mrs. Frances Penn Rush . . . at a suburban nursing-home . . . no service . . . cremation . . .*

David shouted, "When? Here, let's stop it! Order an inquest—"

"Two doctors." Colin nodded to himself. "Two medical certificates. Why didn't I tumble to it at once?"

David was shaking him like a rat. He roused.

"What's that? Inquest my hat! The evidence is gone, Beddoes. Elizabeth's aunt was cremated on Monday afternoon."

Chapter Forty
COLIN SEES

At this instant only did the full horror of it take Alison by the throat.

She had seen Geoffrey Scarpath, spoken with him. Despite every counter-suggestion he had remained for her a somewhat glorified example of the young Englishmen with whom she was becoming familiar—self-centred hedonists, callous perhaps, but mainly from hypersensitiveness. Doesn't a tender spot grow a corn? Above all, men of the Scarpath type rotated in a strictly conventional orbit. She would have said that one whose calendar was regulated by Ascot, Henley, the Eton and Harrow match and the Twelfth of August must be too cautious, too disdainfully lazy, to venture into crime . . .

"Some kink in him, I suppose."

She was fitting it together. Of course Fanny Rush had been murdered! None too skilfully, either, or it wouldn't have been necessary to cremate the remains. She had to die first. Now it was Elizabeth's turn.

David, for a moment a stone figure, was muttering, "Damned neat! At the very time he was spinning the yarn that got Elizabeth away, the old woman was just a handful of ashes."

"Neat or not," said Colin curtly, "it couldn't have been managed without Brodmart's help. The second death certificate proves those two are yoked together. It doesn't make it any easier. You've not found Mrs. Rush's letter?"

"No." Alison's mind groped back. "And that's what disarmed us all. That letter took away Elizabeth's last tiny suspicion—let her go with him, completely trusting. But did Scarpath know it had been written? Did he reckon on it or—"

"Did Elizabeth remark on the handwriting?"

"Oh!" Alison gaped. "You mean *he wrote it himself.*"

David banged the table. "Scarpath! My God, why were we so slow?"

"I've told you," shrugged Colin, "he does most things well."

The theory stupefied Alison. "Not only faked the writing of a woman already dead, but got back the letter so he could burn it. It would have been about our only scrap of real evidence."

"Quite. I was wondering how long it would take you to appreciate that fact."

Simple, daring—*successful.* . . .

Now Alison understood the manner of man with whom they had to deal she felt a deadly sickness at the pit of her stomach. This crazy attempt they were planning, how could it come to anything? Even if by midnight Elizabeth were still alive they had not one chance in a million. Luck must hinge on the actual witnessing of malpractice—and, as Colin had emphasized, a creak, a shadow on the blind, would dynamite the whole scheme. Before another attempt could be made *The Times* would be printing its second death-announcement. This time cremation would not be required.

David was in the bathroom when Colin spied the automatic. "Hide that," he ordered softly.

With hands like slabs of frozen meat she dropped the pistol into her knitting-bag. "Must we? But they *will* be armed."

"Never mind if they are. If we are caught carrying weapons we'll be the offenders. Already to all outward intent they're on the right side of the law. Strengthen their position and we'll crash."

Her eyes were blank with despair. To be caught with weapons or without them, wasn't it the same? Elizabeth would die. David would be sacked from his excellent job—and so would she, not that this detail bothered her. Colin, of course, would forfeit everything—honour, career, livelihood. . . .

"Now, then, none of that!" Colin took her firmly by the shoulders. "Haven't I demonstrated to you there's no other way?"

"I know, oh, I know! Only—well, you can't possibly bring it off. And afterwards?"

He loosed his hold and walked to the door.

It was to Bream, in his office, that he made his confession.

"I can't tell them, can I? The odds are all against our securing one iota of proof."

"You're the doctor." Bream's face was neutral. "I take it you've some notion as to how those two will set about it. Do you know this Dr. Barkstone who appended the second signature?"

"Slightly. He's entirely reputable. If he hadn't been, Brodmart wouldn't have called him in; and now, quite obviously, Barkstone's in a cleft stick. Whatever qualms he may have felt on viewing Mrs. Rush's body he can't admit them. His lips are sealed."

"And so is the accomplished murder. Sealed up for eternity."

"As the new one will be, I'm afraid." Colin's movement was bitter. "Our two criminals are as safe as they would be in a fortified castle. They have a right to be armed. Beddoes's stupidity last night has given them full justification."

Colin drove over the heath.

"No moon. That is a small point in our favour."

"Cat burglars must be feeling the same." Alison winced as they clove through the black, velvety shadows. "Where are we meeting Mr. Bream?"

"At an hotel in Highgate. We must kill time for another hour."

The hotel was dreary, the coffee pale grey. Over it they sat, smoking in jerks, eyes trained on a clock whose hands seemed paralytic. David's bronzed swarthiness showed a sickly green tinge. His eyes were burnt holes. He made but one remark.

"They're at it now. What if it's all over?"

"It will be," snapped Colin, "if we come down on them too soon."

In the car Colin had questioned Alison closely about the cold Elizabeth had caught. She thought of it now, of Sarah Glover's mention of the oxygen tent, and of a whisper to Bream not intended for her ears: *"She's had only eight days to pull up. She'll snuff out like a candle."* These things accounted for the look of doom in Colin's face as he stubbed out one half-smoked Player after another.

She stole a glance at him—and felt a quite different pang in her breast. She knew what had changed Colin—why he was risking his patiently built-up medical practice. It wasn't just any life he was gambling to save. It was Elizabeth's life.

Of course! Imbecile that she had been not to have guessed it at once. Like David, Colin had fallen under the spell . . .

Next instant she was stamping roughly on her ignoble self-pity. What if this thing had happened? Now was no moment to waste tears on the unimportant.

"One o'clock." Bream closed his watch with a click. "Let's go."

Back they plunged to the car, to make with swift sureness for Gambetta Road.

The murky streets grew unfinished. Out of the night familiar landmarks appeared. The Green Dragon, the police station—oh, ironically close!—and now the huge Guinness poster. They slowed by the new villas, to halt opposite the first blank space. Thirty yards ahead loomed the Blythedale Nursing Home. Its front windows were dark.

They got out.

"Follow me." Bream moved towards the deserted premises next door, keeping a wary eye on the empty street. "Mind the gate. It squeaks."

In they filed and round a broken flag-path to the lee of the house. Here, well concealed, lay the two ladders, one short, one long, which Bream that morning had hired from a local builder.

"No one saw me put them here. In fact, there's nothing to suggest there's been the least warning. Wait here. I'll have a look at the back windows."

Silently Bream stole away into the blacker shadows. Alison whispered that there were pitfalls in the other garden—tussocks, withered flowerstalks.

"How can you get a ladder to the house without being heard?"

Colin disregarded her. He was issuing stern orders to David.

"Understand, do you, it's absolutely vital I should go up alone?"

"Oh, I've got it! And if they turn rough?"

"I'll shout. You've got to wait till I do if you have the least hope of saving her. . . . Well, Bream?"

The blurred face came near.

"Dim light in the middle windows. Sashes raised to the limit, curtains pushed aside. Is it what you expected?"

Colin nodded. His lips tightened as he motioned David back.

"We'll give them a little longer, in case one of them's awake."

They went on crouching in the damp and cold. Alison's teeth began to chatter. Colin unwound his knitted muffler and passed it to her along with a pocket flask, but the action was mechanical. It reminded her that she was here on sufferance only, and that being here she must not turn nuisance. Tears she had been fighting back sprang smarting to her eyes. She edged away from the rough contact of a tweed coat and let them slide unseen down her nose. This, she told herself dully, was the end.

Bream left them. Now he crept back with a word which brought the three of them, cramped and stiff, to their feet.

"There's still a light. We must take our chance."

David and Colin took off their coats and handed them into her keeping. Both wore dark sweaters. They might have been thugs.

"Get back to the car," muttered Colin without looking at her. Dismissed, she watched them move along the wall in their rubber-soled shoes, and then slipped wretchedly round the house.

Huddled in Colin's seat, she craned forward, listening. Who but lunatics, she thought, could dream of catching Scarpath and that doctor off guard? All very well to say they were ignorant of being traced. They were astute men, both of them, each with everything to lose. Besides, mightn't their purpose already be accomplished? It was her crushed conviction that those entering—if they did enter!—would find only a small body laid out for burial. A corpse revealing no sign that unnatural death had occurred.

Poor little Elizabeth! Fiendishly cheated out of the life and love for which her gay unselfishness had been fashioned . . .

"Why shouldn't Colin fall for her? She has ten times my charm, yes, and character as well. If he could save her it wouldn't really matter whether it was for himself or for David. It's the certainty that he won't save her that hurts so abominably. All that sacrifice for a heartbreak!"

No, they hadn't got wind of this in time. The victim had been dying fifteen long hours ago. That's why they had given away her shoes . . .

To steady herself Alison thought of the small but important role she was to play if an arranged signal was received. If! Anyhow, the address of the district police-surgeon was in her pocket, and in her head the route she was to take to reach him. Feeling for the slip of paper she gave a violent start. She had forgotten this cold lump dragging down the lining of her camel's hair coat. She looked guiltily about for a place to fling it if necessity arose. At the moment of departure it had made her slightly more comfortable, but even now she was regretting her disobedience to command.

Two o'clock by her watch. Ten minutes had gone by, and still no sound, though within fifty yards of her murder was being committed.

She gnawed her stiff knuckles and sobbed under her breath.

Hoisting the long ladder over the wall was nothing compared with lugging it in silence to the house. The three men were sweating with the strain, but now one ordeal was over, and up above them the light still burned. They could see it clearly, a pendant bulb shaded by a brown-paper cone. Wind had risen. The hanging bulb swayed, but no eclipse indicated movement in its vicinity, nor was there any murmur or rustle to break the dead stillness.

Could the ladder be rested against the house without noise? Probably not. Get it done at top speed.

Up rose the dim shape, tottering precariously. Steadying hands adjusted the summit some ten inches beneath one of the window ledges. Only a slight grating sound. The base, with two to hold it, seemed firm. Colin mounted the rungs.

To his ears the faint creaks made a raucous clamour. Head just topping the sill he dodged to one side. With the edge of a curtain shielding him he peered into the illumined space, stiffened and held his breath.

He was staring straight into the startled, sleep-dazed eyes of Guthrie Brodmart.

He had not been seen, though the man was seated not five feet away, facing the window. Against the yellow light every detail was sharply etched—drab, dry hair in slight disorder, fine puckers criss-crossing the surface of strangely-devitalised skin. Brodmart had evidently just roused from a doze, but his attitude was one of acute vigilance. Two incongruous similes leapt into Colin's mind—a knight guarding his armour, a dog with a bone.

Now he saw that Brodmart was wearing his heavy overcoat, the astrakhan collar drawn up to the ears.

Tucked round him was a mass of soft brown fur. Elizabeth's mink! He had need of it with this cutting winter blast sweeping in on him; and yet the curtain brushing Colin's nostrils gave forth a faint, sickly and unmistakable scent. It was the odour Sarah Glover had mentioned.

God, why must the man sit there blocking the view?

Brodmart had not stirred a muscle. His eyes remained glued to the outer darkness. Slowly he relaxed, looked down and perceived a book sprawling open on the floor. He grunted—telling himself, no doubt, that it was the fall of the volume which had disturbed his slumbers. Picking up his property and methodically marking the place, he seemed about to settle back into position, but no, he was listening, head turned to the right, licking parched lips and sending little furtive glances towards the medical case spread open on a table. Temptation was upon him.

Twice his hand made an abortive movement. Face muscles jerked, all the gallant façade paraded on the lecture platform was cracking and crumbling to show the loathsome rubble underneath. With the eagerness of the sodden drug-addict the physician scheduled for a peerage got up, fumbled in his bag and snatched at a hypodermic syringe.

The mink coat encumbered his feet. Querulously he stooped, and in that moment what lay behind him was revealed.

Colin saw a bed, narrow and white, drawn against the opposite wall. A bed raised high above the waxed linoleum, its cold, hard, surface scarcely ruffled by its huddled and still occupant.

He had been prepared, but now, faced with the actuality, he felt his very soul retch with nausea.

Chapter Forty-One
WITNESSES

Brodmart, back turned, was jabbing the needle deep into his peppered forearm. At the first creak of the ladder he whipped round, glaring with terror, and like jagged lightning plunged for the light switch.

"Scarpath!" he muttered, and in the total blackout he could be heard beating furiously on a door somewhere to the right.

Colin shouted his order to David, making instantly for the bed, only to be headed off by the doctor's dim shape, at bay. Some object swished a pale arc. He felt pain as his jaw was sliced to the bone, and could guess the weapon. A surgeon's knife—nothing deadlier, but perfectly legitimate in the circumstances. Brodmart had weighed every eventuality and meant to remain on the right side of the law.

In the thick darkness Colin sensed rather than saw the wicked blade as it aimed for his jugular vein. Like cats, he and his invisible assailant circled round each other; and then they closed. At the first impact of the grappling embrace Colin knew that conquest would be no simple matter. Brodmart might be unfit, but he was battling for a whole life's prestige. Desperate straits and the shot of cocaine just injected were lending him maniacal strength. A rug slid wildly. Down they crashed, overturning the table. In the same moment the right-hand door was flung back, emitting a thin ribbon of light. Scarpath cannoned upon them, steel glinting in his hand.

Now a head rose to view over the window-sill. Scarpath saw it appear and strode forward to bar the way.

All David saw was the single adamant figure filling the gap. Scarpath—crisp hair electrified, light eyes blazing with hate, whipcord muscles showing through the limp silk of pyjamas. Full in his face a revolver was being levelled, but the trigger was not pressed. Instead, Scarpath seized the ladder and hurled it with savage force away from the house.

Shivering, the wooden structure hesitated, balancing for ten dizzy seconds between earth and sky, only to sway slowly back under David's twelve stone weight. It touched anchorage. David managed to plant a blow in Scarpath's middle even as the sash was being jammed down, but the angle hampered its effect. If he had to fight his way in through broken glass . . . It could never be done. Not with the other fellow armed.

"The light, damn you!" came a croak from the floor.

Scarpath left the window half-closed, dashed to a door and slammed it shut. On the instant David drove the sash upward and took a flying leap into the room.

"Get out!"

In the blackness it was impossible to locate the voice, ice-edged, which had spoken the two words. David got away from the window, whose dim blue revealed his whereabouts, and made for the opposite wall. The light button would be there, by the passage door. Rolling objects impeded him, sounds nearby told him that Colin was fully occupied with the doctor. He blundered against an iron rail. The bed! Groping along it, he touched flesh of such death-like clamminess that he reeled as from a sledge-hammer blow. The job was finished, then. Elizabeth was dead.

Steps crept towards him. Blindly he felt along the edge of a door. A red flame spat. There came a deafening explosion together with hot agony searing his left shoulder.

A crimson haze spread before him. The flash had shown him Scarpath, three paces distant by a chest of drawers. While echoes still volleyed David made a battering-ram of his head, butting the other man to the floor. He scarcely took in the sudden loud pounding on the door behind him or the inrush of some person from another door over to the left. What he did realise was that the opening of this third door had let in a little light so that he could see the opponent who lashed viciously under his weight. Scarpath's body was a steel spring. His gun hand must be immobilised before it could manoeuvre another shot. If not—well, the law would be on the killer's side.

David's right hand gripped Scarpath's throat, his left pinioned the threatening wrist. He bore down, squeezing and choking. Hard. . . .

He saw the face growing purple, the pale eyes beginning to bulge. And then—

Whimpering and snarling, an avalanche crushed down on him. Sharp nails dug into his eyes, teeth fastened into the hand that was intercepting his adversary's aim. The sister! He'd left her out of his reckoning—and he could not throw off her persistent, clinging hold.

Damn her, she'd done the trick! Like an eel Scarpath was on his feet. David, still clamped by the wildcat's teeth, stared into a ring of hot metal.

Once more there was a spurt of fire and a thunderous report.

The first shot had brought Alison tumbling headlong out of the car. As she rushed madly round the nursing-home wall the second brought her to a standstill.

Oh, she had known, she had known!

Breath sobbed in her throat. Two shots—and neither of her men had carried a weapon. Which? Or was it both?

She heard a high, wailing shriek. It drove her onward, but only a few tottering steps. She was chained now by yet another sound. Bumping, slithering. As though a body hurtling from a height was being intercepted in its fall. It thudded to the ground. Her heart turned over.

David or Colin, she would find him beneath the window at the back, most likely with a broken neck. That window was twenty-five feet up. Shots, then the fall . . .

Numbed, she forced her unwilling feet round the corner of the wall. Was she half-witted? No one was here. Only the tall ladder, slanting spectrally up to the sill high above. She couldn't have been mistaken! Not three minutes ago someone had come crashing down, hitting the ladder on the descent. He wasn't here now—unless he had fallen into the area. Fearfully she bent down, trying to pierce the inky shadow of the concreted ditch. Nothing there—and nothing that moved in all the dark expanse of garden. Without and within, silence and desolation. A house of the dead.

Suddenly the windows overhead blazed into hard brilliance, making visible the festoons of grey smoke that writhed out into the night. She heard cries, feminine ones shrill with anger and fright, and the frenzied beating of fists on a door. She could bear no more, but began feverishly to climb.

The ladder sagged and creaked. Heights had always petrified her, but she thought neither of her present peril nor of the graver one about to be met. Up, up . . . the window! Steeling herself, she looked into the room.

It was wrecked confusion—a table and chairs broken or capsized, bottles and instruments strewn broadcast. By the farthermost wall she saw a narrow white bed, but what lay on it was cut off by two stooping figures. Both in dark sweaters! Her heart leapt. One man made a swift movement as though to gather something up into his arms. Brusquely the other checked him, and as he turned she nearly lost her footing. His profile was a welter of blood.

"Colin!"

They didn't notice her scream. It was drowned in the clamour proceeding from the passage. Gingerly hauling herself in she almost trod on a crumpled, middle-aged man who sprawled, weakly coughing, his grey face spattered with red drops. He wouldn't give trouble; but Scarpath? Apparently he was not here.

Her survey fell on a nightmare fantasy. It was Elizabeth's sister-in-law, seated in an arm-chair, surrounded by chaos, smiling vacantly, plucking at foolish lips and uttering little flat giggles! She wore a dingy flannel nightgown, torn at the throat. Her feet were bare, the cramped toes dripped blood.

As she goggled, fascinated by the horrid sight, a small movement on the floor made her look down. The doctor! Prone on his stomach he was dragging himself along, groping, edging furtively—for what? Suddenly his fingers closed. He was on his feet, steadying his exhausted frame with a stupendous effort of will. Before she had grasped his purpose he launched himself bodily at Colin's back. In his hand twinkled a thin, shining blade.

"Stop!"

Alison did not know her own voice. She had drawn David's automatic from her pocket and fired—just in time. Plaster rained down, Colin grappled with Brodmart and hurled him into a corner.

"Thanks." Panting, he laid the lancet on the mantelpiece. "Will you stand over him? We must open this door."

"Oh, Colin, have they killed her?"

He did not answer. Already he was at the passage door, turning the key, motioning curtly to the two women in strange night-attire on the threshold.

"Look!" He pointed to the bed. "I want you to see your patient exactly as we found her. Now!" He swept an arm towards objects stacked behind the door. "You see? Oxygen outfit unused. Cylinders emptied into the air. There's your doctor, what's left of him. Know his little game? Giving a drugged girl gangrenous pneumonia, you can guess how; but that's enough. I want hot bottles, a fire, my kit out of the car. Quick, who'll lend me a hand?"

The thickset younger woman had gasped and turned mottled. The elder one, an ochre-faced witch, tightened with hysteria as she averted her eyes and clung to the wall. Alison smothered a groan.

On the high-pitched bed lay Elizabeth, loosely gagged with a towel, apparently lifeless. Under her—cold, unwrinkled sheet; over her—nothing.

Her body, blue-white and incredibly fragile, was stark naked.

Chapter Forty-Two
COLIN TALKS

It was hours later that Alison waylaid David in the passage. More blood! He seemed unaware that his sweater was a sticky pulp.

"David, you must listen! Wasn't Scarpath here?"

The name at first appeared to convey nothing to him.

"That swine, that rat? Oh, I shunted him through the window! Hell, does it matter now? He'd finished his job."

Savagely he bolted back into the bedroom, closing the door in her face.

Alison sobbed, half laughing. Scarpath—thrown bodily out! Not killed. No, he had got away. Her hysteria dried up. In one way, Scarpath had won. Elizabeth would not, could not recover. Tears ran down her cheeks as she thought of the poor frail candle-flame so soon to be extinguished. Till now there had been so much to do. Now, spent reaction had set in, and the terrible truth must be faced. The police-surgeon was assisting Colin. So was David. Drastic measures were being taken, but what good could they accomplish?

Here was little Bream, kindly jogging her elbow.

"There's a good fire in the matron's room. Sit there, I'll bring you some coffee."

She might as well. Both prisoners were under lock and key, the matron controlling herself in a final effort to save her face, the nurse working like a beaver.

"What about Miss Scarpath? Hadn't we better see why she's so quiet?"

The woman had nearly gouged out David's eyes. There were red scratches all round them. Bream turned the key of the adjacent room and cautiously they peered inside.

In a wicker chair sat Evie Scarpath, simpering and fiddling with some bits of torn newspaper spread on a small table in front of her. Suddenly Alison understood. The jigsaw puzzle. Though her nails were caked with blood her pasty face showed only placidity. She did not look up.

"Gone clean off her rocker," nodded Bream, as he relocked the door. "Result of seeing that precious brother of hers get some of his deserts."

"Some! I supposed the ladder saved him?"

"And yours truly." Ruefully Bream stroked his skull. "He fell on me—laid me out for two ticks. That's how he got off."

"Can he escape?"

"Don't worry, not in pyjamas." Bream noted her slight shrug of indifference. "I agree, these arrests won't fill the bill. I hope, though, you still realise we took the one possible course."

It was his way of breaking it to her that for Elizabeth there was no hope. Well, that she already knew. Poor David. Poor Colin . . .

Crouched by the cosy sitting-room fire she heard the police officers tramp in and upstairs. It seemed another aeon of time before Colin came in, drawn, heavy-eyed, his face cleaned up and a rough cocoon dressing clamped over his cut jaw. She read his expression.

"Then it's too late?"

"There may," he said slowly, "be just a faint chance. She's young, and I'd brought salvarsan. She could have it right away."

"Salvarsan!" She frowned and waited.

He took the cup of hot coffee she had poured for him, set it wearily on the mantel.

"Salvarsan, yes. A remedy for several conditions, among them this particularly vile form of pneumonia. If given in time."

"You knew it would be pneumonia. How?"

"It was the obvious answer—quick, easily fatal, possible to induce. Oh, not by germs! Every one has pneumonia germs lodged in him. We resist them, mostly. The method Brodmart took is almost too horrible to talk about. I guessed, knowing they'd have to drug the victim to prevent outcry. What that charwoman told me clinched matters."

"Sarah Glover? Why, what did she—"

"You didn't hear the last bit. She'd smelled ether in the room. Ether clings, you know, for quite a long while. Those wide-stretched windows were highly suggestive. Nor merely a matter of chilling the patient to the bone. At the finish there must be no ether fumes hanging about. Of course," Colin added, "there was a definite attempt to-night to race things through, due, I imagine, to Scarpath's shindy with David. With Mrs. Rush's death notice already in the press, it wouldn't do to have the police start prying too soon."

"The ether. When was it given?"

"Directly they got her here. She'd had a good tea, you think?"

"I'm sure of it, poor infant! She was so ravenous, you know."

"Well, there you are. A recent meal, undigested by reason of the shock over her aunt and the thumping big shot of morphia Scarpath must have injected to stupefy her. It provided the right conditions, the ether did the rest. Not chloroform, mind. That would have left traces in the brain, detectable in the event of a post-mortem. Soon after the etherisation, nausea set in. They didn't lift her up or turn her head. You see?"

"I don't, quite. You mean—?"

"Simply that she was forced to aspirate. It got the ether fumes and the contents of the stomach well down into the lungs. No better way of ensuring gangrenous pneumonia. It developed at top speed."

Alison clinched her hands. "She's never regained consciousness?"

"They couldn't risk it. She's been fed sedatives, by tube, via the nostrils. I can show you the tube. When she was too far gone to make trouble they'd have let the bromide wear off. There'd have been nothing by way of evidence—not a trace."

Settling into a chair Colin absently drank his coffee. "I felt fairly confident what was happening," he continued, "the instant I knew they'd got the sister acting as nurse. She saw nothing. She was simply a blind."

"Then she is sub-normal! David said so."

"Oh, yes! Rather a typical case—low mentality, starved emotions centered wholly on her attractive brother. She'd have saved him, even when she saw he was a murderer—a fact she can never before have suspected. Every action of hers is characteristic. Note the device she's unconsciously employing now. Whatever comes of this, she won't have to give evidence. She'll have forgotten the whole thing. They'll put her into an asylum, and there she'll remain."

Alison shuddered. Perhaps, she suggested, Scarpath, too, suffered from a taint of insanity?

Colin shrugged. "Certainly his failure to pull this off has been from no lack of ability. The quirk in him hasn't affected his brain. His trouble, as I think I mentioned, is that first and foremost he's the gentleman amateur. Which means that even in the supreme undertaking of murder he lets his personal inclinations interfere. Suppose he'd sacrificed himself to the point of playing the attentive husband? Elizabeth would never have got from under his thumb. Not even David would have shaken her faith. Unsuspicious to the end, she'd have died in accordance with a most admirably-conceived plan."

"But her original illness?"

"Fraud—foisted on her with diabolic cleverness. Don't you see just how it was worked?"

He broke off to listen. The house remained quiet.

"Take the existing circumstances," he resumed. "They not only prompted the scheme, they furnished the ground on which to build. I needn't remind you of what Elizabeth was like—young, much shielded . . ." He moistened dry lips. "Most important, without friends in this country. Brutally cheated in her marriage. Plumped down in surroundings physically and psychologically antipathetic. Can you wonder that her spirits suffered, and in consequence her health? First to give way was her sight. Constant daydreaming disturbed focusing. The trouble is aggravated by too much smoking, till—"

"You're telling me!" Alison interrupted eagerly. "It was like that with a girl in my senior year, who'd lost her fiancé, flunked in her exams and gone nearly blind. On the boat to Bermuda she got engaged again. When she landed her eyes were all right."

"Well, that shows you the cause of Elizabeth's visual trouble. Next, the knee injury—never properly treated till Svendsen took her in hand. I could quote a dozen instances of similar ignorance and neglect; but here it lent itself to a deliberate misinterpretation. The knee was Symptom Number Two; but I'm moving too fast.

"At some time or times, Elizabeth flared up and threatened to leave Scarpath for good and all. If she had done this, Scarpath could never have touched a penny of the money his wife, all unknowingly, was due to inherit. What else was there to do but to kill her? She was proving less malleable than he had expected, his own rooted distaste to the married state prevented the effort to win her back. He had either to forgo the prize for which he had bartered his liberty or keep Elizabeth in subjection till her aunt was dead, then get rid of her before she could make a will. He was counting, you see, on Mrs. Rush's early decease—with good reason. There's not the least doubt Mrs. Rush herself had confided in him her alarm over her health. Probably she drew the picture in bold outlines—made him believe she was due to pop off from stroke at almost any moment. She'd have done that to gain sympathy."

"Yet she never told Elizabeth."

"Certainly not. There was antagonism between them. Isn't it like a woman of Mrs. Rush's type to be secretive with her own sex and open up like a flower with a man who had won her affections? Scarpath is the very sort to fascinate the strong kind of woman, particularly one no longer young—and in this case not over intelligent. It's possible Fanny even dangled her will before his eyes as a bait, hoping he would take her niece off her hands. He was misled, of course, in thinking the fortune would soon be forthcoming. The aunt went on living, and Elizabeth was planning to slip through his fingers. Only illness would keep her at his side.

"It had to be a protracted illness—preferably an obscure one. It was necessary to have medical sanction as well as assistance—and this brings us to Brodmart. As to how he agreed to lend himself to a piece of flagrant malpractice, I'll give you my views. Without pressure his course is unthinkable. The man must already have landed himself in a bad hole financially, and in moral ways let go. Well, both these things are true. Brodmart has been losing heavily on the stock market. Driven by worry and fatigue he has contracted a cocaine habit. Scarpath has known him since the days of the Admiral's last illness. I believe he has even been supplying Brodmart with the excess quantities of the drug. Seeing he could cut the stuff off if and when he chose or threaten a little ruinous blackmail, don't you grasp the powerful leverage it was his to exert?"

"Scarpath has been supplying the cocaine! Surely a doctor can get his own?"

"No. Not above moderate amounts. He'd risk serious challenge. Scarpath, though—that's different. There's a vast quantity of cocaine in London, accessible to those in the know. That party in South Street was an eye-opener; not that I think Scarpath himself meddles with the stuff. I'm positive he doesn't.

"Let's say that Brodmart, spending more than he earns, doping rather recklessly, suddenly is offered a big reward for services easily rendered and involving negligible risk. He caves in, tempted by the chance to see his future clear and pull up. His false diagnosis will never come out. The patient will die at the right moment from a simple, genuine, intermediary illness—and he himself will sign the death certificate. Till the death she must be kept harmless and supine from an alleged chronic complaint. He examines her, and very astutely decides on disseminated sclerosis. It exactly meets the case.

"Disseminated sclerosis is his own speciality. It conforms with Elizabeth's impaired eyesight for no discernible cause, her liability to stumble and fall, her emotional upsets. In the early stage it's so difficult to pin down that no ordinary medical opinion can displace that of an eminent neurologist. The attacks themselves make it plausible to cut the sufferer off from the outside world, turning her literally into a prisoner—and he, Brodmart, can and does produce the attacks."

"How?" demanded Alison.

Colin's eye smouldered. "I don't think I'm guessing. I've questioned Elizabeth pretty closely and formed my own conclusions. Brodmart again showed brilliance—because he employed the very substances present-day science regards as legitimate treatment for the disease in question. He began by injecting typhus vaccine—from five million germs onward. It induced high temperature and great exhaustion, thus lowering Elizabeth's resistance. In time he gave quinine, by mouth. That was the bitter stuff she told us brought such ghastly results. He gave her far too much, the point being that by so doing he created an approximation of the very symptoms correct dosage is designed to relieve—that is, blurred vision reaching almost to blindness and partial paralysis of certain muscles. It was those details that roused my suspicion—and MacConochie's. Add on the starvation diet. Is it surprising she shook like a palsied person, and collapsed on taking a few steps? The knee, remember, was still wrong, and she herself was generally enfeebled from lack of nourishment and confinement in bed. On the last occasion, when Scarpath had got the wind up over David, the overdose of quinine came devilishly near finishing her off. With her aunt still alive! You can picture the blue funk they were in till they'd dragged her back from death's door."

"Cats playing with a mouse." Alison whispered it with loathing.

"Quite—and the intervals when she was allowed to get better pointed to as a peculiarity of the complaint! They might well have been that. Why, disseminated sclerosis has been known to vanish for as long as two years! That was my difficulty. How was I to know I hadn't caught her in one of these deceptive periods? Keeping back her letters," muttered Colin to himself. "Stealing her clothes—letting her read that damned medical treatise!"

Head bent, he hammered his forehead with his two fists.

"Let's drop that part," murmured Alison painfully. "She did slip the cage. Go on from there."

Taking a fresh grip on himself, Colin stared past her.

"She slipped the cage—because our amateur criminal wanted to play golf. It was a knock-out blow, with a worse to follow. The aunt turned up. Scarpath saw his whole beautiful scheme on the rocks. Well, he saved it

224 | ALICE CAMPBELL

from smashing—though it took a clumsy murder to accomplish it. Mrs. Rush evidently told him her intention about altering her will. At one stroke he prevented that and got his wife back into his power—we'll never know exactly how, since the victim's remains have been cremated, and the forged letter that put Elizabeth off her guard is also burned to ashes."

"Was it luck he got hold of Elizabeth before MacConochie could see her?"

"He may have learned of the pending consultation from Mrs. Rush. Quite likely Elizabeth spoke of it. All in all it was a fine piece of engineering, the one snag being the event Scarpath couldn't possibly have foreseen."

"Hats off to Pen. Still, it was David who got her interested."

"Remind him of it, will you? He's blaming himself for the whole cursed show."

"Poor David!" She glanced under her lashes at Colin's harassed face.

"Sheer, black-hearted cruelty." Colin had risen to go. "A man like Geoffrey Scarpath might not deliberately set out to inflict torment on his victim, but he would undoubtedly derive pleasure from making that victim suffer needlessly—particularly when it's a woman. His type can't help being sadistic. Yes, I'd enjoy seeing him hanged."

"Will he be, do you think?"

His gaze narrowed. "No!" he snapped, and quitted the room.

Chapter Forty-Three
THE LONG DROP

Scarpath, fully clothed, stepped into the dark stillness of South Street. All clear; so he had made it. Sliding into his Chrysler, he turned towards Piccadilly, and steered capably through the chill morning gloom. Now! If his luck still held . . .

The pilot's grin, peering forth from the dim Croydon airfield, assured him it did. What if the main passenger services had been warned? Griffin, roused by telephone, had plainly heard nothing. Beaming, he touched his winged cap.

"Copenhagen you said, sir? A bit thick just now. Want to wait another hour or so?"

"No. Make inland, over the fens. We'll strike sunshine above."

In the small, compact cabin the voyager made observations. As he'd expected. Since the scare raised by the happening three years back prudence had again relaxed. He felt in his pocket for the silver flask he had filled at his flat, took a wary survey of the field, and settled into his seat.

The engine pulsed, the private plane swam forward, bumping a little and rising so gently one would not have guessed it but for the easier movement. The huge bulk of the aerodrome dwindled into a sea of mist, and as it was swallowed up Scarpath let his pent breath escape. At the same time his colour, whipped to freshness by the raw air, drained rapidly away. In the mirror opposite he saw a face so grey, so distorted, it might have been a stranger's. Again he touched his flask, but withdrew his hand. Not yet . . .

At this exact moment police officers were bombarding the door in South Street. At the Croydon headquarters a telephone was wildly ringing.

"Worth the gamble," ran the fugitive's thoughts. "Oh, decidedly! It's a satisfaction to know that failure wasn't due to stupidity, as it was with the car. She'll die, of course. Well, let Brodmart stand trial. They won't land me."

He had guessed that the stir over that silly, half-dead girl would cause the necessary delay in informing the police. Luck only that the ladder and the little ass at the bottom had spared him a broken neck, but cool forethought which had made him pick a private garage he could enter unseen and when he chose. In short, he had ensured against all but one unpredictable mischance. He could not reproach himself.

Good speed, now. He wiped the frosted pane and saw pale sun seeping through the upper strata of fog. About here it would be shining thinly on Suffolk lanes with long-tailed pheasants strolling across them; on aged churches, dreaming amidst sere winter landscape. There'd be pools of brown water, sedges, outpost windmills, making this region rather like Holland. Soon it would be time. In the warm, close cabin Scarpath grew clammy. Thinking again! Imbecile, at this juncture. Let his brain be a blank . . .

Life! After all, was it so precious a possession? Even in the most electric moments he had seldom found it so. It was the not wanting anything badly enough—or the not knowing what was most desirable. Money—well, naturally; but that was incidental. A means—to what end? At twenty-eight Geoffrey Scarpath could not answer the question. He would not even try. Yet this brain of his would not be stilled.

Admiration—the centre of the stage—fleeting excitements leaving a bitter taste. What in the sum were they worth? Ashes in the mouth—at Eton, at Brasenose, in the Wimbledon courts, at the piano dabbling over a score he somehow contrived to ruin—no more, no less! With stiff fingers he set his flask to his lips. Good brandy, this—and the last, as was fitting. Why didn't the blur steal over him? The warmth in his stomach did not even extend to his limbs.

The plane had soared to loftier heights, but the thudding in his ear did not come from the engine. Suddenly, ahead, he caught a glimpse of dull, heaving water. The North Sea. In two minutes they'd be over it. He rose, tottering from vertigo.

Suppose the door wouldn't open? Christ, it weighed a ton! He set his shoulder against it, the blood swelling in his neck. The door yielded, swung violently back, and in the yawning vacancy beneath he saw dank swirls of mist. Two thousand feet—or was it more? The nausea was growing worse, his fingers were fastened like steel rivets on the door frame . . . but the sea rushed close! He shut his eyes and let go.

The plane sped seaward.

In a maroon field two labourers gaped at the speck, all arms and legs, which hurtled down, down, from the lead waste of sky. Transfixed, they watched, and then, splashing through puddles, began to run.

"So you were right again!"

As Alison whispered it she had a vision of the broken shape lying deep in East Country mud. It was the best of solutions. There would still be a sensational trial, of course. Guthrie Brodmart, armed with the finest counsel, would fight to a finish, but there was compensation in that feature. Might not the scandal of the medical world lift one young doctor out of obscurity, even bring him a lucrative fame?

She knew that Colin, as he replaced the receiver, was not thinking of this aspect at all. Nor was he thinking of her—hadn't been for days, except as a sexless individual in whom he could confide. Rather forlornly she wondered if this nerve-tearing adventure hadn't provided Dr. Ladbroke with a timely excuse to backwater. She believed that half-consciously he had welcomed the chance of getting safely away from certain dangerous shoals. Well, she might have known it. Alison Young was just an excellent pal, valued only while she kept strictly to this role. What was as natural as breathing to that sad little thing upstairs would, in her, be viewed as outrageous and unbecoming—like darkened eyelids, silvered nails. Yet men adored the feminine graces and allure. Helplessness snared them—and she, fatal blunder, had never learned how to be helpless. . . .

Elizabeth opened weighted eyes. The room about her was medicinal-smelling, but warm and bright. She seemed dimly to know it; but perhaps not. Someone sat by her, broodingly intent. His broad shoulders were etched against the glow of the fire, but his features were all shadow. Who?

In terror she saw the narrow compass of a car, walled in with rain-streaked glass. Geoffrey! Was this he? If so, all that stretched between the sharp stab in her arm and this moment must be hallucination. Under the warm covers she cowered. She was too weak to move had she dared it.

A rough mutter reached her. "Betsy, it's me."

"You!"

He had dark hair. She had edged forth one hand and was touching it, disbelievingly. Palms that were David's cupped her face. She rubbed her cheek against them for comfort.

"Don't talk, Betsy. Listen: It's all right. Everything. Got that?"

"Everything? Not *everything*, David!"

"Every damned thing. Does it hurt you to breathe?"

She considered. "Not much. Why should it?"

He made a gulping sound and bade her lie still.

"I will, if you'll promise to stay . . . David, my bag. Brown suède. Is it there?"

He laid it by her. It was stained with pneumonia serum from one of Brodmart's smashed bottles.

"Open it, David. There's a pipe—for you."

"A pipe!" His voice had the same queer roughness.

"Have you found it? I do hope it's good. Oh-h-h! I can't keep awake. . . ."

Just skirted the brink. If a mind at ease could draw her to safety. . . .

It did. For days, though, the truth had to be kept from her, and then only a portion yielded under a suitable veil. Fanny was dead. Well, that she had expected. Poor Fanny! And, most bewilderingly, she, Elizabeth, would probably come in for the money. It couldn't be much, whatever Geoffrey might have believed. Yet much or little it seemed to have changed David into a being formal and aloof.

Horrid doubts impeded the invalid's gallant struggles towards health. Maybe it wasn't the money. David might be realising that pity wasn't love. Elizabeth strove hard to hide the tears which kept running weakly down her cheeks. It was so ungrateful to let Colin worry about her, only how could she help drooping?

This afternoon she had not slept, merely pretended. Here was David now, fingering his new pipe, staring glumly out into the dusk. Come to say good-bye. His shoulder was healed, he was off to Glasgow—for more than a month. He would speak to her with stiff embarrassment, barely touching her hand. Could her pride let her bear it?

She groped for her handkerchief and found instead a thick envelope bearing a French stamp. Why, what was this?

"David, come here."

He came, only to poise big and awkward, two feet from the bed.

"Read this." She thrust the opened letter on him.

His face altered. "Well," he grunted. "What do you know about that?"

"You see? It's only a tiny bit. Why, even I imagined it would be five times as much!"

Five times was correct. Those concerned might learn that Fanny's stocks had disastrously fallen. They could not guess how a junior clerk, tight on champagne, had muddled dollars with francs. . . .

David was grinning now but still holding back.

"I can't see you," Elizabeth complained. "Here, sit down on the bed . . . David, do you remember the skinny little kid who was too shy to ask you to go swimming with her? You never knew she worshipped the very sneakers you walked about it. How you'd have laughed! Fact, though—and she went on doing it. Ever wonder why you got a bid to her coming-out party? Why she cut an important date to slip off in your car? She hoped, you see, that you might think she'd turned out sort of a nice girl—after Paris and things . . ."

Damn her voice, breaking like this!

"Oh, David, must you make me sorry? You beast, oh, you beast! I . . . oh, *darling*!"

His burnt-out eyes had blazed. Her body was crushed as his lips closed down on her own to linger interminably.

Neither noticed the soft closing of the door.

In the passage Alison shook herself crossly.

"Oh!" she muttered. "I do want my home!"

Colin's blue eyes rested inscrutably on her.

"Is that your reaction? Mine's this." Folding her to him strongly, he kissed her with deliberate and calculated enjoyment.

"Oh!"

The cry was part laugh, part sob. Still startled, she snuggled close to the tweed-clad shoulder for which she had almost ceased to yearn.

"And to think," she blurted disgracefully, "I've been jealous of that poor orphan child!"

"Elizabeth? In God's name, when?"

"Off and on," she mumbled. "Do you despise me?"

"Well!" He held her off and examined her. "Not much of a start for a doctor's wife, is it?"

"Sez you!" It was a last belligerent flash. "And who told you, Doctor Ladbroke, I had any such notion?"

"My mistake, Miss Young! Yes, I dare say you're better off as you are. So you won't face the sausages and mash?"

"Idiot! It's you."

"Life-saver. Always that, aren't you?" Tenderly he stroked her cheek. "Which reminds me: I've never yet thanked you properly for the handy work with that gun."

"So you're taking this way. Listen, Colin, quite sure you aren't just swept off your moorings by relief and—and seeing those two?"

"Am I?" he teased.

"Think hard!" she commanded. "It'll be your last chance. I'd pull my oar, of course, that's understood, but—"

"Oh? Well, that'll give us matter to fight about for some time to come. Not now, though." He stifled a yawn. "Do you know what I propose for the immediate future? That you and I drift down to the matron's room, make a hole in her enticing couch, and—"

"Doctor Ladbroke! One hole?"

"And"—firmly drawing her to the stairs—"go to sleep for a week!"

THE END

Printed in Great Britain
by Amazon

81426597R00139